THE DRAGON PORTAL SERIES

TO KILL A FAE

BOOK 1

JAMIE A. WATERS

Cover Art by Deranged Doctor Designs
Editor: Beyond DEF Lit

ISBN: 978-1-949524-17-8 (Hardback Edition)
ISBN: 978-1-949524-16-1 (Paperback Edition)
ISBN: 978-1-949524-15-4 (eBook Edition)

Library of Congress Control Number: 2019911511
First Edition *September 2019

Chapter One

*A*n owl hooted in warning.

Sabine brushed her fingers against the handle of a throwing knife strapped to her thigh, but she didn't alter her stride. Boots crunched upon the cobblestone street behind her at a steady beat, keeping pace with her. Whoever had decided to follow her this evening hadn't bothered to mask their intent. The weight of the weapons she carried was a small reassurance, but it was no guarantee of safety.

She turned the next corner, angling her head to catch a glimpse of the people trailing her. A shaft of moonlight illuminated both men's features enough to be certain she didn't know them. Not only that, but they were too well-armed to be out for a midnight stroll. She frowned and adjusted her cloak to better cover her silvery-white hair and continued walking. It wasn't an uncommon color in the city, but it was still distinctive and far too recognizable.

Approaching footsteps from an adjacent alley caught her attention. It might be a coincidence, but it wasn't likely in this part of town. Sabine didn't travel to the more affluent areas of Akros often, and when she did, it was rarely on the surface streets. She was too recognizable—being noticed was something she needed to avoid. If she hadn't agreed to meet with a prospective informant with the hope of learning more about the strange rumors surrounding the city council, she wouldn't be in this situation now. Unfortunately, he'd been as clueless as everyone else. No one wanted to talk about what the council was doing—and that was one more thing to make this situation more infuriating.

At the next intersection, Sabine glanced down the adjacent street. It was a dead end. Mentally kicking herself for her earlier cockiness, she debated her limited options. If they were trying to herd her to a place of their choosing for an ambush, another man would be waiting on the next street—she was sure of it.

Stupid. So stupid. What had possessed her to ignore every lesson shoved down her throat since arriving in the city almost ten years earlier? The shadows surrounding her had become like a second skin—one she'd grown accustomed to wearing. Most people barely noticed her presence anymore, unless she specifically tried to draw attention to herself. For her, such behavior was akin to suicide.

Sabine listened to the leisurely pace of the footsteps following her. So far, her would-be assailants weren't in a hurry to engage her. If she could manage to make it closer to the wharf, she'd be back within safe territory. Safer for her, at least. The same couldn't be said for most others, including the ones currently trailing her.

The streets in this part of town were mostly quiet at this time of night. Businesses were closed, and the good citizens of Akros were safely tucked in their beds. Those who wandered the streets usually risked their purses being lifted and any removable belongings stripped by morning. Of course, that was assuming they managed not to have their throat slit. Shadows came out to play at night, and only the clever or lucky usually survived.

For the most part, Sabine didn't worry about the threat of the miscreants who may be lurking within these darkened streets. They knew enough to leave her unhindered; her associates had made sure of that. The fact Sabine was a target now was more than a little curious—and equally worrisome. It was unlikely this ambush was random, especially since the streets were uncharacteristically empty. Not even a few drunks or beggars loitered in any nearby doorsteps.

She frowned and took a deep breath, inhaling the faintest trace of magic permeating the night air. It was subtle enough she hadn't noticed it right away. It had the feel of a witch or wizard's spell, which was part of the reason she hadn't paid much attention. Most witches and wizards were human who relied on nature magic in the form of herbal tinctures and poultices. Only a rare few had enough power to be much of a threat.

Sabine took another deep breath and nearly stumbled as recognition slammed into her. It was definitely a witch, but there was also a trace of a different sort of magic. It took everything in Sabine's power to keep moving at the same leisurely pace when every instinct warned her to flee. Somewhere in this witch's family tree was a Fae, and that type of magic was much more dangerous, especially to Sabine. The witch's spell had been carefully woven to be little more than a suggestion, encouraging mundane passersby to travel another direction. It was a clever bit of magic, and its passive nature hadn't triggered the warding bracelet around her wrist to warn her. Someone had paid a hefty bit of coin for such a spell.

She fingered the hilt of her blade again, preparing for the inevitable. Given the costly spell and the location, it was even less likely this was a coincidence. But something wasn't quite right. If they had guessed her identity, they wouldn't have sent humans after her—even if a part-Fae witch had created the spell. She needed to think, but she had to lose her tail first. Unfortunately, her options were somewhat limited.

She started to turn down another alley but hesitated at the sight of the last man.

"Damn. This is bad," she muttered under her breath. Turning away, she heard the footsteps behind her move faster. She only had a handful of seconds before they intercepted her. Scanning the empty street, she noticed several of the buildings in this area were abandoned rather than simply closed for the evening. Her assailants had chosen well, and she'd been a fool to fall so neatly into their trap. If she was going to do something, the time was now.

Taking a steadying breath, Sabine caught a faint whiff of the nearby sea. She slipped off the warding bracelet and dropped it into her pocket before opening herself to the pulse of the night. Even if she could perform magic while wearing it, she wasn't willing to risk anything interfering with what she was about to attempt.

The moist air tickled her skin, and she allowed the moonlight to penetrate through her protective barriers. Power flared within her briefly before she managed to wrest control of it. The longer she went without actively using her magic, the more difficult it became to suppress it. She wouldn't need too much, but it was dangerous without her usual protections in place.

She inhaled and gathered her power, infusing her very breath with elemental magic. When she exhaled, she projected her magic skyward. The moon slipped behind the cloud cover and darkened the area. She was too exposed to risk using more magic. It would have to be enough. Sabine took the opportunity to duck into a doorway and crouched down to wait.

"Where did she go?" one of the men whispered loudly.

"She's got to be here somewhere," another one snapped. "Find her, or we don't get paid."

Sabine withdrew one of her knives and pressed the poison dispenser on the hilt as she listened to the footsteps hurrying on the pavement. When one of them was close enough, she threw the blade in his direction and rolled forward. A howl of pain signaled she'd hit her mark. The lethal poison would keep him busy—in perpetuity.

Springing to her feet, she pulled another knife free just as someone grabbed hold of her. Lashing outward, she swiped her knife deeply across his forearm.

"Fuck! She cut me!"

The moment he released her, she spun away. The third man grabbed her from behind, jerking her backward. A sharp, stinging sensation burned along her side as his knife sliced across her skin. Ignoring the pain, she stepped down hard on his insole.

Sabine's long, silvery-white braids whipped around as she spun to face her attacker. She slashed with her blade, feeling the soft flesh give way until it met bone. He cried out in pain, and she yanked out the knife. Before she had time to flee, the fourth man appeared and rushed toward her, knocking her to the ground. Her knife flew out of her hand, the metal clattering against the paving stones.

"I've got you, bitch," he rasped in her ear. The stench of stale sweat and cooked onions choked her senses.

Sabine raised her knee between his legs. Sweaty onion man grunted in pain. In one swift movement, she withdrew another dagger and slashed diagonally across his throat.

Blood splashed outward, and she ignored the gurgling noise as she scrambled to her feet.

Two down, but there were two more who needed to be eliminated.

"Kill her already!" a man shouted.

Aha. So not an abduction. They wanted her dead.

A blond man rushed toward her, and she kicked out at him. He stumbled backward as her heel hit the center of his chest. Sabine turned toward the one who had shouted. The scar on his chin was vaguely familiar, but she wasn't sure where she'd seen him before. Grabbing her, he shoved her hard. Her back hit the wall, and she let out an *oomph* as her breath rushed from her lungs.

The flash of a blade caught her attention, and her eyes widened at the sight of the ancient iron dagger and the tattoo on the inside of the man's wrist. Any doubt she had about the randomness of the attack fled. If she were going to survive the next few minutes, she needed to take drastic measures. Hiding in the shadows wouldn't matter if she were dead. Her middling weapons skill was no match against this opponent.

Dropping to her knees, Sabine cut her palm and slapped her bleeding hand against the ground. Pulling the earth's energy up through the paving stones, she held up her other hand and projected the power outward in a sharp blast. Her would-be assailant flew backward, hitting the opposite wall.

"It's her," the tattooed man shouted, pointing in her direction. "Kill her! Now!"

The blond man rushed forward in her direction. His weapon wasn't iron, but it was no less deadly. She couldn't risk performing more major magic and alerting everyone of her presence. Death always happened in threes, and she was one power-pull away from a calamity. She needed to make sure the next person who fell was one of her enemies.

Bracing herself, she remained crouched as the man ran

toward her. A moment before impact, she leaned forward and pushed herself upright with the blade still in her hand. The angle was perfect to pass between his ribs and straight into his heart. Yanking the knife free, she shoved him aside and prepared to throw her weapon.

The last man, the one who'd held the deadly iron dagger and promised to be the most formidable, was on the ground with a puddle of blood pooling beneath him. A dark-haired stranger stood over the body. He yanked his sword free, and Sabine raised her hand, preparing to let her knife fly.

His eyes widened slightly, and he held up his hand in a peaceable gesture. "I swear to you: my word is as strong as the elements. I mean you no harm."

Sabine froze at the irrefutable oath he'd made. The language of Faerie wasn't uncommon within the city, although many of the residents had adopted a bastardized version or used a mixture along with the common tongue. But the ritualistic words he'd uttered were *not* common knowledge nor was the formality of his speech. The oath was enough to stay her hand, but she wasn't foolish enough to lower her weapon.

The man standing before her radiated tightly controlled energy unlike anything she'd seen before. The color of his aura, a rich silvery-blue, reminded her of the night sky after the sun slipped past the horizon. His golden skin and dark hair indicated he wasn't Fae or even a native to Akros, but he might be wearing glamour to hide his true nature. It was too dark to see his eyes, but she wondered if the secrets he harbored would reflect back at her.

Sabine straightened slowly, refusing to lower the knife in her hand. Beautiful or not, no one would know that oath unless they were intimately familiar with the Fae and their ancient customs. He appeared decidedly human, but his energy was something more. It was possible he had some Fae blood in him. It still didn't explain why he was here, especially considering he'd appeared on the heels of an attack. He couldn't lie if he were Fae, but his ability to wield truth *and* lies depended on how much human blood he possessed. Humans could be just as tricky as the Fae.

If necessary, she could kill him later—*after* she questioned him.

Sabine relaxed the hand holding her weapon, acknowledging curiosity had gotten the better of her. She wouldn't kill this stranger yet, but whether she'd trust him was a decidedly different matter.

Footsteps pounded on the pavement. Sabine tensed, her hand tightening around the knife again. A short and stout creature approached, his purple eyes widening at the sight of her.

"Oh, hell's balls. What have you done, Malek?" he croaked hoarsely, the greenish skin of his goblin heritage becoming a sickly hue that was almost the exact shade of regurgitated grass.

Another man, similar in appearance to the one called Malek halted beside him. He frowned at the bodies on the ground before meeting her eyes. He didn't possess the same magnetism as Malek, but he was also a curiosity. If he were completely human, she'd swallow her knife whole, but he *definitely* wasn't full-blooded Fae either. Sabine would bet her last weapon neither one of them were from Akros.

Sabine's eyes narrowed on the familiar goblin. "Pozgil, are these friends of yours?"

Pozgil swallowed and hastily nodded, shifting nervously from foot to foot. His tongue flicked out again before he responded. "I-I was ordered to collect them from the docks. This is Captain Malek Rish'dan." Pozgil gestured to the man who had spoken in the language of the Fae before gesturing to the other. "And this is his first mate, Levin Corynth.

They've just arrived in Akros. I'm escorting them to the tavern to meet with Dax." The goblin paused for a moment, hunched his shoulders, and hastily added, "Wi-With your permission, of course."

Sabine blinked at him. The goblin trembled in terror. She was surprised he hadn't fallen to the ground with the way his knees were knocking together. There wasn't much she could do about dispelling his fears. In any other situation, she'd simply walk away and leave him to his errand. The attempt on her life had changed things. She couldn't afford to back down, not now. But she *could* resolve this entire situation as expediently as possible.

Sabine tucked one of her braids behind her pointed ear, using the gesture to buy a few moments of time while she studied this Captain Malek Rish'dan. He didn't appear like any ship captain she'd ever met. If he were new to Akros like the goblin claimed, it was unlikely he was involved in the recent attack on her. She wouldn't write him off completely, but Dax's goblin messenger would never dream of being involved in a plot against her. Dax was the leader of the local thieves' guild, and he wasn't exactly forgiving when it came to those who betrayed him.

She took a deep breath but couldn't detect any lingering foreign magic in the area. The spell encouraging people to avoid these streets had broken during her power-pull on the earth. She couldn't sense active magic from Malek or his companion either. But still… his connection to the Fae was troubling and curious at the same time.

If Malek had business with Dax, she'd cross paths with him again. Although, Dax's involvement might prove to be inconvenient. Dax was unpredictable at times, and Sabine wasn't willing to risk him killing off the ship captain. It might be considered a weakness, but she wanted to know about his ties to the Fae.

A pained wail broke through her thoughts, and she glanced over at the man she'd struck with the poisoned weapon. It wasn't a death blow, which was nearly impossible with a throwing dagger, but the poison had done the job. He was paralyzed, and the poison was working through his system and burning him up from the inside. Considering the damage was irreversible, there was only one solution.

Walking over to the man on the ground, she gripped his hair and jerked his head upright. With the knife still in her hand, she slashed it across his throat, allowing his lifeblood to spill onto the cobblestones below.

Sabine released his hair and collected the dagger she'd used to dispense the poison, making a mental note to add more mandrake next time. Regardless of his attempt on her life, she couldn't leave anyone to suffer. Leaning down, she wiped her blade on the man's clothing before slipping it into the sheath on her thigh.

"What in the name of the underworld?" Levin muttered.

Pozgil shushed him and whispered, "If you know what's good for you, you'll keep your mouth shut."

Sabine lifted her head to regard the goblin again. Her reputation wasn't the best, but the fear emanating from Pozgil was a little excessive. Most goblins enjoyed it when a little blood was spilled; it was considered something of a sport among their kind. Pozgil's eyes gleamed with a wild hunger, but his fear overshadowed everything else. If Dax's little minion was so out of sorts that he wasn't licking the blood from the cobblestones, the stories floating around about her were even worse than she'd assumed. Perhaps she'd kept herself more isolated over the past few months than she'd realized.

With a sigh, Sabine gestured to the man she'd executed. "I used an experimental poison. It still needs some adjustment."

She paused, considering her words. They probably

weren't the most reassuring. She didn't enjoy killing, but it was sometimes necessary. With a frown, she studied the body and wished she'd had time to craft and dispense an antidote. Now it would be even more difficult to find out who had hired him.

Bending down, she went through his clothing with the hope of finding some clue to his identity or employer. Other than a small pouch of coins at his waist, there was nothing else. She scooped up the pouch and whistled sharply. Tentative footsteps sounded a second later, emerging out of the darkness. Sabine tossed the pouch in the air and caught it, gauging the weight of the coins within. Good. It would be enough.

Walking over to the young boy who stood at the foot of the alley, Sabine dangled the bag in front of him. "For your warning."

His eyes widened as a lock of dark, sooty hair fell over his forehead. He was underweight and filthy, like many of the street urchins. He gripped the bag tightly but didn't turn away. Sabine had noticed him shortly after she'd left her informant, but this young boy had dared quite a bit by trailing behind her attackers. Only someone with strong spirit and intent could have broken past the witch's avoidance spell. He'd taken the extra measure to use an owl's warning call to alert her about the threat. He had potential, and she owed him a debt—Sabine *always* paid her debts.

Keeping her voice and expression neutral, Sabine nodded toward the pouch. "That's enough coin to feed you for a week."

The boy stared at the bag, but he made no move to leave. She arched her brow at him and waited. In her experience, people had to want something badly enough to do what was necessary to make it happen. If this boy couldn't bring himself to ask the question, he wasn't ready.

After a long moment, the boy lifted his head and held out the bag. "I'd like to trade for a wooden coin."

Sabine tilted her head and idly tapped the hilt of her knife with her fingers. The boy's eyes widened, and he swallowed. His nervousness was obvious, but she was more curious about whether he was willing to fight through his fears to accomplish his goals.

Unwilling to make it easy on him, she frowned at him. "That's a lot of coin to exchange for a piece of wood. Are you sure that's what you want?"

His hand clutching the bag trembled, but he nodded. The determination in his eyes was enough to erase any lingering doubt.

"Very well," she agreed and took away the purse. Opening it, she slipped out a coin and infused a bit of magic into it. Out of the corner of her eye, she caught Malek's sudden interest as he took a step toward her, presumably to get a better look.

Hmm. As she had suspected, the captain *was* sensitive to magic. That must have been what caused him to come down the street in the first place.

His magical sensitivity might be a problem, but it also made her question his origins. Anyone who was wholly human wouldn't have felt the magic she'd pulled from the ground, especially while they were hidden behind the witch's avoidance spell. Forcing herself to ignore the intriguing stranger, she focused again on the boy in front of her. "What do they call you?"

"Johnny," he said, straightening his thin body. He couldn't be older than nine or ten, but he had the world-weary gaze of someone who had been on the streets for most of their life.

"Do you know who I am, Johnny?"

A trace of fear came back into his eyes, but he nodded.

Sabine kept her expression neutral, not allowing him to see the sadness that filled her. He may know the name she went by here and the persona she'd carefully crafted, but only a select few knew her true identity. Just like the shadows hid her from view most of the time, so did the surrounding rumors.

Holding out the wooden coin she'd transmuted, she placed it in Johnny's hand and traced her fingernail over its surface. "Choices surround you and dictate possible paths to your future. A baker at the south end of town needs an assistant. He grows older and has no children, but he would gladly pass along his knowledge to one who is eager to learn and serve."

The boy stared in wonder at the loaf of bread now etched into the coin. It was little more than a parlor trick. Anyone with an ounce of magical ability could perform such a thing.

"But there is always another choice." Sabine paused and flipped the coin over before tracing her finger over it again. "If someone is smart, quick, and lucky, they may survive what the future holds. It would be a life of danger, but one with great rewards and greater risk. How much of each depends solely on you. There are no guarantees in either choice, just a chance to unlock a different path than the one you currently walk."

Johnny's eyes lit up, and he opened his mouth to make his choice. She gave him a curt shake of her head, and he froze, clamping his mouth shut. Sabine withdrew her hand, leaving the impression of a knife on the wooden coin in his hand. "No, Johnny. You will think upon your choice for at least one full night. After that, you can make your decision. As long as the coin remains in your possession, the choice is yours and yours alone."

He lifted his head again and closed his fist over the coin, gripping it tightly. "I won't let anyone take it from me."

She inclined her head in acknowledgment of his words. Based on his demeanor, that small piece of wood had just become the most important thing in his life. "You have a fortnight to make your choice. If you wish to become an apprentice, you will take the coin to Bjorn, the proprietor of Batter's Edge. In exchange, he will provide you with a bed, food, and a chance for something more—but only if you're willing to prove yourself. Do you know where his shop is located?"

"Yes."

She nodded. "If you wish to have a chance to learn the craft of those who live in the darkness and dance on the edge of a blade, you will take your coin to Copper's Crossing and find Edvar. Do you know him?"

Johnny nodded eagerly. Sabine resisted the urge to snort. Everyone seemed to know Edvar, a former street rat who had his hands in all sorts of pies. Edvar was going to have to start staying in the shadows. He was incredibly talented but a little reckless at times.

"Very well. If you do nothing or wait longer than a fortnight, the coin will disappear. That, too, is also a choice."

"Thank—"

She held up her hand. "There is no debt between us. Take your choice and go."

Johnny grinned and gripped the wooden coin before sprinting down the alley. Sabine turned and caught a trace of a smile on Malek's lips. The curiosity in his gaze made her wonder if she'd made a mistake. She hadn't wanted Johnny to disappear without paying her debt to him, but she wished no one else had been around to witness such a thing.

Ignoring Malek, she walked over to the body of the man who had carried the ancient iron weapon. The goblin was already busy investigating one of the other bodies and she couldn't allow him close to this one yet. She bent down to search the dead man, discreetly tracing her fingertips over his wrist tattoo to hide it with her glamour. It wouldn't last, but it would stay hidden until the city guards disposed of the body.

Malek crouched down beside her, his gaze straying to the man's wrist. She had the distinct impression he knew what she'd done.

He reached down and picked up the iron knife that had fallen to the ground. She tensed, her hand lingering near one of her weapons. Malek held her eyes as he unbuckled the dead man's knife sheath before sliding the iron blade into the protective leather sleeve and offering it to her. "I believe this is yours."

Sabine frowned and looked into his clear blue eyes. It was as though the sky itself had been captured in his irises. Unable to look away, Sabine reached out and took the weapon, attaching it to her belt by feel alone. She didn't like the idea of having the weapon so close to her, but she didn't have many options. It would be a while before she could discreetly dispose of it, but it was safer with her than in someone else's hands.

She stood and assessed Malek, once again feeling a pull toward him. He was a mystery she'd need to solve sooner rather than later, but the matter of the dead men took prece-dence—as well as the injury at her side and her hand. Unwilling to risk sending Malek off to Dax without some form of protection, she took a step toward him.

"It would seem I also owe you a debt," she said, not speci-fying whether she meant his efforts at killing one of her attackers or his silence about the dead man's tattoo. Either way, all debts needed to be paid. The unbalance hung heavily in the air between them, demanding satisfaction.

He searched her expression for a long time. Finally, he inclined his head. "A debt is due."

Sabine froze for a split second, surprised by the language he'd used. It was the formal exchange of an obligation, even if his words had been spoken in the common tongue. Although many people formalized a debt, few outside Faerie used the traditional wording. Tilting her head, she studied him but didn't see any trace of the Fae in his features or a hint of glamour. There was something about him though—something dangerous and deadly.

Taking a step toward him, she allowed a small smile to curve her lips. "What do you wish of me, Captain Malek Rish'dan?"

Malek swallowed, his Adam's apple bobbing as his heated gaze perused her up and down. If he asked for more than he was entitled to receive, the debt between them would be canceled. She didn't understand why the magic worked that way, but it was one loophole she'd cheerfully exploited a time or two. She waited, curious if he would rise to her challenge or if the debt hanging between them would shatter.

A small shiver went through Sabine at the intensity in Malek's eyes. She had the impression he saw much more than she intended. For a fleeting moment, she wondered if she'd misread him.

"Dinner."

She blinked at him, unsure if she'd heard him correctly. "What?"

His mouth curved upward. "I have no doubt you could have easily dispatched the last man." His blue eyes twinkled with amusement. "As Pozgil mentioned, I'm new to the city. I could easily learn my way around without your assistance, but a shared meal with exceptional company would be preferable."

She stared at him, stunned and a little bewildered. Not only had he neatly avoided the trap she'd left open for him, but he'd also made a request impossible to refuse. He may not be Fae, but he knew enough about their ways for her to be thoroughly intrigued. It had been a long time since a stranger surprised her. She closed the distance between them, unable to deny the magnetism she felt for this captivating man. For whatever reason, her power was drawn to him. It left her oddly unsettled.

"The repayment of the debt has been negotiated. Until it is fulfilled, I leave you with a marker of my promise so that you might call upon me." She held out her hand, both uneasy and curious about what would happen when she touched him.

He placed his much larger hand over hers, and she swallowed. It was just a touch, but she could detect a trace of the muted power within him. She turned his hand over in hers so it was facing palm upward. His fingers were calloused, indicating he was no stranger to hard labor and weapons training. She focused on the rest of his hand, tracing her fingertips over his bare wrist in a pattern. She spoke the words in barely more than a whisper and infused them with a trace of her magic.

He inhaled sharply, and Sabine felt a moment of connection as the debt between them was weighed. With a snap of electricity in the air, her mark settled on his skin. Since the debt was hers to repay, she also accepted the searing pain as though she'd applied it to her own skin. Burying her reaction, she traced the design again. "The agreement is accepted, witnessed, and sealed."

She lifted her gaze to meet his eyes. He appeared equally as affected by her touch. Slightly disconcerted, she added, "Once the debt has been repaid, the mark will fade. If I expire before the debt is collected, the mark will fade. If you pass on before it is collected, the mark will fade."

Malek placed his other hand over hers, trapping her hand between the warmth of his skin. It took everything she had to continue to breathe normally. Something about this man called to her on an elemental level—and for that reason alone, he was dangerous. He squeezed her hand gently. "I look forward to sharing dinner with you soon."

Sabine pulled her hand away, uneasy about what might happen if she continued touching him. She glanced over at the goblin who stared at her open-mouthed. "You are taking them to meet with Dax now?"

Pozgil clamped his mouth shut and straightened. "I'd be honored to escort you too. I'm sure Dax will have questions about this... attack."

She narrowed her eyes. That was putting it mildly. Dax would lose his mind when he found out what had happened on the border of his territory. Until she got answers of her own, she wasn't willing to risk another encounter with the unscrupulous leader of Akros's underworld. "I trust you can relay the events to the best of your knowledge. I have other matters that require my attention."

When Pozgil's skin flushed to that sickly green color again, Sabine relented slightly. Aside from accompanying him and handling Dax herself, there wasn't much she could do except make it clear to Dax that she had refused to go. There would likely be consequences for her decision, but they couldn't be helped—especially since she was bleeding.

She sighed. "Give my regards to Dax. I will see him soon enough."

Pozgil looked pained but nodded. "I'll give him your message."

She darted another quick glance at Malek and pulled her hood over her head. If he managed to survive his encounter with Dax, she'd have a chance to discover more about him. In any event, she'd done what she could to protect him until then.

Heading away from the alley, Sabine gathered some of the

lingering shadows around her. One thing she'd learned years ago was, if she couldn't see the monsters in the dark, they usually couldn't see her either. But the assassination attempt had made it clear the shadows weren't going to be enough for much longer.

Chapter Two

Unable to tear his gaze away, Malek watched the mysterious woman disappear into the darkness. The mark on his wrist still tingled, and he resisted the urge to rub it. Her touch had affected him more than he'd expected. Now he had an almost insatiable desire to discover the effects of having her hands on other parts of his body. The thought was more than a little distracting, and he shook his head to clear it.

Even without that brief taste of her power, her features had been a testament to her mixed Fae heritage. She'd even worn her hair in a braided style more suited to the Fae, but it was her nearly lavender eyes that had intrigued him. They were more blue than anything, but he'd caught a glimpse of the pale purple color—the mark of the Fae.

"Pointed ears," Levin murmured, staring down at the

bodies. "Four bodies, and two of them have pointed ears. Think they're part-Fae?"

Malek made a noise of agreement. The tips of the woman's ears had been pointed too, arching upward in a graceful slope. The trait wasn't as common in the northern cities where they were from. He'd heard some people living in Akros were of Fae descent, but he hadn't realized the strength of those ties until now.

"At least we know we're in the right place," Malek whispered.

The goblin's forked tongue flicked out as he gleefully pocketed another pouch of coins from one of the dead men.

Levin snorted. "I don't know about that. The Fae are supposed to be the keepers of the forests and lakes. I can't imagine someone with a lot of Fae magic living in a city like this."

"Ah, Levin, have a little faith," Malek said with a grin and clapped his friend on the shoulder.

The goblin cocked his head. "You have an interest in the Fae?"

Malek studied Pozgil in surprise. Goblins were one of the lesser Fae, but they had very little magic. It was unlikely he could help them, except to provide some information. "Of course. Tales of their beauty and magic are legendary. Anyone would be intrigued. Are there many Fae living in the city?"

Pozgil grinned, his tongue darting out between his lips. "We have quite a few with Fae blood, but no full-blooded Fae. Those taste of high magic and sex."

"I doubt they'd allow you close enough to take a bite," Levin said dryly. "I've heard the Fae are a bit more discerning in their tastes."

Pozgil shrugged. "The Unseelie Fae are more open-minded than the Seelie. How do you think some of these dead men ended up with pointed ears? When the Unseelie emerged from Underhill after the Dragon War, some took humans as lovers to replenish their numbers."

Levin frowned. "Underhill? You're referring to the Underworld?"

Malek leaned over to study one of the men's ears. Other than a slight point, he didn't see any other sign the man had been Fae. "It's one and the same. The Fae refer to it as Underhill, but the demons and dwarves call it the Underworld. The Unseelie Fae escaped their service to the gods and fled there."

Levin rubbed his chin in thought. "I'd wondered about the difference between the Seelie and Unseelie. You're saying the Seelie remained as servants to the gods and caretakers of the forests?"

"Yes," Malek said.

Pozgil scooted over to inspect the last dead man. He was having a little too much fun playing with the bodies. They'd need to pull him away soon, if he didn't knock it off. They were already running late for their appointment.

Malek turned back to Levin. "The Fae who remained in the light were Seelie, while those who embraced the darkness and abandoned their creators were Unseelie. Their magic is similar, but the Unseelie had to twist theirs into something darker to defend against the demons and dwarves while they were trapped in Underhill."

Pozgil dipped his finger into some of the blood on the ground and licked it off. "You know your history, Captain Malek. I'd think someone with your learning wouldn't be such a fool."

Levin stiffened at the insult and slapped his hand against his sword's hilt. "Watch your tongue, little man."

The goblin huffed and finished searching the last body. "I'll have you know, Dax won't be pleased with you threatening me. You're in *his* city now."

Malek glanced over at Levin and shook his head. Pozgil could hide behind his master all he wanted for the time being, but the minute Malek got what he'd come for, he'd abandon this ruse. "What did you mean about being foolish?"

"You'll find out soon enough." Pozgil straightened and brushed the dirt off his hands. "Now then, we'd best be on our way. The city's guards will be along shortly, and they won't take too kindly to us being here. One near-death experience for the evening is more than enough. Although, I'd rather face down the guards than risk running into Sabine again."

Malek looked down at the body of the man whose tattoo had disappeared with a small swipe of magic. For some reason, Sabine hadn't wanted Pozgil or anyone else to see the design. It had been some sort of dagger with the edge wrapped in ivy. The tattoo had been distinctive enough that Malek intended to learn more about it—and hopefully about the mysterious woman who had hidden it.

The goblin started heading out of the alley, and Malek walked alongside Levin, taking the opportunity to study the city. As first impressions went, Akros wasn't particularly remarkable. Though it was a little rough around the edges, it was similar to dozens of other cities lining the coast. The biggest difference was, it was the gateway city to the southern lands, housing one of the largest mixed magical communities in the world.

Pozgil pinched the bridge of his pointed green nose. "How'd you convince Sabine not to kill you?"

Levin smirked. "He has that effect on women."

Malek shrugged, not bothering to explain. He suspected her hesitation had been the result of his hasty attempt to speak the language of the Fae. He'd caught the surprise in her eyes. "What do you know about her?"

Pozgil darted a quick look at him. "I know enough to stay

away. Dax won't be happy when he finds out what happened —or about your dinner invitation. You'll be lucky if he doesn't kill you right off."

"Please tell me she's not involved with the leader of the thieves' guild," Levin muttered.

Pozgil nodded. "She's under his protection. The fact you helped kill one of those men might be the only thing that saves you. I'd suggest canceling your dinner plans and be ready to board your ship as quickly as possible if things go bad."

The mark on Malek's wrist tingled as though it possessed its own awareness. He glanced down at it, but the triangular pattern hadn't changed. It wasn't common to formalize such a small debt between two people, but she'd wanted to mark him for a reason. If Sabine was involved with Dax, that might be a problem, but he needed to learn more about her. The mark was a guarantee he'd see her again. Otherwise, he wasn't sure he would have allowed her to walk away. Her power had been like a beacon calling to him from the docks when he'd disembarked from his ship.

"I'm not concerned. It's only dinner," Malek said, continuing to walk through the darkened streets. The buildings in this area of town were more run down and a number of them were abandoned. Even though the streets appeared to be empty, he could feel the weight of eyes upon them.

Pozgil snorted. "Dinner. Right." The goblin looked around and lowered his voice to a hushed whisper, "The last man who looked at Sabine the way you did was found floating in the canal. His limbs had been ripped from his body and were never recovered. The guards said they thought it happened while he was still alive."

Levin shot him a warning look, but Malek ignored him and continued walking. He'd hoped to have been here a bit longer before offending the disreputable guild master, but he wasn't about to abandon his purpose.

They turned a corner, and this street was markedly different. Lanterns lined the path, and the street was more congested. It was still a poor area of town, but a handful of prostitutes lounged against the wall calling out a greeting to them as they passed.

A few other people were milling around nearby. Some were a little too sharp-eyed considering the location and time of night, which led Malek to believe they were some of Dax's men. He'd heard the majority of the city was locked down by Dax's people, which was why he'd requested this meeting in the first place. Supposedly, Dax had the pulse of almost everything that went on within Akros's underworld and even in some of the surrounding villages.

At the end of the street stood a brightly lit tavern. Pozgil led them right up to the entrance and pushed open the heavy wooden door. Malek wasn't sure what he'd expected, but it wasn't the warm and welcoming sight that greeted them. Tables were scattered throughout the overly large room with dozens of people gathered together and enjoying a companionable drink or two.

The bar itself was unlike any he'd seen before. The base was carved out of a single tree, with detailed carvings of leaves and animals perched in the branches. The top of the bar was almost equally captivating, with what appeared to be fractured glass that caught the light of the candles, reflecting it throughout the room and giving the surrounding walls a warm, cheerful glow.

Several more doxies made the rounds throughout the tavern, most of them more appealing than the ones lingering outside. The patrons, on the other hand, enforced the idea this wasn't the most reputable of areas. They had the sharp eyes and hardened lines on their faces that made it clear they were intimate with a darker side of life. Each one of them appeared heavily armed, and more than a few had scars from previous run-ins with a blade.

Pozgil pushed past the bar and headed directly to a man standing guard in front of another door. The man's eyes narrowed on Pozgil, and he crossed his arms over his chest. Undeterred, the goblin straightened his body. "I've brought Captain Malek and his first mate to see Dax."

"It's all right, Campho. They're expected," a man said from behind them.

Malek turned to find another man with mixed Fae heritage. He had the same light hair and eyes as Sabine, but there was a coarseness to his features Sabine had lacked. The tusks jutting out of his mouth made Malek question if he carried a bit of troll in his bloodline. Malek detected a faint trace of power surrounding him, but it was more Fae than troll.

"A-apologies, Javyn, er, sir," Pozgil sputtered, his eyes wide at the approaching Fae. "I didn't realize you were here."

Javyn frowned at the goblin. "Dax expected you earlier."

Pozgil swallowed audibly, his coloring deepening to a sickly green. The metallic and bitter scent of the goblin's fear was enough to make Malek's nose itch.

The goblin hopped from foot to foot. "Uh, we ran into some trouble. But everything's okay. We handled it. Yep. Everything's fine. Nothing to worry about."

"You can explain your delay to Dax," Javyn said before turning toward Malek. "You're the ship captain?"

Malek inclined his head. "Captain Malek Rish'dan of Obsidian's Storm."

"Welcome to Akros. The name's Javyn. If you'll follow me, I'll take you to see Dax." Without waiting for a reply, Javyn headed into the tavern's back rooms. Malek exchanged a look with Levin before following Javyn. Apparently, polite niceties weren't high on the thieves' guild's list of priorities. It was just as well. The sooner he met with Dax, the faster this entire sordid affair could be resolved.

The back area of the tavern wasn't quite as welcoming as the front. A few closed doors lined the hallway with lanterns tucked into stone alcoves, illuminating the darkness. Some of these rooms were under guard, but other than a few curious glances, no one said anything as they passed. Javyn led them toward a steep staircase and headed downward, not bothering to check if they were still behind him.

Malek couldn't help but think about Sabine again, comparing her more delicate features with the man they followed. If it weren't for her skin and hair coloring, he'd wonder if Sabine were a full-blooded Fae. Her voice had the same musical lilt and accent that marked someone of Fae descent, but her appearance was far too human. Part of him wished he'd had a chance to hear her speak more of their language to determine if she carried that same inflection in her words. The few pure-blooded Fae he'd known had the ability to cause a reaction simply by speaking. That was part of their gift and power. Some of their words could cause ecstasy while others could drive someone mad. During the last war, Fae captives had to be gagged to prevent them from singing their way to freedom or inciting mass panic.

At the bottom of the stairs was an expansive corridor. The air was heavier down here, with a trace of moisture, and Malek detected the faint sound of rushing water, most likely from one of the canals. A set of heavy double doors was built into the wall, and Javyn pushed them open and led them into a larger room. This had the appearance of a meeting room with an elongated table set up in the center. A handful of people were gathered around the table talking, but it was the man standing at the head of the table who commanded Malek's attention.

Levin inhaled sharply, and Malek had to force himself not to react or reveal his surprise. For all his inquiries into Dax and his group, no one had even hinted the man he stood before was a demon. Most of them were confined to the underworld, unable or unwilling to venture into the sunlight, which weakened their magic significantly. If Malek had known the guild leader's identity, he would have handled this entire endeavor differently or even possibly dismissed Dax as a potential resource. This new development made Malek even more curious about Sabine and her ties to a demon.

If legends were true, the dwarves and demons shared the same origins as the Fae. The demons, with their penchant for violence and working the underworld forges, took up residence in the deepest levels of Underhill. They became the caretakers of the molten rock and fires burning deep within the world's core.

Demons twisted their brand of magic into weapons, lashing out with fire elemental abilities—and it was that same fire ability that concerned Malek now. He only hoped the warding necklace around his neck was powerful enough to mask his true intent. The witch who had crafted it for him had assured him of such, but they hadn't anticipated the need to deceive a demon.

Levin whispered, "We might want to rethink this plan. Demons have ties to the Fae, but this is too risky."

Malek shook his head as Javyn approached the demon standing at the head of the table. In a voice too low for anyone else to overhear, Malek said to Levin, "Not just yet. This might still work out to our benefit."

Levin frowned at him, but Malek didn't elaborate. Even though they were in a cellar underneath the tavern, Dax shouldn't be able to live within a mostly human city cut off from the magic of the underworld. Perhaps Akros had a larger source of magic than rumors claimed, or maybe Malek didn't know the full truth about demons. Either way, he intended to get to the bottom of it.

The man standing at the head of the table was a powerful and massive man, with skin the color of the darkest obsidian. He was a true master of the night—even the light from the lantern seemed hesitant to touch him. The room fell silent as Javyn leaned in close and whispered something to the demon. Dax lifted his horned head, his amber eyes holding the flame of his ancestors as he pinned Malek with his gaze. No matter what he'd hoped, Malek couldn't deny the truth: Dax would be an adversary who would require careful handling.

Pozgil approached the table and bowed low, almost touching the ground with his forehead. "I-I apologize for the delay, sir. We ran into a bit of trouble, but I've brought Captain Malek and his first mate to discuss a business opportunity with you."

Dax didn't respond right away. Instead, he motioned for a woman to roll up the maps they'd been studying. As she moved forward and began clearing the table, Dax sat down in his chair, leaned back, and steepled his hands together.

"What sort of trouble?"

Pozgil shifted from foot to foot, rubbing the back of his neck. Malek half expected his knees to start knocking from the way he was panicking. When Dax arched his brow, Pozgil stammered, "Ah, er, well, we happened to run into Sabine."

A sudden stillness fell over the room at the mention of Sabine's name. Everyone's attention became focused on the goblin trembling in front of Dax.

"Is that so?" Dax questioned mildly, but the sudden rigidity in his shoulders made it obvious he was more than a little interested in Pozgil's response.

"Ah, yes. She... well, some men..." His voice trailed off

and his shoulders hunched, clearly uneasy about spilling the full story.

"Dammit, Pozgil. Spit it out already," another man muttered. This man also had the look of the Fae in his chiseled features, equally as strong as Sabine's had been. With his nearly white blond hair and pale blue eyes, he could have passed as one of Sabine's close relatives. But unlike Sabine and Javyn, Malek didn't sense even a faint hint of power from him.

"Right. Sorry, Verin," Pozgil said with an eager nod. "Some men attacked her, but she's okay. She's fine. They're all dead."

"I see," Dax murmured, drumming his fingertips on the arm of his chair. "And where did this happen?"

"Over by the butcher's shop on East End Lane." Pozgil clasped his hands together tightly. From the way his gaze darted around the table, he was obviously fearful he'd be blamed for the attack.

Verin frowned. "How long ago did this happen?"

"Right before we arrived here. The bodies are probably still warm and their blood still wet." Pozgil snickered, his forked tongue slithering outward as though he could still taste the blood in the air.

Dax motioned toward two of his men. They both nodded and hastened out of the room. When they were gone, Dax leaned back in his chair again. "And what of Sabine?"

"She, uh, she…" Pozgil cleared his throat. "I believe she'll see you soon. She sends her regards."

"Does she?" Dax murmured with a trace of a cruel smile.

A heavily armed woman with a long scar down the side of her face spoke up. "Should we attempt to track her?"

"That won't be necessary. You won't find her unless she wants to be found. She'll reappear soon enough," Dax said with an absent wave. "Was there anything else, Pozgil?"

Pozgil gestured to Malek eagerly. "It was fortunate Captain Malek arrived. He helped Sabine kill one of them."

Dax arched his brow, sweeping his gaze over Malek. Despite Pozgil's claims, the look wasn't overly friendly. "Sabine is under my protection. If you aided her, it would seem I owe you a debt."

The mark on Malek's wrist tingled, almost in warning. "That won't be necessary. The debt belongs to Sabine, and it has been settled between us."

Dax froze, his features hardening. He studied Malek for a long time, and Malek felt the weight of his gaze as Dax caught sight of Sabine's mark on his wrist. A brief flash of anger streaked through his amber eyes, turning them to a sharp silver before they reverted to their normal color. For whatever reason, Dax wasn't pleased with this newest development.

Dax pushed up from the chair. "In that case, perhaps we should discuss why you're in *my* city."

Malek inclined his head. The introductory message he'd sent had outlined his intent, but the demon obviously wanted Malek to go through a song and dance for his benefit. "As my messenger detailed, my purpose here is two-fold. In addition to establishing Akros as part of a regular trading route, I represent some individuals who are interested in acquiring certain rare artifacts—discreetly, of course."

"I'm aware of your request for assistance in smuggling merchandise through the trading blockades." Dax turned away from the table and paced the length of the room. "Tell me about the items you're looking to offload."

"Rare wines, ale, textiles, and other specialty items from the southern dwarven city all the way north as far as the Sky Cities." Malek wondered if he might need to approach this from a different angle. He had the impression Dax might not be receptive to such an offer, and now Malek was curious how steep the price tag would be to elicit the demon's agreement. But the smuggling was inconsequential compared to his true purpose. He *needed* those artifacts found, and Dax's position left him best suited for the task. The smuggling was only a way to access Dax's underworld contacts.

"Why should I consider your proposal over the others who have reached out to me?"

Malek took a step toward Dax, refusing to show any signs of weakness. Demons only respected those they considered equals or more powerful, but Malek needed to strike a balance to elicit Dax's confidence.

"I don't know what the others have offered you, but in addition to giving you a cut of all trading profits, you'll also have first pick of the available merchandise. As you know, trading is almost nonexistent with the northern Sky Cities. Through my contacts, you'll have access to the rarest and most costly merchandise available."

When Dax arched a brow, Malek buried his smile and added, "As a gesture of our goodwill, my people have been instructed to deliver a crate to you in the morning which will contain a sampling of the items we're prepared to provide you. Consider it a gift."

"A gift," Dax murmured, his gaze turning suspicious. The demon was clearly intrigued, but he was equally cautious. He likely wouldn't have lasted long in his position if he trusted easily. "Very well. I'll consider your request and let you know my decision after we assess your merchandise. In the meantime, Javyn will show you to a room. You may remain here for the duration of your stay. We will discuss the rest of your request later."

"Your hospitality is generous." Malek suspected the offer was more of an order than a request. He'd prepared and even hoped for such a thing, but that was before he'd known Dax was a demon. This entire endeavor had just become more challenging, and the chances for success had taken a swift nosedive into murky waters. Unfortunately, failure to acquire the artifacts he was hunting would have much more far-reaching repercussions.

SABINE SLIPPED BEHIND A COLUMN, holding the darkness around her like a thick cloak. The wound at her side throbbed; otherwise, she never would have ventured here. The two men's voices grew louder as they approached the room. The door creaked open, and Sabine held her breath as they moved deeper into the room.

"Enough, Evo. I'm not prepared to consider his request at this time," Bane said with a trace of irritation in his voice.

"I understand your reservations, sir," Evo argued, "but we could use the extra manpower. We're getting more requests from farther away, and it would benefit our cause to have a presence in other cities. Would you at least consider taking on some additional recruits if I personally vetted each one?"

Bane was quiet for a long time, but his footsteps moved toward the desk. "I suppose you already have a list?"

"Yes."

"Very well. I'll take a look at your other alternatives in the morning," Bane agreed and then sighed. "Close the door on your way out, Evo."

"Of course. Goodnight."

The floorboard creaked, and Sabine leaned against the column, listening as Evo's footsteps moved toward the door. The door shut, and Sabine heard the clink of glasses before Bane said, "I just acquired a new case of dwarven ale. You might enjoy this one."

Despite the pain from her injury, Sabine smiled and moved around the column to face the demon. Bane's darkened skin shone in the lamplight, and the two jutting horns on his otherwise bald head indicated the expansive power at his fingertips. He could be a formidable opponent against his enemies, but there was no sign of that now. Instead, he stood beside the bar on the opposite end of the room and held out a glass toward her.

"You always know when I'm here," she complained, walking over to him.

Bane smirked. "You always make it easy for me."

Her eyes narrowed, but she took the proffered glass. She sniffed at it and then wrinkled her nose in distaste. With the way he drank, one would think Bane was a dwarf. It was a stark reminder of their differences.

"Try it, little one, and stop making that face." Bane took a drink. "If you visited more often, I might be tempted to acquire a case of your preferred wine."

"If you get hold of a case of my wine, I might consider it," she agreed but took a sip. Dear gods. It was as bad as the smell had warned. Placing the horrific brew back on the bar, she turned to him. "I'll never understand how you can drink that swill. I've crafted more palatable poisons."

"I suppose it's an acquired taste." Bane put down his drink and took a step closer to her. "I'm assuming you're here for another reason. How badly are you hurt?"

Sabine frowned and lifted her shirt. Exhaling slowly, she released the glamour masking the injury. It wasn't as serious as she'd feared, more of a surface wound than anything but it was still bleeding. If there hadn't been so many of them, her attacker never would have managed to get a lucky strike with his blade. But she couldn't risk allowing it to heal naturally. She'd temporarily stopped it from bleeding with her magic, but it was already failing. Magic was in her blood, and hers could be dangerous—especially if the wrong people discovered it.

Bane's eyes roamed over her. "You *could* release all of your glamour, Sabine. It's been a long time since you allowed me to see your truth."

Sabine turned her head away, her long hair offering a protective curtain to hide the emotion his words evoked. Over the years, she'd only risked lowering her glamour in times of great need. It was painful holding on to it all the time, but she'd grown accustomed to it. When one lived with constant pain for so long, it became part of their psyche. But part of her still yearned for freedom.

"Don't push, Bane. Not here. It makes it harder to hold on to it when you say such things."

He fell silent and trailed his fingers over her side. His touch was gentle, but Sabine winced as he brushed against the injury. When he spoke, a sharp edge of fury laced his tone. "Who's responsible for this?"

She turned back to him. "Fix it and my hand. Then I'll tell you what I know."

Bane scowled and continued to trail his fingers over her skin. When nothing happened, she narrowed her eyes at him. "You're as stubborn as Dax. Heal it or back the hell off."

"Don't compare me to him," he growled, threading his power through his fingertips and into her skin.

Despite what many people believed, healing wasn't a pleasant experience. The body would repair itself naturally over time, but a forced healing made the recipient relive the original injury—only worse. For every action, there was an equal and opposite reaction. Magic was the same. Every small bit required a type of sacrifice. Her own brand of magic was no different.

When she'd killed those men, she's stolen part of their life's energy and had been holding it in reserve. Through touch, she now gifted some of it to Bane in exchange for his healing. He eagerly accepted the offering, easing the balance of debt between them and erasing the burden from her soul. His fingertips became more heated as they trailed over her skin, healing her injuries. He leaned toward her, putting both his hands on her waist and pulled her closer. With a growl, he lowered his head and kissed her.

Sabine immediately stiffened, surprised at his lapse in control. But this was Bane. He never would have kissed her unless he needed her and what she could offer. Relaxing her body against him, she sent more of her magic toward him in a gentle wave. He deepened his kiss, and his touch became more demanding. She placed her hands against his chest, and he broke the kiss.

Breathing heavily, he gazed at her with a wild, heated look in his eyes. It was both unnerving and thrilling. Instead of backing away, she lifted her chin to meet his eyes. Any sign of weakness could be used against her. Bane was dangerous on the best of occasions, but he always pushed himself too far, especially with her.

"What do you need from me, Bane?"

He gripped her tighter before releasing her suddenly. Turning away, he started to pace the room. He ran a hand over his head in agitation, and Sabine glared at him. She was tired of these games.

Sabine took a step toward him. "You don't want to be compared to Dax, but you're both equally stubborn. Why can't you tell me what you need? It's *not* a weakness. I've never refused you when you've asked for my magic or needed an outlet for yours. That was our agreement all those years ago."

Bane whirled around and punched the wall. Plaster broke free as he removed his fist. If he were more frustrated, he'd end up taking out the entire wall. She'd seen it happen before. Sabine watched for a moment and then turned to pick up the glass of dwarven ale she'd barely touched. She wouldn't drink it, but Bane likely needed it. She held it out, and he snatched it from her.

Taking a healthy swallow, he muttered, "You shouldn't provoke either of us."

Sabine's eyes narrowed, and she jabbed her finger against his chest. "*You* kissed *me*. I'm not going to pretend it didn't happen. Now, do you want to have this discussion, or would you rather learn what happened tonight?"

Bane scowled, placing the glass on the desk hard enough that she was surprised it didn't break. "Who went after you?"

It figured. Neither Bane nor Dax were willing to resolve the myriad of issues between them. Fine. She sighed and leaned against the wall, trying to resist the urge to bang her head against it. May the gods spare her from stubborn demons and foolish pride. "Four men. They herded me to the border of Dax's territory. One of them wore your mark."

"The fuck did you say?" he snarled, taking a step toward her.

Sabine grabbed his wrist and held it out to prominently display the dagger tattoo on his forearm. It had been crafted with blood and magic, among other things. All of Bane's men carried the mark. "It was one of your men, Bane. An assassin. Someone is setting you up."

"Don't move," he ordered and stormed toward the door. He flung it open and bellowed, "Evo, get your ass in here now."

Footsteps pounded on the stairway, and Sabine sighed. She sat on the edge of the desk and glanced over at the bar, debating whether to try Bane's new ale again. The taste wouldn't have improved, but it might make the next few minutes more tolerable.

"What's going on?" Evo's footsteps faltered as he entered. "Sabine? I wasn't aware you were here."

Sabine gave Evo a curt nod in greeting. She didn't care

much for him, and Evo wasn't overly fond of her either. But Bane trusted him, even if she'd rather drink a case of that ale in lieu of spending another moment with Evo. If she were being fair, it wasn't exactly Evo's fault. He was loyal to Bane, and Evo believed her presence caused problems for his boss. As long as Dax considered Sabine under his protection, he would continue trying to meddle in Bane's affairs, especially when she was around.

"Sabine, describe the man." Bane shut the door a bit more forcefully than necessary.

She shrugged. "Human. A bit taller than me, short brown hair, scar on his chin, smelled like leather and oil."

Evo darted a quick glance at Bane. "Who is she describing?"

Bane didn't stop his pacing. "A man wearing our emblem attacked her tonight."

Evo's frown deepened. "I'm assuming the man is dead?"

Sabine arched her brow, trying to bury her irritation. "I think my presence is answer enough."

Evo blew out a breath. "It sounds like Naphor, one of our newer men."

Bane pointed a finger at Evo. "*This* is why we're not opening our doors to more recruits. I want a list drafted of all his closest associates immediately. Bring me everyone who was recruited shortly before or after him. I want everyone questioned. *Tonight.*"

Sabine slid off the desk and stretched. Thanks to Bane's healing abilities, her side felt remarkably better. Now that she'd given Bane sufficient warning, she needed to figure out how her attackers knew where to find her. Only a couple of people had known her plans to speak with the clerk working in the city council's office, and she needed to question each of them.

She headed toward the window. "Do what you must. I have other things requiring my attention."

"Sabine," Bane called out, and she turned toward him.

He held her gaze for a long time, indecision warring on his face. She waited expectantly, but he didn't say anything else. It wasn't surprising. Bane might want to keep her safe, but he wouldn't dare try to keep her here against her will. He knew she'd never volunteer to remain if she had a choice.

Instead, she gave him a small smile. "Goodnight, Bane. If you need me, you know how to find me. Otherwise, I'll see you soon."

Without waiting for a response, she climbed back out the window and headed toward the commercial district. It was time for the hunted to become the hunter.

Chapter Three

The following evening, Sabine pushed open the door and stormed into the dimly lit tavern.

"Dammit. Get Dax. Now," One of Dax's guards ordered.

A man hastened toward the back rooms, but she ignored him as she scanned the seating areas. Her target was in here somewhere. Dax would take a few minutes to arrive, and it might be enough time to get the information she needed without his interference.

"Sabine? Can I get you a drink?"

She didn't respond to the bartender's attempt at distracting her. Instead, she hung up her cloak to allow more freedom of movement. Taking a step down into the main seating area, another one of Dax's men stepped in front of her.

"Sabine, always good to see you. Are you looking for someone?"

She spared the briefest glance at Javyn. "Which one is Riven?"

Javyn frowned and didn't reply right away. Sabine narrowed her eyes on him, dropping her hand to the hilt of her knife. Javyn was the only one of Dax's men who would dare consider challenging her presence, but only up to a point.

Lowering her voice to barely above a whisper, she threatened, "Do *not* push me on this, Javyn. Point out Riven, and your task is done."

Javyn nodded toward the southernmost table. It was enough for her to pick out a man fitting the description she'd been given. Riven, the man who had sold information about her whereabouts, was drinking with several others at the table. Judging by his animated gestures and loud voice, he was more than a little intoxicated.

She moved quickly to the table and kicked out Riven's chair from underneath him. He fell over backward. Everyone else at the table jumped up, but they immediately backpedaled when they sobered with recognition. None of them made any effort to help their drinking buddy.

Pressing her boot against Riven's throat, she withdrew one of her knives. "I got a message you were looking for me."

His eyes widened in fear. She pressed down a little harder. "Who paid you, Riven?"

He opened his mouth as though trying to speak. Sabine eased up her foot, and he managed, "I-I-I don't know what you're—"

She cut him off by pressing down again with the heel of her boot. Turning the blade in her hand so the light caught the metal, she leaned forward. "Shall I start removing your body parts until your memory returns? We can start with your pretty blue eyes."

His eyes bulged, and he tried to shake his head. She eased

up again, and he held up his hands in surrender. "P-please, Sabine. I haven't done anything. I'd never betray Dax. You have the wrong man."

"Is there a problem here?"

Sabine bit back the urge to curse. Dax had arrived a little too quickly.

She took a step away from Riven and turned around to face Dax. He was an intimidating figure with a powerful physique. His intense amber eyes were focused on her, and she returned his gaze evenly. Inclining her head, she gestured to the man on the ground. "I'd say so. It seems your man's been selling information about me, Dax."

His eyes flashed to silver and narrowed on the man at her feet. "Is that so?"

Riven sat up halfway and rubbed his neck. "I swear I'm loyal to you, Dax. I'd never do anything to betray you."

Dax scowled and crossed his arms over his chest. "Which is it? Are you calling Sabine a liar? Or have you been selling information?"

Sabine leaned against a column as Javyn and Campho moved forward and hauled Riven to his feet. Riven's expression was full of panic now, and he searched the room for anyone who might intervene. The fool. No one would challenge Dax, especially when his eyes were silvered.

"I-I... She must be mistaken. I would never—"

Dax took a step toward him. "Who did you sell information to?"

Sabine waited, feigning boredom as Riven sobbed and denied any involvement. Dax tended to draw these things out, but she couldn't interfere any further with his men watching. It was one thing to handle matters when he wasn't around but another to interrogate one of his people while he was there.

Javyn withdrew his knife and pressed it under Riven's right eye. "Which eye did you want keep as a trophy, Sabine?"

She tilted her head and pretended to consider it. "I'm partial to the left."

Dax nodded. "Take his eye, Javyn."

"Wait!" Riven shouted, his panicked gaze darting back and forth between them. "It was Terrance. I had no idea he would send someone to ambush Sabine. He said he wanted to talk to her. He swore he wouldn't raise a hand to her."

Dax took a step toward Riven, his gaze murderous. "What did Terrance give you in exchange for this information?"

Riven's chin trembled. "He paid off my debts. I only told him she'd planned to meet with the city clerk's assistant around midnight. That's all. I swear!"

Sabine straightened. Dax wasn't asking about this person named Terrance, so he had to know him. Judging by the hardened glint in Dax's eyes, neither Terrance nor his informant would be breathing much longer. Dax would likely execute both men before she had the chance to question them. Dammit. She couldn't let that happen. She needed to learn more about the man who'd hired Riven.

Putting her hand on Dax's arm, she infused her touch with a trace of magic to catch his attention. "Don't kill him yet, Dax. Who's Terrance?"

Dax narrowed his eyes at her, but she held his gaze, unwilling to back down. Dax would cut her out of this investigation if she let him, and there was too much at stake. Her life was at risk, not his.

"If you won't tell me, then give me ten minutes with Riven. Call it compensation for *your* man selling information about me."

Riven's eyes widened. She started to move toward Riven to question him, but Dax grabbed her arm. She wasn't surprised. He'd never let her interrogate one of his men once he was involved. Demons were impossibly controlling, and Dax was no exception.

In one smooth movement, she withdrew her knife and tried to move forward. Dax yanked her backward and she started to spin away, but he wouldn't relinquish his grip. Stepping hard onto his foot, she tried to sidestep. He pushed her up against the column, using his heavier body mass to trap her. It was nothing more than she'd expected. Dax had been training her in fighting techniques and weapons for the past several years. Fortunately, she'd learned to anticipate some of his moves. They'd done this particular dance many times, and she wasn't above being sneaky.

Sabine pressed her knife against his abdomen and smiled sweetly. "We can play later, Dax. I need answers first."

He gave her a wicked grin, his eyes flashing with the thrill of the hunt and the challenge she offered. "Haven't I told you never to draw your weapon unless you intend to use it? From you, this is the equivalent of foreplay."

Despite herself, she laughed and relaxed her grip on the knife. Dax trailed his hand down her arm and encircled her waist. He leaned in close and whispered, "Don't run away until I'm finished here, beautiful. Otherwise, I *will* hunt you down, and you know how much I love the chase."

She didn't reply, and he chuckled before turning back to Riven. Dax's comment wasn't exactly an agreement to share information, but he knew she wouldn't remain here for long if he wasn't forthcoming.

Dax walked over to the man on the ground. "You disappoint me, Riven."

Riven's chin trembled. "I swear, I didn't know what Terrance had planned. I never would have betrayed you. Terrance said he needed to talk to her without you knowing about it."

Sabine winced. That was the wrong thing to say. Apparently, Dax agreed.

He stormed toward Riven and grabbed the man around the throat. Yanking him up, Dax shoved him against the wall and snarled, "*That* is betrayal."

Riven started thrashing, trying to escape Dax's ironclad grip. Sabine turned away, not willing to watch any further. Riven screamed, but Sabine knew his night was just beginning. Dax would probably keep him alive for a few days to make an example of him. It would be some time before anyone else considered betraying Dax again. Unfortunately, that meant any information she needed would have to be elicited from Dax himself. He'd never let her anywhere near Riven now, even if she insisted. For all his flaws, Dax took his oath to protect her seriously. They just disagreed on what that entailed. But it wasn't an oath to *her*, so her opinion apparently didn't matter—or so the old argument went.

Sabine walked over to the bar and slid onto an empty stool. A loud *crack* sounded behind her, and from the piercing scream that followed, she guessed Dax had broken something. She blew out a breath, debating whether to slip away. Sometimes Dax enjoyed torture a little too much, but she suspected he'd meant what he said. Dax would come after her if she left. He wouldn't hurt her when he found her, but he'd take out his anger on everyone else around him. If she remained, she'd at least have a chance to diffuse the worst of it.

"Take him downstairs and chain him up," Dax ordered, and Riven's screams became garbled whimpers as though he'd been gagged or was in more pain than the human body could handle. "Find out what else he knows, but keep him alive. I'll see to him later."

She didn't turn around to look. Henry, the bartender, had gone pale as he stared over her shoulder, presumably at Dax.

Henry had seen a great deal over the years, so she had to assume it was particularly bad.

Sabine drummed her fingers on the top of the bar. "What do you have to drink tonight?"

Henry blinked at her, and she nodded toward the bottles behind the counter. He needed to snap out of it before Dax got over here.

Henry swallowed. "Ah, sorry about that. We have—"

"Get her some of the wine we just received. There's a bottle behind the bar," Dax ordered from behind her and pressed his hand against her back.

She started to turn toward him, but she caught sight of the ship captain, Malek, sitting at the end of the bar. She stared at him for a second before forcing herself to turn away. It wouldn't be a good idea to show any interest in Malek while Dax was in a foul mood.

It was hard to resist not taking another peek. The magnetism between them undeniable, but something wasn't right. She'd marked Malek. She should have sensed his presence before now. There were rumors about items that could interfere with a mark or bond, but she'd never experienced anything like that before.

Dax trailed his hand down her back. Her eyes narrowed on the demon in warning, but he simply grinned and sat on the stool beside her. The bartender put a silver goblet in front of her. She picked it up, inhaling deeply and breathing in the heady scent of the fruits and forest. Her eyes widened in surprise. Faerie wine was difficult to come by, and the price very dear. That Dax was willing to go to such lengths made her wary of his motivations. He wasn't usually known for his generosity. Knowing Dax had procured it for her made her feelings toward him soften a bit. Perhaps that had been his intention.

His fingers stroked the thin material of her shirt as she

took a sip of the wine. Her eyes unwittingly fluttered closed as the taste of home settled on her tongue. It was rich with earthy undertones, and the memories of the forest and laughter flashed through her mind. There was something else under the surface, lurking at the edge of the memory.

Before she could focus on it too much, Dax leaned in close to her and whispered, "I'm tempted to take you and that bottle downstairs. I bet I could make you forget about everything, more than any glass of wine."

Sabine blinked up at Dax, not terribly surprised the threat of torturing Riven had incited some of his other appetites. Even if she rebuked his invitation, he'd shrug it off and find someone else to share his bed. It wouldn't require much effort either. The tavern was currently full of women who would happily accept any invitation he made to them.

They had a complicated understanding between them, so he wouldn't care either way. On some level, she *did* care about him, but their relationship was built out of necessity, not from any tender feelings. Most people didn't understand their arrangement and assumed they meant more to each other than they did. Then again, most of those people were more human than *Other*. Humans had some bizarre notions about intimacy and sex that hadn't dissipated even though they'd come to this world through the portal thousands of years ago.

Sabine swirled the wine in her glass while deciding on an appropriate response. "Maybe if you tell me what you know about Terrance, I'll be more inclined to consider your offer."

"Ah." Dax settled back in his seat and motioned for Henry to get him a drink. "Terrance is recently new to the city. He's only been here a few months, but he's been busy making a name for himself."

She frowned and took another sip of her wine. The effect was immediate—both calming and relaxing. It was probably why Dax had wanted her to drink it. She wouldn't put it past him to use the wine to lower her defenses, and this was an excellent way to accomplish his goals. Sadly, Faerie wine was still a rarity here and she wasn't about to abandon her glass. It tasted different than she remembered, but it had been a long time since she'd been able to enjoy such a delicacy. Each winemaker had their own special flavor of magic, so some variations were expected.

"I haven't heard of him. Where can I find him?"

Henry put Dax's glass in front of him. Judging by the greenish color of the bubbling liquid, it contained his preferred beverage distilled with hops and the sweat of goblins. That might be part of the reason Pozgil was always so terrified of him. Dax wasn't picky about where the goblin sweat came from.

Dax didn't answer right away and instead took a long drink. Her gaze fell upon Malek again, and she idly took another sip of her wine. He watched her too and wasn't making any effort to mask his interest. His mouth curved upward, and heat pooled in the center of her belly. It was both intriguing and worrying that only a look elicited such a strong reaction in her.

Sabine lifted her glass again, drinking more deeply this time. Sharing wine with the fascinating ship captain might be interesting. Malek possessed magic, of that she was certain. She just didn't know what kind or how much. Part of her wondered if the memories contained within the magic of the wine would be hers alone or if he could walk the path with her. She was tempted to find out.

Dax put down his glass. "I understand you met Malek yesterday."

Sabine didn't reply right away. Dax had obviously caught her interest and wasn't particularly pleased about it. Like most demons, Dax was possessive, and it probably rankled that she'd decided to mark Malek. Dax had been trying to incite her into marking him permanently for years, but she'd managed to avoid it. She wasn't inclined to give him more leverage over her than he already had.

At least her temporary mark on Malek's wrist had kept him alive so far. Dax wouldn't dare harm the ship captain while it was present.

Sabine swirled the wine in her glass again. "Avoiding my question, Dax? I thought you were going to tell me about Terrance and where to find him."

His eyes narrowed on her, and he lifted one of her many braids. He trailed his fingers down it and murmured, "Shall we talk about avoidance, Sabine?"

She stiffened, something in his tone making her uneasy. "What do you want in exchange for information about Terrance?"

Dax's mouth curved in a wicked smile. "Many things, but I doubt you'll pay the price I want. Not for one such as him anyway."

Sabine was quiet for a long time before picking up her wine again. Dax was intentionally trying to keep her off guard for some reason, but she didn't know his game. She peered at him over the rim of her goblet. "I might not object to your price."

Dax's face became unreadable, and Sabine realized she'd made a mistake. Underneath his teasing and flirting, he was truly angry. It couldn't only be because of Riven's betrayal. There had to be something else—most likely related to her.

His jaw hardened. "How badly were you hurt last night, Sabine?"

She swallowed, the wine on her tongue almost sour as the pleasant memory it offered fell away. Dax must have spies reporting back to him. She darted an unobtrusive glance at Malek sitting at the end of the bar. It was unlikely he'd been the one to give any information to Dax. He hadn't seen her injuries. She'd made sure of it.

Swirling what was left of the wine in her glass, she didn't reply. Until she had confirmation of what Dax had learned, it was better to keep her mouth shut.

Dax held her gaze, his eyes narrowing. It usually wasn't a good idea to piss off a demon, but Dax wouldn't hurt her— too much. He leaned forward and growled, "Don't fuck with me, Sabine. Why did you go to *him* last night?"

Resisting the urge to curse, she put down her glass. "Is Bane aware you have people watching him?"

"I don't give a fuck what he knows. If you want me to kill him, keep pulling these little stunts. I warned you what would happen if you went to him again," Dax threatened, the sudden flash of anger shifting his eyes from amber to a sharp silver.

She couldn't stop the small shiver that went through her at the sight. If she pushed him much more, he'd turn completely, and nothing less than violence would assuage his instincts. No one in the bar would be safe if that happened. She didn't like backing down, but she wouldn't risk anyone being harmed as a result of her issues with Dax.

Pushing away her wine, Sabine jumped off the stool and yanked up her shirt to show where she'd been stabbed. Dax's gaze gravitated downward, and as she knew he would, he trailed his fingers over the slight mark she'd embedded into her glamour. His touch on her skin was disconcerting, but she ignored it and continued to glare at him. The mark would fade soon enough, at the same time as the real one, but the evidence of Bane's magic on her skin would linger for a while longer. It was Bane's residual magic, and hers, that Dax was siphoning off her skin.

She tossed back her braided hair and let her temper shine through her eyes. Dropping her shirt again, she poked Dax in the chest. "It was *necessary*. Don't you dare drag me into your argument. I won't choose sides. If you kill your brother, that's on you."

Dax grabbed her finger and yanked her close. "If I thought killing him would get me what I want, he wouldn't survive the night."

She wouldn't rise to his bait. Instead, she demanded, "Tell me about Terrance."

Dax's mouth curved upward, and he released her. He picked up his glass and took another drink. She eyed him warily and slid back onto the stool. He was up to something. She tentatively lifted her wine and took a sip. The flavors exploded on her tongue once more, and she debated stealing the rest of the bottle so she could enjoy it at her leisure.

"As I mentioned, Terrance is new to the city, which is why you haven't heard about him," Dax said, putting his mug back down. "He opened a fairly profitable gambling hall about two months ago. I've been keeping an eye on it, but our relationship until now has been mutually beneficial."

Sabine frowned. "He's been paying you?"

"Yes. I'll likely install one of my men to head his operation now. In the interim, I'll send some of my men to pick him up and bring him back here for questioning."

"I'm going with them," Sabine declared, pushing away her glass again and trying to shake off the fuzziness plaguing her. The wine affected her more strongly than she remembered, and she needed to try to keep a clear head.

"I think not."

Her jaw clenched, and she glared at him. "I didn't ask for your permission."

Dax grinned. "You're not going anywhere. Especially not now."

Her face paled, and her gaze flew to the almost empty wine glass. She'd detected something strange, but Dax had kept distracting her before she could fully analyze it. He'd drugged her, knowing she couldn't resist Faerie wine and the reminder of home.

"You bastard," she whispered, betrayal coursing through her as she drew her knife.

Pressing down on the poison depressor, she shoved it into Dax's stomach. He roared and jumped back, flinging her to the side. She hit the floor, and the world started to spin—whether from her fall or the wine, she wasn't sure. She tried to push herself up, but Dax grabbed her and hauled her back to her feet. His eyes had turned to pure silver, and she felt a flash of fear rush through her. He wouldn't kill her, but he might kill everyone else in his rage.

"Release her!" Malek shouted, leaping toward them and unsheathing his weapon.

"Stay back!" Sabine held up her hand to stop Malek's approach as Dax's silvered gaze narrowed on the ship captain. Panic flooded through her, understanding the malicious intent in Dax's eyes. It took everything Sabine had to focus on stopping Dax before he lost control completely. Wrapping her hands around his wrist, she poured her magic into him, searing him with her touch.

A strangled scream ripped through him, and he shoved her away again. Malek caught her this time, pulling her close and away from Dax.

"I've got you." Malek angled himself between her and Dax.

She struggled to lift her head against the effects of the drug, but Dax had chosen well. It was subtle but potent, and it grew more difficult to resist the call of the darkness. At least Dax's eyes had turned back to their normal amber color, and he was in control once again. But Malek's interference between her and Dax had put the ship captain in a great deal of danger. She touched Malek's mark on his wrist and infused it with a secondary protection enchantment. Her wrist burned as she accepted the pain of the debt marker, as though the original mark hadn't taken to him quite right.

"Malek is under *my* protection until the mark fades. You will *not* hurt him," she managed, speaking in the language of Faerie and infusing her words with power.

Dax's eyes flashed with temper at her order, but it was enough. He'd have to obey and keep to the oath he swore years ago to protect her. Harming Malek would hurt her, leaving the debt between them unresolved. Leaning heavily against Malek, Sabine stopped fighting the effects of the drug and slipped into unconsciousness.

Chapter Four

*M*alek wrapped his arms around Sabine, holding her tightly as her body went limp. Levin moved forward, taking a protective stance beside him with his weapon drawn. Malek didn't fully understand everything that had happened between Dax and Sabine, except she'd most likely saved everyone still inside the tavern. A number of people had fled the minute she stabbed Dax, but there were still too many onlookers. When Dax's eyes turned silver, Malek had thought he might have to abandon his subterfuge to stop the demon from killing everyone. He wasn't sure how, but Sabine had managed to bring Dax away from that dangerous edge. It only reinforced Malek's earlier belief that Sabine had been touched by the Fae, especially after hearing her speak words of power. No one with only a trace amount of magic could have such an ability.

Javyn, the man who had helped restrain Riven earlier, moved toward Sabine. Through the tusks jutting from his lips, he demanded, "Give her to me."

"Not going to happen," Malek retorted, refusing to release Sabine.

It wasn't simply a matter of his protective instincts when it came to her. Until he knew what Dax planned to do with her, he wasn't letting Sabine out of his sight. Right now, she was his best chance at finding someone with enough Fae magic to serve his purposes. If Dax intended to harm her, he'd have to go through Malek first.

Dax yanked Sabine's knife from his stomach and clutched his wound. Black blood oozed down his midsection, and he leaned heavily against the counter. Sweat trailed heavily over his obsidian skin, and Malek suspected she'd poisoned him just like the man who'd attacked her in the alley.

In a raspy voice, Dax said, "Let Malek bring her, and have someone locate Esmelle. She was downstairs earlier."

Without waiting for a response, Dax staggered toward the back rooms. Javyn motioned for Malek to follow him, stopping only to issue instructions to a few of Dax's people. Malek bent down and lifted Sabine into his arms. She was lighter than he expected, and he caught a faint scent of the night-blooming flowers he'd noticed last time she'd gotten close to him. Having her in his arms was strangely disconcerting, and a surge of protectiveness filled him as he breathed in her alluring scent. It was another indicator of the potency of her Fae magic if she could affect him this strongly even while she slumbered.

"Are you sure about this?" Levin whispered, still holding tightly to his weapon. "If you're wrong about her, we've just alienated our biggest potential ally."

"I'm sure," Malek said, prepared to come up with another plan if his beliefs were unfounded. He wasn't willing to allow anything to happen to Sabine. He wasn't sure why he felt so strongly about her, but he doubted the mark she'd left on his wrist had anything to do with it. Even before she'd marked him, he'd been drawn to her. It was why he'd searched for the burst of magic he'd felt that night. It had called to him.

"In here." Javyn led him into a large bedroom suite. A few pieces of highly decorative furnishings were situated in the room, but there were no personal mementos. It had the appearance of being a temporary room, and not one that was frequently used.

Dax staggered over to a chair and slumped down on it.

Javyn gestured to the bed. "Put her down over there."

Malek carried Sabine to the bed and gently placing her on it. One of the braids binding her hair fell across her face. He brushed it aside, allowing his fingers to trail over her soft skin. Looking at her in this unguarded moment made it easy to understand why even the gods had succumbed to the allure of the Fae. And Sabine was only part Fae.

"Take her weapons, Javyn," Dax muttered, dropping Sabine's poisoned knife on the desk with a clatter. "The key to the chest is on the table beside the bed. Lock it when you're finished and toss me the key." He rubbed his abdomen. "Fuck, this hurts. Where the hell is Esmelle?"

"Verin's bringing her," Javyn said, walking toward the bed.

Malek moved to stand in front of Javyn. Until he was sure they didn't intend to harm Sabine, he wasn't about to let them take her weapons. "I want your word you won't harm her."

Dax's eyes narrowed. "Sabine may want you alive for some reason, but you're in *my* den. I'll flay your skin from your body if you continue to interfere."

Levin cleared his throat. "Malek, maybe we should—"

Malek held up his hand to stop Levin's objections and

turned back to Dax. "Your word, Dax. Or I won't allow your man to get near her."

Despite being wounded, Dax pushed up from the chair and his eyes flashed silver briefly before reverting to amber. "You're trying my patience, ship captain. Sabine is *mine*. You will allow her to be disarmed, or I swear by the last memory of the exiled gods, you won't leave this room alive."

Malek arched a brow, making it obvious he wasn't intimidated by Dax's threat. Dax may be a formidable opponent, but so was Malek. The warding necklace around his neck warmed against his skin, serving as a warning that his suppressed power was quickly rising to the surface.

Javyn studied Malek, considering him thoughtfully. "You have my word Dax does not intend Sabine any harm, and her weapons will be returned. If she's armed when she awakens, she may try to kill Dax again and she may be harmed accidentally if he has to physically remove them." He darted a meaningful look at Sabine's knife lying on the desk where Dax had dropped it. "This is only a precaution to prevent another... incident."

While he wouldn't blame Sabine for trying to kill Dax, Malek couldn't fault Javyn's logic. Stepping aside, he watched as Javyn began removing her weapons. The deference Javyn displayed while disarming her was somewhat surprising. He seemed to avoid touching her as much as possible, making each movement deliberate as though aware two powerful predators were carefully observing him.

Malek counted at least a half-dozen weapons, including a set of silver throwing knives. Each one appeared to be extremely high quality, and even the weapon sheaths were intricately designed. It wasn't something he expected to find among this band of ruffians, but then again, nothing was exactly as he'd anticipated.

Javyn opened the chest and placed Sabine's weapons

inside just as a woman with an explosion of red curls and vivid green eyes ran into the room. Her clothing was equally bold, a kaleidoscope of colors that didn't quite fit in with the serious tone of the other tavern patrons.

She gasped and skidded to a halt, her eyes widening at the sight of Sabine on the bed. "What happened to her? Should we call Bane?"

Dax scowled. "She's fine, Esmelle. I need you to figure out what the hell kind of poison she used on me. This one is stronger than the last."

Esmelle hesitated, darting her gaze back and forth between Dax and Sabine. After a moment, she took a step toward Dax. "Where's her weapon?"

Dax gestured to the knife he'd tossed on the desk. Esmelle walked over and picked it up, making sure not to touch anything other than the hilt. Holding the blade up to her nose, she closed her eyes and inhaled deeply. Her eyes flew open almost immediately, and she stared at Dax in shock.

"This is a lethal poison. It would have killed anyone else. Why would Sabine use this on you?"

Dax glared at her and continued clutching his stomach. "If one more person questions me, people are going to start dying. Can you create an antidote or not?"

"Not until I get an explanation, and if you even think about laying a hand on me, Sabine really will kill you when she wakes up," Esmelle snapped, a trace of temper in her green eyes. "I'm not going to get dragged into your arguments. If Sabine poisoned you, there's a good reason."

Malek arched his brow, fascinated by the argument. It would appear Dax deferred to Sabine, at least in part. That didn't quite fit in with what he'd heard about the demon.

Javyn sighed. "Esme, he's in pain. Just see what you can do. Dax had a bottle of Sabine's favorite wine drugged earlier. She wasn't pleased when she realized what had happened."

"She's going to kill you one day if you keep pushing her," Esmelle muttered, putting the knife back on the desk. "I believe this is one of her newer creations. But yes, I can probably craft an antidote provided Sabine didn't use anything too unusual. I'll need to run back to my shop for supplies. Can you hold out while I'm gone? Or do you need me to try to find something here that'll lessen the effects?"

Malek leaned back against the wall and crossed his arms. He wasn't inclined to help Dax, but Levin was right; they needed to keep their options open. If Dax took too long to recover from whatever Sabine had used to poison him, they might miss their window of opportunity to find the artifacts they were hunting. "What supplies do you need? I may have a few with me."

Esmelle turned toward him and cocked her head. "You're the ship captain, aren't you?"

"I am," he said, inclining his head in greeting.

"Hmm. I've heard about you." She studied him with a great deal of curiosity. "Sadly, unless you're carting around a full herbal regimen, I don't think you'll have what I need."

"Check in there," Dax managed, gesturing toward a large cupboard in the corner.

Esmelle appeared skeptical, but she walked over and opened the door to reveal dozens of glass bottles lining the shelves. She let out a low whistle. "Sabine left some of her supplies here? I thought she'd moved everything out when she left." Esmelle picked up a few bottles and placed them on the table. She opened one and sniffed at the contents. "Perfect. This is extremely potent. I should have what I need."

While the woman continued to pick up different bottles and sniff them, Malek glanced over at Sabine as she slept peacefully. It was difficult to imagine her living here.

Although, it was slightly reassuring not seeing any of Dax's personal effects around. It made him even more curious about their relationship.

Javyn walked over to Dax and offered him the key to the chest. Dax waved him away and gestured to Sabine again. "Take her hairpins too."

Javyn's brow furrowed in confusion. "Her hairpins?"

Esmelle dumped some herbs in a mortar and began crushing them. "Mm-hmm. She's been using hollowed out needles filled with poison and braiding them into her hair. Rather clever, if you don't mind me saying. If you're trying to remove them, be careful. I'd rather not have to craft a second antidote if you stick yourself."

"Great," Javyn muttered and walked back over to Sabine. He carefully started unbraiding her hair and pulled out several pins, placing each of them on the nightstand.

Malek walked over to take a better look at them, surprised by the elaborate carvings at the end of each one. They were made of some type of wood, and each pin appeared to have a different design representing a facet of nature. He picked up one of them, holding it up to the light to better see the carving. The handle had an intricately carved leaf that was astounding with its realism. It wasn't painted, but instead the artist had used the natural shading of the wood to give it more depth. "These are extraordinary."

"Careful you don't end up dead," Javyn advised, removing another pin and placing it beside the others.

Dax removed his shirt, wiped the blood off his abdomen, and gingerly touched his injury. "The poison in her pins isn't lethal."

"No, it's not." Esmelle dumped the crushed herbs into another vial and added a few more items to the mix. She swirled it around and added, "Sabine uses a paralytic in them. It won't kill you, but you'll be unable to move for at least an hour."

While Javyn finished removing all her hair pins and headed back over to the chest to deposit them, Malek turned back to Sabine. The effect of seeing her hair loose around her face was dramatic. It gave her a softer appearance, and her delicate features were even more Fae-like. It was difficult trying to reconcile the peaceful sleeping woman before him with the fierce warrior he'd first met.

Esmelle handed Dax the concoction she'd crafted. "Drink and let me see how bad the wound is."

Dax swallowed the brew and put the bottle back on the table. While Esmelle kneeled down to assess his injury, Dax turned toward Malek. "Are you still interested in smuggling your goods regularly into Akros?"

Malek paused, the question taking him off guard. Dax had been intrigued when they'd delivered a chest of rare items to the tavern, but he hadn't brought up the business side of things until now. "I'm interested."

"Good." Dax leaned back, allowing Esmelle to poke at his injury. "I'm willing to grant you rights to dock in the port as often as you need. My people will circumvent customs and help distribute your goods. One of our warehouses will also be at your disposal for storing your merchandise."

Malek arched his brow. He wouldn't be opposed to having unfettered access to Akros, especially given what he'd discovered so far about their residents. But he hadn't heard the price yet. "And in exchange?"

Dax's expression became calculating. "As previously discussed, I retain first rights to your merchandise and an equal cut of all profits. You will also agree to transfer Sabine's mark to me."

Esmelle froze and Javyn tensed. Their reaction was telling in itself, but Malek wasn't sure why Dax would request such a thing. The mark was trivial, little more than a formal acknowledgment of a barely negligible debt. Dax was giving it far more weight than he should, unless he knew something Malek didn't. The mark on his wrist tingled, and he resisted the urge to rub it. Malek wasn't in a hurry to get rid of it, least of all to someone like Dax. He didn't know everything about debt markers, but he wasn't inclined to agree until he knew the possible repercussions.

"While I appreciate the offer, I must refuse your terms. The mark simply represents a debt. The terms have already been agreed upon."

Before Dax could respond, Esmelle blew out a breath. "You'll live, Dax. You consumed enough of her magic that you're healing without my interference." She picked up his discarded shirt and wiped off her hands. "Although, if Sabine finds out you tried to buy her mark, not even *my* efforts will save you."

Dax didn't reply. Instead, he motioned to Javyn. "Take a few men and go down to Terrance's gambling hall. I want him brought back here for questioning before Sabine wakes up."

"And if he resists?"

Dax narrowed his eyes. "Make it clear this isn't a request. I want answers, and I don't particularly care how I get them. If he wants to survive the night, he'll cooperate. Otherwise, start cutting off limbs. He doesn't need hands to spill his secrets."

Javyn inclined his head. "I'll grab Verin and we'll leave immediately."

Malek frowned. He didn't want to leave Sabine, but Esmelle was currently checking on the sleeping woman. He suspected Esmelle wouldn't allow anything to happen to her, and he needed to learn more about this plot. Right now, Sabine was the most promising candidate to fulfill his purposes, but Javyn and Verin had Fae in their bloodlines. It would only prove beneficial to his purposes if he helped them resolve the situation. "I'll accompany you."

Javyn paused, glancing over at Dax with a question in his eyes. Dax scowled and tossed his shirt back onto the table. "Fine. Take him with you."

Chapter Five

A warm hand stroked Sabine's bare stomach. She opened her eyes to stare up at Dax. Before she could even form a coherent thought, he bent down and kissed her. Her eyes automatically closed again, and she tasted his lips and the herbal concoction on his tongue. His hand lowered to her hip and he deepened the kiss, sliding his leg in between hers.

It had been a long time since she'd kissed him like this. Need and desire welled within her, but something tugged at the edge of her memory. There was a reason they hadn't been intimate in months, but with his power trailing over her skin in the same pattern as his hand, it didn't seem terribly important.

Someone pounded on the door, but Dax ignored it and slid his hand up under her shirt to cup her breast. She broke their kiss and pressed her hands against his chest. "Someone's looking for you, Dax."

"I'm busy," he murmured and kissed her again.

Her lips curved against his mouth. His single-minded determination at trying to seduce her was a character trademark. She ran her hands up his bare chest and encircled his neck. He groaned and pulled her even closer.

Whomever was outside pounded on the door again. "Dax, we have news about Terrance."

Sabine froze as her memory flooded back.

Dax muttered a curse. "What are the chances you're willing to forget what you just heard?"

"Bastard," she hissed, digging her fingers into the injury in his abdomen.

He shouted a colorful oath and pulled back enough for her to escape. She didn't bother checking to see if he'd disarmed her. It would have been the first thing Dax would have done. Scrambling out from underneath him, she grabbed a glass from the nightstand and threw it at him.

"Dammit, Sabine!" he shouted and rolled off the bed.

He made a grab for her, but she dove away and grabbed a glass bottle containing some of her herbs. She held it up, prepared to throw it. "Where are my weapons?"

He tackled her, and they crashed into the desk, breaking it apart. "Not until you calm down!"

She jerked her knee up in a cheap shot, and he grunted, allowing her to escape once again. Grabbing part of the broken desk, she reared back and brought it down over his head. It broke apart, splintering in her hand. Dax had always had a hard head. "You drugged me, tried to seduce me, and now you think I'm going to calm down? I'll cut you to pieces, you manipulative piece of garbage."

Dax roared. He leapt to his feet and slammed her into the wall, the force enough to steal her breath. He grabbed her wrists and yanked them over her head, angling his body to pin her against the wall. Sabine narrowed her eyes, preparing to unleash her remaining magic on him. He'd taken quite a bit already when she'd subdued him earlier, but she always kept some in reserve.

"Your weapons are locked in the chest," he admitted, accurately guessing he'd pushed her too far this time. "You can't blame me, Sabine. You're a pain in the ass to try to keep safe. I should have refused your Beastman when he first brought you to me and made *you* beholden to me instead."

She hesitated, holding back her power at the mention of Balkin. The agreement Dax had made with Balkin had saved her life more times than she could count, but like so many other promises, this one harbored a jagged edge. Dax swore a blood oath to Balkin to protect her. In return, Balkin had demanded she regularly exchange power with Dax, tempering his demonic energy to allow him to live freely aboveground. They owed Balkin a blood debt for saving their lives, so they'd agreed to his terms. In truth, she and Dax had needed each other to survive here in the city.

Their arrangement didn't stop Dax from wanting more. He wanted the debt tying them together to be between them, outside of Balkin's involvement. If anything should ever happen to Balkin, their arrangement would end. Unless they agreed to renew it between them, Dax would be forced underground. No one entered into a blood debt like theirs easily.

Her life in this city was temporary, and Dax knew it. If the Fae ever found out where she'd been hiding for the past ten years, they'd raze the city trying to find her. Dax was the only reason she'd managed to survive unnoticed this long. Contrary to most beliefs, demons had the ability to hide some magical abilities and skew the Fae's ability to track their quarry. If she agreed to tie herself to him, they both knew Dax would never let her go, and that could *never* happen. A prison without walls is still a prison.

Sabine wasn't foolish enough to think Dax had any real feelings for her. She was simply the reason he was able to live within the city unlike most other full-blooded demons. Although, she sometimes wondered if Dax had decided to make his headquarters in the tavern's basement because its underground location was still a seat of power for him.

She lifted her head to meet Dax's predatory gaze. Underneath, she caught a hint of the vulnerability he kept hidden from the world. The sight was enough to ease away most of her anger, but she didn't dare remark upon it.

Sabine released a sigh. "Where is the key to the chest, Dax?"

His lips curved in a smirk, and he kissed her neck. "My pants. Do you want to go looking for it?"

Despite herself, she laughed. He was a scoundrel who frequently pushed his advantage, but they'd always walked a fine line with each other. He'd managed to gain the upper hand earlier, but she'd make him pay for the consequences of that decision. It was his nature to want to suppress her, and it was hers to keep resisting.

"You lost that chance when you drugged me."

"I could convince you to forgive me."

"Not tonight you won't," she said, meaning every word.

If Javyn hadn't interrupted them and mentioned Terrance, she likely would have allowed it. Dax could be charming when it suited him, but he often couldn't be bothered. She always demanded more than his usual conquests, but he'd never complained. Sometimes she thought the demon in him relished the challenge she offered. Few could match a demon's strength, either physically or with magic. He exceeded her in the former, but she held the advantage over him with the latter.

"We'll see about that." He released her.

She held out her hand for the key, and he withdrew it from his pocket. After handing it to her, he headed toward the door.

Sabine bent down to unlock the chest. Javyn and Malek entered the room, and Malek swept his gaze over her, sending a rush of warmth through her at his perusal. She felt more vulnerable without her weapons than if she'd been standing naked in the room. But despite that, she felt a surge of gratitude toward Malek with the way he'd tried to intervene between her and Dax before she'd passed out. She tilted her head and gave him a small smile in appreciation for his efforts. His eyes warmed, and he gave her a barely discernible nod.

"Where's Terrance?" Dax demanded, crossing his arms over his chest while she pulled out her weapons. If his irritation was any indication, Dax hadn't missed the way Malek had been looking at her or their exchange.

Javyn winced. "I'm sorry, Dax. He's missing."

Dax's eyes narrowed. "Explain."

"We went down to his gambling hall, but his assistant hasn't seen him for two days. No one knows where he's gone."

Sabine started equipping her weapons, trying to suppress her frustration. If Dax would stop trying to control every situation involving her, she could have accompanied them. Javyn was skilled, but he could have missed something. Her ability to read a place's energy far surpassed everyone in Dax's employ. "Where is his gambling hall located?"

"Past Elm in an abandoned warehouse on the edge of Dax's territory," Javyn admitted with a frown. "We searched his office, but we didn't see any clue about where he'd gone."

"I want you to stay away from Terrance's establishment until we get to the bottom of this, Sabine," Dax said sharply.

She arched an eyebrow and secured her throwing knives on her thigh. Straightening, she put her hands on her hips. "Are *you* dictating to *me*, Dax?"

"Don't fight me on this, Sabine," he said, his voice tinged with a hint of a growl. "If Terrance has hired someone to kill you, I want you as far away from him as possible."

She tilted her head and walked toward Dax, putting the slightest bit of a swing in her steps. His gaze immediately became suspicious, but he stood his ground. Trailing her finger down his chest and over his wound with a trace of her magic, she reminded him, "I can take care of myself."

His nostrils flared, and he grabbed her wrist. "And you were at my mercy less than an hour ago. I want your word you'll stay away from his gambling hall."

She jerked her chin up to meet Dax's gaze. From the stubborn set to his jaw, she guessed he'd do anything within his power to stop her—including trying to keep her here. Recognizing the need to retreat before the situation became such that neither one of them would walk away unscathed, she pulled away from him.

"I'll agree to stay away from the gambling hall... for twenty-four hours."

His scowl deepened, but he didn't argue. She'd have to figure out a way to find out more about Terrance without breaking her word or involving Dax. Picking up her hairpins, she placed them in the sheath with one of her daggers. It would take more time than she could spare to braid her hair.

"We also went to his home," Javyn continued with a frown. His hand rested on the hilt of the sword as though uncertain who he should try to protect if things continued to devolve between her and Dax. "There were signs of a struggle, and it appeared to have been searched, but he wasn't there. I'm going to post a few men near both establishments to keep watch. If he shows up, we'll know about it."

Dax started pacing the room, reminding her of a caged beast. "Reach out to our contacts within the city guards. I want a city-wide search conducted immediately."

Sabine turned and started to head out of the room. Dax stopped her with a hand on her arm. "Where do you think you're going?"

She glared at him. "I don't answer to you, Dax. You do what you must, and I'll do the same."

"I want you staying here until this threat is resolved."

"Be careful making demands of me," she warned, sending a trace amount of her magic through his hand. It was enough to make her threat clear. He hastily released her arm and scowled. Without waiting for a response, she headed out of the room. It was time to find out who was responsible for orchestrating this attack and stop them.

SABINE RAISED the hood of her cloak as she left the tavern. Even with the glamour she wore, her features were too recognizable. Under normal circumstances, she would have shifted her appearance slightly. She'd used too much magic to bring Dax back to himself after she'd stabbed him. Until her magic naturally replenished itself, she needed to conserve her strength. If someone *were* hunting her, she couldn't afford to make any more mistakes. Some of the Fae or those who were part of the Wild Hunt had ways of dispelling a secondary glamour. It had taken her years to develop and strengthen her current mask so it wouldn't fracture using any of their usual tricks.

The moon shone brightly overhead, illuminating the streets better than the lanterns hanging along the path. Her boots crunched on the cobblestone street until she gradually softened her footfalls as she moved away from the tavern.

Once she was far enough away to avoid prying eyes, she gathered the surrounding shadows until she was mostly hidden from sight. It was a minimal display of power, but it had served her well for years.

Sabine reached into her pocket and withdrew one of the golden coins she habitually carried with her. Infusing it with a trace of her power, she transmuted it into wood and traced the first letter of her name. The heat of her magic formed the mark, settling into the wood as though eager to do her bidding.

An old, blind woman was hunched over in front of an abandoned building, her empty cup beside her in a silent plea for an offering. Without saying a word, Sabine dropped the wooden coin into the cup with a hollow *thud* and continued walking. The woman inclined her head as Sabine passed, but neither one needed to exchange words. Bane would receive the message she needed to speak with him, and he'd reach out to her soon enough. Contacting Bane might cause more problems with Dax, but she needed information. Bane would have completed his interrogation of his men by now, and he'd hopefully have some insight to share.

Sabine reached into her pocket again and withdrew a few more gold coins. This time, she didn't bother transmuting them. For her next contact, gold carried far more weight than anything else. Turning a corner, she headed toward a more affluent area of the city—one with a heavy human influence.

Akros was something of a remarkable city, founded more than a millennium ago by worshippers of the gods. It was later taken over by humans who had fled the war between the gods and the dragons. Once the portal collapsed and trapped the humans, they'd attempted to recreate their lost homeworld in this city. Although it was a melting pot of human and magical races, they didn't always live in harmony.

Pockets had emerged over time, with the non-magical humans claiming certain areas of the city while specific species gravitated to different ones. No other city in the world had such a diverse mix, and living in a place with a large population of iron-loving humans was one of the last places the Fae would ever look for her. Or so she hoped.

Sabine sighed, trying to bury her fatigue and focus on her surroundings. The streets weren't nearly as congested at this time of night.

Walking in the direction of the local market, she rounded another corner. A young boy leaned against a wall feigning boredom, but the sharp look in his eyes made it apparent he was hunting for his next mark. Like many of the people in this area, Caleb was wholly human without an ounce of magic in his blood. He relied on his skills as a thief to keep coin in his pocket and food in his belly. It broke her heart a little to know how some humans treated their young.

Children were precious amongst the Fae and many other magical races. Perhaps it was because they were slow to reproduce, though even wild animals typically cared better for their young than some humans. Although, she'd been a child once too—one with a death threat hanging over her head, forcing her to flee her home. Maybe the Fae weren't as dissimilar to the humans as she'd once thought.

Pushing aside the memories of a past better left forgotten, Sabine caught Caleb's eye and nodded toward an alley. He slipped around the corner, and she followed him, halting once they were both out of sight from anyone who might be passing by.

He offered her a quick grin as she dropped the coins into his outstretched hand. "What do ya need from us, milady?"

She paused, studying Caleb in the moonlight. He was possibly a dozen years in age, but he carried the same worldly weight in his eyes as many of the street kids. At least he wasn't as malnourished as he'd been when she'd first met him more than a year ago. The realization warmed her. She couldn't save them all, but Caleb would survive and hopefully, even thrive.

"I'm looking for information about someone named Terrance. He's been running a gambling hall with Dax's permission for the past few months."

Caleb nodded. "Aye. I know 'im. There's some hefty purses to lift near there if you're quick enough and catch 'em on the way in to gamble."

Her mouth twitched in a smile. "I bet. Do you go there often?"

He shrugged. "Nah. Better coin here. Whatcha wanna know about 'im?"

"He's disappeared. I need to locate him before Dax finds him," she said quietly, and Caleb frowned at the mention of Dax. "Talk to Edvar. He'll know who to speak with to find out what I'm looking for. I'll stop by the crypt tomorrow evening to get the information from Edvar directly."

Caleb dropped the coins into his pocket. "I can ask around for ya, Sabine."

She wouldn't put any of these children in a position to go up against Dax. Edvar was a bit different, but she wouldn't endanger him either. Pride was a delicate thing to maneuver, especially when Caleb had fought so hard to prove his worth to her. She smiled gently and shook her head. "Only if Edvar agrees. Let him know I don't want any risks taken and to stay away from Dax's men."

He nodded. "I'll let 'im know. We 'eard some other rumors too." Caleb glanced around and leaned in closer, the overly ripe stench of unwashed adolescent affronting her sense of smell. "You know the stuff they found in the catacombs?"

Sabine nodded.

"They've gone an' split it all up. They've been moving the treasures around the city and hired more guards to sit on 'em. We think they're expectin' Dax to hit the places."

Her eyebrows rose. Now *that* was interesting. Dax had been itching to get his hands on whatever they'd found in the catacombs.

Some of the city builders had been making repairs to the ancient plumbing in one of the oldest parts of the city. They'd broken through a wall and had discovered a treasure trove of valuable artifacts. Ever since then, Dax had been salivating at the thought of stealing whatever they'd found. He'd asked her to make some discreet inquiries while she investigated some of the other strange rumors floating around about the city council. That's what had prompted her to meet with a prospective informant the night of her ambush.

"Do you know where they've moved the items?"

"Some are at City Hall, but we think Baxter Rasten took the best treasures to his home. You want me to find out for ya?"

Sabine frowned. The councilman's home wasn't as secure as the vault at City Hall. It didn't make sense why he would have moved them there. She didn't have a good feeling about this.

Not wanting to get Caleb involved in something that might get him hurt or worse, she said, "No. If they're under heavy guard, it's better if Dax handles it from here."

Caleb nodded. "Is there anything else I can do for ya?"

Sabine studied Caleb again and his eager yet filthy face. Her mouth twitched in a smile. "What are the chances I can talk you into taking a bath?"

Caleb wrinkled his nose. "Aww. The smell keeps the guards from chasing too hard."

Sabine laughed. "Then go. Good fortune to you, Caleb."

He grinned and scampered out of the alley to relay her request for information about Terrance to Edvar. It would take some time before either Edvar or Bane had any information to share with her. She yawned and stared up at the moon overhead. Whatever Dax had used in the wine had left her more than a little tired. Unfortunately, she needed to shake a few more tree limbs before finding a bed for the night.

Turning back around, she headed out of the alley and toward the tavern again. The best source of information was Dax, but she wasn't up to going another round with him. However, there was someone else who might be willing to help her.

She located a well-worn familiar trellis and swiftly climbed until she was able to pull herself up to the roof. The streets were much faster, but they weren't as safe as the rooftops. They were known as the thieves' highway for a reason. Keeping her footsteps light to avoid disturbing anyone who slumbered below, she hopped from roof to roof, intent on her destination.

Sabine slipped through the window and into the bedroom. Malek whirled around, a knife in his hand as though prepared to strike. She paused, tilted her head, and gave him a small smile.

"Expecting trouble?"

Malek lowered his knife, his expression turning curious. "Always. But I'll take your brand of trouble instead."

She made a noncommittal noise. Malek's bedroom was an attic room over the main floor of the tavern, but larger than some rooms Dax rented out to guests. Both beds appeared to have been used recently, leading her to believe

Levin, Malek's first mate, shared the same quarters. It made sense, especially if they didn't trust Dax. And only a fool would trust a demon implicitly.

Sabine walked over to the bed closest to Malek. "I haven't been up here in years."

Malek put away the weapon and leaned against the wall. He continued to watch her with that unnerving intensity of his. "Is it the same as you remember?"

"For the most part. Things don't change around here very often," Sabine admitted, trailing her fingers along the frayed edge of the blanket. It was well-worn, like so many other things in Akros. Henry, the bartender, and Martha, his wife, had done a remarkable job keeping everything running smoothly for so long. Dax was fortunate to have them.

Sabine walked over to the desk closer to where Malek stood. A few papers were on top, but they didn't appear to be anything other than his ship manifest and a few maps. A quick glance at the manifest told her Malek was transporting several profitable items but nothing overly remarkable. Although, if it were her, she'd never keep sensitive information anywhere in plain sight. Any of Malek's secrets were probably on his ship or hidden elsewhere.

A small engraved box caught her attention, and she traced the pattern with her fingertips. It was embedded with several colorful stones in a starburst pattern that was both beautiful and deceptively simplistic in its design. Such work was clearly the mark of a master artist.

"Would you like to see what's in it?"

She pulled away her hand and lifted her gaze to regard Malek. He smiled and opened the box to reveal a small metallic tube nestled inside. It looked similar to a spyglass used by ship captains, but it was much smaller than any she'd ever seen. He picked it up and offered it to her. "Take a look."

Curious, she took it from him and looked through the

end. Colors, vibrant and bold, exploded in her vision. She jerked it away, and Malek chuckled. She frowned and studied the piece of metal, trying to figure out how it worked.

Malek leaned in closer, and she caught a whiff of incense clinging to his clothing. It was an exotic scent, captivating and alluring, and one more reminder he was completely foreign. Part of her wanted to inhale his scent again, but humans could be strange about that sort of thing.

Malek gestured toward the tube. "Look again. I'll show you how to make it work."

After the slightest hesitation, she held it up to her eye again and took another peek. He placed his hand over hers, his light touch causing her stomach to flutter with a strange awareness. She swallowed, trying to suppress her instincts and not respond with her magic.

"What do I do?"

"You turn the end like this," he whispered, his voice husky and almost right next to her ear. It was enough to send a small shiver through her. Gods. If he could cause this sort of reaction with nothing more than a slight touch, she was at a disadvantage.

Keeping his touch light, he turned the end of the tube, and Sabine gasped. Colors shifted and merged in a hypnotizing and silent dance.

His warm breath tickled her ear as he murmured, "It's called a kaleidoscope."

"It's beautiful," she whispered, unable to tear her gaze away from the swirling colors. "I've never seen anything like this."

His fingertips brushed against hers again, and she lifted her head to find him studying her intently. He searched her expression for a long time. "If I offered it to you, would you accept it?"

Sabine frowned and reluctantly put it back in the box. For him to ask such a question might mean he suspected her origins. It could be innocent, but he'd also caught her using major magic on the night of the attack and then using glamour to cover up the tattoo. One incident might be explained away, but she'd been careless lately. Even using her magic to temper Dax's rage earlier had been a mistake. Too many coincidences could force her into betraying all her secrets.

It was regretful, but spending too much time with him was probably dangerous. At the very least, Malek had some knowledge about the Fae. It wouldn't be difficult for him to draw his own conclusions. His life would be forfeit if he discovered the truth. Dax or Bane would kill him without question. She didn't want anyone else's blood on her hands unnecessarily.

"Your offer is generous, but I'm wary of accepting gifts."

He nodded and closed the box, hiding the wondrous creation from view. "I can understand that. Perhaps you'll reconsider once you get to know me better."

She didn't respond. Instead, she studied one of the maps spread out on the desk. Many of the ports were marked off with different symbols, but there was no way to know what they meant. "Have you been to all these locations?"

"Yes," he admitted, looking down at the map. "What about you? Have you traveled much?"

She shook her head. "No. I haven't had the chance. Do you have a favorite place?"

Malek leaned against the desk. "Several. One of the most unique was Razadon."

Her eyes widened. "You've been to the dwarven city?"

He chuckled. "The last time was about two months ago. They're selective about who they'll trade with, but it's always profitable."

She closed the distance between them, wanting to learn more. "What's it like?"

His smiled deepened, and his eyes warmed at her interest. "It's more astounding than the stories you've probably heard. They have trading stalls set up outside of the city, but the entrance is nestled within a mountain where they've carved out the side of it and underneath. That's their true home. The city itself is completely underground, but there's magic within their walls."

Sabine bit her lip, trying to imagine the scene he described. She'd read some ancient texts when she was younger, but the colorful illustrations had only piqued her curiosity. A few travelers had passed through Akros on their way to or from the dwarven city, and she'd eagerly listened in on some of their stories.

"Is it true that each carving holds the traces of the artist's memories?"

"That's what they say," Malek agreed and studied her for a long time. "As it happens, we're planning to return in the next few weeks. If you're interested, you're welcome to join us. There's room on the ship for one more."

Sabine paused, somewhat surprised by the suggestion. It was a nice thought if she were truly human, but it was too risky to travel there, especially with him. She might be able to hide her identity for a short time, but it would be impossible in close proximity on a ship. Besides, she ran the risk of her glamour being stripped away the minute she stepped foot inside the dwarven city. It was rumored the dwarves had wards in place that could negate such magic. She didn't know if it was true or not, but she couldn't take that chance.

Turning away, she walked over to the bed, feeling the weight of Malek's gaze on her. He hadn't pushed, but each of his questions and comments had been carefully designed to chisel away at her façade. Over the years, she'd found the questions that weren't answered could tell her more about someone than if they had answered outright. Malek was a little too appealing, and it was time to return the favor by setting *him* off balance.

Aware of his interest in her, she sat on the edge of the bed. She tucked her loose hair behind her ear and gave him a small smile. "I came here tonight because I hoped you might be interested in making a trade."

He slowly perused her up and down, the heat in his gaze warming her from within. He took a step toward her, his mouth curving upward. "I'm listening. What sort of trade did you have in mind?"

She bit her lip and lowered her gaze, hoping he wouldn't disappoint her. He wasn't Fae, but he knew enough about their ways that he might prove to be fun to barter with again. It had been a long time since someone had surprised her the way he had with his dinner invitation.

Trailing her fingers over the blanket, Sabine said, "Nothing too difficult. I'm simply looking for some information." Lifting her head, she peered at him through her lashes. "What would you like from me in return?"

He paused and then chuckled, shaking his head. "Having you on my bed is giving me all sorts of ideas, which I'm sure is exactly what you intended." His gaze roamed over her again, this time more thoughtfully. "I think I need to hear what information you're interested in before we discuss the terms. I'm afraid you'll have the advantage, though, because I'd like to keep you exactly where you are."

Her smile became genuine, and she stood. She affected him, but he was also wary. Good. He *was* going to be fun, but she wouldn't toy with him too much. The magnetism between them was potent enough to make seducing him more than a little appealing, but she needed to learn more about him before deciding. Sadly, that would have to wait while other pressing matters were pursued first.

"You went with Javyn to retrieve Terrance, correct?"

His brow furrowed. "Yes, but as Javyn mentioned, Terrance is missing. I came upstairs not long after you left, so I don't know if Dax has heard anything more yet. Why? Do you want me to find out what's going on?"

Sabine made a noncommittal noise. It was a sweet offer, but Dax would do everything in his power to keep Malek out of it. Dax wasn't a fan of competition, preferring to eliminate any potential threats immediately. If she had more time to spare, she could wait on word from Bane or Edvar without pulling Malek into a messy situation. But time was a luxury she couldn't afford. If the Fae were targeting her, she needed to know right away. No one in Akros would be safe if the Fae, or even worse, the Wild Hunt, descended upon the city.

Sabine approached Malek until he was within touching distance. Lifting her chin, she looked up into his eyes. "I understand you went to Terrance's office and home. I'd like you to tell me where he lives."

Malek became quiet for a long time. "You promised to stay away from the gambling hall but not his home. I'm assuming you came to me because you don't want Dax to know what you're planning?"

She gave him a small smile. "Dax can be... somewhat overprotective at times. I don't think either of us is willing to go another round tonight."

Malek frowned. "I'll give you the information you want, but in exchange, you will allow me to accompany you."

Sabine froze and narrowed her eyes. "I work alone."

Malek shook his head. "Not tonight. That's the price for my help."

"Then there is no deal between us." She turned back to

the window, but his voice stopped her before she could withdraw from his room.

"Someone is trying to hurt you, Sabine. I know you can take care of yourself, but if these people are determined, another weapon by your side may help."

Turning back around, she studied him, trying to figure out his motivation. "Why would you offer this?"

He hesitated, and she had the impression he was trying to come up with a believable reason. "I know we've only just met and you don't have a reason to trust me yet, but I'd like to help you. Something about you… I'm not sure I can adequately explain, but I feel protective of you. I'd also like to get to you know you better, although I believe you already knew that."

Something wasn't right. Sabine glanced at the mark on his wrist. She'd deepened it with a secondary protection when he'd tried to intervene between her and Dax, but the mark was only supposed to go one way. He'd somehow managed to block her from sensing him when she'd visited the tavern earlier too.

Malek smiled, his blue eyes twinkling with humor. "No, it's not your mark. I enjoy it. It's a connection of sorts."

She frowned, wondering if he was somehow resistant to her magic. "You shouldn't be able to feel anything from it."

Malek paused. It set her even more on guard. He was hiding something. An air of magical energy surrounded him, but it was suppressed somehow, as though his power was warded against detection. Maybe that's why her mark wasn't working correctly. Those type of wards were extremely rare and usually crafted by powerful witches. She could try asking Esmelle, but her witch friend didn't usually dabble with that sort of magic. Another witch at the behest of Bane had crafted the warding bracelet she usually wore, but it was only designed to warn her against magical attacks.

"Sabine," he began hesitantly, taking another step toward her. "I can't tell you too much, but my promise to you still stands. I swear I mean you no harm."

She believed him. It was strange to trust him; she hardly knew him. In a way, he reminded her of Dax and Bane. He wasn't a demon, but she could sense a similar power slumbering within him. It was skewed, as though it hovered right outside her field of vision. If she turned quickly enough, she might be able to catch a glimpse.

Dax and Bane had come into her life for a reason, and if she hadn't trusted them, she never would have survived the past ten years. Malek was different, but the gods had brought him to her too. If she were honest with herself, she felt protective over him too. Otherwise, she never would have risked marking him. Such things were *never* done lightly, even when the mark was trivial.

The realization was enough to make her discard her earlier objections. She tucked her loose hair behind her ear. "How do you feel about heights?"

Malek arched his brow and his mouth twitched in a smile. "I don't have a problem with them. Why?"

Sabine smiled. "Come along, Captain. If you're determined to join me, we're going the scenic route."

Chapter Six

Sabine climbed out the window and pulled herself onto the roof. Malek managed to follow her with little trouble, even though he significantly outweighed her. This only elevated her opinion of him. She bit back a smile and motioned for him to follow. If Malek had such skill as a ship captain, it wasn't surprising he'd found smuggling to be profitable.

"Which direction?" she asked when he crouched down beside her.

"Back toward the docks, but we'll need to head to the surface streets when we get closer. I'm not familiar enough with the city to identify the landmarks from here."

She nodded and climbed over a parapet wall onto a lower section of roof. "You handle yourself well up here."

"Do you travel the rooftops often?"

"Only when I'm trying to avoid attention," she admitted,

pointing out an area where the roof appeared a bit weaker. It would support her weight, but probably not his. He nodded and moved behind her while she led him across several more buildings and toward the edge of Dax's territory. The city guards patrolled this area, but many of them were in Dax's pocket. She wasn't sure what instructions he'd given regarding her, but it was safe to assume she needed to avoid them.

"The night we met... were you *trying* to draw attention? Was that why you weren't traveling the rooftops?"

She frowned. "No. I was careless that night."

Malek arched his brow. "Most people wouldn't have admitted that."

"I'm not most people."

"I'm learning that," he said quietly.

Sabine darted another glance at him. He studied her again with that unnerving intensity of his. She frowned and turned away, determined to focus on their destination. Malek was a mystery she intended to solve, but she had to keep reminding herself to be patient.

Moving forward, she leapt over the railing of a low terrace and climbed up to the adjacent rooftop before crossing to the next building. An owl hooted in the distance, and she paused at the edge of the roof. Closing her eyes, she inhaled deeply and took the pulse of the night. Everything was quiet, as though even the few stray people wandering the streets were being respectful of the night's silent embrace. The owl was just an owl this time, not a warning.

Sabine opened her eyes and waited for Malek to crouch beside her once again. For such a large man, he had the uncanny ability to wrap himself in the shadows and move silently. Her suspicions deepened that he was much more than he pretended. But then again, they all were pretending to some degree.

"Does this look familiar?" she asked softly, reluctant to disturb the night's silence.

"I believe so." He gestured farther down the street. "Is there a butcher's shop down that way?"

Sabine nodded. The area he referred to was more congested, but she'd have to take the chance on being recognized. Gesturing toward a trellis which had been a common climbing point for her over the years, she said, "We can get down to the street from here."

Leading the way, she lowered herself using the trellis as a makeshift ladder. She dropped down the rest of the way once she was low enough and brushed off her hands while Malek started his descent.

Malek jumped off the trellis, landing lightly on his feet beside her. She started, and he chuckled. "You don't have to look so shocked. I may not be accustomed to your rooftop traveling, but while my mischievous little sister was growing up, she often found herself in out-of-the-way places, particularly when she was trying to get out of her studies. I usually had to hunt her down before our parents discovered she was missing. It led me to climbing some rather tall trees and onto a roof a time or two."

"You have a sister," she murmured, touched he'd taken it upon himself to look out for her. From the way his eyes softened when he spoke of her, it was obvious he held a great deal of affection for his sister. "You two are close?"

"Aye," he agreed, considering her thoughtfully, and then his lips curved in a smile. "Her name is Kaia. It's been a few years since I last saw her, but I imagine she's still getting into quite a bit of trouble. I just hope she's better at getting herself out of it now." He paused for a moment. "What about you? Do you have any siblings?"

"A brother." Sabine looked away, not wanting to revisit the shadows of her past. Sometimes it was better not to speak of such things, especially when the night was eager to capture careless words and send them back to those who might be listening.

Without waiting for a response or giving him a chance to ask more questions, she headed down the alley and toward the main thoroughfare. Sabine leaned forward, peering down the street. A couple of guards were patrolling farther down the block, but their gait was leisurely and unhurried.

Sabine frowned. In a quiet voice, she said, "Once the guards pass, we can move down the street. Dax has probably paid them off to keep an eye on this area, and I'd rather not be spotted by them."

Glancing in the direction she indicated, he nodded and then stepped back into the shadows. She followed him and leaned against the wall. Closing her eyes, she listened for footsteps. Malek didn't say anything else, but she could feel him watching her. Expectation and anticipation hung in the air as they waited.

Only a handful of minutes had elapsed before the sound of the guards' approaching footsteps interrupted the silence.

"Hey, you," a man's voice called from the same direction as the footsteps. "Move along. You can't sleep here on the street."

Sabine's eyes flew open, and she grabbed Malek's arm to pull him away. He shook his head, pointing toward a building across the street from where they were hiding. An unconscious man with a bottle in his hand was in a nearby doorway, and the guards had obviously decided to chase him off.

Sabine tensed, scanning the dead-end alleyway for a place to hide. If they climbed the trellis again, they'd be spotted. It was too risky to try to use her magic to shroud them from view, but if the guards turned around, they'd be in clear view. It was unlikely the guards would trouble her too much, but

Dax would kill Malek if he found out he'd accompanied her. Not even her mark on Malek's wrist would stop him.

Yanking off her heavy cloak, she tied it around her waist to cover her weapons and give the appearance she wore a dress. With her hair unbraided and covering her ears, it might be enough for the guards to overlook them. At the very least, they might not recognize her right away and would assume they were two lovers engaging in a quick tryst in the alley. Malek's expression became quizzical, but she ignored him and gripped his shirt tightly.

"Kiss me," she whispered urgently, aware they only had seconds to pull off this ruse.

"What?"

She pulled him toward her just as footsteps rapidly approached. Awareness filled his eyes, and he lowered his head, pressing his lips against hers. She put her arms around his neck, listening for the guards.

Malek wrapped his arms around her, drawing her even closer. Focus was critical, but his nearness affected all of her senses. Oh, this was a *very* bad idea. The taste of his lips and the scent of his skin were heady, threatening to overwhelm her from pure sensation. Despite the danger of the approaching guards, he took his time, tasting and exploring her mouth. Malek *did* have magic, but she couldn't tell how much because it was tightly controlled and suppressed.

She whimpered and softened against his body, unable to resist him. Part of her was tempted to claim she was merely playing a part, but she wanted this. She wanted *him*. Unlocking his magic wouldn't be difficult, but she wasn't willing to force him into revealing his secrets before he was ready. This kiss was only a hint of what could be between them, and she suspected this brief taste of him was never going to be enough. But the timing wasn't right—for either of them.

The footsteps faded, indicating their ruse had worked, but she couldn't bring herself to pull away just yet. She nipped at his lower lip, and he groaned, his hand sliding under her shirt and brushing against her bare skin.

Sabine broke the kiss suddenly. If she continued kissing him, she'd forget why they'd come here tonight. The temptation to trace her power over his skin was overwhelming. Running her hands down Malek's chest, she managed, "I think they're gone."

Malek's breathing was as rapid as hers, and she could feel his heart pounding beneath her fingertips. He searched her expression for a long time. "We could pretend the guards are still here."

Despite herself, she laughed. "You're very tempting."

"That's not a no," he said with a grin, trailing his fingers under the edge of her shirt to brush against her skin in a light caress.

She bit her lip, reluctant to pull away. Their attraction to each other was undeniable, but sex was viewed differently amongst other races. Depending on how much humanity was within him, she couldn't risk allowing him to form any attachments. She didn't trust herself enough with him to hold back her power. Magic could be addictive, especially when coupled with intimacy. If that kiss was any indication, he could easily cause her to forget herself, and that could be dangerous for both of them.

With a small smile, she said, "No, it's not. But we should keep moving."

Malek's eyes filled with something akin to regret before he moved away from her. She missed the warmth of his body almost immediately, but the space between them brought some clarity. With a sigh, Sabine focused on what needed to be done, namely getting to the bottom of who was behind the attack.

Chapter Seven

*M*alek crouched down beside Sabine in the alley and studied her profile. Part of him was surprised he'd been able to convince her to allow him to accompany her. Everything about her was fascinating. Each time he got a glimpse of one of her pointed ears hidden underneath her hair, he wanted to trace its graceful slope with his finger. She smelled incredible too, like the forest and moonlight.

His reaction to kissing her had also surprised him. He'd been ready to forego years of tutelage and preparation within seconds of having his hands on her. Releasing her had been more difficult than he'd expected.

She glanced over at him with cheeks that were still slightly flushed. With her silvery hair loose around her face and sparkling lavender eyes, he couldn't help but stare. She was exquisite. Unfortunately, judging by Dax's earlier reaction, the guild leader also thought so. He was getting some mixed information about their relationship though. She didn't appear quite as enamored with Dax.

"It's the building up ahead on the right," he said, slipping into the language of the Fae. It had set her off guard before, and part of him wanted to see how she'd respond again.

"Which floor does he live on?" she asked in the same tongue, leaning forward to get a better look.

He paused in surprise, her pronunciation making her normally sultry voice even more captivating. At the very least, one of her parents was Fae. Her inflection with those few words was completely natural. She turned to look at him, a small frown on her face.

He cleared his throat, trying to focus again on her question. Having her so close made it difficult to form any coherent thoughts. "His living quarters take up the entire top floor."

She nodded. "I don't see any other guards other than the ones we already passed. Dax probably hasn't moved his people into position yet. We'll need to hurry before that happens."

"Right." Malek moved forward and away from her, even though all he wanted to do was get her alone. If he had his way, he'd take her back to his ship and spend the next several hours getting lost in her, breathing in her scent and exploring her delectable body. The Fae's ability to charm and seduce was legendary, but he hadn't believed the talent would be so potent in anyone with a shared heritage.

He walked up the steps toward Terrance's building and led Sabine inside. There were three floors in this building, and it overlooked the ocean. The area was a bit run-down compared to the more affluent areas of the city, but the view was spectacular. Malek gripped the rickety banister and started climbing the stairs. Sabine's footsteps behind him were completely silent, so much so that he kept checking to make sure she was following him.

They'd closed the door to Terrance's apartment when they left earlier, but Javyn hadn't bothered to lock it. Malek opened it to find nothing had changed. The apartment was still in shambles, making it obvious the entire living quarters had been thoroughly searched. Sabine moved into the room and swept her gaze over the furnishings. Books and cushions had been tossed around, and papers littered the floor. Her frown deepened, and he followed her into the room, curious to learn what she'd hoped to find.

Sabine trailed her fingers over a table, her tactile exploration making him wonder what it would be like to have her hands on him. He'd noticed she'd done the same thing when she'd been in his room earlier. It was an endearing quality, but it might be more than that. Some magic users could read energies through touch. If that was one of Sabine's talents, it could be extraordinarily useful depending on how powerful it was.

She crossed the room, stopping at a small bar area. He turned to see what had caught her attention, but it was simply a bottle of a very expensive dwarven ale. Sabine picked it up and studied the hand-drawn label.

"Have you tried that?"

She nodded and placed the dwarven ale back on the bar. "Yes. It's a bit of out of place here though."

Malek studied the rest of the bottles on the bar. Most of them had been opened, and there were a few homegrown liquors. She was right; such a costly brew didn't quite fit in with the rest of the selection. Malek picked up the bottle in question, but it was still sealed. Unusual, but it hadn't been here long.

"It's a shame to let this go to waste," he murmured, debating whether to take it with him.

Her mouth twitched in a smile. "We can't have that, can we?"

He chuckled. "It would be a travesty. What are the chances I can convince you to share a glass with me?"

She tilted her head, and the tip of a pointed ear peeked through her hair. "It's not really to my taste."

He nodded, unsurprised by her admission. "You prefer Faerie wine, right? I happen to have another case of that on my ship. You have my word none of those have been drugged."

Sabine arched her brow. "You have me intrigued, Captain. Is it safe to assume Dax acquired the wine from you?"

"Indeed, but I can assure you I had no knowledge about what he planned to do," Malek said with a frown. If he *had* known, he would have put a stop to it. "I picked up a couple of cases from a merchant in Karga after I left the dwarven city. Dax took one of those cases off my hands."

Sabine studied him thoughtfully and took a step toward him, closing the distance between them. "Dwarven ale is difficult to come by too. Did you bring any of that with you?"

"Actually, yes," Malek admitted, trying to recount how many cases he'd offloaded since he arrived. "I'll have to check my inventory lists, but I know we brought several crates to shore. Dax received one of them, and I believe he handled the distribution of the rest."

Sabine reached for the bottle in his hand, her fingers brushing against his. "When was it distributed?"

"The items were moved to a warehouse the first day we arrived in port."

"When did you arrive? The night we met?"

He shook his head, unsure where she was going with her inquiries. "We arrived the day before, but Dax wasn't available to meet with us then. My first mate, Levin, made the arrangements to distribute the goods with the dockmaster. He's the one who agreed to coordinate an introduction to meet with Dax so we could secure Akros as a regular trading port."

She tapped the cork on the bottle. "Could this bottle have come from your supply?"

"It's possible. Why? What are you thinking?"

Sabine gave a halfhearted shrug and moved away to investigate the rest of the apartment. His eyes narrowed slightly, watching as she moved throughout the room.

She disappeared into the bedroom, and Malek followed her. Clothing was strewn around the room; even the mattress had been cut open and searched. A bookshelf was toppled on its side with the contents scattered on the ground. Sabine walked the length of the room, paused at the wall, and then turned back around. Her footsteps were silent, but she almost seemed to be listening for something as she moved toward him.

Running her hand along the wall, she paused at a corner and took a step backward. She stared at the wall for several heartbeats before bending down and touching the floorboards.

With a frown, he put the bottle on the messy dresser. "Did you find something?"

"There's something here," she said, crawling along the floor and pressing down. Her fingers located a knot in the wood, and she pulled up a loose floorboard. Reaching into the dark hole, she withdrew a small book.

"What is that?"

She turned the pages and frowned. "I'm not sure."

"May I?" he asked, and she offered it to him.

It was a small leather-bound book that appeared more like a ledger than a notebook. Symbols, numbers, and seemingly random letters were scribbled inside. The handwriting was atrocious, but he'd seen coded entries like this before. "It's a ledger written in code."

"You know what it means?" She moved closer to him.

He leaned over to show her the different columns. "If he's running a gambling hall, these could be people who owe him money. I believe the first column may represent a date. The next set would be the name of the person, and the last is probably the amount they're up or down."

Sabine frowned. "Is Riven on that list?"

"It's possible. Figuring out which entry belongs to him might be the key to unlocking the rest of the code."

She lifted her gaze, and he was taken aback once again. Her eyes were the palest of blues, but in the right light, the lavender deepened. It made her appear even more Fae-like. She placed her hand on his arm, and the mark on his arm warmed as though it recognized her. "Do you know how to break the code?"

He paused, wondering whether she would agree to accept his help. She hadn't been willing to accept the kaleidoscope as a gift, much to his disappointment. If he had any hope of convincing her to trust him, he needed to make it clear there was no obligation in return. Otherwise, she'd likely cut him out of her investigation. "I enjoy solving these types of puzzles. I've seen enough of these codes that I can probably decipher it, but it'll take some time."

She gave him a small smile, drawing his attention back to her mouth. The urge to kiss her again was overwhelming. This woman was going to drive him to the edge of all distraction. Sabine looked up into his eyes. "Perhaps you'll share with me what you learn."

"I'd be happy to keep you updated on my progress," he offered, fully prepared to spend however many hours it would take if he could keep that look in her eyes.

Her hand stayed on his arm as she studied the room again. He wasn't in a hurry for her to pull away, so he remained still.

"I don't think there's anything else here," she said and closed her eyes for a moment.

He could feel the slightest brush of her magic move outward and sweep across the room. The warding medallion on his neck prevented most magic from directly affecting him, but he'd never been more inclined to yank it off so he could experience the full scope of her power.

He cleared his throat, forcing himself to bury his desires. "You've found more in only a handful of minutes than we did when we searched earlier. We wrongly assumed whoever searched this apartment had already found what they were looking for. I'm wondering if you might have better luck at the gambling hall."

Sabine pulled her hand away and tucked her hair behind her ear. "I might, but not until tomorrow evening. Dax will likely order his people to search the gambling hall and his home more thoroughly if Terrance doesn't show up soon. We should probably leave before they arrive."

Malek placed the ledger in his pocket and picked up the bottle of dwarven ale again. Unable to resist touching her, he placed his hand on her back and led her toward the door. She looked up at him but didn't make any move to pull away. He needed to go for a dip in the ocean to cool off after tonight.

They headed downstairs together, and she halted right at the door. Leaning into him, she whispered, "We need to see if there's a back exit. I just saw one of Dax's men."

Malek frowned and studied the downstairs of the small lobby. There wasn't another exit as far as he could tell. He handed the bottle of ale to Sabine. "Take this and meet me in the alley where we kissed. I'll go distract him for you."

She bit her lip again, and he nearly groaned at the sight.

The ocean swim might not be enough to distract himself. He leaned in close and whispered, "I won't say no to another kiss for my efforts in keeping your presence hidden."

Her mouth curved in an amused smile. "That can be arranged."

He grinned, shoved his hands in his pockets, and whistled a tune as he walked out the front door. The possibility of having to deal with an enraged demon had never been more attractive. Malek had the feeling another kiss from Sabine would definitely be worth the cost and so much more.

SABINE BARELY RESISTED the urge to laugh. Malek was a little too charming. Even if he hadn't suggested it, she wanted to kiss him again to see if the first time had been a fluke. She had the feeling their next kiss would only fuel the flames even hotter.

She ducked down as he headed out the door as though he was simply out for a pleasant stroll. Dax's man would probably recognize him and ask him why he was here, but his presence would be easier to explain than hers. He should be safe enough as long as Dax didn't learn Malek was helping her. Making sure to stay within the shadows, she slipped out the door and headed for the alley.

Malek joined her only a few minutes later. She offered him the bottle of ale, and he took it with a mock bow. "I'd ask for my kiss now, but it's probably not a good idea to stay here. I'm not sure if Dax's man believed my excuses."

She gave him a teasing smile. "Then we'll have to see about settling my debt when we're alone."

His eyes sparkled. "You won't hear any complaints from me. Shall we?"

Sabine tucked her hair behind her ear and led him back

toward Dax's territory and the tavern. If Dax or any of his men saw her from this point onward, it wouldn't matter. She might not be able to lie, but it wouldn't be difficult to lead them to assume their meeting was simply a coincidence.

Thankfully, she'd managed to get some information from Terrance's home, but it had raised more questions than answers. If Malek managed to decipher that notebook, it might lead her to the person who had hired him. Her only other option was to go through Dax again, but she wasn't inclined to ask him for any favors.

"How long have you and Dax known each other?"

She frowned. Normally, she wouldn't answer such personal questions, but Malek had earned the right to know some truths. "Several years. I met him when I came to the city."

"Where are you from originally?"

Sabine shook her head, refusing to answer the question. Even if she trusted him, the truth was too dangerous to share. "Our past may shape who we are, but it doesn't define us."

"Fair enough," he murmured, keeping pace with her as they walked down the mostly empty streets. It was only an hour or so before dawn; people would be waking up soon. "Some of Dax's men tried to warn me away from you. I was under the impression the two of you were involved."

Sabine frowned at him, suddenly wary. "You were asking about me?"

Malek hesitated. "In a manner of speaking. The night we met, Pozgil mentioned Dax tortured and killed the last man who was interested in you. Then, earlier this evening, Javyn suggested it would be beneficial to keep my distance from you. He indicated Dax would have an issue with it."

She sighed. Some of Dax's men were bigger gossips than the fishwives who gathered at the docks. Javyn was usually more discreet, but he probably thought he was protecting Dax and her by warning Malek away. Pozgil, on the other hand, was typical of most goblins and relished stirring up trouble. If Pozgil wasn't careful, Dax would toss him into Martha's stewpot and eat him for lunch.

"The goblin was talking about Cristof, but he wasn't killed *because* he was interested in me. Dax caught him stealing from him. He's always dealt with traitors harshly."

"Ah, so it's safe to assume I should avoid listening to rumors?"

Sabine paused and turned to face Malek. "That would be wise, but I'd like to give you another bit of advice too."

He arched his brow. "I'm listening."

"Don't underestimate Dax. He's smart and ruthless, and not even my mark on your wrist will protect you for long. Tread lightly around him, Malek."

Malek's lips twitched into a hint of a smile. "You believe I need protection?"

She glanced down the street to make sure it was empty before looking up at him. "You claim you've come to Akros to establish a profitable trading route, but no one comes to this city to secure a fortune. Everyone's either searching for something or hoping to forget something. As long as you're claiming anything different, Dax will never trust you."

He studied her for a long time. "Why are *you* here, Sabine?"

"I'd like to forget," she murmured and lowered her gaze. There were so many things better left forgotten, but her past was reluctant to release her from her chains.

"Hey," Malek said gently and touched her arm. She lifted her head, somewhat surprised by the genuine remorse in his eyes. "I'm sorry if my question upset you. I didn't realize it was a painful subject."

Sabine nodded. "You may want to be careful asking too

many questions in Akros. You have few allies here, and you'll have even less if Dax decides you're trouble. I won't be able to help you if that happens."

Reaching out, she touched the mark on Malek's wrist and infused it with more of her magic. It flared to life briefly before dimming again. Malek wasn't shy about asking her probing questions, and it would be better for both of them if she allowed him to walk away now. Even though it was the smart decision, she couldn't bring herself to part ways with him permanently yet.

Gesturing down the street, she said, "Take this street to the end and then turn left. The tavern will be at the end of the road. You should be able to find it without much trouble. I'd take you there myself, but it would be better for me to stay away for now."

Malek placed his hand over hers, his touch searing her like a brand. "When can I see you again?"

She smiled, unable to hide her pleasure at the question. Before she could respond, he tensed and looked at something over her shoulder. His hand flew to the hilt of his knife, but Sabine took a step toward him. Placing her hand against his chest, she urged, "It's all right. He's a friend."

He paused and arched his brow. "Are you sure? I'm not getting particularly friendly vibes."

Her smile deepened, and she glanced behind her. Bane was hidden in the shadows, but she knew he was there and waiting for her. It was curious Malek had also sensed his presence and one more indicator the enigmatic ship captain had magical inclinations.

"Yes, but I should go before he gets impatient. I need to tell him about Terrance."

Malek frowned. "Very well, but I would like to see you again."

She bit her lip, feeling the steady beat of his heart underneath her fingertips. It wasn't smart, but she wanted to see him again too. "A friend of mine is an herbalist with a shop not far from here. I use her workshop to create the poisons I use for my weapons."

"Esmelle?"

Sabine tilted her head, regarding him with surprise. "You know her?"

"We met earlier tonight. She helped create an antidote for Dax."

"Ah," she murmured, making a mental to note to ask Esmelle what she'd thought about Malek. "Her shop is called Witch's Brew. I'll be there in the afternoon, if you'd like to meet me."

Malek reached down and captured her hand. Raising it, he brushed a soft kiss against it. "Until tomorrow."

Charmed by the gesture, she smiled. "May peace walk with you even in your dreams, Malek."

Turning away, she headed toward the demon waiting in the shadows. Bane stepped into the light as she approached. He smirked and nodded toward Malek. "New conquest? The kiss on your hand was a nice touch."

"Behave," she said, continuing to walk down the street.

Bane chuckled and fell into step beside her. "I'm surprised my brother hasn't killed him yet. We both know how Dax feels about competition."

She made a noncommittal noise. Dax was probably counting down the minutes until she lost interest in Malek. "I've marked him. Dax will leave him alone for now."

"Or try to find a way around your mark," Bane muttered with a hint of a growl in his tone, indicating he wasn't pleased she'd marked Malek either. "What do you know about this stranger? And why the hell would you mark him?"

She gave him a sharp look. "I'm not discussing him with you."

"Very well. I'm assuming you're on your way to Esme's shop. We need to discuss a few other things, like the people hunting you."

She nodded and continued heading in that direction, more than a little weary. She needed to get some rest before she collapsed. "Yes, but we can talk inside. Dax has people watching the outside of Esme's shop, and I'd rather they not hear what we discuss. If you go around back, I'll lower the wards for you so you can slip over the wall."

"That won't be necessary. My men chased Dax's people away from Esme's shop earlier. After I got your message, I assumed you'd be heading here tonight." Bane gestured toward an alley where he had someone standing watch. She didn't recognize the person, but she wasn't as familiar with Bane's people.

Sabine blew out a breath and muttered, "Great. More trouble. Dax is going to *love* that."

"I can handle my brother." Bane put his hand on her lower back to lead her toward Esmelle's front door.

Sabine traced a pattern on the door and infused it with her magic. The warding shimmered with a bluish light before falling away. Witch magic typically flared blue when it was triggered or deactivated. She didn't quite understand why various colors were associated with different types of magic, but most people couldn't see them. They might catch a trace of light or a shimmer in the air, but not much else.

Pushing open the door, she led Bane inside the warm and inviting shop. It didn't matter what time she showed up; Esmelle always seemed to know when to expect her.

The fire had been banked, but it provided enough warmth in the shop to eliminate the worst of the night's chill. Sabine pulled off her cloak and hung it on the hook. Esmelle had left a pot of tea on the counter with a note.

Sabine picked up the message and smiled at the hand-written script.

Don't argue. Just drink the damn tea.

It figured. Esmelle might be human, but she was also a rather talented witch who enjoyed dabbling in charms and elixirs. Unfortunately, that meant Sabine was frequently volunteered to be a test subject in Esmelle's creations. Her friend meant well, but Sabine tried to escape from Esmelle's experiments whenever possible. Her magic was much better than her cooking and brewing abilities, which could be quite harrowing at times.

Lifting the top of the teapot, Sabine inhaled and then wrinkled her nose at the pungent aroma. Apparently, Esmelle was worried about the effects of Dax stealing her magic earlier. In addition to a magical enhancement herb, she also caught a faint whiff of another plant that encour-aged relaxation. The two herbs were in direct contrast to each other, not only with their intent but also with their flavors.

Sabine motioned for Bane to carry the pot while she picked up a jar of mint and two cups. If she had to drink the foul concoction, Bane could suffer too.

"I'm not drinking that," Bane said, warily eyeing the two cups she'd grabbed.

She headed up the stairs toward her room, trusting he'd follow her. "I'm going to add some mint."

"I've tasted Esme's brews. You don't have enough mint in that little jar to cover up the taste. Maybe not even in her entire garden."

She grinned and pushed open one of the doors at the top of the stairs. "Don't be a baby. You'll hurt Esme's feelings."

"At least I won't be hurling my guts out," Bane muttered, walking into the bedroom Sabine used on occasion. She didn't stay at the shop all the time, but often enough Esmelle had offered her a private bedroom. Sabine suspected Esmelle would prefer if she moved in permanently, but she wasn't willing to endanger her friend. Too many people might be inclined to hurt Esmelle if they knew how much Sabine adored the human witch.

"That happened once, and she's gotten a lot better." Sabine motioned for him to place the teapot on the dresser. She opened the jar of mint and doctored the tea to mask the worst of the taste. Leaving it to steep, she put her loose hairpins on the dresser and then sat on the edge of the bed to pull off her boots.

Bane wandered over, picked up one of Sabine's hairpins, and studied it. "Are you going to tell me why you're not wearing these tonight? You don't normally keep your hair down."

"I do when your brother's being a pain in the ass," she muttered and started pulling off the rest of her weapons.

He arched his brow. "What did Dax do now?"

"The bastard drugged me."

Bane's mouth twitched in a smile, and she glared at him. He chuckled and held up his hands in surrender. "Dax has never been the most tactful. Did you hurt him?"

She snorted. "I got to test out a new poison made from sewer rats. Even with Esme's antidote, he's going to be uncomfortable for a few days."

Bane laughed. "You're good for him, I'll give you that much. He'll think twice about doing that again."

She made a noise of agreement and placed her throwing knives on the small table beside her bed. "He knows I went to see you last night."

"Is that so?"

Sabine stood and walked back over to the teapot. She poured each of them a cup and then walked over to Bane. Offering it to him, she said, "You need to talk to him, Bane.

I'm getting tired of being caught in the middle of your argument. The more time passes, the harder it will be to resolve."

Bane took the cup and sniffed it but made no move to drink it. He placed it back on the dresser. "What did you learn about the attack?"

She narrowed her eyes at his refusal to discuss Dax. It was tempting to throw one of her poisoned blades at the brother standing in front of her. They needed to fix this mess before she strangled both of them.

Perhaps part of their argument *was* her fault, but she'd made her decision out of necessity. Unlike Dax, Bane had the ability to manipulate someone's lifeforce. He typically used that ability to steal someone's life, making him a very effective assassin. But they'd found his magic could also be used in reverse. It was much more difficult to heal using demonic magic, but they'd found it worked better if he carried her mark and was sworn to protect her.

Dax hadn't been pleased when he'd learned about it, and it was still a point of contention between them. The knowledge his brother could live aboveground due to her protection mark chafed. If she had known it would cause so many problems between the brothers, she might have reconsidered her decision. Bane didn't seem to have the same controlling tendencies as Dax, which was the main reason she'd agreed in the first place. Although, she suspected Bane was simply better at hiding the worst of his demonic traits. May the gods save her from volatile demons and the headaches they created.

Irritated by the whole mess, she snapped, "Don't push me tonight, Bane. I'm exhausted, and I've had a rough few days. Drink your damn tea or get the hell out of my room."

His amber eyes flashed silver for a second before they faded. He wasn't as quick to temper as Dax, but she'd had it with both of them. She waited, tapping her foot impatiently, and arched her brow at him.

He held her gaze and picked up the tea, took a drink, and grimaced. Placing the cup back on the dresser, he crossed his arms over his chest and glared at her, as though daring her to challenge him further.

She wouldn't. Someone could only push a demon so far, even one as even-tempered as Bane.

Sabine took a sip from her cup and wrinkled her nose. It wasn't horrible, but Bane was right; it was barely palatable. She'd have to talk to Esme again about masking some of the more offensive herbs.

Placing her cup on the dresser, she pulled open one of the drawers to find an oversized shirt to wear to sleep.

"Last week, Dax asked me to reach out to some of my contacts to see if I could get any information for him. He was interested in some strange happenings with the local politicians over the past two months. Money has been changing hands, and there's been a heavier presence of armed guards in certain key areas around the city."

Bane arched his brow. "I've heard similar complaints from some of my men. It's made moving unseen a bit more difficult. Do you know why?"

She hesitated. "Not exactly. I've only begun putting bits and pieces together, but most of this is supposition. Some of Edvar's street kids heard rumors about a cache of ancient artifacts that was recently discovered in one of the catacombs under the city."

Bane snorted. "Let me guess, my brother wants to steal them?"

She smiled and nodded. "Most likely. At the very least, he wants to know what they found. Dax believes they've hired mercenaries to help guard the items, but they keep moving them around. So far, everyone's been tight-lipped about it.

His contacts in the city guard don't even know what they're hiding."

"How is this related to the attack on you?"

Sabine picked up her tea and took another sip. "I contacted Thomas, the owner of a nearby general store, and asked him to arrange a meeting with an informant in the city council's office."

Bane frowned. "Thomas? Dax's fence? What does he know about the city council?"

She shrugged. "Nothing, but his cousin works as a clerk for the city council. When I stopped at the general store, I didn't realize one of Dax's men was in the backroom unloading some merchandise that had arrived by ship. Riven overheard my conversation about the planned meet. He told someone named Terrance where I was going to be. I believe Terrance orchestrated the attack, but I don't know if he was ultimately responsible."

Bane scowled. "I've met Terrance. Dax allowed him to set up a gambling hall not far from the docks. If he's the one responsible for this, I'll handle him."

Sabine frowned and started unfastening the laces of her shirt. It seemed as though everyone else knew about Terrance, except for her. She'd wanted to put some space between her and Dax, so she'd decided to take a step back from some of Dax's dealings. Now she wondered if that had been a mistake.

"Terrance is missing, and Dax has people searching for him. How much contact did you have with him?"

Bane leaned against the wall, watching as she pulled off her shirt. Nudity was common enough amongst her people and his, but Bane had already slipped once the other day by kissing her. She arched her brow at him, and he grinned.

"You can't blame me for looking, little one. A beautiful woman should always be admired. But to answer your question, I had very little interaction with Terrance. He hired us to kill someone a few weeks ago, and it's possible that's how he came into contact with one of my men. Naphor was assigned to the task."

Sabine frowned and pulled on her nightshirt. Naphor had been the man from the alley with the tattoo, indicating his allegiance to Bane and the assassin's guild. Everyone who wore one celebrated the dark masters, those gods who were responsible for death, revenge, and chaos. Bane had his own version of the tattoo on one of his arms, and it was an easy way to identify others who followed their credo.

"You don't normally talk to me about your assassination contracts."

"No, and I'm not giving you details. But in this case, you need to know the connection between my people and Terrance."

She nodded and reached down to unfasten and slip off her pants. "Do I need to know who the target was?"

"Not right now. I'm investigating any connection to you, but I don't believe there is one. It wasn't a difficult target, which was why one of my newer recruits was tasked with killing the mark."

Sabine tucked her loose hair behind her ear. "There might be another possibility. Your feud with Dax isn't a secret, and most people believe I'm the reason for it. I think it's interesting Terrance hired one of Dax's men for information about me, and then he hired one of your men to kill me."

Bane straightened. "You believe someone's trying to play us against each other?"

Walking back over to the bed, she opened the drawer of the nightstand and withdrew the iron dagger she'd collected from Naphor. Even through the leather sheath, the cold iron warmed her skin enough to make it uncomfortable. Direct contact would burn her; not even water would quench the flames. "It's a possibility, but he had this."

She offered the knife to Bane, and his eyes flashed silver once again. This time, they stayed that way for almost a full minute while he tried to get himself under control. She waited, knowing his anger wasn't directed at her, but it wasn't a good idea to push him too far in this state. Dax's temper was explosive and immediate, but Bane's could be much more dangerous when it was fully unleashed.

Bane exhaled slowly and gripped the knife. "Someone knows who you are."

"Or suspects, yes." She folded down the blankets in the bed. "Many people believe I'm more Fae than human, so this may be a coincidence. It could even have been part of the payment. Iron weapons are rare, even here in a city where the metal can be more easily tolerated."

"Did you tell Dax about this?"

She climbed into bed and looked up at Bane. His eyes had returned to normal, but it wouldn't take much to set him off again. "Not yet. I planned on telling him tonight before he decided to be an ass. If someone is hoping to take advantage of your disagreement, it's up to both of you to resolve it."

Bane's jaw clenched, and she sighed. It was too late at night to deal with a brooding over-protective demon. The sun was going to rise soon, and she needed to get some rest before Esmelle's clients started showing up.

"I'm going to bed. Are you staying or leaving?"

He was quiet for a long time. "I'd like to stay for a bit."

"All right," she said and listened to him remove some of his weapons.

Bane wouldn't fall asleep, but he'd stay with her long enough until she did. Demons didn't love the same way as humans or other magical races, but she knew he cared about her. Bane was worried about what she'd shared, but the real reason he would remain was a little more practical: he simply needed access to her magic. It fueled him enough to enhance his senses and allow him more mobility aboveground, but he didn't like being dependent upon it.

Any form of intimacy, even small touches and caresses, helped strengthen their connection through the mark on his wrist. It allowed him to go longer periods of time without having direct access to her. Part of the reason Dax wanted Bane to stay away from her was because Dax wanted Bane's mark to fade. Stupid, jealous demons. If Dax would quit trying to control and manipulate every situation involving her, Sabine might consider marking him too. Instead, she was the equivalent of a shiny toy both demons wanted to possess.

Bane slid into bed beside her, and she scooted over next to him. He was always so warm, like a giant heater. Wrapping his arm around her, he pulled her closer. "I'm putting guards on you around the clock, little one. I have a handful of people who are loyal and beyond reproach. They'll be the ones to watch over you."

Resting her head on his chest, she said, "Just don't get angry when I lose them. You know how I feel about people tracking me."

Bane ran his hand down her back and murmured, "Fair enough. Will you tell me about the man from earlier?"

Sabine yawned. "His name's Malek. And no, you're not allowed to kill him either."

"I wouldn't ask permission," he said with a chuckle and kissed her hair. "If you won't tell me anything more, go to sleep."

"You didn't tell me what else you learned," she grumbled, closing her eyes and burrowing deeper against his side.

"Nothing much. It'll keep. We'll talk more after you've had a chance to rest."

"All right," she whispered, thinking back to the events that happened earlier. Something still troubled her, and she wouldn't be able to sleep until she got an answer. She opened her eyes again. "Where did you get the dwarven ale you were drinking the other night?"

He arched his brow. "The one you barely touched?" When she nodded, he frowned. "I'll have to check with Evo. He managed to acquire a case from a smuggler."

"Was it a full case?"

Bane frowned. "I'm not sure. Why?"

"I went to Terrance's home earlier tonight. He had a bottle of the same ale. Malek mentioned it was rare and took the bottle with him. I'm wondering if it came from the same case."

Bane narrowed his eyes. "You need to tell me more about this Malek. If he had a hand in this—"

"I don't believe he's responsible for the attack," she interrupted, refusing to let him continue with that line of thought.

If Malek had meant her any harm, she wouldn't have been able to mark him with protective magic. The mark wasn't working quite right, but she should have been able to sense malicious intent. That was part of the reason she'd done it, but she didn't intend to admit that to either Bane or Dax. They had a habit of killing off any perceived threats, regardless of whether they were real or not.

Sending a calming wave of her power over Bane, she continued, "Malek's a smuggler. That's how Dax managed to drug me earlier. He used a bottle of Faerie wine from Malek's supplies. The dwarven ale we found may have originated from the same shipment, but I don't believe Malek had anything to do with the attack."

Bane caressed her back, sliding his hand under her shirt to touch her bare skin. "When did he arrive in town?"

"The day before the attack," she admitted, cuddling

against Bane once more. "Dax let him sit at the docks for a full day before granting him an audience."

"Of course. Dax always enjoys lording over his subjects," Bane muttered and then sighed. "Get some sleep, little one. I suspect you're going to need it."

Chapter Eight

A bell chimed in greeting as Malek pushed open the door to Esmelle's shop. The magical ward protecting the shop tickled his skin and heated his necklace, but he ignored it, recognizing it was only to prevent anyone from entering who may intend harm.

The store was busier than he expected, and a couple of the customers glanced over at him briefly before turning back to the shelves they were browsing.

Bottles of liquids and dried herbs lined the shelves on the walls, while plants in various stages of drying were tied to racks overhead. A fire crackled cheerfully in the fireplace, and several candles were placed around the room, providing a cozy atmosphere. An older woman was seated in an over-stuffed chair by the fireplace sipping from a steaming cup, a teapot on the table next to her.

Rather than the cold and dank atmosphere he'd experienced in some other witches' shops, this entire store felt more like a warm and inviting home. It only elevated his opinion of Esmelle. She obviously didn't need the traditional trappings to encourage business.

The woman he'd met the day before flitted around the shop, smiling and laughing with customers. Esmelle was once again wearing bright and vivid colors, and she smiled as she handed one of her customers a small cloth pouch. "Add a small pinch of this mixture to your bath water. You'll be feeling better in no time."

"Bless you, Esme," the elderly woman said, clutching the bag tightly to her chest. "I thank the gods every day for bringing you to Akros. I don't know what we'd do without you."

Esmelle beamed a smile at her and walked the old woman to the door. "You know it's always a pleasure to have you visit me, Lenore. But next time, I hope it's just because you'd like to share a cup of tea."

"Oh, I'll be back soon enough. You couldn't keep me away."

Esmelle closed the door behind the woman and turned to face Malek. Her eyes twinkled in amusement. "I was told a handsome ship captain might be visiting my garden today."

Malek chuckled. "Oh?"

"Mm-hmm." She gestured toward a door at the back of the shop. "I think you'll find my garden quite... fascinating. There are all sorts of lovely flowers and a few poisonous ones. You might want to step lightly."

Before he could respond, Esmelle swirled away in another wave of color and toward another customer. Malek grinned and headed for the heavy wooden door. This time, when he opened it, there was no sensation of the warding, which led him to believe it also encompassed the garden area. But what he hadn't been expecting was the explosion of colors and scents permeating the air.

The garden was a wonder with almost every type of flower and plant imaginable. He paused, unable to do anything but take in the sight of the unusual oasis in the middle of the disreputable city. It reminded him of the gardens from home, especially the one that had been lovingly tended by his grandmother for years until she'd passed away. He'd never thought to see their equal again.

Malek took a few steps on the cobblestone path and then halted as a furious buzzing noise rapidly approached. He turned to see a tiny man wearing a pair of overalls flying in his direction. The small pixie wielded a miniature spear and brandished it in his direction.

"Halt! State your purpose, stranger."

The high-pitched sound of other voices could be heard, and Malek caught sight of several other pixie faces peering at him from the foliage. Making an effort to keep the smile off his face, he held up his hands. "My name is Malek. Sabine's expecting me."

"Sabine? You must have the wrong garden. There's no pixie named Sabine here. Begone," the pixie sneered, still waving his weapon threateningly.

"Hush, Barley!" A tiny female pixie flew out from underneath a large leaf. Her bright-yellow dress put him in mind of one of the flowers gracing the garden. She darted close to him, looking him up and down curiously. "Don't mind Barley. Sabine put him in charge of defending the garden. He takes his job *very* seriously."

"I can see that," Malek agreed, both curious and fascinated by the pixies.

Pixies were particular about inhabiting certain gardens, choosing their homes with care. They naturally gravitated to areas with a Fae presence, and it shouldn't have surprised

him to see them in the southern lands. But he hadn't anticipated seeing them in a city garden plot.

"I'm Blossom. I'll take you to Sabine."

"I'd appreciate that." Malek glanced over at a scowling
Barley. The little pixie still hadn't bothered to lower his
weapon.

"I'm watching you," Barley warned, waving his spear in
Malek's direction and causing a shimmer of pixie dust to
flutter to the ground. "Any sudden movements and you'll feel
the sharp edge of my thorn."

Blossom giggled, a light, merry sound reminiscent of
bells. She motioned for Malek to follow her and flew down
the path. He kept to the cobblestones laid out as a charming
walkway and moved deeper into the garden. Everywhere he
looked, more exotic plants and flowers greeted him. The
sound of trickling water caught his attention, and he
wondered if they had a private spring here too.

As he turned a corner, he nearly stopped in his tracks.
Sabine knelt a short distance off the cobblestone path in a
patch of sunlight as she collected some plants. She hummed a
wordless tune as she worked, and he was taken aback at the
vaguely familiar melody. Her hair was once again braided,
but this time flowers had been woven into the braids instead
of poisoned hairpins. For the first time since he'd met her, he
had the feeling he was seeing the real Sabine.

She looked up as he approached and gave him a warm
smile that caused his heart to skip a beat. Brushing the dirt
off her hands, she picked up the plants she'd chosen. "You
managed to find me."

"So I did," he said, forcing his hands to stay by his side to
keep from touching her. In the daylight and with the sun
caressing her skin, she was even more captivating. It was
going to be next to impossible to focus on why he was here.

Blossom landed gracefully on Sabine's shoulder and

whispered something in her ear. Sabine grinned, her eyes twinkling with amusement. "Mmm. I agree. Perhaps I will."

Blossom giggled at Sabine's words, and the little pixie darted off back into the underbrush.

Sabine tilted her head. "I need to take these plants to the workshop. Will you walk with me?"

"Of course." Malek fell into step beside her. "This garden is extraordinary, and not just because of the plants. It's been a long time since I've been around pixies."

Sabine glanced up at him. "You've been around pixies before?"

"They used to visit my grandmother in her gardens when she was still alive. They disappeared around the same time she left this world. I didn't connect the two until now."

Sabine nodded. "Pixies can go into mourning when they lose a loved one. They search out sources of nature magic, but when it's gone, not even the life in the garden can sustain them when they're grieving. Many times, they'll abandon a garden in search of a new source."

Malek studied the flowers surrounding them, but he only caught a few flashes of color before the pixies disappeared again. It was impossible to know how many were living in the garden. "They appear to be flourishing here."

"Esmelle's a very talented nature witch."

He made a noncommittal noise. Esmelle might very well be a talented witch, but he suspected Sabine was the real reason the pixies had decided to take up residence here. It wasn't a secret pixies preferred to be around those with Fae blood.

Sabine led him toward a small wooden structure that was completely open on one side. It offered some protection from the elements, but it had been constructed in such a way to make it blend in with the rest of the gardenscape.

A large table had been built directly into one of the walls of the structure. On top were several bottles filled with various liquids and dried herbs. Sabine placed her plants on the table, and Malek caught sight of another pixie darting out from beneath the underbrush. This one wore bright-pink, which was the only way he was able to identify it was a different pixie than Blossom. A pink flower in her hands matched her dress. The pixie perched on Sabine's shoulder, placed the flower in one of Sabine's braids, and then giggled as she flew away. Sabine didn't react, which made him think this was a common occurrence.

Malek's mouth twitched in a smile. "The flowers in your hair are a nice touch."

"What?" Sabine frowned and patted at her braids. She gave him a sheepish smile. "Be careful, or you'll end up with some too. They like doing sneak attacks."

Malek chuckled. "I'll keep an eye out. What did Blossom say to you before she disappeared?"

Sabine gave him a mischievous smile. "She said you're extremely handsome, even though you're much too tall for her."

Malek arched his brow, determined to thank the little pixie next time he saw her. "Oh?"

"She also thinks I should take you as a lover."

Malek paused, remembering Sabine's response to Blossom's comment. Damn. He wasn't about to let that go. "*Perhaps* you will?"

Sabine bit her lower lip as though trying to suppress a laugh. "Mm-hmm. I'm considering it."

"I think we can do a bit better than that," Malek said with a grin and moved in closer.

She looked up at him, her eyes sparkling with humor. Unable to resist her for a moment longer, he lowered his head and kissed her. This time, there was no threat of approaching guards and he could take his time.

She tasted even better than he remembered, like berries or something else equally sweet. The scent of blooming flowers surrounded him, and when her body softened against his, he wrapped his arms around her and pulled her closer. He swept in, taking control of their kiss, and when she whimpered in response, his thoughts fractured.

He wanted this woman with an urgency that defied all logic or rational thought. No one had ever come close to eliciting this same level of response. She ran her hands up his chest and wound her arms around his neck. It only flamed his desire for her even hotter.

Lifting her, he placed her on the table and she wrapped her legs around him, drawing him closer. It still wasn't enough. Her magic flowed over his skin, inciting him to respond, but the warding necklace he wore prevented it from happening. Malek nearly yanked it off, but only barely managed to restrain himself. He wanted Sabine in every way imaginable, but it was too risky. If his suspicions about her were correct, she'd never allow him this close again when she learned who he was. The realization was enough to cool some of his ardor and replace it with regret.

Malek forced himself to break their kiss, but he couldn't bring himself to release her. He hesitated, desperately wanting to kiss her again. She blinked up at him with passion-filled eyes that were almost his undoing. If he knew she wouldn't run, he'd damn this entire operation for just one night with her. But he suspected one night would never be enough.

He reached up to tuck one of her braids behind her pointed ear and trailed his hand downward along her soft skin. She trembled at his touch, and he had the sudden urge to nibble on her ear. Without doubt, she was the most alluring and captivating woman he'd ever met—and he wanted to possess her completely. Even now, he couldn't stop touching her.

"I think you almost have me convinced," she said with a teasing smile, running her hands under his shirt and up his bare chest. She infused her touch with a hint of magic, and it was enough to fracture his weakening resolve. The thought of having her hands on other parts of his body was one of the most erotic things he'd ever envisioned, and he wasn't going to be able to hold back much longer.

Several pixies called out a warning, and a few seconds later, footsteps crunched on the cobblestone path toward them. He spun around, slapping his hand to his weapon as Esmelle and Javyn approached. Javyn's eyes narrowed on him, his expression anything but friendly. Dammit. Dax would definitely hear about this, and that would require some tactical adjustments to his plans.

Esmelle froze and then winced. "Ah, er, sorry. Didn't mean to interrupt. Javyn has an urgent message from Dax."

Sabine hopped off the table. "What is it?"

Javyn's jaw clenched, but he walked over to Sabine and held out a scroll. Sabine frowned and took it, unrolling it to read the message. She lifted her head. "When does he need this?"

"Before tonight."

Sabine frowned and rolled up the parchment. She offered to Javyn. "I'm not interested. Tell him to find someone else."

Javyn didn't take the message. Instead, he held out a small engraved box. "Will you reconsider? Dax is willing to pay whatever you believe is fair, and he wanted me to offer you a gift."

Sabine tilted her head to study the man but made no move to accept the box. "Are *you* asking for my help, Javyn? Or are you asking me on behalf of Dax?"

Javyn frowned and lowered the box. "The gift is from

Dax, but I'm asking that you at least consider his request." He paused for a moment and then added quietly, "No one else can do what you can in the time allotted. If necessary, Dax will do this without you. But it will greatly increase the risks to everyone involved, including Dax."

Malek frowned. He didn't trust Dax, especially after he'd drugged Sabine, but it wasn't his place to intervene. Regardless of what had happened a few minutes earlier between him and Sabine, it didn't erase the history she shared with Dax.

Esmelle huffed. "Come on, Sabine. You know you're probably going to give in anyway. Let's see what sparkly Dax decided to give you this time." Without waiting for a response, she took the box from Javyn and opened it. She wrinkled her nose and muttered, "It's pretty, but I like it better when he gives you jewelry."

"That's because you end up wearing most of it," Sabine retorted and took the box. Curious about the type of gift that would appeal to Sabine, Malek took a step toward her to look inside. His eyes widened. Within the box was a highly stylized silver dagger. The hilt was extremely intricate and embedded with several precious stones. Such a gift had probably cost a small fortune.

"Oh," Sabine murmured and stared down at it, indecision clearly warring on her face. "This is a dwarven dagger, isn't it? Damn him. He knows I can't resist such workmanship."

Esmelle snickered. "You're too easy, Sabine. He's probably had that sitting in his vault waiting until he pissed you off again."

Sabine looked up and shrugged, but she didn't dispute Esmelle's words. Putting the box on the table, she lit the brazier and burned the message. "You can tell Dax I'll do it, but this is going to cost him. And if he pulls another stunt like the other night, it'll be the last time."

Javyn's shoulders relaxed at her agreement, and he nodded. "I understand, and I'll let him know. Do you know when you'll have the information?"

"A few hours. I'll come to the tavern once it's done," Sabine said, turning off the brazier. One of the pixies darted into the ashes and proceeded to make tiny, sooty footprints along the table. Another one squealed and dove into the mess, tossing ash into the air like confetti.

Sabine scooped up the confetti-throwing pixie and blew the ash off its wings. "You know you're not allowed on my table, Acorn. It took days for your wings to heal last time you knocked over one of my jars."

Barley swooped in. "My apologies, Sabine. I will ensure this young troublemaker will be suitably punished." He scowled at Acorn. "Move it, soldier! I'll have you whipped into shape in no time."

The young pixie's eyes widened in fear. He threw his little body down on Sabine's palm and begged for forgiveness. Sabine's mouth twitched in a smile. "I think herding the caterpillars away from Esme's garden this afternoon should be sufficient. No whipping will be necessary."

Barley saluted Sabine. "You heard her, soldier! Let's go!"

"I wish they listened to me half as well," Esmelle muttered as the pixies flew away. "I'm still finding pixie-sized hand and face prints all over my windows."

Sabine brushed the ash off her hands. "Put out some sugar water or a honey cake. Tell them they need to clean the windows before they can have any. It'll get done in record time."

"Hmm. I'll have to try that."

Sabine turned toward Malek and gave him an apologetic smile. "I'm afraid I need to take care of something."

"So I gathered," he murmured, wishing he'd had an

opportunity to get a look at the message from Dax. "Do you need help with anything?"

Before Sabine could respond, Javyn interrupted. "Dax would like a word with you, Malek. He sent a message to your ship requesting an audience. I'll be happy to escort you to him."

Malek resisted the urge to curse. The last thing he wanted was to deal with Dax, especially when he'd just had Sabine in his arms. He still didn't know *what* Sabine saw in the demon nor did he understand the connection between them. If he didn't need to worry about offending the master thief, he'd say to hell with Dax. But until he found what he came for, Malek needed to continue this charade.

Esmelle cleared her throat and picked up the box containing the silver dagger. "I'll take this inside for you, Sabine. You can pick it up whenever you're finished... doing whatever it is you need to do. Come on, Javyn. You can wait for Malek in the shop."

Javyn scowled and shot Malek a warning look before turning and following Esmelle. His meaning was clear: he wasn't happy about Malek getting close to Sabine. That was too damn bad.

Sabine reached out and brushed her fingertips across the mark on his wrist. It flared to life briefly at the contact and then settled down, but he knew she'd infused more of her magic into it. Even now, it coursed through his body in an erotic wave of heat.

Sabine placed her hand on his chest. "I'm glad you stopped by, Malek. Maybe we can continue this later?"

He barely resisted the urge to groan. This woman had managed to get under his skin already. One small touch from her was enough to make him want to pin her against the table again. He lowered his gaze to her mouth, tempted to kiss her again, but he wasn't sure he'd be able to stop. He needed to figure out a way to convince her to trust him, before she learned the truth. It was only a matter of time before he gave up trying to suppress his instincts when it came to her.

Reaching up, he caressed her face. "You couldn't keep me away."

Her mouth curved upward, and she pressed a light kiss against his lips. "You should go. Dax gets grumpy when he's kept waiting, but I look forward to seeing you again soon."

SABINE WATCHED Malek head back to Esmelle's shop and leaned against the table for support. She'd never been so drawn to someone before, and it had thrown her completely off balance. Years of lessons with Dax and Bane had taught her critical skills in self-control, especially when it came to her magic, but she'd finally met someone who challenged that foundation. Balkin, the Beastman who'd helped her escape the Fae years ago, was going to be furious if she jeopardized everything.

Blossom swooped down and perched on her shoulder. "I knew it! You *are* going to take him as a lover, aren't you?"

"I'm not sure that's a good idea," Sabine admitted, even though she thought Blossom was probably right. If Javyn hadn't interrupted them, it might have happened much sooner than she intended. "Did you pick up on any magic from him? I can't quite get a read on him."

"He's definitely not fully human, even though he's pretending like you," Blossom said, her wings buzzing close to Sabine's ear. "He was wearing a ward. I couldn't get close enough to find out. Barley tried too."

Sabine frowned. "Yeah. I sensed the ward. I think that's the reason my mark is breaking down so quickly. I have to keep refreshing it. I wish I knew why he's holding on to it. I even tried enticing him a little with my magic to get him to lower it, but that didn't work either."

Blossom pulled on one of Sabine's braids, most likely adjusting one of the flowers. "He likes you. Maybe he's hiding too. Maybe you are meant to be together, like fated lovers from the old days."

Sabine sighed. "That doesn't happen anymore, Blossom. We've corrupted too much of the natural magic of this world since the portal closed. It's nothing more than a faery tale now."

Blossom flew off her shoulder and faced Sabine. Putting her hands on her hips, Blossom said, "But you're helping to bring it back! You're returning the balance. Maybe he can help you."

Sabine shook her head and pushed away from the table. It was a pretty thought, but it was impossible. If he were full-blooded Fae, she would know it. "Dax has another job for me. I need to get some information for him, so I'll be gone for the rest of the day. I know you're hoping Malek is special, but I want you to stay away from him. No following or spying. It's too risky in the city."

The pixie's wings drooped. Sabine automatically held out her hand, allowing Blossom to perch on her palm. Blossom's bottom lip stuck out in a pout, and the pixie crossed her arms over her chest. "He won't catch us."

"He's been around pixies before," Sabine reminded her gently. "You're very talented, but it's too dangerous. If it weren't for all of you, this city would have been unbearable for me to live in. I don't want to risk losing you."

Blossom wrapped her arms around Sabine's thumb and hugged her. When she finally had to leave Akros, she would miss Blossom and the rest of her family. It was sometimes difficult for pixies to abandon a garden once they'd established roots. Sabine had made it a point to warn them against doing such a thing. This wasn't a permanent spot for them, and they'd only temporarily claimed it. Pixies lived in large family colonies, and at last count, this garden had forty-three tending it. She knew each one of them by sight, with their own peculiarities and personalities.

Blossom had been the first to find her, but it hadn't taken long for other pixies to take up residence. She cared about all of them, but Blossom would always have a special place in her heart. Sabine smiled at the little pixie and sent a wave of her magic over her. Blossom trilled in happiness, and a wave of pixie dust scattered around her.

"Will you come back later?"

"Probably not. It's not safe to stay at Esme's too many nights in a row. I'll try to visit tomorrow. Will you collect some mint from the garden tonight? Esme's getting a little low."

Blossom nodded. "It's a good moon. It should be potent tonight. I'll have some of my sisters help me."

A pixie shrieked somewhere deeper in the garden, and several giggles followed. Sabine grinned as Blossom took off in search of the mischief makers. Plucking the flowers out of her hair, she headed for the shop. It was tempting to leave them in, but it didn't exactly fit the image she'd cultivated. The pixies seemed to enjoy braiding her hair, so she usually let them do it while she worked in the garden. They frequently got a little carried away.

She pushed open the door of the shop to find Esmelle busy helping an older woman, so Sabine simply waved to her before grabbing her cloak and heading out into the sunlight. Night was the preferable time to travel, which allowed her to either gather the shadows to help hide her identity or traverse the rooftops. But she couldn't risk using the thieves' highway in the daylight. The chances of someone seeing her were too great.

As she moved through the busy streets, she used glamour to make small changes to her features and mask her appearance. With each step, she darkened her skin, elongated her nose, and added a few wrinkles for good measure. She'd spent too long in Akros and was becoming too recognizable. She was reluctant to leave the small family she'd created here, but it might be safer for all of them if she moved on. The thought filled her with regret, but she wasn't willing to risk endangering any of them if her identity was discovered.

The city streets were crowded with merchants hawking their wares and trying to solicit prospective patrons. Sabine ignored them and made her way toward the oldest section of the city, relaxing slightly as the crowd thinned. The remnants of ancient power drifted upward through the cracks in the cobblestones lining the street, a residual effect from the time the gods still walked this world. It was rumored the worshipers of a mated pair—Ethos the Keeper of Shadows, and Brymis, Mistress of Twilight—had originally built Akros. They had long since abandoned the world with the rest of the gods, forced into exile during the Dragon War. The touch of their magic still remained, and it was their lingering power that helped Sabine hide in the city.

She approached the abandoned temple that had once been a great place of gathering and community. After the exile of the gods more than a thousand years earlier, countless sacrifices had been made in an attempt to recall them to this plane of existence. Even now, Sabine could detect the echoes of spilled sacrificial blood as she walked across the cobblestones. She released her modified glamour and surrounded herself with the shadows, using them to ward against the strongest lingering emotions. Even those without much sensitivity to magic could feel the effects, which was why this part of the city was mostly abandoned. It could be unsettling, if someone didn't know how to ward against it.

Sabine pushed open the creaking gate to the large grassy courtyard of the temple. Ivy and other foliage had begun to reclaim the building, but the magic of this place had prevented it from fully taking it over. That might happen one day, but it wouldn't be for a long time yet. The gods had protected this place well, and most of their magical protections still worked.

Turning away from the temple, Sabine headed toward the rear of the building where the burial stones and crypt remained. The burial stones were large obelisks carved with runes. Some were traced with protections, while others detailed the names and feats of those who were buried within the crypts. The language was old, from a time before the humans had come to the city. To her knowledge, no one except the oldest magical races could read the language or access the magic of the stones. This was the greatest source of power within the city, but only if you knew how to properly tap into it.

A young boy emerged from behind one of the burial stones, his eyes lighting up at the sight of her. Sabine gave him a warm smile. "Good afternoon, Toby. Any problems today?"

He shook his head and grinned, revealing a gap where he'd lost another tooth. Toby had been a fairly recent addition to Edvar's little band of rebels, but he appeared to be thriving. There were too many orphaned or abandoned children in the city. It broke her heart a little, but it was impossible to help them all.

Sabine approached one of the largest crypts and traced a pattern on the door, using the surrounding magic to unlock it. She'd originally intended to make this her own private getaway to escape from Dax and Bane when they irritated her, but she'd quickly seen others had more pressing needs. With so much lingering power, she'd been able to teach the human children how to manipulate some of the magical doorways in this area. It offered them a measure of protection and a place where they could live safely without fear.

The rune glowed in acknowledgement of the power she offered, and the door slid open with a groan. Stepping into the dark hallway, she formed a light in her hand—one of the earliest magics she'd learned as a child. It was bright enough to chase away the darkest of the shadows, but not enough to eliminate them completely. After all, the shadows were what gave this place its power. They could be used but never destroyed without creating an imbalance.

At the bottom of the stairs, Sabine traced another rune onto the wall. A hidden door opened, and she released her summoned light source before stepping inside the old stone building. It was part of the crypt but couldn't be easily accessed if one didn't know the path to walk or the correct combination of runes. Deeper within the building, she heard laughter and other voices.

Sabine paused for a moment to listen. It always warmed her heart that these children could still find reasons to smile when life had been so cruel to them. She'd once laughed that way too, but it had been stolen from her a long time ago. It had been years before she'd learned how to smile again, but some semblance of safety had to be achieved before she could embrace those emotions. She still wasn't safe and probably wouldn't ever be, but she'd come to terms with that.

She wasn't sure if these children felt the same way or if they'd released their earlier burdens when they embraced the sanctuary of the crypt. Either way, every time she came here and saw them, her soul lightened. Dax didn't understand why she bothered with these forgotten children, and even Bane had been somewhat perplexed. Esmelle, on the other hand, seemed to sympathize with their plight. The witch regularly asked after them and left small sacks filled with children-sized clothing and other items on Sabine's bed for her to take to them.

A teenage girl, maybe a dozen years younger than Sabine, stepped out from one of the rooms. Her eyes widened and a broad smile crossed her face. "Hey, Sabine! I heard the door and thought Toby might have been coming in."

Sabine smiled at Talia. "No, he's still outside. How are you feeling?"

"Much better! The tonic you sent over from Esme worked great. Edvar's even sending me on a job tomorrow." The dark-haired girl grinned and tucked one of her braids behind her ear. She'd started trying to wear her hair in a similar style to Sabine's several months ago. One of these days, Sabine might try to bring Talia to visit the pixies. They'd enjoy meeting her.

Sabine nodded. "Good. I'm looking for Edvar. Do you know where he is?"

"He was in the dining hall a few minutes ago. Do you want me to let him know you're here?"

Sabine shook her head. "That's all right. I'll find him."

Ignoring Talia's curious look, Sabine headed down the hallway in the direction of the voices. Talia's surprise wasn't unusual; Sabine didn't interact with most of the residents on a regular basis. They all knew who she was, and she'd recruited a few of them. It was better if she kept her distance. The more relationships she developed here, the harder it would be when she finally had to leave. As it was, Edvar and Talia had come to mean a great deal to her. Her departure would affect them the most, but she'd warned them it was inevitable.

Sabine entered the dining area, which had previously been empty and abandoned for generations. Edvar and the other children had spent months trying to return it to some semblance of its former glory. They'd done a remarkable job with their limited resources. The walls were stone, and the table itself was a heavily carved piece of wood that was ancient in origin. The magic of this place had prevented it from falling in complete disrepair, but the enthusiasm of the children had brought it back to life.

Unwilling to interrupt, Sabine leaned against the wall and watched as Edvar doled out tomorrow's assignments to everyone in the dining area. He was older than the children who lived here, and she guessed he was somewhere in his late teens or early twenties. His operation wasn't as large or as profitable as Dax's, but it served as a feeder group to Dax's crew. Sabine once thought Edvar would have wanted to join Dax's crew, but he'd insisted on remaining here instead. That suited her fine; she couldn't afford to be more entwined in this operation than she already was. Between Edvar and Talia, they had everything well in hand.

Edvar pushed his dark-blond hair out of his eyes and handed a rolled-up document to a young girl no more than nine or ten. She gave him a wide smile and darted out of the room. Edvar looked up and met Sabine's gaze. She nodded at him in greeting, and his eyes warmed.

He walked over to her, and she noted he wore some of the clothes she'd dropped off for him a few weeks earlier. He was almost as tall as Dax now, and his shoulders were almost as broad. Only a faint trace of his former youthfulness remained. She'd met him when she was still fairly new to the city. One of the city guards had been a little too rough after he'd been caught pickpocketing. He'd managed to escape to this part of the city, which was where Sabine had found him, bleeding and on the verge of death.

Sabine had taken him to Esmelle's shop, and the two of them had nursed Edvar back to health. Once he recovered, she showed him how to navigate the crypts and helped him set up his operation. Talia had been the next to join them, and the other children followed after that.

Edvar shoved his hands into his pockets. "We weren't expecting you until later tonight, but I'm glad you're here. That vendor with those cakes you like set up his cart not too far from here. I think Talia's on her way out to pick some up."

She smiled, touched by his thoughtfulness. "I just ran into her. If she gets back before I have to leave, I might steal one to take with me."

"It's not stealing if she's going out specifically for you," Edvar said with a grin. "Oh, I got your message yesterday. The kids have started looking for Terrance, but they haven't had any luck yet. They're supposed to check in with me again later tonight."

"I'm actually here on another matter." She glanced at the younger children. "It would be better to discuss it privately."

"Of course." Edvar motioned for her to follow him. Edvar's bedroom was down the hallway, right next to the room she used when she spent the night. That wasn't often, but she tried to mix up the places she stayed. One of these days, it would be nice to have a more permanent place to call her own.

She swept her gaze over the room as Edvar hastily picked up clothes from the floor and tossed them into a corner. "Can I get you a drink?"

"Maybe later. Unfortunately, I can't stay for long." Sabine walked over to some papers scattered on the desk and picked up a hand-drawn picture of Talia. The likeness was uncanny. He'd managed to capture Talia's inquisitive nature perfectly. "This is wonderful, Edvar."

"Yeah? I thought it came out pretty good, but I need to fix a few more things on it," he said, looking away as though he were embarrassed by the compliment. "I plan to give that to her when it's finished."

"I'm sure it will be a treasured gift." Sabine put the picture back and caught sight of another one. She arched her brow at him, and Edvar winced.

"Sorry. I know you don't want me to draw you, but…" He gave her a sheepish smile and shrugged. "I couldn't resist. I-I can get rid of it, if you want."

The last was said almost with regret. Sabine didn't answer right way. Instead, she picked up the drawing and studied it. It was very good—a little *too* good. She was laughing in the image, and Edvar had enhanced her features as though he'd seen through most of her glamour. Artists possessed their own special brand of magic.

The thought of destroying something belonging to Edvar filled her with regret. He'd already lost so much, including his family. She couldn't bring herself to take this from him too. With a sigh, she said, "I won't ask you to do that, but I can't risk allowing this to fall into the wrong hands. If someone looking for me were to find it…" Her voice trailed off, and she shook her head.

"I would never do anything to put you in harm's way, Sabine," Edvar said quietly and rubbed the back of his neck. "It's only a picture. You can tear it up. I… I *needed* to draw you. I can't seem to get it quite right though. I've been working on it for weeks."

She gave him a small smile. Edvar didn't give himself enough credit. Instead, he'd attempted to reconcile the truth of her appearance with what she presented to the world. "I can't bear to see your creations destroyed. I trust you, Edvar. Just don't allow it to leave the crypt."

"Of course. Whatever you want." Edvar paused and frowned. "Do you mind if I show Talia when I'm finished? I won't show anyone else."

"That's fine." She returned the picture to the desk.

In another place, Edvar might have an opportunity to do something great with his artistic talent. She'd once suggested he consider going to one of the northern cities to study art, but Akros was his home. She hadn't pushed. One thing she'd learned over the years was everyone had their own destiny to follow.

Turning back to Edvar, she focused on the reason Dax had asked her to come. "Do you know Baxter Rasten?"

"The councilman?"

Sabine nodded. "I need a drawing of his house. I've been inside a few times, but I don't have your artistic talent."

"Sure." Edvar picked up his sketchpad and sat on the edge of his bed. "Do you want the exterior or interior?"

"Both. We're running a job there tonight, and I need to have a detailed floorplan for Dax and his crew."

Edvar frowned and started to sketch. "I can do that. I remember the outside of the house well enough. I used to pickpocket not far from there when I was a kid. Festin was working that area until a few days ago. He said there's been some commotion lately, and they've increased security. They're using mercenaries, though, not city guards. Do you think it's tied into the stuff they found in the catacombs?"

Sabine walked over and sat beside Edvar, watching as the image of the house came to life in front of her. His recollection of the building was better than she expected, but Edvar had always had an eye for this sort of thing.

"Perhaps. It would explain why Dax wants to break in tonight. There's something going on with the city council. They've been making a lot of changes. I'm not sure what it means for everyone living in Akros, but I've been trying to get more information. You may want to give the kids a warning and ask them to lie low for a while."

Edvar snorted. "No one pays attention to street kids, Sabine. You know that."

She nodded. "You're right, but it may be worth it to issue a warning. I have another request too."

"Anything," he murmured, continuing to draw the outside of the house.

"You should never make such an offer in a place of magic without hearing the terms first," she reminded him gently. When he rolled his eyes at her, Sabine laughed. They both knew she wouldn't take advantage of him, but others might if he gave them the opportunity. "There's a ship in the harbor right now called Obsidian's Storm. Do you know it?"

Edvar's brow furrowed. "Yeah. Smuggler ship. It got here a few days ago. Dax approved the docking and made the arrangements with the dockmaster."

Sabine smiled. Edvar had always been well-informed. "Yes. Can you have one of the children work the dock area for a few days? I'd like to get more information about the crew, especially the captain."

He frowned. "Sure, but I can handle that for you."

"You're a little too recognizable now, Edvar," she teased lightly. "That's why Dax doesn't go out on jobs much anymore. It's hard to stay in the shadows when everyone knows who you are."

Edvar shrugged and ran his finger over the paper, shading the drawing to give the image some depth. "He still goes on some jobs. Like tonight. If he's asked you for information about the councilman's home and it's surrounded by mercenaries, he won't let you go in alone."

Sabine was quiet for a long time. Dax was protective of her, and Edvar tried to emulate the demon's behavior. The biggest difference was, Edvar was protective of *all* the children living and working for him, while Dax primarily looked out for himself. She was the only exception.

When Edvar completed the rough sketch of the exterior, he turned the page and waited for her instructions on the inside. Sabine started to describe what she remembered, but there would be some estimations. Dax hadn't given her enough time for much more than that, and it had been several months since she'd last been inside the councilman's home.

"There are two floors, plus a cellar. I've been in most of the rooms, and it's unlikely they would have changed much since then."

Edvar began drawing. "I thought you avoided places like this."

"I usually do," she admitted, pointing out an area that needed to be enlarged. "Baxter has one of the largest libraries in the city. He doesn't notice when I borrow a book or two. It's fairly easy to sneak in and out to replace them and grab more."

He grinned, his hair dropping down into his eyes. He absently brushed it away and resumed sketching. "You're the only person I know who steals books and then returns them."

"Borrow," she reminded him with a laugh. "Although, he has some excellent wines in his cellar. Those, I don't borrow. But tonight, we won't be shopping for books or wine. Dax is hoping for a big score. We'll see if he actually manages to pull this off."

Chapter Nine

*M*alek rested his hands on the edge of the table while he studied the sketches scattered on top of it. Dax had managed to steal drawings of some of the artifacts discovered in a recently excavated catacomb underneath Akros. One of them was particularly promising. Most of these items appeared to be from the time before the Great War, but he wasn't certain if they were the magical objects he sought. Even if they weren't, a seer might be able to use them to locate other items that had been created around the same time. It was imperative he locate the artifacts used to seal the portal more than a millennium ago.

Dax stood on the opposite side of the table, along with Javyn and a few others from Dax's crew. The demon still believed Malek was simply seeking valuable items for some unknown client, and Malek had no intention of correcting his assumption.

Malek straightened and gestured to the drawings. "I'm willing to offer you one chest of gold for each item you're able to acquire, provided they're authentic, of course."

Dax crossed his arms over his chest. "Two chests of gold, and another one filled with gems from the dwarven mines." He leaned forward, his eyes flashing silver before he gave Malek a sly smile. "Or I'm willing to accept one chest of gold and Sabine's mark."

Javyn frowned at Dax but remained silent. No one else had any reaction, which led Malek to believe Javyn knew why Dax wanted the mark transferred to him.

Malek's jaw clenched. The price Dax demanded was more than he was willing to pay. He wasn't about to turn over Sabine's mark to the demon.

"One chest of gold and one chest of precious gems for each artifact you acquire. Sabine's mark is *mine*." He pushed away the sketches. "There's no guarantee these items are the ones I'm seeking."

Dax leaned back and studied the mark on Malek's wrist, his expression calculating. Malek narrowed his eyes. If Dax attempted to use Sabine as further leverage in these negotiations, he might be inclined to pin the demon to the ground and rip out his throat. The warding medallion around his neck warmed against his skin.

"Do we have a deal?" Malek prompted.

"You may keep Sabine's mark for now," Dax replied with a trace of amusement in his tone. "The deal is set at one chest of gold and one chest of gems for each artifact we recover."

Forcing himself to relax his shoulders, Malek asked, "When can I expect delivery?"

"The first of these items will be collected tonight. Delivery will be made to you upon receipt of payment. We're still locating the other artifacts. They've been moved to other locations within the city, although we have reports some may have been transported farther south."

Malek paused, wondering if the message Dax had sent to Sabine was related to acquiring the artifact. If she was instrumental in Dax's efforts to locate the items, perhaps he might be able to convince her to help him without the demon's involvement. Keeping his expression neutral, he spoke over his shoulder, "Levin, make the arrangements. I want the chests for the first artifact delivered by morning."

"I'll make sure it's done," Levin replied.

Dax's lips curved upward, his expression a little too smug. The demon was up to something, but as long as Malek got what he'd come for, he didn't give a damn what games Dax played.

Dax called over to Javyn, "Tell everyone to gear up. We're leaving in less than an hour."

Javyn nodded and started issuing orders to the people who had been standing around watching the negotiations. It appeared to be a rather large undertaking, including at least a half-dozen people. More than a few of them had some trace of magical abilities, but Malek couldn't tell how much or what kind of powers they possessed. The warding necklace he wore caused too much interference, but at least it still worked to mask his secret.

Dax walked around the table toward him, his eyes trained on Malek's wrist. "How many times has Sabine refreshed the mark?"

Malek glanced down at his wrist and didn't respond. Sabine had made it a point to touch the mark every time he'd seen her, infusing more magic into the design. Now that he studied it closer, he could see some slight changes to it, almost as if it were fading.

"It burns her every time she has to reapply it, like liquid fire trapped under her skin," Dax said with a malicious smile on his face. "Sabine would never allow someone to accept the pain on her behalf, taking it upon herself instead. If you want to play human and ward yourself against external magic, don't play with powers you don't understand."

The last part was said with a sneer. Malek's body went rigid as Dax's words registered. The mark must not have settled on his skin properly due to the warding necklace he wore. He resisted the urge to curse. Sabine had been refreshing it to try to protect him, but she'd never said a word about it. Dax had known it was fading when he started negotiating the price for acquiring the artifacts, and Malek had foolishly fallen into the demon's trap.

It was a minor marker, but he'd just made his interest in Sabine abundantly clear—even to the point of endangering his purpose here. If Dax believed his protection of Sabine extended to eliminating the pain she felt at reapplying the mark, the demon might try to force a confrontation. Malek needed to tread carefully, but he wasn't willing to back down either.

Dax chuckled. "You may hold her temporary mark, but Sabine is *mine*. The moment it fades and our business is done, I'll enjoy peeling your skin from your body. Perhaps I'll wear it as a cloak."

"Good luck with that," Malek retorted, allowing his power to rise and beat against the warding. He wouldn't unleash it yet, but it was a very near thing. Levin moved into a defensive position beside him.

An unfamiliar woman entered the room, sweeping her gaze over everyone before settling on Dax. She hesitated for a moment before Dax demanded, "What is it, Leia?"

She winced and hastened over to him, offering a rolled parchment. "An urgent message just arrived. It has Balkin's seal."

Dax took it, breaking the seal with his magic and sending

a waft of sulfur into the air. He read it quickly, his scowl deepening, and then crumbled it. His eyes flashed silver as flames erupted from his hand, engulfing the message until it was nothing more than ash.

"Javyn, when did you last see Sabine?" Dax snapped.

Javyn jerked to attention. "A few hours ago. I believe she intended to come here after acquiring the information you requested. Is there a problem?"

"I want her found. Now."

Javyn gave Dax a curt nod. "Shall I contact Bane?"

"Do it. Tell him to run a tracking spell on her immediately," he ordered, turning and pacing the length of the room. "Leia, go to Esmelle's shop and see if she's there. Verin, I want you to locate one of the street kids lurking in the market. Have them get a message to Edvar and find out if he's seen her."

Malek frowned and took a step toward the demon. "Is Sabine in danger?"

Dax scowled at him, but before he could respond, the door opened again and Sabine entered, carrying some rolled-up parchment. Malek scanned her up and down, but she appeared much the same as when he'd left her. Although, the flowers were now missing from her hair. She otherwise appeared unharmed.

She paused, arching her brow at the serious faces in the room. Her mouth twitched in a small smile. "Problem?"

Dax crossed the room toward her in a handful of steps. His hand whipped out blindingly fast and hooked around the back of her neck. Pulling her tightly against him, he whispered something into her ear.

Sabine's face paled as she listened to the demon. She wrapped her hand around Dax's wrist. "No. Did he say why?"

Dax's voice was little more than a growl as he said, "Why

the fuck do you think, Sabine? Tell me about this knife. Where is it?"

"I gave it to Bane after I left here last night. You would have known about it sooner if you hadn't drugged me," she said, shoving the rolled parchment in his direction. "Here. Either back off or find someone else to help you tonight."

Dax's jaw clenched, but he grabbed the parchment and walked back over to the table. "I'm not letting you out of my sight until I get to the bottom of this, Sabine. We'll discuss the rest after we finish the job."

Sabine's eyes narrowed, but she didn't argue. Instead, she headed over to the table where Dax was unrolling the parchment. Javyn and the other members of Dax's crew hesitantly approached.

Levin frowned and gave him a questioning look. Malek shook his head, indicating he didn't know. It was unlikely this was related to the dagger Dax had given Sabine as a gift earlier. The timeframe didn't match, and Dax was furious he hadn't known about this mysterious knife.

Malek studied Sabine as she listened to Dax detail the plan for the tonight. Bane could have been the man he'd seen waiting for her last night. Malek had recognized the energy signature as belonging to a demon, which made sense if Bane and Dax were brothers. It was possible the knife in question was the same one he'd picked up after killing one of Sabine's attackers. He'd been surprised to see an iron weapon here, but now he was almost positive Sabine's Fae heritage was even stronger than he'd originally believed.

"—you'll coordinate with them to take out the men located along the perimeter if an alarm is raised," Dax said to Javyn. "Tasha, while he's distracting them, you'll need to open the door on the north side of the building to give us entry. Eliminate any guards you find on the way."

"That may not be necessary," Sabine said, pulling the

sketch over to her. She pointed to an area on the parchment. "This second-floor entrance is rarely locked, but even if it is, it's only a simple lock and easy to bypass. The guards only go up here when they're patrolling. Otherwise, just the family and a few servants go upstairs. We can access the balcony through the gardens." She tapped on another location on the map. "The rest of the interior crew can gain entry to the lower level through the servants' quarters entrance here. That should keep loss of life to a minimum."

Dax arched his brow. "Do you know the location of the safe?"

She nodded. "Safes. There are at least two. One is in the library, which is right off the second-floor entrance I showed you. The other is in the councilman's bedroom, which is here." She pointed to another location on the floorplan. "There's also a downstairs wine cellar where he has a hidey hole. Larger objects may be stashed there. If there are more safes or hidden locations, I don't know where they are. I wasn't searching for them."

"How many times have you been in there?" Tasha smirked.

Sabine lifted her head and winked at her. "Enough to know one he's got one of your favorite ales in his cellar."

Tasha laughed. "Looks like I'll be checking out this hidey hole then."

Dax nodded, studying the diagram. "Fine. Sabine, you're with me. After the distraction to lure the guards away, we'll enter on the second floor. Everyone else, keep to your positions and the original plan. I want us to be in and out of there fast."

Malek looked down at the elaborate floorplan and then at Sabine. If she was the key to locating this artifact, he needed to see how it was done. "I'm going with you."

Dax narrowed his eyes. "And what makes you think I'll allow that?"

"The fact I'm paying you." Malek held Dax's gaze, refusing to back down. "I'm providing you with a great deal of coin to secure this artifact, and I intend to make sure there are no problems. This is *not* a request."

Sabine blinked, regarding him with surprise. "This item is for you?"

Malek nodded at her. "Yes. I've hired Dax and his crew to acquire this artifact."

"Out of the question. This was not our agreement. You'll receive it as previously discussed," Dax snapped, crossing his arms over his chest. "I will *not* take an untested observer along with my crew. Not only that, but I don't trust you."

"Name your price," Malek challenged.

Before Dax could argue further or make another outlandish request, Sabine put her hand on the demon's arm. "Another weapon on our side may tip the balance in our favor, Dax. If they're moving the artifact out tomorrow, you know we need to do this tonight. We haven't had time to properly case the place. Malek knows how to walk in the shadows. I think you should allow it."

The air shifted around the demon, and Malek had the sudden insight Sabine was sending a small wave of her magic into him. She gave the demon a small cryptic smile and barely discernible nod.

Dax turned back to him with a look of disgust. "Very well. You may accompany us. In return, you will deliver another chest of coin at the same time as the rest of the payment. If you are the reason this endeavor fails and we are unable to secure the item, the full payment is still due."

Malek inclined his head in agreement. He wasn't sure why Sabine had helped convince the demon, but he wasn't going to argue. The sooner he completed his mission and left this city, the better. As Sabine had warned him, Dax was growing more suspicious and less tolerant of Malek's presence. He just hoped he might be able to convince Sabine to come with him when he left.

SABINE STOOD in the alley behind Dax with Malek standing beside her. Everyone was in position, waiting for Dax's signal. He turned to Malek and pulled out a knife, flipping it over and offering it hilt first. "A blood oath is required, or you will wait here in the alley." His eyes flashed silver. "*This* is not a request."

Malek narrowed his eyes but didn't take the blade. "What oath?"

Sabine tensed, knowing this could get ugly. She had the impression Malek was as much a predator as Dax, and neither one was willing to back down. It was probably foolish of her to intervene in their argument earlier, but Sabine was curious about why Malek wanted to come along. She'd wrongly assumed Dax would have regulated him to accompany Javyn, but Dax had decided to keep Malek with them instead. If she had to guess, she'd say Dax was still trying to manipulate the situation so he could eliminate Malek.

She might understand and respect Dax's reasonings for the oath, but Malek wouldn't. Deciding it would be best to intervene again before either one decided to shed blood, she took the knife from Dax. He scowled at her. She ignored him and turned away, taking his silence as reluctant agreement he'd accept her handling of the situation.

Sabine looked up at Malek, whose expression had softened to one of curiosity. The oath she was about to ask him to make was one that had to be adhered by both magic users and mundane humans. It wasn't something done lightly, and she wouldn't normally ask such a thing. If Malek refused, Dax would kill him right here and now. And she would have to stand by and let him.

Hoping she wasn't wrong about Malek, she chose her words carefully. "The night we met, you offered me your word you didn't intend me any harm. Tonight, I ask you to make it official. By blood and moonlight, I ask for your oath you will not reveal anything you see, hear, or learn tonight."

Malek straightened, darting a quick glance at Dax before focusing on her again. The ship captain nodded and held out his hand, allowing her to place the hilt of the blade in it. A surge of relief rushed through her at his quick acceptance. Malek flipped the knife around, much in the same manner Dax had done, and sliced open his non-weapon hand.

He curled his injured hand into a fist. "By blood and moonlight, I swear I intend you no harm. I further swear not to reveal any secrets that might be seen, heard, or learned tonight without your leave to do so."

Sabine held out her hand, and he placed his injured hand over hers. His blood spilled onto her hand. She froze, staggered by the raw power in his blood.

Her gaze flew up to meet his, but he kept his expression neutral. Only the slight tension in his shoulders belied his nonchalance. She swallowed her unease and blew softly over his hand, infusing her breath with the magic of her ancestors to seal their bargain and heal his wound. She wasn't a healer by any means, except for this one ability granted by a promise and gift of blood.

Still somewhat shaken by the unexpected rush of power in Malek's blood, she managed to complete the ritualistic words. "By blood and moonlight, I accept and bind your oath."

Sabine started to pull away, but Malek captured her hand.

He held her gaze, lifted her hand, and placed a gentle kiss on it. Charmed by the romantic gesture, she gazed up at him and gave him a shy smile. It might be a small thing to others, but no one had ever treated her like this before.

Dax scowled, snatched his knife back, and re-sheathed it. "Sabine, it's time."

Reluctantly, she pulled her hand away from Malek and nodded. It was time to honor her part of the debt they'd forged years earlier. One caveat to their original agreement was if Dax's coffers dropped below a certain amount, he had the right to call upon her for assistance. He'd been spending quite a bit of coin lately trying to get information about the city council and paying off guards, but part of that was because he was trying to expand his territory. She knew Dax sometimes manipulated the situation as it pleased him, particularly when he was in a mood and she wasn't feeling accommodating. But they always adhered to their agreement.

Sabine removed her cloak, needing more freedom of movement. Dax took it from her, tossing it out of the way and deeper into the alley. They'd retrieve it later, or one of his men would. Dax's hand wrapped around her neck, the skin-to-skin contact necessary for what they were about to attempt. It was only when he was hiding her presence in this manner that she could safely tap into the full scope of her magic. Otherwise, those who hunted her would be drawn to her power like a beacon.

She paused for a moment, wondering if the magical burst she'd exhibited during the ambush had drawn attention to herself. Perhaps that was the reason Balkin was returning to Akros. He'd told her he would come for her when it was time to bring her home, but it was still too soon. The timing wasn't right yet.

Dax stroked her neck in a warning, and she pushed aside

the errant thoughts to focus on the task at hand. Dax had never been overly patient, and they had a job to do. Although major magic could be worked without blood, a few drops helped make it easier and allowed her to keep excess power in reserve. It was also risky because blood contained power, especially hers.

Sabine pulled out her dagger, pricked her finger, and allowed two drops of blood to fall to the cobblestones. In the language of her birth, she whispered, "By blood, by magic, by rights of both, I call upon the memory of the gods who have abandoned this world. May the darkness fall and shadows dance freely within the night."

Clouds, dark and ominous, streaked across the sky, stealing the light of the moon. Sabine pricked another finger and allowed two more drops to fall to the stones below. She knew without looking the first ones had dissipated the moment the magic consumed her blood. "By blood, by magic, by rights of both, I call upon the memory of the gods who have abandoned this world. May the light shine brightly within those who embrace the darkness."

A sharp and biting wind blew through the streets, causing fallen leaves and debris to scatter. As the magical wind caressed Dax's men, it would infuse them with power, giving them enhanced speed and luck for the duration of the magic.

She cut a third finger and held it up. Dax leaned forward, catching her blood on his tongue before the drops could fall to the ground. He closed his eyes for a moment, and she could feel her magic rushing through him and filling him with purpose. Until the moon returned and the magic exhausted itself, his power would be magnified far beyond his normal abilities. His ties to this world were once again cemented, and he was now as powerful here as he would be trapped in the underworld. Stolen blood could never be used for this purpose, even though many had tried over the centuries. The magic flared bright and true only when offered as a gift or a bargain was struck.

Dax stroked her neck again, indicating it was done. He released her and moved forward to the end of the alley, waiting for Javyn to initiate the distraction. The moon's disappearance was the prearranged signal for Dax's men to move into position.

Sabine glanced over at Malek to find a stunned expression on his face. Underneath was a covetous and predatory look, which caused her heart to race. She hesitated for a moment, concerned she'd misread him. But anyone with the strength of magic he possessed shouldn't have been able to make the oath he did and still intend her harm. She bit her lip, hoping she hadn't been wrong.

As though sensing her unease, his expression gentled and he reached out, brushing the backs of his fingers against hers. He gave her the slightest hint of a smile as his eyes warmed. It was enough to make her relax. Oh, he might still hurt her. But the *intention* wouldn't be there. Besides, the heart was always at risk when emotions became involved. She wanted to trust his intentions were honorable. She just hoped she wasn't being foolish.

A birdlike whistle pierced the night, the only signal they'd receive to let them know the guards were being lured away. Dax hastened out of the alley and leapt over the wall to the garden, quickly disappearing from sight. She followed, jumping over the wall and trusting Malek was behind her. Landing softly on the ground, she ran toward the building. Like the magic she'd unleashed, those who sought the cover of the shadows tonight would have an easier time moving unseen. They still needed to hurry because the more people who were involved, the faster the magic would dissipate.

Dax bent down, offering her a foothold. She ran, using the momentum to throw herself into the air and over the second-floor balcony. She could have made it without his assistance, but she needed to conserve her remaining magic until after they escaped. Kneeling in front of the double doors, she tested the door to find it locked. Withdrawing her knife, she pricked her finger again and coated the tip of the blade with a drop of blood. At this rate, she was going to run out of fingers. Pressing the point of the dagger into the door lock, she listened for the almost silent *snick* of the lock disengaging.

Dax climbed over the balcony, dropping down silently. She moved away from the door, allowing him to take point. Malek appeared almost a second later, moving closer to the building and deeper into the shadows to hide from anyone who may have a view of the balcony.

Dax leaned against the wall at the edge of the door and glanced down at her. She gave him a nod, indicating it was unlocked. Dax pressed his hand against the door and closed his eyes, undoubtedly using his abilities to search for any lifeforce present on the other side. After several heartbeats, he opened the door and slipped inside. She motioned for Malek to stay close as they crept behind Dax.

The councilman's home was more of a mansion than a house, with hand-carved furniture and rich tapestries. The faint scent of a cigar tickled her nose. Sabine rubbed it absently as she gazed longingly at the floor-to-ceiling shelves filled with books on almost every subject. It had been a few months since she'd last visited, and it appeared the councilman had obtained a few more tomes.

Pushing aside the temptation to explore these new treasures, she headed directly for the safe embedded in the wall. It was unlikely it contained the item Dax was looking for, but they couldn't move on until they checked. Sabine moved aside the picture hiding the safe and stepped back, allowing Dax to begin working on the lock.

Malek positioned himself close to the window to watch the streets below for the guards. Sabine didn't bother. Javyn would keep the guards busy for a while. Instead, she ran her fingers over the books on the shelves and studied some of the newer titles. The councilman had been busy collecting books on magical items. She didn't remember any of these from her last visit. Curious, she pulled one out and flipped it open to a marked page.

Malek approached her and placed his hand against her back, leaning over to see what had caught her interest. She glanced up at him but didn't pull away. Malek seemed to take every opportunity to touch her, and she'd found she enjoyed it far more than she expected.

The book she'd picked up appeared to be little more than nonsense. It was a madman's ramblings, most likely a human who was running tests on items forged with magic. A lot of it was speculation about things he didn't understand. When the humans had become trapped on their world and the portal closed, they began hunting for ways to adapt to living amongst the magical races. The first witches and warlocks were created using these methods, trying to steal magic from others and forcing it to bend to their will.

Like the offering she'd made to Dax, magic needed to be gifted or part of a bargain for it to remain effective. The humans eventually realized this simple truth, which ended up being part of the reason there were so many mixed heritages. Even Esme was mostly human, but somewhere in her family line was a dryad who had mated with a human.

The notes scribbled in the margins of the book were a little more interesting. Someone, possibly the councilman, had made several references to the light and the dark. It wasn't a concept humans typically embraced, preferring a more simplistic view of good and evil. He further went on to write about how the dark could be trapped by the light, and vice versa. Sabine frowned, wondering if the councilman had been experimenting with magic and whether this had anything to do with the strange rumors circulating in Akros. If Baxter had discovered the artifacts were magical items, he might be trying to use them for some unknown purpose. It would explain some of the secrecy.

Dax opened the safe, and Sabine slid the book back onto the shelf. She'd have to come back at a later time and investigate more thoroughly. Leaning over Dax's shoulder, she watched as he pushed aside some papers to reveal a box tucked into the back of the safe. He pulled it out and flicked it open, studying the sparkling diamond necklace resting inside. It wasn't dwarven workmanship nor magical in nature, and only somewhat pretty. Dax arched his brow in a silent question. She wrinkled her nose and shook her head.

He nodded, withdrew the necklace, and tossed the empty box back into the safe. If she had indicated she liked it, the jewelry would probably make its way into a gift of some kind for her. Since she was ambivalent about it, Dax would likely sell it and distribute the profits to his crew.

It clearly wasn't the item they were hunting, so Dax put it in his pocket, closed the safe, and moved the picture covering it back into position. Malek glanced at her with a question in his eyes. She shook her head to indicate they needed to keep looking.

Dax moved to the door leading out into the hall. Pressing his hand on the door, he closed his eyes again and breathed deeply. His shoulders tensed and he jerked his head in her direction. Sabine grabbed Malek's hand and pulled him into the corner of the room just as Dax moved in front of them. Reaching out, she touched Dax's hand and focused on gathering the surrounding shadows just as the door swung open.

The light in the room changed slightly, but not enough to alert anyone of the deepening shadows. It wasn't an invisibility spell. Such things were impossible, but perceptions and lighting could be changed to hide someone from view. It was also possible to plant a suggestion for people not to notice them, encouraging them to slide their gaze past them as though they were a fixture or furnishing. The magic flowed over them, not penetrating Malek's warding, but it didn't matter. The type of magic she was using wasn't designed to affect him directly; it was simply necessary to mask his presence.

Footsteps moved across the floor of the library, most likely from one of the guards patrolling the house. Dax silently slid a knife out of its sheath, but he wouldn't break her shadow illusion unless the guard got too close. Sabine kept her breathing quiet and glanced over at Malek to see he'd also angled himself protectively in front of her and had drawn a weapon. Despite the danger, she smiled to herself at the gesture. She could handle herself fine, but it only reinforced her earlier decision to trust him.

The moment the guard was gone, Dax slipped his knife back in its sheath and jerked his head toward the door. Sabine released the magic masking their presence and followed him. Some of Dax's people were probably still searching downstairs. Either Javyn or Verin most likely already had contacts amongst the servants, allowing them to move downstairs a bit easier. The second floor was more dangerous, which was why Dax had wanted to handle this part himself.

Even with her ability to manipulate the shadows, moving around unseen with three people was far more challenging than if she'd been alone. But with the guards or hired mercenaries lurking around, Dax would never have agreed to allow her to break into the councilman's home without him. Malek carried himself well though. He hadn't panicked, which was always a concern when someone was new to this type of activity. It made her even more curious about his background and where he'd learned some of his skills.

They moved down the hallway toward the master bedroom—the other location with a hidden safe. Thievery had never been her primary motivation. She'd originally broken into the councilman's home years earlier because she had been looking for information about the political climate in Akros. When she'd seen his expansive library, she knew she'd never be able to stay away.

Dax opened the door to the bedroom. Sabine slipped inside and immediately felt the unmistakable pulse of magic in the room. She grabbed Dax's arm and whispered, "Wait."

He froze, allowing her to move farther into the room. She closed her eyes to better focus on the threads of power calling to her. It was subtle and elegantly crafted, but it was difficult to sort through all the layers. She shook her head and tried to bury the unease plaguing her.

Dax moved beside her. "What is it?"

"Fae magic of a sort. Ancient. But it's different from anything I've felt before. It's been changed somehow…" She let her voice trail off, unable to fully explain what she was picking up. It was almost as though there was a component about the magic that had changed from its original purpose.

Malek arched an eyebrow. "Do you know where it's coming from?"

She swallowed and nodded, walking over to where she knew the safe was hidden. Unlike the safe in the library, this one was seated in the floor. She moved aside the heavy woven rug covering it, and Dax knelt beside her, studying it.

"Any traps?"

She frowned, placing her hand directly on the safe. She closed her eyes and sent her awareness outward, but she didn't pick up anything except the strange magic. "I can't be sure. Something is strange about the item in there. It may be interfering with my senses."

Dax muttered a curse under his breath. She frowned, but it was impossible to offer him any real assurances. Something wasn't right, but she couldn't tell any more than that.

"Malek, watch the door," Dax ordered and pulled out his lockpicks.

Sabine sat back on her heels, waiting for him to work through the lock. In a few quick movements, he'd slid the tumblers into place and wrenched open the door. A black velvet bag was inside, the shape revealing the object was longer than the length of her hand.

Dax started to reach inside, but she grabbed his wrist. "Wait. Let me."

His inquisitive gaze flew to her, but she couldn't put it into words. She knew this item was dangerous to *him*, but she'd didn't know how. Leaning down, she picked up the cloth pouch, the heavy weight somewhat surprising. When nothing happened, she relaxed and opened the bag to ensure this was the item they were seeking.

It was a golden chalice encrusted with several precious stones. The workmanship was remarkable and unlike anything she'd ever seen. She held it toward Dax to show him, and he thrust his hand into the bag. His back bowed and a shout exploded out of him, his eyes flashing silver and staying that way. His skin shimmered, the color deepening to a sickly blue-black.

Sabine gasped, terror flooding through her as Dax's tenuous grip on his demonic abilities faltered. Something was draining his lifeforce and pulling his demonic powers to the forefront. His hand tightened around the chalice, and his body started to tremble uncontrollably. Flashes of gray light snaked up his arms, pulsing in time with the magical trap surrounding the chalice. Sabine fumbled, trying to pull out her knife as Dax let out an ear-deafening roar that undoubtedly alerted everyone within the surrounding buildings to their presence.

Malek swore and dragged a dresser in front of the door to barricade it. "If you can snap him out of it, you need to hurry. We won't have much time until they break down the door."

Sabine blew out a breath, knowing they had even less time than that. The gray color of the magic imprisoning Dax could only be the work of a necromancer or one of its minions. Necromancers always corrupted the natural order of things to suit their purposes. They sipped on souls the same way she might enjoy a glass of Faerie wine. If she couldn't bring Dax back under control of himself, he'd rend a path of death and destruction in his wake until the spell killed him.

The only thing that might work was to counteract the death magic with a source of life. Slicing open her hand with the edge of her blade, Sabine slapped her bleeding hand against Dax's mouth. He latched on, drinking it as she poured her blood and power into him. Hopefully, it would be enough to break the chains tethering him to the chalice.

It fell out of his hands with a clatter, but he continued drinking until Malek wrenched him away from her. Dax's eyes were still silver, but he was power-drunk and would remain that way for some time. Even worse, her efforts hadn't worked. The gray magic of the necromancer still surrounded him.

She scooped up the fallen chalice, understanding she needed to break the magical link Dax had formed with it. Until she did, none of them would be safe and it would continue draining his lifeforce. The power she'd offered him was only a temporary boost, and she didn't know how long it would last until it started stealing his life again.

Excruciating, white-hot pain lanced through her. She struggled against succumbing to it and tried to focus on the magic affecting Dax. A ward, vaguely familiar to one she'd seen before, had been embedded over the chalice. This was the source of the gray magic attacking Dax.

Her hands trembled. The magic contained within the chalice itself was even greater than the trap. But she couldn't afford to be distracted by it right now. Whatever the chalice was, it wasn't killing Dax. A necromancer had crafted a lich ward, a nasty piece of spellcraft specifically designed to drain someone's lifeforce. Dax must be the intended target, which was why she could still see the gray magic surrounding him. It was impossibly complex, and Sabine didn't have enough time for a more traditional severing of its hold over Dax.

She turned her attention to the chalice itself and the source of power she sensed within it. Some long-dormant part of her knew it was crafted by the Fae. She explored it carefully, searching for a way to use it to break the hold over Dax.

An unfamiliar scene flashed through her mind's eye. A ritual. Drums. Words etched into her mind, unlike anything she'd heard before. It was a memory, but it had never been hers. The scent of sulfur and burnt leaves filled the air, but it wasn't from Dax's power or even from the necromancer's trap. It was a long-forgotten remnant from the time the chalice was first forged.

In her hands was an object of power. Like the Faerie wine she enjoyed drinking, the chalice offered her a shocking insight. Only a Fae could wield the chalice and claim its power. The trap itself was a perversion, fixed in place using a combination of undead and demonic blood. It was clumsy and coarse compared to the elegance and beauty of the magic contained within the artifact.

It might be possible to use that power to break the necromancer's spell. All magic demanded a sacrifice, even if it was hers. Blood dripped from her hand and she smeared it over the chalice, coating the gemstones in an offering.

She gasped as the magic of the chalice rushed through her, strong and more potent than anything she'd ever experienced. Sabine's glamour fell away as she grappled the tidal wave of power, attempting to direct it to break its hold over Dax. Her skin began to glow, her hair lightening into an impossible shade of silver that could never belong to a human. The winding, silver thorn tattoos that were the hallmark of her heritage reappeared on her hands and arms, pulsing with magical intent.

Someone or something thudded against the door, trying to break it down. She ignored it and gripped the chalice tightly, refusing to release it. The power from the chalice rushed through her, trailing up her hands and arms, burning along the path of the markings on her skin. The magic was both Unseelie and Seelie, before they had ever been sundered. The chalice was an ancient relic, forged from a time when the gods still walked this world. It was flavored with their power.

Items of power had their own awareness, and this one was no different. Sabine had never held one before, but she recalled the lessons she'd learned as a child. Understanding what it wanted, she stopped fighting. Instead, she poured her power into the chalice, connecting with it and letting its power flow over her. It recognized her as worthy, and the magical attack ceased abruptly. The golden cup fell from her hands, clattering to the ground, and she slumped over, gasping for breath.

Malek reached for her, but Dax growled. "Don't touch her."

"Dax," she whispered, recognizing most of her magic had been used trying to break the trap holding him. Dax wrapped his arms around her and pulled her to her feet. The pounding at the door continued, and she dimly heard the sound of wood splintering. At least Dax seemed to be in control of himself once more and one crisis had been averted.

Dax scooped her into his arms and carried her over to the bed. "Do you have enough strength to hide yourself?"

She blinked, trying to fumble with her limited magic, and nodded. It would be a crude undertaking, but it was imperative it be done. The glamour settled over her skin, a thousand pinpricks as she fixed the illusion in place.

"We need to get her out of here," Malek warned, pushing another piece of furniture in front of the door. They'd break it down any minute, and she couldn't risk being caught here in her weakened state.

"There's an attic access in the sitting area," she managed, leaning against one of the posters of the bed and trying to fortify her remaining strength. It would take some time and rest before her magic naturally replenished itself.

Dax yanked open the attic access, studying the darkness. "We can escape to the roof and over to the adjacent building. Can you climb?"

Sabine winced. "I don't think I have much choice, but I might need some help. The chalice should be safe to pick up for now, but use the bag, just in case. I don't have enough magic left right now if you trigger it again."

Dax walked back over and carefully used the bag like a glove to pick up the fallen artifact. He slid it back inside and pulled the drawstring tight, hiding it from view.

Malek frowned and motioned toward the attic entrance. "They're going to be through the door in another minute. We need to leave. Now."

Dax affixed the bag to his waist and frowned. "Malek, take her back to the tavern. Keep her off the main streets and out of sight."

Malek moved over to her and wrapped his arm around Sabine, pulling her to her feet. She was still unsteady, but that wouldn't get any better until she had a chance to rest. Peering up at Dax, she asked, "What about you?"

"I'll stall them." Dax slid his sword from its sheath. He turned back to Malek, his eyes flashing silver. "If any harm comes to her, I'll hunt you to the ends of the world and beyond."

Malek's jaw clenched. "*Nothing* will happen to her. I won't allow it."

Dax gave him a curt nod. Malek started to lead her toward the attic access, but she stopped beside Dax and looked into his eyes. "Come back to me, Dax."

His mouth curved upward into his telltale smirk. "Run along, little Fae. I have people to kill."

She reached out, placing her bleeding hand against his sword arm. "By blood and magic, I offer you my strength and demand you return to me."

His eyes flashed silver as her power flowed toward him, and he jerked away. In a voice barely recognizable, he roared, "Go! Now!"

Without waiting for her to say or do anything, Malek swept her toward the attic access and pushed her up the ladder. It was none too soon as the door splintered and crashed open behind them.

Chapter Ten

*M*alek glanced at Sabine. She'd been leaning on him heavily for the past ten minutes, but her usual grace was absent as her steps became even more sluggish. He bent down and scooped her into his arms. She didn't object. Instead, she trailed her fingertips over his chest.

"There's an old temple east of here. We need to get to the burial stones."

He frowned. "What's there?"

Her eyes fluttered shut as she murmured, "A crypt. Tell Edvar to call Bane. He can lead you through the tunnels under the city, but you have to show him…"

Alarm flooded through him as her voice trailed off. He squeezed her gently. "Keep talking to me, Sabine. What do you want me to show him?"

She blinked open her eyes, but they were unfocused. Whatever she had done inside the councilman's home had stolen all her strength. She swallowed. "I won't be able to stay awake much longer. By blood and magic, I release you from the confines of your oath to share your knowledge of what happened tonight with Bane and Edvar."

His brow furrowed. "You want me to tell them everything?"

"They're both sworn to keep my secrets. Show Bane your mark. He won't kill you."

Malek fell silent as her remaining magic settled over him, shifting the confines of his oath so he could reveal her secrets to this other demon. Malek frowned, debating whether to abandon this entire charade. Sabine was exhausted, and he needed to get her to safety. It was tempting to steal her away from the city until she recovered, but she trusted these people. If he had any hope of convincing her to trust him too, he needed to play by her rules for now.

Keeping his voice gentle, he urged, "I'll take care of everything. Just rest."

She nodded and leaned her head against his chest again. He felt her relax in his arms a few minutes later, and he knew she slept. He paused in the alleyway, breathing in her intoxicating scent, and battled his instincts. It was getting more difficult to stay in character the longer he remained in her presence. Now that he'd had a glimpse of the real Sabine, the one hidden underneath layers of intricate glamour, he needed to be even more careful. In his wildest dreams, he'd never expected to find a full-blooded Fae hiding within the city, much less one with her level of power.

Malek continued walking, staying in the shadows and off the streets as much as possible. Except for the maps he'd studied in preparation for his arrival, he didn't know the city very well. The temple she spoke of was deep within the oldest area of the city.

People hadn't worshiped the old gods for centuries. As a testament to their abandonment, the surrounding area was mostly deserted. Moss and vines covered the cobblestone streets, reclaiming the territory. An uneasy chill went through him, and he walked silently, feeling eyes tracking his progress.

The gate surrounding the temple was falling in some areas and completely collapsed in others. A strange stillness filled the night as though even the spirits haunting this place held their breath. He paused and swept his gaze over the area. Someone was definitely watching, but he didn't see any sign of them.

Malek pushed open the gate and headed inside, toward the back of the temple where the burial stones should be located. The giant stone obelisks were scattered throughout the grounds, each one dedicated to a different god. At the rear of the crumbling temple stood two stone figures, a god and goddess, pressing their frozen hands together in a show of solidarity. Magic hung heavy in the air, and Malek ignored the oiliness that coated his skin as the ward around his neck tried to fend it off.

He took a few steps toward the statues and called out, "I know you're there. I have a message for Edvar."

After almost a full minute, a young boy, no more than seven or eight years in age, stepped out from behind a burial stone. In a wavering voice, he whispered, "She's not dead, is she? Did... did you hurt her?"

"No." Malek studied the child a little closer. He was even younger than the boy Sabine had spoken with in the alley when they first met. "She's alive, but she needs help. Are you Edvar?"

The boy shook his head and motioned for him to follow. "No, but I'll take you to him."

He scampered behind the burial stone again and moved aside some bushes. A tunnel descended into darkness.

"Stay close. Walk in my steps. Light doesn't work here, but I know the path."

Malek arched a brow but followed the boy's instructions. The moment he entered the tunnel, the strong chill of magic crossed over his skin. It was different from the source of power he felt from Sabine, but it was similar. Someone with Fae blood had placed wards here—powerful ones. Sabine's warning about needing an escort suddenly made sense. If a Fae had set traps here, no one would be able to pass without severe consequences. He doubted even the warding around his neck could protect him.

The boy stepped forward, and a trail of green illuminated his footsteps. Malek's eyes widened in surprise. It was some sort of moss generating its own light. Someone, most likely Sabine, had shown the child where he needed to walk. He had the suspicion anyone else who tried to infiltrate the crypt would find themselves hopelessly lost or trapped.

"What's your name?" Malek asked, making sure his footsteps followed the exact same path of the boy.

"Toby," he said without looking back over his shoulder. He stopped at a small alcove and traced a pattern over it with his finger.

The wall shimmered briefly and disappeared. Malek inhaled sharply at the realization it was simply an illusion. He'd swear Toby was human, but the child had manipulated the magical protection with no small measure of competence. Someone had spent a great deal of time teaching him. From the heavy scent of magic coating the air like a blanket, the entire area could be an illusion. He'd seen enough magic over the years to know one misstep or incorrect rune would likely mean the death of anyone who attempted to navigate this place without an escort.

Malek followed the boy down the corridor, stepping on the same moss-covered stones that continued through here. They turned down different paths enough times to convince Malek they were traveling in circles. But such was the nature of Fae magic. It wasn't a coincidence people could go missing for years after falling afoul of them.

He glanced down at Sabine still in his arms. With the strange green glow offering a bit of illumination, Sabine appeared even more Fae-like. He didn't think he'd ever forget the memory of her true appearance. She was exquisite, and he understood why she'd hidden her appearance underneath layers of glamour. No one who ever saw her true appearance could ever mistake her as anything other than Fae.

Malek couldn't help but wonder how she'd learned about these tunnels and whether she'd been the one to teach Toby how to navigate them. It would explain the worry he'd seen in the child's eyes that something might be wrong with her. Sabine was shrouded in secrets and mystery as thick as the glamour that protected her.

Toby paused at a third wall and traced another symbol. It flared briefly, and Sabine murmured something unintelligible in her sleep. Malek frowned and focused on a narrow stairway leading upward. Toby started climbing and stopped right outside a door. Without bothering to knock, Toby pushed on the silver handle and the heavy wooden door swung open without making a sound.

They entered a small chamber-type room, and the boy whistled loudly. A teenage girl wearing a simple but clean dress in the style of a maid or servant entered the room. Her eyes widened at the sight of Sabine in his arms. She took a step forward and urged, "Toby, run and get Edvar. He's in the training room. Hurry."

"Don't worry, Talia. He says Sabine ain't dead." Toby darted down the hallway without waiting for a response.

Talia swallowed and gave Malek a questioning look. "Was he telling the truth? Will she be okay?"

"She's sleeping, but I must speak with Edvar right away."

Talia nodded, her shoulders slumping in relief. "Thank the gods. There's a room Sabine stays in sometimes. I'll show you."

He followed Talia down another hallway. She turned down an adjacent corridor and unlocked a heavy wooden door. Pushing it open, Talia gestured for him to place Sabine on the bed. Malek's gaze swept the small room. It was bare but functional, consisting of only a small bed and chest. If Sabine spent any time here at all, there was no trace of her to be seen.

He carefully laid her down, brushing his fingers against her cheek. Her skin was cool and paler than he'd like, but she didn't seem to be in any discomfort. She just seemed weak and tired. He didn't know what exactly she'd done power-wise, but it had cost her greatly.

Talia took a step toward him. "I've only seen her like this once before. It scared me then too."

Malek frowned. "What happened?"

Talia hesitated, tugging on the edge of her smock. "It was when she brought Toby to us. He almost died, but she saved him somehow. She collapsed afterward, and it took Toby a long time to recover too. D-did she save you tonight? Or someone else?"

"I'm sorry, but I swore an oath not to discuss what happened," he admitted, wishing he knew exactly what she'd done. Dax had been out of control, trapped in some sort of magical enchantment tied to the chalice. Malek was going to intervene, but then she'd done something by cutting her hand to bring him back from the brink. "Sabine asked me to bring her here before she passed out. She knew she'd be safe here. She must trust you a great deal."

Talia smiled and tucked her braided hair behind her ear, the mannerism reminding him of Sabine. "None of us will ever betray her. Most of us owe our lives to her in some way."

Malek sat on the edge of the bed, trying to appear less formidable. "Does Sabine live here with you?"

Talia shook her head. "No. I think we all wish she'd stay here, but she worries about drawing too much attention to us. I try to change the linens in here every so often, but she won't let me do more than that."

Footsteps sounded outside in the hallway, and a young man rushed into the room with Toby right behind him. At the sight of Malek, his hand immediately went to the weapon at his side. "Get away from her," he snapped.

Malek arched a brow and stood, but he didn't move away from the bed. "Are you Edvar?"

He inclined his head but didn't release his weapon. "Yes. Who the hell are you?"

"I'm Malek. Sabine's unconscious but otherwise unhurt. Before she passed out, she asked me to bring her here—to you. She wants you to call Bane."

Talia's face paled. Toby backed away a few steps, his eyes wide in fear.

Edvar muttered a curse. "Talia, go clear the lower levels of everyone except Raf and Shari. Toby, lock down the crypts."

Without a word, Toby disappeared. Talia hesitated. "She can't mean for you to bring him here, can she?"

"Go now, Talia," Edvar ordered. "Sabine wouldn't have used those words unless that was what she needed. She trusts him, so we need to do the same."

Talia swallowed and ran from the room.

Edvar walked over to the chest and opened it. He withdrew something that appeared to be a small wooden disk and drew his knife from its sheath. He took a step toward the bed, but Malek moved in front of him.

"I think you need to tell me what you plan to do with that first."

Edvar narrowed his eyes. He might be on the cusp of manhood, but there was a depth to his gaze as though he'd lived a lifetime already. "I don't know you or owe you any explanations. Sabine wanted you to bring her here for a reason. Now, move aside and let me do what I must."

Malek held his gaze for a long time. He was tempted to push the issue, but Sabine likely wouldn't appreciate him bullying someone she wanted to protect. If his suspicions were correct, Sabine was protecting all the children within these walls.

Malek stepped aside, and Edvar dropped to his knees beside the bed. His hand trembled slightly as he lifted Sabine's uninjured hand. Malek had stopped to bind the wound on her other hand once they were away from the councilman's home. Sabine had been frantic about stopping her bleeding, which made sense given her true identity.

Edvar used the knife to prick her fingertip. Blood welled to the surface, along with the heady scent of the forest and wild magic. Malek froze as Edvar coated the wooden disk with Sabine's blood. It soaked the surface almost immediately.

"*Saivere,*" Edvar whispered, and the disk began to glow. He pressed it again to Sabine's finger and more blood soaked through. The disk became even brighter, almost humming as power in the room began to build. It was threatening and furious all at once, but it was gone a moment later.

With shaking hands, Edvar placed the disk in Sabine's open hand. Malek leaned down to see the wound on her fingertip had disappeared. The strange light had done something to heal the injury. Unfortunately, Sabine didn't look any better. If anything, her skin was even paler. Panic rushed through him as he reached downward to check for a pulse. Her heart was beating, but it was slow. Something wasn't right.

"What did you do?" Malek demanded, glaring at Edvar. "She's weaker."

Edvar shook his head, his expression alarmed. "That can't be. She told me what to do, and I did it exactly as she said. It's supposed to summon Bane."

"Who is Bane to her?"

Edvar stared at him. "He's an assassin. *The* assassin. He runs the assassins' guild here in Akros."

"Are you mad?" he roared, bending over to lift Sabine back into his arms. Edvar flashed his knife, and Malek spun around, slamming him against the wall. He disarmed the young man and tossed his knife aside. With a scowl, Malek said, "An assassin? You called an assassin here when she's this weak?"

"Bane won't kill her," Edvar argued, jerking away from him.

"No, I won't," a man said from the doorway.

Malek narrowed his eyes at the newcomer. It figured. Another demon, and this was the same one who had been on the street waiting for her the night they searched Terrance's home. This must be Dax's brother. Rumors about demon siblings claimed they frequently competed and even killed each other when they reached maturity. Apparently, that hadn't happened yet.

Bane swept his gaze over Malek, and his mouth twisted in a smirk. "The ship captain, I presume?"

Malek inclined his head a fraction. "You'd be correct."

Bane grunted and walked over to the bed. Malek moved forward to block his progress. "Hurt her and you die."

Bane chuckled. "Move aside, ship captain. She *Called* me here. You may carry her temporary mark out of obligation, but I was gifted with her mark as a sign of trust." He flashed his wrist, the complete pattern more intricate and vibrant than the one on Malek's skin. It reminded him of the tattoos he'd seen on her arms when her glamour had fallen. "Now, move aside so I can help her."

It pained him to do it, but Malek allowed Bane to pass. Sabine trusted him, just like she seemed to trust Dax.

The demon sat on the edge of the bed and frowned. "How long has she been like this?"

"Almost two hours," Malek admitted, trying to bury his unease. He should have ignored the consequences and gotten her safely away before now. "She wasn't this bad until Edvar called you here."

Bane muttered a curse and picked up the wooden disk. He wrapped his hand around it and when it opened, the disk crumbled to dust. "She was too weak to risk a Calling."

Edvar swallowed. "Can you help her?"

Bane didn't reply right away. Instead, his gaze roamed over Sabine and his frown deepened. He unbound her cut hand, but it was already healed. "I don't see any other injuries. Activating the disk would have healed most of her wounds. What *exactly* happened?"

Malek rubbed the back of his neck. He'd been replaying everything in his head, but he still didn't understand everything that had occurred. "I've been trying to figure it out. Dax picked up an artifact and had a bad reaction to it. It caused his eyes to silver. Sabine managed to bring him back to himself using her blood, but then she did something to disable the magical protection around the chalice. She was weaker afterward, but not this bad." He stared at the sleeping woman, wondering if the entire thing had been a trap. "We got pinned down and couldn't get out. Dax told me to get her out of there while he created a distraction. Sabine asked me to bring her here."

Edvar nodded. "Sabine was here earlier tonight. She needed floorplans drawn up for the councilman's home. I think they were going after some artifacts that were found in the catacombs."

Bane's shoulders tensed. "Did Sabine touch Dax after she picked up the item?"

Malek frowned. "Yes, when we were trying to escape. She was already weak by that point. Would she have transferred more of her power to him?"

Bane nodded. "Unfortunately, yes. If she thought Dax was in danger, she would have made every effort to prevent him from falling into complete bloodlust. I took a trace amount of energy from her the other day, and I can share some of it with her now. In her current state, it won't be enough. I need to return her to Dax. He can return more of what he's taken from her."

Malek clenched his teeth. For some reason, and even though he didn't have any right to feel that way, he didn't like the idea of her sharing magic with Bane. Such a thing could be extraordinarily intimate. It was also a sign of trust. Most people avoided demons, but Sabine had embraced both of them and shared power with them. That wasn't an act done lightly, especially between Fae and demons.

Bane reached down and took Sabine's hands in his. The air shimmered around them, but it was barely discernible. If Malek hadn't been watching for it, he never would have noticed.

Sabine's eyes fluttered open. "You came," she said softly.

Bane chuckled. "You Called me with blood and magic. Yours is always impossible to resist."

She gave him a weak smile and grasped his hands. "Will you lead Malek back to the tavern through the tunnels? The guards will be looking for us. I don't think …" She shook her head as though trying to clear it. "I don't think I'll be able to stay awake long enough to show him the way."

He arched a brow. "I'm not in the habit of saving lives other than yours, little one. But for you, I will do as you ask and return you both to the tavern. I'm assuming Dax is waiting there for you?"

Sabine nodded and closed her eyes again, and Bane's shoulders tensed. He shook her awake and demanded, "What have you done, you beautiful little fool? How much power did you share with Dax?"

She blinked several times, but it was apparent she was struggling to stay awake. "Not Dax's fault," she slurred. "It was a lich ward. Embedded over the chalice and activated by touch. I broke the hold over Dax, but not… without consequences."

"Where is this chalice?"

"With Dax, but it's old, Bane. Very old. Both Seelie and Unseelie. Light and dark fused together, like the book said." She gripped his hand tightly and tried to sit up. "My glamour failed. Dax couldn't shield me. He was fighting off the effects and offered himself as a distraction so I could get away."

"My brother was a fool to take you with him," Bane muttered and pulled her off the bed. "I'll take you to Dax, but I will *not* leave you with him. There will be repercussions from this, Sabine."

"You can't interfere with our agreement," she managed, struggling to stand on her own.

When she faltered and Malek reached for her, Bane hissed at him, his eyes flaring silver. Malek's hands curved into fists, regarding the demon with irritation. If he forced the issue, Sabine might get hurt, but standing down was one of the most difficult things he'd ever done.

"Don't," Sabine whispered, placing her hand against

Bane's chest. "Malek helped me. I wouldn't have gotten away if it weren't for him. The magic you gave me is already fading. We need to hurry."

Bane glanced down at her and back at Malek with a look of disgust. He lifted Sabine into his arms. "Follow closely, ship captain. She wants you alive, but her safety is my priority. I won't wait for you if you fall behind."

Malek nodded and followed the demon back down the corridor. Sabine had already slipped back into unconsciousness, and Bane shifted her over his shoulder. Malek suspected he moved her so he could have his weapons hand free. Bane might have agreed to honor Sabine's request, but he'd likely try to wriggle out of it at the first opportunity. Malek wasn't overly concerned, except he'd need to break his own warding if it came down to a fight between them.

The thought of wards brought him back to Sabine's earlier comment. He'd heard of lich wards, but he hadn't known it was possible to escape from one once it had been triggered. "What did she mean about a lich ward?"

"I don't know everything she was talking about, but whatever Dax tried to steal, the ward may have been designed to target him specifically. Dax has been causing trouble for the city leaders, and they've been trying to shut him down for some time. My brother likely wouldn't still be alive if it weren't for Sabine."

Bane placed his hand on the wall and traced a pattern. A symbol flared briefly with a potent red light before the wall disappeared from view. Whatever magic Bane had poured into the mark had shifted the barrier hiding the passage. Malek suspected no one other than a demon could have opened that particular wall. The way into the crypt might normally be closed to Bane, except for this one time when Edvar had summoned him.

Malek walked quickly down into a tunnel that smelled

like it was connected to the sewers. His nostrils flared, but he ignored the stench. It was a powerful deterrent for anyone who might want to explore this area, but he was more concerned about Sabine.

"Will she recover?" Malek asked, following Bane across the raised platform. A quick glance over the side confirmed his earlier suspicion. Sewer water flowed below them.

"Eventually," Bane said, shifting Sabine again before he leapt over a narrow break in the platform. "The trap they set burned through a great deal of her power. She poured what she could into Dax, probably to ensure he'd survive once she left him. If he burns through too much of her transferred power, it'll leave her vulnerable for longer than I'd like."

Malek nodded, relieved by the demon's words. Vulnerable wasn't ideal, but he could ensure she remained protected until she fully recovered. That was assuming she allowed him to remain close once she learned the truth about why he was here. He thought back to the book she'd been studying in the library.

"Sabine picked up a book in the councilman's library. It spoke of the light and dark."

Bane snorted. "It's a trademark of humans to want to identify everything into light or dark, good or evil."

Malek made a noise of agreement and ducked under a low-hanging beam. He considered the rest of what Sabine had told Bane, particularly about the Seelie and Unseelie. As Bane had mentioned, good and evil was a human perception. The Seelie and Unseelie were simply different facets to the same people.

During the last war, the Fae who rejected the claims of the gods were labeled as Unseelie and sought refuge with the dwarves and demons underground. The Seelie were the ones who remained in service of the gods and supported their return. If Sabine were an Unseelie Fae, it would explain her willingness to consort with demons.

The realization made him straighten. Sabine might actually be inclined to help him with his mission when she learned the truth. Although, that might be false optimism. The Unseelie were still Fae, and all Fae viewed his kind as their enemies. Malek thought for sure she'd known what he was when he made his oath earlier. She'd been uneasy, but she hadn't said anything. It was possible she'd never met one of his kind before. His people rarely traveled this far south.

Bane stopped at another wall, tracing another rune with his hand. It flared red again, and the wall dissolved. He stepped through, and Malek followed closely, glancing backward to see the wall had already reformed behind him.

The sound of weapons sliding from their sheaths cut through the quiet. Malek's hand immediately went to his sword, drawing it in preparation for an attack. Bane's body remain relaxed, and he didn't bother to draw his weapon.

"Lower your weapons and I'll allow you to live," Bane said in an almost bored tone to the two men blocking their path.

One of the men nodded toward Sabine. "We're under orders. Give her to us and walk away."

Malek moved to stand next to Bane and into a more defensible stance. He didn't recognize either of the men, but that wasn't unexpected. He hadn't gotten to know many of the people here yet, but they were probably Dax's men. They didn't have the look of city guards or even of the mercenaries he'd seen outside the councilman's home.

The second man hesitated, and then slid his blade into its sheath. "Stand down, Aharis. If you try to take her from him, neither of us will survive."

Aharis scowled at his companion. "Dax will kill us if we don't return her to him."

Bane ignored Aharis and regarded the second man. "I recognize you. You're Jacoby, correct?"

Jacoby inclined his head. "Yes, and you're not welcome here, Bane. Dax has ordered a search of the city to locate Sabine. Your efforts in aiding her are appreciated, but Dax won't be pleased if we allow you to trespass. Will you allow us to take her to him?"

"Sabine will not leave my sight," Bane said with a trace of a growl in his voice.

Malek sheathed his weapon but kept his hand on the hilt. Keeping his expression neutral, he said casually, "Perhaps we should take Sabine back to my ship. Dax asked me to return to the tavern with her, but if his people impede our efforts…" He trailed off and shrugged. "I'm not willing to risk Sabine being harmed if it comes to a fight. I doubt Dax will appreciate anyone putting her in harm's way either."

Aharis paled and lowered his weapon while Jacoby frowned and regarded them both warily. Bane snorted in amusement. Malek smirked. At least he'd made his point.

Jacoby sighed. "Very well. We'll take you to him."

Chapter Eleven

The rest of their trip through the sewers moved swiftly after the initial confrontation. They encountered a few more of Dax's people, but no one else challenged them. If anything, they appeared relieved to know Sabine was being returned to Dax, although a few of them seemed apprehensive about her physical state. She still hadn't regained consciousness, and Malek was starting to get concerned.

Malek followed Bane up a narrow stairway and into a building. He studied the hallway, recognizing the same stonework that was present in the tavern's cellar. It made sense for Dax to have multiple escape routes in the building where he conducted most of his business.

Javyn skidded to a halt in front of them, his eyes wide. "Tell me she's still alive."

"She is, but we need to see Dax immediately," Bane said, continuing to carry Sabine over his shoulder. "Where is he?"

"Probably tearing apart the tavern," Javyn muttered and motioned for them to follow. "I'll let him know she's returned. He won't be pleased to see you, Bane, especially in his current mood."

"Is her old room still vacant?" Bane asked, apparently unconcerned by Javyn's warning.

"Yes. Dax won't allow anyone else to move in there. Can you awaken Sabine? She may be the only one who can calm him down."

Bane shook his head. "I'll handle Dax. But you need to hurry. I can't wake her up again without his help."

Javyn gave him a worried look but nodded and disappeared to another part of the tavern. Malek opened the door to the room Dax had taken her to after he'd drugged her. The shattered bottles had been cleaned up and the broken furniture replaced or repaired. It was as though nothing had ever happened.

Bane placed Sabine on the bed, and Malek frowned. Her face was still too pale, and even her breathing seemed to be labored. Judging by Bane's pinched expression, the demon was also concerned. He'd never thought to see a demon worried about anyone else's welfare, and it surprised him.

Dax entered the room only a handful of heartbeats later with Esmelle running behind him. His eyes were silvered, and he glared at Bane. Demonic magic filled the room, recognizable by the telltale sulfuric scent. "*You*! You dare come *here*? In my presence?"

Without waiting for a response, Dax charged toward Bane. The two demons locked horns and crashed into the wall, claws and blades flashing. Esmelle's eyes widened. With a muttered curse, she ran back out of the room. Malek jumped toward the bed, intent on protecting Sabine while the demons fought within the confines of the small bedroom.

Moving at a speed too fast to ever be considered human, they fought with weapons, horns, teeth, and claws. They crashed into the desk, splintering it apart.

"Sabine is *mine*," Dax roared, trying to connect his claws with the soft flesh of Bane's stomach.

Bane blocked the attack and gripped Dax's horns, shoving him backward against the wall. Malek had the distinct impression Bane wasn't trying to kill his brother, but the same couldn't be said for Dax.

Esmelle ran back into the room with a large pot of water. She tossed it over the two demons and shouted, "Grow!"

The water covering the two demons transformed into a vined plant, pinning them both against the wall. It made them pause long enough to focus on Esmelle standing defiantly in front of them. Malek stared at the redheaded witch in surprise. Such magic was far beyond a witch's normal ability. He'd only thought a Fae or a dryad had the power to transmute water into plants.

Esmelle lowered the pot and put her hand on her hip. "Are you two quite finished?"

Dax scowled and sliced through the vines with his claws. "You dare much, little witch."

"Me?" Esmelle demanded and gestured to Bane. "He brought Sabine back here, and your response is to what? Kill him for it? You're both supposed to protect her, but Malek's the one standing guard over her. Now knock it off. Both of you. If I'm going to try to help her, I can't waste my magic trying to tie you two up."

Bane cut the vines restraining him. "She's right. We don't have time to revisit old arguments. Sabine is dying." He glanced at Sabine's unconscious form. "I don't know if your healing skills will be sufficient for this task, Esmelle."

Esmelle glared at the demons and pushed past them, intent on reaching her patient. Malek moved aside to let her pass, but he wasn't willing to let the demons approach until he was sure they were back in control.

Dax watched Esmelle check Sabine over, and his silvered eyes reverted to his normal amber color. Bane's eyes had changed back almost immediately after the water had hit him. Malek sheathed his weapon and stepped aside.

Esmelle made a clicking noise with her tongue and headed toward the cabinet where the herbs were stored. "Dax told me what happened at the councilman's home. I don't see any physical injuries, but she's far too weak. I can barely sense her magic. I might be able to brew something that'll help strengthen her, but we need to get it down her throat."

Dax sat on the edge of the bed. "She wasn't this bad when I last saw her. What happened?"

"A Calling," Bane said in a dry tone. "I gave her what I could, but I've not taken much of her magic lately. She told Edvar how to summon me."

"The boy's a fool," Dax growled, reaching over to brush his fingertips against her skin. "Sabine never should have taught him such magic. She was already weak after breaking the trap on the chalice, but then she tried to gift me more magic while I killed the guards. I stopped the transfer before it became too dangerous for her."

Esmelle dumped some herbs into a mortar. "Did you use all of it? She's still weakening for some reason."

Dax scowled. "It's gone, except for the smallest trace. It's not enough to bring her back to stasis. Other than knowing Sabine was still alive, I couldn't sense her. If she was in that godsforsaken crypt, it explains why I couldn't locate her."

Malek had been listening to the two brothers and the witch discuss the problem. None of them seemed to be paying much attention to him, which suited him fine. But something was troubling him. He studied Sabine and the paleness of her skin, trying to figure out what his mind was trying to tell him. After a long moment, he straightened.

"The glamour. Can any of you break glamour?"

Esmelle stopped crushing the herbal mixture and arched her brow. Dax and Bane turned to him, their eyes flashing to silver. Malek froze, his fingers itching to draw his weapon, but the threat of violence would only incite the demons. He didn't know Esmelle well enough to speculate.

Esmelle cleared her throat and asked carefully, "You've seen Sabine without her glamour?"

"The chalice stripped it, and I was unable to shield her," Dax snapped, pushing up from the bed. "He's sworn a blood oath for silence. He technically didn't break it just now, but a suggestion is close enough."

"This keeps getting worse," Esmelle muttered with a sigh. "Okay. We'll deal with that later. Why are you asking about her glamour, Malek?"

Forcing himself to project a calm he didn't quite feel, Malek said, "If Sabine's still weakening, it's because she doesn't have enough magic. The glamour could be the reason for it."

Almost in unison, Dax and Bane blinked, and their eyes returned to normal. Esmelle gave a curt nod and dropped a pinch of the contents from another vial into the mortar.

Dax frowned and turned back to Sabine. "You may be right about the glamour, but Sabine is the only one who can remove it."

Bane studied Malek carefully, his gaze suspicious as he crossed his arms over his chest. "What do you know of glamour?"

"Not a great deal," Malek admitted truthfully.

None of his people possessed such abilities, and they

didn't have a way to remove it either. Glamour was one of those tricky magics that usually worked because everyone believed it to be true. Some lesser creatures could have theirs broken by disbelieving it, but the Fae were the strongest of all magical creatures when it came to that talent. To his knowledge, not even another Fae could break it. He'd hoped whatever ties Sabine shared with the demons might be enough to allow them to manipulate her magic.

Bane swept his gaze over Malek again. "You're not human."

Malek paused before responding. "No, I'm not."

Dax frowned. "What the hell does that have to do with anything? No one can break glamour."

"What are you?" Bane demanded, narrowing his eyes on Malek.

"I'm no threat to Sabine," Malek replied evenly, unwilling to divulge his identity. He'd eventually need to tell Sabine who he was, but he didn't owe these two demons the same courtesy.

Dax pushed off the bed. "He's warded. Sabine's been refreshing his mark to keep it active."

Bane studied the mark on Malek's wrist, and his mouth twisted in a cruel smile. "Interesting. What is it you're hiding behind a ward, ship captain? You're obviously some kind of magic user."

Esmelle arched her brow. "You're not a witch. Part Fae maybe? The pixies said Malek knew about them."

Malek frowned, wondering what else the pixies had said. "I'm *not* Fae."

"No, you're not. Sabine would have known, so you must be something she wouldn't recognize." Bane took a step toward him. The demon's hand lifted, and Malek immediately raised his to deflect a fire attack.

"Dragon," Dax hissed, his eyes flashing to silver and

staying that way. He drew his weapon and started to advance. Bane grabbed his arm and spun him around, slamming him against the wall. Dax roared out a challenge, but Bane didn't release him.

Esmelle gaped at them, darting a worried glance at Sabine sleeping on the bed.

"Think, brother," Bane ordered, holding Dax in place. "He's here for a reason."

"I don't care about his reasons," Dax hissed. "The dragon dies."

"Try it," Malek snapped, prepared to yank off the ward around his neck. If he needed to kill both demons, so be it.

"Enough!" Bane shouted, using his body to keep Dax contained. "Sabine doesn't know what he is or she never would have offered him a mark of protection. She trusts him, perhaps foolishly, but we may be able to use him to help her."

Malek paused in surprise. He wasn't sure what the demon intended, but if it helped Sabine, he'd consider it. "How?"

Dax scowled, but he'd stopped fighting Bane. "No. I will not allow him near her. Balkin will be arriving in the city either tonight or tomorrow."

Esmelle straightened. "Balkin and Sabine are linked, right? Can't he share power with her?"

Bane arched his brow. "The Beastman is coming here?"

When Dax gave him a curt nod, Bane muttered a curse and released him. "Balkin may be too late. During the short walk here from the crypt, Sabine weakened a great deal. She's fading." Bane held out his arm to show the mark on his wrist wasn't as vibrant. "I don't know if she'll last another few hours, much less until tonight."

Malek's gaze fell on Sabine, and a heavy weight pressed on his chest, making it difficult to breathe. Not only had he started to care a great deal for her, but she was the best chance he had to save his people. "You believe I may be able to help her?"

Dax scowled. "She won't thank any of us if we allow a dragon near her now that we know the truth."

Bane didn't respond right away. Instead, he continued to regard Malek thoughtfully. Such rational behavior from a demon was suspect, but it was better than Malek being forced into killing Sabine's friends. Besides, trying to shift into his dragon form here would endanger everyone—including Sabine.

"Why are you here?" Bane crossed his arms over his chest. "You've made an effort to get close to Sabine. Why?"

Malek held Bane's gaze. He could refuse to answer, but it would be unlikely either brother would allow him to help Sabine. And he *needed* her to survive.

"I've spent the last several years trying to track down the artifacts used to close the portal. I heard a rumor some ancient artifacts had resurfaced in Akros, so I brought my ship here and requested an audience with Dax."

Bane nodded. "And you were seeking those with enough magic to power them?"

"Yes," Malek admitted, glancing down at Sabine again. "The Fae have closed their forests to all outsiders. I had hoped to find someone in the southern cities with enough magic to use the Fae artifact once I discovered it. I'd originally believed Sabine might have a close relative who was a full-blooded Fae."

"You're a fool," Dax said with a sneer. "Dragons imprisoned and slaughtered her people for generations, and you believe she'll *help* you?"

Malek's shoulders tensed. "I believe, once I have a chance to speak with her, she'll consider it. Sabine is unlike anyone I've met. I've never heard of another Fae caring for demons, human witches, and orphaned children. Yet, in the short time

I've known her, I've seen the depth of the ties Sabine's forged in this city."

"He swore a blood oath earlier tonight that he intended her no harm," Dax said, his mouth twisting in a smirk. "Even if Sabine refuses his offer, she's protected from any retribution. But I'd rather just kill him. Problem neatly solved."

Malek glared at Dax. "Even without swearing to it, I still wouldn't harm her. You can try to kill me, but it won't end well for you."

"Can you breathe dragonfire while in human form?" Bane asked, his words seemingly casual, but Malek didn't believe that for a minute. Malek didn't answer, unwilling to give his enemies any insight into his abilities.

Esmelle's brow furrowed as she shook her head. "Uh, Bane? I don't know much about dragons, but there has to be another way. Sabine won't be happy if we allow him to use magic on her, especially while she's unconscious and defenseless."

Ignoring Esmelle's objections, Bane focused on Malek and gestured to Sabine. "She marked you, which has created a tie of sorts between you two, even if it's temporary. If you can send your power through the mark, it should be enough to awaken her so she can drop her glamour."

Taken aback by his suggestion, Malek glanced at Sabine's still figure. "Dragonfire could kill her."

"It won't kill her if you send it through the mark," Bane said, taking a step away from Sabine and toward him. "I've studied enough about your kind to know dragonfire won't harm *you*. If you can filter your magic by sending it into your body first through the mark, it should be enough to bring her back to some semblance of consciousness."

Malek hesitated. He was protected from dragonfire and most other forms of fire, but the thought of attempting to infuse Sabine with it made him uneasy. What Bane had suggested was possible, but sharing such magic wasn't something done lightly—especially with its potential to harm the recipient. He wasn't sure it would work without a mating bond. If Sabine's mark on his wrist worked the way Bane believed, she should have sensed his magic before now.

Apparently, Dax agreed because he crossed his arms over his chest and said, "No. Sabine is mine to protect. I won't allow a dragon to experiment on her."

Bane snorted. "And if she dies? You swore to protect her. She won't survive until morning if we don't try *something*. No one else has enough of a connection with her to attempt such a thing. We're running out of options."

Dax fell silent, looking down at Sabine again. After a long time, he lifted his head and met Malek's gaze. "Can you do this? Infuse her with dragonfire without harming her?"

Malek frowned. "Bane's reasoning is sound, but I've never attempted such a thing. In all honesty, I don't know what will happen. Dragonfire is designed to kill. It's only safe when used with our mates, but that's because they inherit a resistance to the negative effects."

Bane nodded as though Malek's words had strengthened his argument. "Dax, this must be done. If he wears her mark of protection and he's sworn a blood oath not to harm her, the dragonfire will not hurt her. The magic won't allow it."

Dax scowled, not looking pleased by the prospect of allowing Malek close to her. He pointed his finger at Malek. "If this harms her in any way, you *will not* leave this room alive."

Malek narrowed his eyes at the demon. "I would not even consider attempting such a thing if your brother hadn't suggested it. I have no intention of harming Sabine. Ever."

Bane made a gesture toward Sabine. "Then begin. We are wasting time arguing while she grows weaker."

Malek took a step toward the sleeping woman, drawn to her on a level that was more than simple attraction. So much depended on this. He'd do everything he could to save her, but it didn't diminish his need for her assistance. He wanted her to know the truth about him, but it had to be done carefully if there was any hope of salvaging the fragile trust he'd started to build with her.

"Before I do this, I ask you all to agree not to tell Sabine my secret."

Esmelle's mouth formed a thin line, and the witch shook her head.

Dax glared at him. "No. She *will* learn the truth of your deception."

"I'm not disputing that," Malek agreed, glancing down at Sabine again. He wanted to believe she wouldn't regard him as an enemy, but he didn't know her well enough to guess either way. "I will tell her. I'm simply asking that you give me the opportunity to tell her the truth myself."

Esmelle huffed. "Fine. I won't tell her right away. It would be better coming from you anyway. But if you don't tell her, I will."

Bane studied him for a long time and then nodded. "You have one day. If this works and she recovers, you will have one day from the time Sabine regains her full strength. If you falter or attempt to deceive her in any other way, we will tell her the truth—and kill you."

Dax gave him a curt nod. "One day, and no more."

Malek curled his hands into fists. If it came to a battle between a dragon and two demons, it would be interesting to find out who would win. Based on the silver shining from Bane and Dax's eyes, they agreed and were even eager for the fight.

Malek inclined his head. "Very well."

Bane and Dax moved aside, allowing him to sit on the bed

beside Sabine. He reached for the warding necklace around his neck and unfastened it. The power he'd been suppressing rushed through him. It had been more than a month since he'd last shackled himself, and he relished the brief moment of freedom before focusing on what needed to be done. He needed to shift into his dragon form soon to release some of his building magic.

He brushed one of Sabine's braids away from her face, trailing his fingers over her soft skin. She didn't stir. Focusing on his intention to help her and his feelings for her, he lifted his wrist and blew gently against the fading mark.

Nothing happened.

It was as though some barrier prevented the magic from filtering back to her.

Malek frowned and turned to Dax. "You said it hurts her every time she's needed to reapply the mark and she's been taking the pain unto herself. How is that possible?"

Dax shrugged. "I've never claimed to understand Fae magic."

Esmelle's expression became thoughtful. "This is just speculation, but Sabine has difficulties causing pain to others. She can kill when necessary, but it has never come easily for her. She once told me it was a bit easier to take a life, knowing either Dax or Bane would steal that taint from her soul. They thrive off of consuming someone's lifeforce or magic, but I believe Sabine's natural magic rejects harming others. She must shift it somehow so she takes the cost upon herself."

Malek paused, glancing back and forth between Bane and Dax. Was it possible that was part of the reason they'd formed an agreement to protect each other? Too much didn't make sense though. He still didn't understand why she'd left Faerie and pretended to be mostly human. Pushing aside these questions for the time being, he asked, "Her magic is tied to her blood, correct?"

Dax narrowed his eyes. "As much as yours, *Dragon*."

Malek held up his hand in a request for latitude. "I have a reason for these questions. Sending the dragonfire through the mark won't be possible, but I may be able to connect with the magic in her blood."

Bane's brow furrowed. "Explain."

"I made a blood oath not to harm her," Malek began, watching as both demons nodded. "That oath is tied to *my* blood and magic. It was accepted and the wound was healed by Sabine in acknowledgment of my vow. Going by that logic, I should be able create a similar wound and use my blood to provide her with some resistance to the dragonfire."

"Clever," Bane murmured thoughtfully. "As ideas go, it has merit."

Dax frowned. "And the effects of dragon blood on a Fae?"

Malek winced and shook his head. In dragon form, his molten blood could be a weapon, burning his enemies alive. In his current form, it shouldn't be dangerous, but he'd never shared blood *and* magic with a Fae. Intent was a large part of magic, and the last thing he wanted was to harm her. "It hasn't ended well for the Fae in the past, but to the best of my knowledge, no one had a mark that connected them. I won't say it's completely without risk, but I believe it's our best option."

Bane glanced over at Dax. "Can you get a message to the Beastman to see if he can get here sooner?"

"No," Dax grumbled and rubbed his chin in thought. "Balkin's message came by bird, so it's likely he's already on the move. A seer in his village had a vision of the Wild Hunt rising again. She foresaw an iron dagger being used in an attack against a woman of Fae heritage. Balkin's coming here because he believes Sabine's in danger."

Malek cocked his head, wondering again about this Balkin. He'd never had the opportunity to meet one of the Beastpeople. They primarily lived within the confines of the Silver Forests surrounding Faerie. From what little he knew about them, they were sworn to serve the Fae. During the Great War, the Fae formed armies of Beastpeople by twisting the magic of the gods and making some of the animals in their forests more humanlike. Some resembled lions, wolves, foxes, bears, and even birds of prey had been used.

They were the ruthless defenders of Faerie, and some of the Beastpeople were dedicated not only to protect Faerie but also to serve certain families. If this Balkin considered himself Sabine's protector, it was surprising he hadn't remained by her side. What was even more curious and troubling was two full-blooded demons appeared to defer to the Beastman.

"We don't have a choice then," Bane muttered with a curse. Focusing again on Malek, he asked, "What do you need to attempt this blood connection?"

"A small cut on her hand and mine will allow my blood to enter her wound and offer her some measure of protection." Malek turned back to Sabine and took her hand in his. Running his fingers over her palm, he said, "From there, I can breathe the dragonfire directly into her."

The dragon within him roared in anticipation. Malek wanted to do this, he realized with a trace of surprise. The thought of sharing blood and magic, as well as forging a deeper connection with Sabine, was more than alluring—it was intoxicating.

"Then do it," Dax said, gesturing for him to get on with it.

Malek withdrew his knife and cut his hand first before turning the knife on Sabine. He hesitated and then shook his head. "One of you needs to make the cut. My oath prevents me from any harm, even if the end result will help her."

Dax nodded and took the knife, cutting a small line on Sabine's palm. She murmured something unintelligible in her sleep but didn't awaken. Blood welled to the surface of her hand. Malek clasped his hand over hers, allowing their blood to intermingle. Her magic, potent and beguiling, surged through him and he closed his eyes, breathing in her power. She was exquisite. Her raw energy was more enticing than anything he could have imagined.

He opened his eyes to look down at her, willing her to awaken. Intention was an important part of this magic, and he needed to focus on protecting and reviving Sabine.

Still grasping her hand, he pressed his lips against hers and exhaled the dragonfire into her body. Sabine's mouth parted on a gasp, and she murmured his name. In the throes of her healing slumber, Sabine didn't resist him or the magic he offered. He cupped the back of her head with his free hand, continuing to infuse her with his power. The smell of night-blooming flowers he'd begun to associate with Sabine filled the air and co-mingled with the sharper scent of smoke and burnt leaves from the dragonfire.

Reluctantly, he eased away, but the sense of awareness and connection remained. Sabine blinked open her eyes, her brows furrowing in confusion as she whispered, "Malek?"

"Little one," Bane interrupted before he could respond and crouched beside the bed. "You need to remove your glamour and recharge your magic. Dax and I will watch over you until you're recovered."

Her eyes widened, and she started to sit up. "Where's Dax? Is he all right?"

Bane gently eased her back down and brushed one of her braids away from her face. "He's well. We all are, but you need to rest and recover. We don't have any more magic to give you."

Dax took a step toward the bed. "I'm fine, Sabine. Remove

the glamour so it'll stop draining you. When you're better, we're going to talk about that stupid move you pulled in the councilman's home."

Sabine gave him a small smile, settled back, and closed her eyes with a sigh. A moment later, the glamour fell away and she was once again asleep. Malek didn't move and couldn't tear his eyes away from her. She was beautiful and far more exotic in appearance than he'd first thought.

Her hair was nearly white with strands of silver reminiscent of moonlight. Her skin was still fair, glowing softly with the remnants of her power. Intricate marks of silvered vines wound up her hands and wrists, continuing upward where they disappeared under her clothing. He'd heard the tattoos were markings of power, given to Fae children at a very young age as their magical abilities took hold. They were supposed to be painful, blending both blood and magic together and then pierced under the skin. She'd obviously spent a great number of years living among the Fae.

Bane nodded. "Good. Her coloring is better. Let me check her hand."

Malek hesitated, wanting to continue touching her but knowing he needed to pull away. Reluctantly, he released her, and Bane took her injured hand. The air around her hand shimmered with a strange energy, and the wound began to fuse back together.

Malek arched his brow in surprise. "Interesting. I wasn't aware demons could heal."

"Only Sabine," Bane said, pushing off the floor. "Esme, she'll need some of your tea when she awakens next."

Esmelle nodded. "I'll finish preparing it. I can sit with her until she wakes up again."

Malek stood, barely listening to the conversation as he gazed down at Sabine. He was tempted to remain with her until she recovered, but he suspected her demon protectors and witch friend would have a problem with that. As though sensing Malek's internal conflict, Dax took a step toward him.

"Be careful," Dax warned, his eyes flaring silver briefly. "Right now, the fact you helped stabilize her is the only reason you're still alive."

Malek held Dax's gaze, refusing to look away now that Dax knew the truth. "I'd like to inspect the chalice we acquired earlier this evening."

"Not until Sabine awakens," Dax retorted, crossing his arms over his chest. "Until the magic has been completely disabled, it won't be leaving my vault. You may remain here in the tavern until then. If you try to leave, I'll have your crew executed and your ship sunk."

Malek cocked his head. "You believe I intend to betray Sabine?"

Dax gave him a cruel smile. "I take Sabine's protection *very* seriously. Until we've determined you're not a threat to her or planning to divulge her secrets, I'll be keeping a close eye on you."

"So be it," Malek said, fastening the warding necklace around his neck and trying to ignore the uncomfortable sensation of his magic being suppressed. He hadn't intended to leave now that he'd found Sabine, and Dax had just made his life much easier. Without another word, he turned and left the room.

Chapter Twelve

Sabine opened her eyes to stare at a familiar ceiling. She had no recollection of how she'd ended up back in her old room at the tavern. A scraping noise caught her attention, and she turned her head.

Esmelle glanced up from where she was weaving herbs on a new drying rack. "Oh, good. You're finally awake. We were starting to get worried."

Sabine frowned and sat up, rubbing her eyes. "How long was I out?"

"Almost a full day," Esmelle said cheerfully, putting the small portable rack to the side. "You got up once or twice, but you were pretty out of it. I'm not surprised you don't remember. Bane and Dax have been nuisances, refusing to let anyone near you."

"Except you," Sabine guessed, wondering what sort of problems had emerged with both demons together in the same space. It was probably too much to hope they'd resolved their issues, but at least they hadn't killed each other yet. She should probably be grateful for such small favors.

Esmelle grinned and picked up a pot of tea from the table. She poured a cup and said, "Mm-hmm. I told them they'd have to deal with you if they tried to keep me away. I swear, they're the two scariest people in this city and they're terrified of you."

Sabine yawned and stretched. "If they knew what was good for them, they'd be more scared of you. One little waggle of your fingers and you'd turn them into toads or hang them from a tree by their horns."

Esme laughed and handed her the cup. Sabine sniffed at it, but it was a simple combination of complementary herbs. She took a sip. "This is pretty good. Blossom gathered more mint for you?"

Esmelle nodded. "She did. I think she's worried about you."

Sabine lifted her head to meet Esmelle's gaze. "How so?"

Esmelle put her hand on her hip, tilting her head and causing a red curl to fall across her forehead. She brushed it aside absently. "Something about the moon disappearing? A magical explosion that brought another family of pixies to my garden? She had a fit and said she was going to track you down if you didn't show up soon."

Sabine squeezed her eyes shut and groaned. Blossom was probably beside herself at being unable to communicate with her. If Blossom knew the other pixie clan, it was unlikely their arrival heralded good news. The other option was even worse. If her magical workings had drawn the attention of an unrelated clan, that meant the ripple effects of her power had scattered far beyond the boundaries of Akros. Pixies flocked to any powerful source of magic, and she'd essentially hung out a welcome mat announcing her presence to anyone in the vicinity.

"On another note," Esmelle said, "that ship captain came in to check on you a few times. I thought Dax or Bane were going to kill him, but they seem to have reached an uneasy truce of sorts. I talked to him a little bit while we were waiting for you to wake up. I wasn't sure about him at first, but I can see why you're interested in him."

Sabine frowned and looked down at her arms, but her glamour was back in place. She had a vague recollection of Malek kissing her and Dax and Bane telling her to release the glamour. She must have reapplied it one of the times she'd woken up, but she knew Malek had been there when she'd lowered it. She just didn't remember his reaction.

Taking another sip of her tea, she said, "Malek saw through my glamour. Did he say anything?"

Esmelle shook her head. "No, but he didn't have to say a word. Sabine, a man doesn't face down two angry demons and a witch so he can check on a woman five times in less than a day unless he *really* likes her. From the sparks you two were putting off the other day in the garden, I'd say it goes both ways. To hell with your glamour. I'd say he likes you in any form he can get you. I just want you to be careful. You... you don't know him very well yet."

Sabine hid her smile behind the rim of her cup. She had every intention of getting to know him much better.

Esmelle laughed. "Good. Now that we've got that settled, Dax arranged to have some clothing and personal items brought to you. They're in the chest. I'll let you get cleaned up and dressed. Henry's wife made a huge pot of vegetable stew for you, and it's simmering in the kitchen. Bane threatened to hurt anyone who got near it before you woke up."

"Martha cooked for me?" Sabine sat up straighter at the

prospect. Martha was a fantastic cook, and her food was one of the things Sabine missed most about staying here.

Esme grinned, her green eyes twinkling with humor. "Yes, but Martha snuck me a bowl when Bane's back was turned. It's absolutely delicious. Not even Bane's threats are going to keep people away for long if you don't get out there. It's been driving everyone crazy all day." She paused, her expression becoming more serious. "I'm glad you're okay, Sabine. You had all of us worried."

Sabine tilted her head and smiled. "I think I worried myself a bit this time too."

Esmelle nodded and returned her smile. "I'll let you get dressed. Come out whenever you're ready. I need to run back to the shop and check on things, but I'll be back soon. Bane and Dax are running around somewhere. I'll let them know you're awake before I go."

After the door closed behind Esme, Sabine stood and rubbed the kinks out of her neck from sleeping so long. She put the empty cup on the table and caught a glimpse of herself in the mirror. Dax must have undressed her while she slept, only leaving her in an overly large shirt and nothing else. She opened the chest, but there was only another one of his shirts folded inside along with undergarments. Her weapons were missing too. She *could* run naked through the streets relying solely on her glamour, but her magic hadn't yet recovered enough for such an undertaking. Dax clearly intended to make escaping difficult.

Muttering a colorful curse, she ran her hand through her hair to find he'd also unbraided it and taken her hairpins too.

"I'm going to kill him," Sabine muttered, snatching up the shirt and heading into the small room next to the bedroom.

Lifting the pump handle, she poured some water into the basin and washed herself quickly. By the time she finished taking care of her immediate needs, her stomach grumbled a complaint. Pulling Dax's shirt over her head, she scowled at the realization it only fell to mid-thigh. She wouldn't be walking around the main floor of the tavern or leaving until she acquired more clothing, which was why Dax had stolen hers. She huffed and left the bedroom, heading in the direction of the kitchen and the source of the delicious smells permeating the air.

The kitchen was empty when she entered, but she could hear what sounded like a card game being played in the next room. Ignoring it, she walked over to the large wood-burning stove and the pot simmering on top of it. She grabbed a cloth and lifted the lid, her stomach making another appreciative rumble as the heavenly aroma escaped.

Sabine scooped out a large bowl of the soup and replaced the lid before heading over to the table. She took a bite and let out a moan of appreciation. Martha had gone above and beyond, even including some of her favorite vegetables and spices. It was a complex blend of flavors, all perfectly complementing each other and proving some humans had their own brand of magic.

A cheer went up from the next room, but she ignored it and ate several more bites before putting the bowl to the side. Walking over to the cupboards, she started searching for one of the bottles of wine Henry had hidden for her. Such a meal deserved nothing less.

"You're awake," Malek said behind her.

She spun around, gripping the edge of the counter tightly. His eyes warmed as he perused her up and down, lingering overly long on her bare legs before meeting her eyes. Her face heated at his frank appraisal, but she couldn't bring herself to look away as he took a step toward her.

"How are you feeling, Sabine?"

"Better," she said quietly, wishing she had her weapons on her. Even though she didn't intend any harm to Malek, she felt surprisingly vulnerable without them. Although, part of that could be because he knew some of what she was hiding. Other than Esmelle, Dax, and Bane, no one outside of Faerie had seen her without glamour.

Malek crossed the room toward her, stopping only when he was within touching distance. He searched her expression, and the conflicted emotions on his face were surprising. Sabine frowned, wondering if Esmelle had misread the situation and his interest in her.

"What do you remember?"

She tilted her head to study him, getting the impression he was worried about her answer. "Not much. Only bits and pieces. I remember escaping from the councilman's home, heading toward the crypt, but not much else. Little flashes. Esme said I woke up a few times, and you came to check on me."

He frowned. "That's all?"

"I remember you kissing me," she admitted with a small smile.

"At least I'm somewhat memorable," he murmured, a trace of a grin on his lips. Reaching up, he tucked some of her hair behind her ear and trailed his fingers down the side of her face. She closed her eyes, leaning into his hand and relishing his touch.

Something about this man intrigued her. Perhaps it was the power she sensed below the surface, but she didn't think that was quite right. He called to her on a fundamental level, more so than anyone she'd ever met. Taking a step toward him, she closed the distance between them and placed her hand against his chest.

"You're a little more than *just* memorable."

Malek cupped her face and lowered his head, pressing his lips against hers. It was just a gentle pressure as though she were impossibly fragile, but the heat lurking beneath the surface of his kiss was undeniable. He pulled back far too soon for her liking but didn't move away. Instead, he trailed his thumb across her cheek and murmured, "In my wildest dreams, I never expected to meet someone like you. You could easily cause me to forget everything, Sabine, including my entire purpose for coming here."

Her heart soared at his words. In her mind, he could easily do the same to her. She gave him a small smile. "Sometimes fate takes us in unexpected directions, but we always end up where we're supposed to be."

"I'd like to believe that," Malek murmured, lifting some of her hair and rubbing it between his fingers.

The shadows in Malek's eyes were troubling, but she wouldn't pry. They both had a past, and sometimes reliving it could be painful. Perhaps she could connect with him another way.

"There's a bottle of wine in the cabinet behind me. Will you share a glass with me?"

He reached over to take the bottle off the top shelf. "This is Faerie wine, right? The same kind Dax drugged?"

Sabine smiled and nodded. "Yes, but this one is safe. Dax won't try anything like that again for a while." Selecting a clean goblet from the cabinet, she walked over to the table and placed it beside her bowl. "Martha made a wonderful stew. If you'd like some, it's on the stove."

"That's all right," he said, sitting beside her and opening the wine. He poured some into the cup and recapped the bottle.

Sabine lifted the goblet and swirled the contents. "Have you ever shared wine before?"

Malek arched his brow. "Your tone makes me think there's some sort of ritual that goes beyond simply sharing a drink."

"Very perceptive, and yes," Sabine agreed with a laugh and

put the goblet down between them. "It's not exactly a ritual, but more of a way to share a memory or an experience."

"I'm intrigued," he admitted. "How does this work?"

She lifted her gaze to meet his and tried to ignore the familiar fluttering in her stomach that seemed to occur whenever he looked at her. "If you were Fae, we could simply drink from the same cup to share a memory. Since you're not, I'd like to share some of my power with you so you can get the full experience."

Malek frowned. "Sabine, you've spent the last day and most of this evening in a restorative sleep. I'm not sure you should attempt anything else until you're fully recovered."

Touched by the concern in his eyes, she smiled at him. It had been a long time since anyone had looked at her that way without any expectations in return. Reaching over, she placed her hand over his. "This isn't major magic. It's simply a sharing of power with very little cost. The magic itself is in the wine. I can unlock it so you can experience it too."

"How?"

"Will you allow me the use of your knife?"

Malek unsheathed his weapon and passed it over to her hilt first. She took it from him, admiring the expensive weapon. It was excellent dwarven workmanship, both serviceable and decorative. She pricked her finger with the tip of the blade and squeezed it until two drops of blood fell into the wine. Malek's eyes widened.

She gave him a small smile. "Will you allow me to give you a gift of my blood?"

He glanced at her finger and nodded. She squeezed her finger again until her blood welled to the surface. Holding out her finger, she offered it to him. Malek held her gaze as he wrapped his hand around her wrist. He lifted her hand and wrapped his lips around her finger. Her mouth parted on a gasp. Malek's mouth was warm, almost hot, as his tongue encircled her finger, catching the blood and the power she offered. The gesture was erotic and sensual, and her heart pounded at the rush of desire that flooded through her.

He pressed a kiss against her fingertip. "You honor me with such a gift."

"You saved my life, Malek. I owe you much more than this."

"No," he said quickly, squeezing her hand. "There is no debt between us. I will explain why soon, but for now, please do not feel you owe me anything."

She studied him for a long time, gauging his sincerity. Unlike the Fae, humans and some other magical races could lie. She had the impression Malek was being honest, but he was also hiding something. It wasn't in her nature to pry, especially when staying silent about her own secrets had saved her life over the years. Everyone was entitled to keep their own counsel.

Picking up the goblet again, she swirled the wine to mix it with her blood. Sabine lifted it to her lips, drinking deeply and tasting the memory of the forest. The rich scent of the trees, including the revered silver oaks, tickled her nose. The memory of her home filled her with a combination of peace and longing.

She offered Malek the goblet, and he took it, taking a sip of the wine. His eyes widened and then closed, and he took a deep breath. His voice, when he spoke, was filled with awe. "The Silver Forest. It's the forest that protects the home of the Fae."

"Yes," she said quietly, pleased he could see it.

His eyes opened, and he gazed at her with wonder. "I had no idea this was possible. Every time you drink Faerie wine, this is what you experience?"

Sabine laughed and shook her head. "No. Each vintner

has their own specialty, and each bottle is identified by the memory it may evoke. A bottle with a green mark on the top, such as this one, usually contains the memories and magic of nature or the forest."

Malek chuckled. "I had no idea. Now I'll need to check the rest of the cases on my ship. What do the other colors mean?"

"It depends on who crafted it and the magic of the person drinking it," she admitted, reaching for the goblet again. "Usually, a purple label will draw upon the creativity of the drinker. You may hear music or revisit a book you loved. Blue is more soothing, perhaps holding a memory of a peaceful place you once visited. Red is the color for passion, and that wine is usually shared between lovers."

"Hmm. I wonder if I have any of the red bottles."

Sabine laughed and took a sip, once again allowing the memory of the forest to fill her with a peaceful calm. She offered it to him. "This time, close your eyes and take a drink. I want to show you one of my favorite places in the forest."

He did as she asked, and she placed her hand over his and closed her eyes, reaching for the connection between them. When she opened her eyes again, the tavern's kitchen had faded away and they were standing in a small clearing in the middle of the forest. Birds chittered in the trees, their songs an accompaniment to the soothing sound of the rushing river.

Malek stared at the trees overhead in amazement.

She approached him quietly. "I wasn't sure you'd be able to see it this vividly."

At the sound of her voice, Malek turned toward her and froze. His heated gaze roamed over her, and he swallowed.

Sabine looked down at herself and the Fae markings that traveled up her arms. She wore a simple dress in the style of her people, which showcased the patterned marks she'd attained during her younger years.

She gave him a shy smile. "Here, you see me as I really am without any glamour. Or at least, how I see myself in my mind's eye. Illusions don't always work for the Fae when we're lost in memory."

Malek closed the distance between them. He reached up to tuck her loose hair behind her ear and trailed his fingers down in a gentle caress, their path sending a surge of heat through her. "You're the most beautiful woman I've ever seen, Sabine." He paused and his brow furrowed. "Is this dangerous for you? Can anyone else see you?"

Sabine shook her head, touched by his concern. "No. We'll hear if anyone comes into the kitchen, but they won't see anything other than two people sitting at the table with their eyes closed."

Malek reached down to take her hand in his. "How much of this magic is real?"

"As real as any magic or memory," she said with a shrug and looked at the canopy of trees overhead. The sunlight filtered down, causing the shadows to dance through the leaves. It was beautiful, but it saddened her to know she may never see it again.

"Will you tell me about this place?"

She nodded, continuing to hold his hand as she led him toward the river. "I spent a lot of time here as a child. Whenever my brother and I wanted to avoid our lessons, we used to sneak away and come here. We spent far too much time reenacting the last war, but we always won in a sweeping victory."

"You mentioned your brother before. Is he still with the Fae?"

Sabine frowned. Even in this place of memory, mentioning certain names could draw unwanted attention and allow some creatures to listen in. Dreamwalkers and Memorywalkers were rare, but not unheard of, especially among the Fae and some of their allies. "It's better not to say too much."

He squeezed her hand. "I never thought to see the inside of the forest. Your people don't allow outsiders to come here."

"It's not forbidden, but it's not done lightly either," she admitted, watching the sunlight dance over the water. "The forests are sentient, and once permission is given, it's difficult to revoke it. It's only one of our defenses, but it's very effective."

Malek looked upward again at the trees. "This entire place is incredible. I can see why you'd want to visit it like this."

Sabine smiled, glancing up and trying to see it through his eyes. She hadn't traveled much, but the protective trees didn't exist anywhere else in the world. Others had tried to steal saplings and transplant them in other areas without success. They fed off sunlight and Fae magic, which was why they were so rare. The leaves were a deep green like any normal oak tree, but the veins of each leaf were streaked with silver, like the marks of power etched on her skin.

Malek reached out and touched the bark of one of the trees. "It's so real. The smell, the feel of it, everything. This place is extraordinary. How long does the magic last?"

"Only until the wine is gone," she said, secretly pleased by his reaction. "Some of our Elders enjoy their wine a little too much, getting lost in their memories of the past instead of embracing the present. But it's a way to share experiences with each other, and a way to learn from our past through reflection."

He glanced over at her. "If you bring someone into your

memory with you, does whatever happens here also extend into the real world?"

Sabine hesitated. They were a little too close to discussing knowledge forbidden to outsiders. She might have fled her home to save her life, but she wasn't willing to betray her people. "What do you mean?"

"If I kiss you here," he began, taking another step closer to her, "will I be kissing you in the real world too?"

Her mouth curved into a smile, and she shook her head. "Not usually. It can be done, but the intention needs to be there. Sometimes, the duality of physical intimacy both here and in the 'real world' can be rather... intense. Pleasurable, but intense."

"In that case, I'm definitely going to have to see if we have a bottle of that red wine on my ship," he murmured, cupping her face and kissing her gently.

Her eyes fluttered closed, and she softened her body against his as he deepened the kiss. The magnetism between them ignited, and she ran her hands up his chest, feeling the heat from his body and the strong play of muscles under his clothing. Here, in the relative safety of this memory, she didn't have to pretend to be something she wasn't. Malek might not know all her secrets, but he knew more than most people. For that reason alone, this kiss meant far more to her than it probably should.

The sound of footsteps interrupted them, and Sabine pulled away, sliding them from the memory and back into the tavern's kitchen. She blinked, staring over at Bane on the other side of the room. His hands were curled into fists as he glared at Malek with silvered eyes.

Malek muttered a curse and leaned back, returning Bane's scowl. Sabine frowned at Bane and stood, not particularly pleased with the angry demon vibes he was throwing off. He turned his gaze on her and blinked, the silver fading almost immediately. She relaxed as he crossed the room toward her.

"I was just coming to check on you. Esme said you were awake." He scanned her up and down. "How are you feeling?"

She smiled at him and stood on her toes to kiss his cheek. "Better. Although I'd be happier if Dax hadn't stolen my weapons and clothing."

He chuckled. "My brother has always been talented at riling you up, but in this instance, I was the one who suggested we take your belongings. Balkin's going to be here soon. We need you to stay here until then."

Sabine blew out a breath, having forgotten all about the Beastman's visit. Given the circumstances, Bane's decision made sense.

Bane studied the table, the wine bottle, and the goblet that had been between them. "You're sharing wine? With *him?*"

Sabine frowned at his sharp tone. Bane wasn't usually as possessive as Dax, so this was somewhat surprising. "Yes. Is that a problem?"

Bane was quiet for a moment as though trying to reach a decision. Finally, he sighed. "Dax needs you. He just came up from the cellar, and he's been in one of his moods since you were injured. Javyn asked me to see if you'd be willing to help run interference."

She glanced toward the closed door. The voices were more muted, but no one was screaming. "Has he killed anyone yet?"

"No one important," Bane said with a shrug. "He'll come tearing in here once everyone finds out you're awake. I suggest you go to him before then. I'll clean up the wine."

Sabine nodded and turned back to Malek and smiled. "We'll talk more later?"

Malek returned her smile, but there was a slight tension around his eyes. "I look forward to it."

She started to head toward the door but stopped and put her hand on Bane's arm. The way Bane and Malek were regarding each other made her uneasy, as though something was going on between them. In a quiet voice, she asked, "Does Dax really need me? Or are you trying to get me to leave?"

"I won't kill the... *ship captain*," he said with a trace of a sneer, still glaring at Malek. "At least not right now."

When she frowned at him, Bane waved her off. "We will be out in a moment, and I won't touch a hair on his head while you're gone. But Dax will likely kill someone if you don't reassure him you're alive and well."

Sabine grinned and kissed his cheek again. Turning away, she squared her shoulders and headed toward the door, mentally preparing to tame the other demon in her life.

Chapter Thirteen

*M*alek kept an eye on Bane as Sabine headed out of the room. The experience of sharing wine with her had been beyond anything he'd expected, and he was still a little disconcerted. As soon as the door closed behind Sabine, Malek got to his feet.

"You didn't tell her," Bane said with a low growl in his voice. He stormed over to the table and snatched up the goblet of wine. Putting it to his lips, he downed the rest of it. A moment later, shock colored his expression and his gaze flew to Malek. "Of all places, she took you *there?*"

Malek frowned, irritated Bane had been able to intrude on a private moment between them. He didn't know enough about how such magic worked or he would have stopped Bane before he'd touched the goblet.

When Malek didn't say anything, Bane shook his head and stared at the empty cup. "Sabine doesn't share such things lightly, but for some foolish reason, she trusts a *dragon*. She offered you a piece of herself and you took it, yet you continue to deceive her."

A cold hand gripped Malek's heart. Bane was right, but Malek couldn't regret sharing the experience with her. "It's not my intention to hurt her."

"You will." Bane walked over to a sack in the corner. He grabbed a handful of salt and dumped it in the goblet to break the magic completely. Leaving the salted cup on the counter, he picked up the bottle of wine and put it away. When he was finished, Bane pressed his hands against the counter and lowered his chin to his chest. His voice was quiet when he spoke, and it lacked his earlier anger. "Tell her soon, ship captain. *Before* she falls in love with you. If it isn't too late already."

Malek didn't respond. There wasn't anything he could say, especially when Bane was right. When Sabine found out who he was, she might not forgive him. He hadn't intended to mislead her, and the longer he waited, the worse it would be when she learned the truth.

Leaving Bane to his thoughts, Malek headed out of the room in the same direction Sabine had gone. The game of chance Dax's crew had been playing was more muted, with each of the players darting surreptitious glances at Dax and Sabine standing in the corner of the room. They were speaking too low for him to hear what they were saying, but their body language made it apparent Sabine had calmed the worst of Dax's anger.

Her hands were pressed against Dax's chest, and she was giving him a teasing smile. In return, Dax gazed down at her with an expression that spoke of a long-shared history and intimacy. The sight, especially after what Malek had shared with her in the kitchen, elicited a sharp pang of jealousy. The dragon within him wanted to yank her out of Dax's grasp.

The warding medallion heated around his neck, warning him to get control of his emotions. Unmindful of Malek's presence or his internal conflict, the demon lifted his clawed hand and trailed the back of it across Sabine's cheek. Such a move could be considered a threat if it weren't for Dax's teasing expression and Sabine's laughter. She wrapped her hand around the demon's wrist, leaning into him and saying something that made the demon chuckle.

The sight was a sharp cry from Dax's response after Malek had revived Sabine. The demon had been furious and out of control, lashing out at everyone and anyone who happened to be nearby. Javyn had suggested Dax might want to take out his aggression on Riven, the man who had betrayed Sabine by selling her location. The resulting screams had lasted for hours and could be heard throughout the tavern and even into the streets. The distraction had offered a brief reprieve for Dax's other men, though, and Malek had tried to keep some distance between himself and Dax since then.

"You joining us for the next game?" Javyn gestured to the empty seat Malek had occupied earlier.

"Very well," he agreed, sitting down while Javyn dealt him in.

They were playing a variation of Skulls and Crossbones he'd never seen before, as evidenced by how quickly he lost the last round. That's how he'd ended up running into Sabine in the kitchen.

"You can deal me in too," Dax said from the corner. Wrapping his arm around Sabine's waist, he led her toward the table.

The young man sitting next to Malek jumped up. "You can take my seat, Dax. I'll sit out this round."

Dax didn't respond but slid into the seat, pulling Sabine down with him and onto his lap. He didn't spare Malek a glance, and instead, put his hand on Sabine's bare leg. She rested her head against Dax's shoulder while Javyn collected the thin, flat wooden disks and shuffled them. Each wooden disk was painstakingly illustrated with images of different races. It was essentially a makeshift battle, where each player decided what moves and countermoves they should make, depending on the makeup of the disks in their hand. At the end of the round, the person with the most well-balanced group usually won. A bit of luck didn't hurt either.

Bane emerged from the kitchen area carrying a bowl of stew and put it on the table in front of Dax. "She needs to eat something."

Sabine frowned. "I had a few bites."

"Not enough." Bane's tone brooked no argument, and he turned away and walked back into the kitchen.

"Eat, Sabine," Dax ordered, nodding toward the bowl.

Sabine shrugged and pulled the bowl closer to her. Everyone else at the table gave the bowl covetous looks. She arched her brow. "Martha made a huge pot in there. I can't eat all of it."

Javyn chuckled as two of their players jumped up and ran to the kitchen. He started dealing out the cards. "Same rules as before. The last player standing wins, unless you get the crossbones. Then you have an automatic death throw at the person of your choice."

While Sabine ate, Dax nuzzled her neck and murmured, "I want you staying here until Balkin leaves the city. He should be here no later than morning, unless something comes up."

Sabine made a small noise of agreement. "All right. I'd like him to look at the chalice too. I'm not sure how the lich ward was embedded over it, and he might have an idea. What did you do with it?"

"It's in the vault," Dax said, reaching for the wooden disks

Javyn passed to him. "If you stay longer, I could be persuaded to give you another silver dagger."

Sabine paused. "Dwarven?"

"If you'd like," Dax agreed, studying the wooden disks in his hand. "What did you think of the other one I sent over to you?"

"It's very pretty," she said, going back to her stew. "You knew I wouldn't be able to resist it."

Dax chuckled and tossed a few coins on the table to place his bet. Malek studied his wooden disks, debating how much to wager.

Sabine glanced at him. "You know how to play?"

"It's a bit different from the versions I've played before, but I'll catch on."

"Show me what you have," Sabine said, leaning toward him.

He held out his hand enough so she could see them, and she pointed to two of them—a troll and a goblin. Picking up a few of the coins they used for betting, she tossed them onto the table and winked at him. Dax didn't appear pleased with her offer to help him, but the demon could get over it. Malek wasn't in a mood to consider Dax's wishes when Sabine was curled up on his lap.

"You're not eating," Dax reminded her. He selected one of the playing disks in his hand and tossed it onto the table. Sabine huffed, but she resumed eating. Javyn slid Dax a replacement disk and looked at Malek expectantly.

Malek studied his hand, curious about the two disks she'd pointed out to him. If he'd been playing the way he usually did, he'd have selected to discard different ones, probably the human and the dwarf. Trusting Sabine, he picked up the two she indicated, and she gave him a brilliant smile, her eyes twinkling with humor. Passing them over to Javyn, he decided it would be worth it for that look in her eyes even if he lost.

Javyn handed him two more illustrated disks. He got a witch and another troll, but this troll had a higher number of bones on the card, indicating its power level. Sabine pushed aside her nearly empty bowl and leaned toward him again to see his pieces. Her eyes lit up, and she gave him a nod of approval.

Dax scowled and put his hand on her leg again. "If you want to play, we can deal you in."

"I'm probably going back to bed after this," Sabine said with a yawn and stretched. Her shirt slid upward, exposing more of her bare legs. Malek's gaze lowered to them, wondering if the glamour also hid markings on other parts of her body. He swallowed, trying to pay attention to what was happening as each player went around the table playing their game pieces.

She leaned against Dax's shoulder again, positioning herself so she could watch the game unfold and see Malek's playing pieces. On Malek's turn, Javyn tossed down a witch marker. He started to pull out his higher-level troll, identified by the number of bones on the card, but Sabine shook her head and pointed to the witch in his hand. He arched his brow but went ahead and played it, curious about her reasoning.

Javyn paused, darting a look at Sabine who smiled sweetly at him. He chuckled and passed both disks to Malek, indicating he'd won that round. "If Sabine's helping you, maybe we should just hand you the winnings now."

"I have no idea why that hand won," Malek admitted.

Sabine laughed and flipped over the wooden pieces they'd just played. She pointed to an area he hadn't noticed. "See the etchings on here that indicate a wind is blowing? Javyn played an air witch. Yours had flames around the edges, which indicates a fire witch. Even though your game piece was lower level, wind will only enhance the fire witch's ability by causing the fire to spread. Your witch won by default."

Malek leaned back in surprise, taking the opportunity to study the details on each wooden piece, including the ones still in his hand. Sabine was right. Their version of the game was more multi-faceted than he had expected. In addition to the bones on the card indicating their level of power, each race also had other subtle variations on it denoting the type of magical ability or strength of that game piece.

"This deck is extraordinary. It adds more nuances to a relatively simplistic game," Malek said, the realization only elevating his opinion of Dax's crew. They might operate on the shadowed side of the law, but they had proven themselves to be extraordinarily clever.

With much more confidence now, Malek played the troll marker. Sabine settled back against Dax again, and the demon tossed out another game piece. Javyn passed both of them to Dax. The game proceeded for another few rounds until Bane emerged from the kitchen. He looked down at Sabine, whose eyes had closed at some point. "Good. She's sleeping again. I'll take her."

Dax nodded and leaned back to allow Bane to pick her up. "Put her in my room."

"Not a chance," Bane retorted and headed back out of the room with Sabine in his arms.

Dax chuckled as though unsurprised by his brother's reply and organized his remaining game pieces. Javyn glanced over at the closed kitchen door where Bane had disappeared. "Did you tell her we found Terrance?"

"No. Not until she recovers completely."

Malek straightened. He hadn't realized they'd located him. "Did Terrance say anything about the attack?"

Javyn frowned and tossed another game piece on the table. "Nothing to say. One of our people found him floating in the harbor with his throat cut. Looked like it may have been done by someone from the assassins' guild."

"It wasn't." Dax took the wooden disks Javyn passed to him. "They would have weighed down the body better, not left it for us to find. Someone wanted us to believe it was one of Bane's people."

Javyn's brows furrowed, and he muttered a curse under his breath. "They're trying to pit us against Bane's crew?"

"Appears that way," Dax said with a shrug.

Malek frowned, selected one of his remaining game pieces, and pushed it toward the center of the table. His mind wasn't really on playing anymore. Instead, he was considering the ledger Sabine had discovered in Terrance's home. He'd started trying to decipher it, but there were a lot of things that didn't make sense.

He'd planned on sharing his thoughts with Sabine first. Given the news of Terrance's death and Sabine's weakened state, he needed to reveal the information to Dax now.

"Sabine and I went back to Terrance's home the other night. She discovered a ledger under one of the floorboards. It was written in some kind of code."

Dax's eyes narrowed. "You did *what?*"

Javyn winced and slid a little lower in his seat.

Malek held Dax's gaze. "She wanted to search his home. I accompanied her so she wouldn't go alone, especially since someone is seeking to harm her. It's a good thing she went, since she managed to discover a ledger everyone else missed. At her request, I've been working on unlocking the code. We originally assumed it was a list of debts and winnings from his gambling hall, but I no longer believe that's the case."

"Show me this ledger." Dax pushed away from the table.

Malek handed Javyn his game pieces and stood. Dax

followed him back out to the main tavern room, which was in full swing and would be for several more hours. A few people he'd begun to recognize nodded at Malek in greeting, but at the sight of Dax, they didn't call out or interrupt. Although, Dax's thunderous expression might have had something to do with that.

Malek climbed the stairs and pushed open the door to his empty room. He'd sent Levin back to the ship after he'd infused Sabine with his dragonfire. Malek hadn't shared his reasons for asking Levin to leave the tavern. His oath prevented him from telling Levin what happened, but Malek didn't want to put his first mate and closest friend at risk.

Levin was a wyvern, one of the lesser dragons. In a battle between a demon and wyvern, Dax would likely be the winner. Levin was crafty and quick, but he wouldn't be a match for such a formidable opponent. Besides, if Malek failed or fell for any reason, someone needed to send word back to the Sky Cities that his efforts hadn't been successful.

Walking over to the desk, he unlocked the box containing some of his maps and pulled out the ledger he'd hidden underneath them. He handed it to Dax, who flipped it open and glanced through the pages with a frown.

"You've deciphered some of this?"

"Not exactly," Malek began and pointed to the various columns. "I originally thought these were dates, client names, and then corresponding amounts. I tried to figure out the symbols I assumed represented the coin amounts, but they weren't adding up."

"How so?"

Malek pointed to the last column. "There's no method for tracking the overall wins or losses. Too many of the center columns were duplicates, which is why I originally thought they were names. I still think they're names, but the last column are locations, not amounts."

Dax studied the ledger for a long time. He placed it on the desk and grabbed a blank parchment. Malek handed him a piece of charcoal and the demon started sketching some symbols. It was similar to what Malek had been doing, looking for crossover between them. Three sets of symbols were repeated regularly.

"If he wasn't already dead, I'd kill him again," Dax said with a scowl and tossed the charcoal down. "Terrance was tracking Sabine, Bane, *and* me."

Malek frowned and studied the parchment. "How do you figure? The symbols don't match up with the letters in each person's name."

"I've seen codes like this before. You were close, but you didn't have all the information. Sabine used to be called Sabinthea. She'd been in Akros almost two years before Esmelle suggested she shorten her name to Sabine. She thought Sabinthea sounded a little too Fae."

"But the name Sabine would be more acceptable for a human with Fae ancestry," Malek murmured, taking another look at the symbols. Dax was right. They matched up perfectly if you knew the alternative form of Sabine's name. "How many people knew she used to go by Sabinthea?"

Dax rubbed his chin, staring at the flickering light in the lamp. "Too many to reliably track. At the time she shortened her name, Bane hadn't yet split off on his own. When he left, a handful of my crew decided to follow him. All of them knew her original name, and Bane still calls her that on occasion."

"Bane mentioned he thought someone was targeting you," Malek said, recalling what Bane had told him about the lich ward on the chalice. "He said you've been causing problems for the city leaders."

"Yes, and it's likely they're responsible," Dax admitted. "After what happened at the councilman's home, the iron dagger used during the ambush, and Terrance paying one of my men for information, it's obvious someone with deep pockets is behind this. If all three of us were being tracked, there are some common threads we can use to flush out anyone else who may be involved."

Malek nodded, suspecting Dax and Bane were going to be cleaning house very soon. "What are the chances this is an attack on Sabine instead of you? Why is she hiding in Akros?"

Dax picked up the ledger. "You may return to your ship. You're free to remain in the harbor until we've determined the ward on the chalice has been fully removed. After that, we'll conduct the trade as originally agreed and you can depart from the city."

Malek straightened and narrowed his eyes on Dax. He folded his arms across his chest, deliberately using the motion to display Sabine's mark on his wrist. "Sabine and I still have unfinished business. I won't leave until it's concluded."

Dax clenched his jaw and didn't respond. Instead, the demon turned and headed out of the room, slamming the door behind him. Malek frowned and shook his head. Time was running out very quickly. When she woke up next, he'd need to speak with Sabine privately and tell her the truth. He just hoped he didn't lose her in the process.

Chapter Fourteen

Sabine yawned and stretched, feeling much better than she had the last time she'd awakened. Her magic flowed through her at full strength once again, and she wove a trace of it through her glamour to soften any jagged edges left as a result of her previous and hasty application.

The blankets next to her were disheveled, and she caught a faint trace of Bane's scent on them as though he'd just recently gotten out of bed. Sabine smiled, pleased he'd stayed the night. Even if she'd suffered some unfortunate effects from trying to interrupt the lich ward, at least it had forced Dax and Bane together again under the same roof. Hopefully, they could resolve some of their differences.

She climbed out of bed to find someone had washed and folded her clothing. It had been left neatly on top of the chest, along with her weapons. Eager to feel their welcome weight against her skin, she quickly dressed and equipped her knives. In some ways, she'd felt more vulnerable without her weapons than her magic. It was a testament to how much she'd changed since coming to live here.

Very few of the Fae would ever understand why or how she'd come to care about the people living here. It probably hadn't dawned on them she'd been living in a city surrounded by humans and mixed magical races. It hadn't been something she'd considered, until Balkin had made the choice for her after he helped her escape from Faerie. Humans, for the most part, were viewed as the weakest of the races and one of the most destructive. Her father had once compared them to insects with a propensity for multiplying out of control and ignorant of the magic of their world. Sabine had come to know another side of them, and their strength of spirit and ability to persevere in almost any situation had opened her eyes.

Sliding the last of her knives into the sheath on her thigh, she pushed open the door and headed in the direction of the wonderful aromas that beckoned to her. Sunlight streamed in through the windows of the kitchen, and Martha hummed a wordless tune as she pulled out a batch of freshly baked bread. Martha was an older woman with a rounded figure, a testament to her ability to create mouthwatering delicacies.

The gray-haired woman's mouth curved upward at the sight of Sabine. "Good! You're awake. Have a seat and I'll fix you something too."

Martha gestured to the table where Bane was already sitting. The demon grunted at her, but he was too busy shoveling food into his mouth to respond.

Sabine beamed a smile at Martha. "If it tastes half as delicious as it smells, it promises to be as divine as your stew last night."

Martha laughed and shooed her to the table. A moment later, she placed a plate with some sort of meat and vegetable pie in front of Sabine. "I've missed having both of you here. Taste this and let me know what you think. I'm trying out something new."

Bane was still busy digging into his food, a sure sign of his approval. Sabine grinned and picked up the spoon. The moment the first bite touched her tongue, she closed her eyes and moaned. The flavors exploded in her mouth, the tang of the spiced meat complementing the savory herbs and vegetables Martha had used. Some of these must have come from Esmelle's garden because she could taste the faint trace of pixie magic on her tongue.

"This might be better than your stew last night," Sabine admitted, pulling the plate closer to her. Bane gave another grunt of agreement and took another bite.

"I'm so glad to hear it, dear," Martha said, bringing over a pitcher and pouring each of them a drink. "Balkin should be here any minute, and Dax asked me to prepare something special for him."

Sabine swallowed the bite she'd been chewing and frowned. "I forgot about that. He hasn't arrived yet?"

Bane paused and glanced out the window. "He should have been. We were thinking he'd be here either last night or this morning, but it's already past midday."

"Have you seen Dax?" Sabine asked, trying to bury her unease.

The village where Balkin lived was situated at the edge of the Silver Forest, less than a week's travel from Akros. By the time Dax had received the message announcing Balkin's imminent arrival, he should have been no more than a day or two away. The message had been worded as a warning, and Balkin would have made haste traveling here, unless something had delayed him.

To her knowledge, the Fae weren't aware he'd helped her escape after her mother had been murdered. It had been one of Sabine's tutors who had taken her to Balkin's village that night. She later learned her tutor had been executed.

If her father ever discovered Balkin was still watching over her, his life would be forfeit too. She didn't even want to think about what they'd do to the rest of his family. Balkin had taken a terrible risk helping her escape, and every time he came to her, he endangered himself again.

Bane frowned. "I haven't seen Dax since I woke up. We were working on a project together for most of the night."

"I think he's in the war room. I'll take care of those plates if you need to speak with him," Martha offered, a trace of worry deepening the wrinkles around her eyes.

Sabine nodded at her. The war room was where Dax usually spent his time organizing his people and assigning them tasks. It was nothing more than a glorified meeting room. She didn't know why it had been named such, except Dax tended to enjoy violence. "The meal was wonderful, one of your best. But I'm afraid this can't wait."

Martha gave her a smile. "Go ahead, dear. I'll save your plate." She turned to Bane. "Shall I put yours away too?"

Bane sighed and pushed it away. "I've missed your cooking, Martha. Are you sure I can't convince you to come work for me? I'll pay you double whatever Dax is paying."

Martha laughed and shooed him off. "Shame on you. Go before you get me in trouble."

As they headed out of the room, Sabine grinned. "Don't you dare try to steal her away. I've been trying to smooth things over between you and Dax. If you convince her to leave, he'll never forgive you and I won't either."

Bane chuckled and wrapped his arm around her waist, navigating her toward the stairway that led to the lower levels of the tavern. "You could always come too. I've been trying to convince you to stay with me for the past few years."

She shook her head. "And all my efforts at repairing the rift between you and Dax will fall apart."

"Ah, but some things might be worth it," he suggested with a teasing grin. Leaning in close, he whispered, "Just think, we could even leave the city. My business isn't dependent upon staying here. You could live in the forest again. I'd take a few jobs here or there, but you'd never have to step foot in a city of stone and metal ever again. How would you feel about having the trees as your ceiling once again?"

Sabine darted a quick glance at him and didn't answer. He knew how much she missed the forest. She'd shared her memories with him over a glass of wine almost six years earlier. One night, after they'd downed an entire bottle, she'd broken down and told him everything. Bane knew far more about her history than even Dax. The next day, Bane convinced her to mark him, claiming it was another way to protect her.

On the one hand, it had helped make living in the city easier with his shared resistance to metals, but she knew Bane wanted the same thing Dax did. No matter how much they might pretend to be otherwise, they were both demons who dreamed about being able to walk in the sunlight without consequences and still retain their full strength. There was a reason the gods had limited their power and dominion to the underworld. Demons were a force to be reckoned with, and left unchecked, their potential for destruction could be devastating.

She might care about and trust Bane up to a point, but she could never risk forgetting what he was and who she was. She would always be Fae, one of the sworn protectors of this world. Allowing a demon to use her magic to walk the world unchecked would go against her very foundation and purpose. A short-term and controlled agreement between them was one thing, but anything more was too dangerous.

Over the years, Bane had occasionally brought up the possibility of them leaving the city, but it was always with a hint of teasing. Bane was much more subtle about wanting to keep her to himself, but in many ways, he was like Dax. He might project himself to be more tolerant and less intense, but he was simply more skilled at controlling his tendencies than his more volatile brother. In short, he was far sneakier and more manipulative.

As though sensing he'd crossed a line again, Bane fell silent as they walked through the empty hallways toward Dax's meeting room. Before they descended the stairwell, Bane stopped her. "Sabine, I want you to be careful around Malek. You should keep your distance from him."

Surprised by the abrupt change of subject, she lifted her head to regard him. His face was carefully neutral, and he was impossible to read when he set his mind to it.

"I'm not discussing him with you."

Sabine started to turn away, but he grabbed her arm. She frowned, looking up into his amber eyes that reminded her so much of his brother. Bane shook his head. "He's not who you think."

Without waiting for a response, he walked down the steps and toward the meeting room. She stared after him and shook her head. Something obviously bothered him about Malek. She just wasn't sure if it was because she'd shown an interest in the ship captain or if there was something else going on.

For all the years she'd spent with Dax and Bane, sometimes it felt as though she barely knew either of them. They were as foreign to her as the humans that surrounded them. It had led to a lot of mistakes made by all of them, but they'd tried to avoid them whenever possible.

Sabine blew out a breath and continued descending the stairs. Trying to corner Bane wouldn't get her anywhere.

He'd eventually tell her what was troubling him, but not until he was ready or it suited his purposes. Sabine followed him into the meeting room where Dax was sitting slouched low in a chair, his hands steepled together. She halted at the sight of Terrance's ledger on the table in front of him. Parchments with scribbled markings were scattered around him, leading her to believe he'd been there for hours.

"You're still working on it?" Bane asked, circling the table and looking over Dax's notes.

Dax ignored Bane and met her eyes, a faint trace of temper in them as he gestured to the chair beside him. "Have a seat, *Sabinthea*."

She froze. It had been years since Dax had called her that. It wasn't her real name, but it was close enough his use of it made her uneasy. Even more disturbing was the sight of the book and Malek not being anywhere near it. She couldn't sense him through the mark, but that might not mean anything. It still wasn't working right.

"Where did you get the ledger? And where is Malek?"

"Your new *friend* shared it with me last night." Dax stood, his eyes flashing to silver and staying that way. "Sit. Down. Now."

Sabine narrowed her eyes at Dax, sending a sharp lash of her power toward him in warning. It struck him like a whip, a not-so-subtle reminder she would never bow to him. "Have you forgotten who you're talking to, Dax'than Versed, son of Kal'thorz? I will *never* obey your commands."

Dax glared at her, his breathing heavy as though he were struggling to get control of himself. Sabine remained where she was, waiting and hoping he wouldn't force the issue. Balkin had repeatedly warned her about allowing a demon to issue orders. Dax might make a request, which she could decide whether to accept or decline. But once someone allowed a demon to circumvent their will, it was much more difficult to retain their autonomy. So far it had proven to be sound advice, but the path she walked was treacherous. Sometimes she thought demons were more dangerous than the Fae who wanted her dead.

Bane crossed his arms over his chest, still studying the parchment on the table. He would be no help in this, which indicated he wasn't particularly happy with her either. She just didn't know why. Something more than just jealousy or possessiveness was going on.

Dax grabbed the edge of the table and hurled it across the room, causing it to splinter apart. Her heart thundered in her chest, but she didn't move. It was never a good idea to run from a predator, especially one such as Dax. It took everything in her to keep her expression neutral and her body relaxed as she held his gaze. Feigning nonchalance, she arched her brow. "Well, that was rather unnecessary, don't you think?"

Dax snarled and prowled toward her. Despite her false bravado, he was starting to scare her. She took a half-step backward before she caught herself, but it was enough to give Dax the advantage. He closed the distance between them and wrapped his arm around her, yanking her even closer. "Give me one good reason why I shouldn't bind you to me right now."

Sabine blinked up at him and placed her hand against his chest. "You could try, but I would destroy you before you had a chance."

Without giving him an opportunity to respond, she blasted him with her power. Dax flew backward, hitting the wall with enough force the stone support behind him started to collapse. Broken plaster and a piece of wood fell from above him, the dust coating the top of his head and his horns.

Straightening her shoulders, she approached him. Infusing her words with magic, she reminded him, "*You* are not my equal, Dax'than Versed. You walk freely under the sun only because *I* will it. If you ever try to force a binding between us, I will banish you to the underworld and be done with you."

"You've made your point, Sabine," Bane said in a dry tone and picked up the ledger from the ground where it had fallen.

Dax laughed, a cruel and harsh sound. She frowned as he got to his feet and brushed himself off. Seemingly unconcerned by what had happened, Dax smirked at Bane. "She's back to full power."

"Yes, she is," Bane agreed, flipping through the pages of the ledger. "The twenty-four-hour grace period begins now."

Sabine's gaze darted back and forth between them. "What in the name of Underhill is going on?"

Bane glanced up at her. "Dax wanted to make sure you were fully recovered."

Her mouth dropped open. "And you didn't think to just *ask*?"

"Not nearly as much fun," Dax said, picking up some of the papers and handing them to Bane.

Sabine threw her hands up in surrender. "May the gods save me from foolish demons. I could have hurt you, Dax."

He shrugged. "A bit of foreplay never hurt anyone."

Sabine rolled her eyes and picked up one of the papers from the floor. Someone, most likely Dax based on the handwriting, had been working on deciphering the code. "Where's Malek? I thought he was trying to decode this."

"He's... otherwise engaged."

Sabine jerked her head up and narrowed her eyes on Dax. "What did you do to him?"

"He's alive and unharmed for the moment, but whether he remains that way is yet to be seen," Bane said with a shrug. He walked over and handed her the ledger. "Terrance was tracking our movements for the past two months—mine, Dax's, and yours. We believe he may have paid off some of our people to acquire this information."

Sabine frowned. "To what end? I'm hardly involved in either of your operations anymore, and none of Edvar's kids would sell information about me."

Dax nodded. "I suspect you're correct. That's why we believe Terrance paid off Riven to find out your whereabouts. Your name was listed much less often in the ledger than either Bane or myself. Terrance foolishly considered you the weak link between us, and I was the actual target."

Sabine looked at the ledger again and shook her head. "What reason would he have to target you? You said Terrance was new to the city, and you'd given him rights to operate his gambling hall with little interference."

Bane shrugged. "He was probably hired to track us or to determine a way to have Dax eliminated."

"And framing the leader of the local assassins' guild for my murder would be the quickest way to have you and Dax turn on each other," Sabine murmured with a sigh. "I suppose the old adage is true. Send a demon to kill a demon."

"Indeed," Dax agreed, dropping the papers on a chair. "The most likely culprit is the councilman whose home we burglarized. The heightened security and addition of the mercenaries was enough to pique my interest. He laid a trap by embedding a valuable object with a lich ward that was targeted to me."

"So we've been dancing to the councilman's tune ever since he spread word about artifacts being discovered in the catacombs under the city." Sabine didn't bother to hide her disgust, but it still didn't answer her earlier question about Malek and Bane's cryptic warning. "If you think Malek had a hand in this plot, you're wrong."

Dax chuckled and approached her with a shrewd look in

his eyes. "Have you fallen for the ship captain? Is that why you're so quick to defend him?"

She slapped the ledger against Dax's chest, refusing to answer his questions. "He isn't responsible. You were likely planning to go after the items even if Malek hadn't negotiated a deal to acquire them. Now, tell me about Balkin."

Dax tossed the ledger onto the nearby chair. "He hasn't arrived yet, nor have we heard anything more from him. I know he's still alive, but beyond that, it's impossible to know."

Sabine frowned, that uneasy feeling beginning to fill her once again. Dax had been marked by Balkin years before she'd come to Akros. Dax was able to sense him, but unlike the mark she shared with Bane, Dax couldn't track Balkin. Such an ability had to be gifted or inherited.

Sometimes, pixies could track the Beastpeople, since they'd also been created from Fae magic. She could try to ask Blossom to locate him, but she was hesitant to send her away, especially with the arrival of a new pixie clan.

A noise in the hallway caught her attention, and she turned to see Javyn escorting a hooded individual into the room. Her heart thudded in her chest as he lowered his hood, revealing pointed ears and a face more animal than man. More than a millennium ago, when the dragons and other races started slaughtering her people en masse, the Fae infused their magic into some of the most dangerous creatures of the forest. They became one of their most lethal forms of defense, sworn to protect their creators, much as the Fae had once been created to serve the gods.

Balkin walked upright on two legs like the humans, but there could be no confusing him with anything other than one of the Beastpeople. Sabine suspected Balkin's family were descended from one of the larger predatory cats. He was covered with a pelt of fur from top to bottom, but the golden hair on Balkin's head was even longer, reminding her of a lion's mane. His snout was elongated, and he possessed whiskers that twitched when he was annoyed or found something amusing. They'd twitched a great deal when she'd been a child. At least, until she'd been forced to flee Faerie.

"Balkin," she whispered as memories from the past crashed over her. She rushed toward him and he swept her up in his arms, holding her tightly against him.

"Sabin'theoria," he murmured in a voice quiet enough no one else could hear.

She squeezed her eyes shut, ignoring the tears that escaped as the welcome scent of the forest and home surrounded her. It had been so long since anyone other than Balkin called her by her true name. His chest rumbled in a purr, and she smiled against his neck. She hadn't seen him for more than a year, and she'd missed him dearly.

She sniffed and wiped her eyes. Balkin leaned back, his golden catlike eyes scanning over her with no small amount of affection. Sabine's mother had trusted him above all others, and he'd been a near-constant fixture and protector while she was growing up. She gave him a small smile. Taking his furred hands in hers, she sent a gentle wave of her power over him. His purr grew louder, and he returned her smile.

"My kitten has become a fierce warrior, much like her mother," Balkin said with pride. His voice was raspy as though unaccustomed to speech, which was likely if he'd been spending most of his time in his village. His people relied more heavily on thought-based communication rather than typical speech patterns. They could also speak to the Fae through mind contact, but demons didn't share in that ability.

Dax approached them and motioned for Javyn to withdraw. As soon as the door closed, Dax said, "We were expecting you much sooner, Balkin. Was there trouble on the road?"

Balkin's golden eyes began to glow as they focused on the demon. "There is always trouble when dealing with the treachery of the Fae. You have been negligent in caring for my charge, Dax'than Versed. The Wild Hunt will fly again soon."

"What's happened, Balkin?" Sabine asked, trying to bury the fear his words evoked.

The Wild Hunt was a Fae creation. Once, it had been used as the army of the Unseelie Fae to seek out those who were oath-breakers or to battle against their enemies. After the portal closed and their original purpose was no longer necessary, the magic changed. It was wild magic, neither Seelie nor Unseelie, but something in between and outside of anyone's control.

Balkin turned back to her, blinking away the golden light. "Whispers have reached Faerie concerning a Fae who possesses dual facets of power, both light and dark, Seelie and Unseelie. Your father has heard these whispers and knows you still live. He will come for you soon."

Sabine's mouth went dry. "And my brother?"

"Rhys'ellesar has agreed to rouse the Wild Hunt, in accordance with his father's wishes. It is no longer safe for you in Akros, my darling kitten."

Sabine blanched, and the entire world started to tilt. Faster than any normal mortal, Balkin wrapped his arm around her before she collapsed. She gripped his cloak and whispered, "Why would Rhys do this? He has to know I had nothing to do with the death of our mother."

"Your father has been whispering in his ear for more than a decade, Sabine," Bane said, taking a step toward her. "We all expected it would come to this. Your brother and father must die to ensure your survival. With your leave, I will head to Faerie and take their heads."

Dax gave Bane a nod of approval. "I will accompany you. With Sabine's marks upon us, we can move safely through the Silver Forest."

Sabine's eyes widened, and she darted a glance between all three of them. Their expressions were grim, but she couldn't allow them to do this. Pulling away from Balkin, she took a step backward and shook her head. "No. You will not kill my brother, and you won't be able to get close to my father. I will not agree to this."

"Your brother is planning to summon the Wild Hunt. He doesn't deserve your loyalty," Bane said, his eyes flashing to silver.

Her hands curled into fists. "Rhys doesn't know the truth! If I speak to him or get a message to him about what happened that night, maybe—"

Balkin shook his head, his gaze filled with sorrow. "Rhys'ellesar will ascend to the Council of Eight in less than six moon cycles."

Sabine's heart fell into her stomach. She turned away to stare at the crumbled wall where she'd thrown Dax, a fitting representation of her chaotic emotions.

After the portal had been sealed with magic provided by a renegade goddess, widespread war had occurred between the races as territories were divided and reorganized. When the Fae began to face certain annihilation, they'd banded together, both Seelie and Unseelie, and formed the Council of Eight as the ruling body of the Fae.

Sabine's mother had been one of the Unseelie representatives and her father one of the Seelie. Upon her mother's death, Sabine had been expected to take her place. But that was before her father had tried to have her killed.

"This decision has been approved by the rest of the Council?" she asked quietly, already knowing the answer.

"The seat has been empty since you left," Balkin said gently and rested his clawed hand on her shoulder, the gesture a comfort and painful reminder of everything she'd lost. "Your father still retains his place. Your brother will now join him."

"Rhys is Seelie," she whispered, turning back to look into Balkin's eyes. "That seat has always been held by an Unseelie. Why would they allow this?"

"The Seelie do not wish more of the old magic returning. They will do anything, including trickery and deceit, to accomplish their goals."

Sabine frowned, suspecting Balkin was right. The Seelie had always been threatened by the darker magic the Unseelie embraced. It had been centuries since the Unseelie left Underhill to rejoin the rest of Faerie, but the division between the two groups still remained.

Bane took a step toward her. "He has a point, Sabine. From what you've told me, your parents' union made your brand of magic possible. I wouldn't be surprised if they started killing off the rest of the Unseelie to prevent it from happening again."

Dax crossed his arms over his chest. "Sabine, you need to be practical about this. Your father knows your continued existence is now a threat to your brother, which is why he's probably pushing for your brother's ascension so quickly. He's trying to force a confrontation and lure you out of hiding."

Balkin glanced over at him and nodded. "Your protector speaks the truth. Rhys'ellesar needs your death confirmed before the ascension, or he risks jeopardizing his standing among the Fae. Your father has declared him your mother's legal heir."

Sabine laughed—a harsh, bitter sound. "My mother *never* would have allowed a Seelie to take her place and allow them ruling control over the council. Rhys knows that."

"That's probably why he hasn't called for your death until now," Bane said with a shrug. "But it sounds like your father has forced him into this path. His efforts at killing you failed years ago, and he's now assigned your brother to the task. Do not sacrifice yourself to protect someone who doesn't deserve it. If you aren't willing to strike, my brother and I will act as your weapons."

"No," she snapped, curling her hands into fists again and infusing her voice with power. "I will *not* allow you to kill my brother. You would do well not to ask me such a thing again."

Without waiting for a response, she stormed out of the room. The hallway was clear, most likely on Dax's orders. With Balkin's arrival, he would have made sure to keep everyone away. Balkin was too recognizable as being connected to the Fae, and he didn't possess the ability to glamour himself. The lack of curious onlookers was for the best. In her current mood, she didn't want to see or talk to anyone.

Pushing open the back door of the tavern, Sabine stumbled out into the sunlight and bent over, resting her hands on her thighs as she tried to breathe through her tumultuous emotions. The smell of stone, dead wood, refuse, and human frailty and sickness filled her nose. She squeezed her eyes shut, trying to find a calm oasis in her mind. It was always so difficult here, without the forest and nature surrounding her. She stared up at the sky, thinking of Rhys and how things could have come to this.

He was asleep the night she'd snuck out and followed her mother deep into the forest to find out who she was meeting. It shouldn't have mattered that Rhys hadn't accompanied her. He knew her better than anyone. Or rather, he *had*.

Sabine shook her head and wrapped her arms around herself, not wanting to believe her brother thought she was capable of killing their mother.

The evidence against her was fairly damning. Her father had made sure of that. Her escape from Faerie had been used against her too, but she wouldn't have survived if she'd remained. She'd been too young and inexperienced to fight against opponents who'd had centuries to hone their skills. Even now, she still couldn't match their magic. She might have raw power, but she lacked finesse. Her years of living surrounded by humans and suppressing her magic had made sure of that.

Part of her had held out hope that once she returned, her brother would have joined her side to help clear her name. She'd thought, perhaps foolishly, her brother wouldn't have believed she'd been responsible for their mother's death. Twins were supposed to have a mystical connection to each other. Sadly, she'd never shared anything like that with Rhys.

"Are you all right?"

Sabine brushed away her tears and turned at the sound of Malek's voice. She managed a weak smile and then shook her head. Lies came so easily for humans, but the Fae couldn't lie. Sometimes she thought it might be easier if she could.

"I don't think I've been all right for a long time."

Malek frowned and moved closer to her. "Is there anything I can do to help?"

She swallowed and glanced at the closed tavern door. Bane or Dax would probably come looking for her any minute, and she didn't want to talk to them right now. Their solution was simple; once Rhys and her father were dead, she'd be safe. That was the way of demons and one of the sources of contention between the two brothers. Find a problem and kill it.

But she wasn't a demon. It would destroy something

inside her to allow them to harm her brother. The only reason she'd left him behind years ago was because Balkin had assured her he would remain safe. After all, Rhys was her father's chosen heir.

Balkin had made it clear he would support Rhys's execution. The thought was enough to twist her stomach into knots. She looked up into Malek's concerned eyes. "I don't think…"

Her voice trailed off, and she glanced at the closed door again. Her emotions were too volatile when it came to her past. Some space might help provide a bit of clarity.

She straightened her shoulders. "I need to get out of here for a bit. Will you take me on a tour of your ship?"

Malek paused, his eyes widening in surprise. "My ship? Ah, of course. I'd be happy to show you."

"Perfect," Sabine said and fell into step beside him.

Malek was quiet as they headed for the docks, both of them seemingly lost in their own thoughts. His silent presence was more comforting than she expected. His hand brushed against hers, and that slight touch made her heart flutter in appreciation at the reminder she wasn't alone.

Perhaps Bane was right and she was starting to fall for Malek. It was more than the power she sensed within him. She'd started to care about him. It had been a long time since she'd thought someone might feel the same way about her, and not just because her magic allowed them to walk under the sun.

She'd been lonely for a long time. It might be smarter to push Malek away, but the constant secrets and subterfuge were beginning to wear upon her. She darted a quick glance at Malek, wondering how much more she could trust him.

Wanting to distract herself, she asked, "Will you tell me about your ship?"

Malek gave her a smile, his eyes twinkling in amusement.

"Ah, well, the ship is your typical smuggler's vessel. It's designed to look like a merchant ship, and more or less functions as one. We have a crew of about fifty but with the capacity for many more."

Her eyes widened. For all the time she'd spent living close to the sea, she hadn't spent any of it on board a ship. "I didn't realize so many people lived there."

"It takes more people than you might expect to keep things running smoothly. The crew works in shifts around the clock, but on occasion, they need to pull double duty. Any fewer than that number and you begin to run into problems."

They approached the docks, and the wind brought the strong scent of salt and fish along with it. Akros was a port city, but it wasn't wealthy like some others. Many merchants elected to take their wares someplace else where their merchandise could fetch higher prices. They had some quality artisans, but many of them paled in comparison to cities which specialized in exotic textiles, wines, weapons, and other items.

Malek's ship was larger than she'd expected, with the center mast reaching higher than the tallest warehouse. She stared in surprise, feeling a bit out of her element. Although most Fae didn't have a problem with water, very few of them ever elected to spend time on a ship made from dead wood. Some creatures who claimed the sea as their dominion wouldn't take too kindly to any other magical race trespassing. Sabine had enough problems with the ones on land. She didn't need to add more enemies to the mix.

A wooden plank bridged the gap between the dock and ship. Malek took a step onto it and held out his hand toward her. She hesitated only for a moment before allowing him to help her on board the ship. Despite its large size, the ship swayed lightly under her feet, and each of her footsteps sounded hollow as she stepped onto the dead wood.

Some of Malek's crew were on the deck and called out greetings to their captain while also giving her curious looks.

Malek put his hand against her back and leaned in closer. "I can give you the grand tour, if you'd like. Or if you'd prefer some privacy, we can go to my cabin and talk."

Sabine swallowed, searching the dock for any familiar faces. Dax would have some of his people working in the area. Word she'd boarded Malek's ship would reach him quickly. "Privacy would probably be better. I can't stay long."

He nodded and led her toward the rear of the ship just as another man ascended the nearby stairs. Levin's eyes widened at the sight of her, and he grinned.

"You joining us when we depart, Sabine?"

Sabine halted in her tracks.

Before she could say anything, Malek frowned at his first mate. "She's simply here to see the ship. Can you arrange to have some tea sent to my cabin?" He glanced at her. "Is tea acceptable? Or would you prefer wine?"

"Tea would be good," she said, unwilling to get lost in more memories, especially on the heels of Balkin's news.

"Of course," Levin said easily but with a trace of his smile still in place. "I'll take care of it."

He moved aside to allow them to pass, and Malek led her up some stairs to a deck area where the wheel of the ship was located. Behind it were two doors, and Malek opened one of them, gesturing for her to enter. She did, somewhat surprised to see a rather large bedroom with a desk, shelves, and several chests in the corner. It wasn't as spacious as the attic room in the tavern, but it was bigger than she'd expected.

"Levin's cabin is next door. The rest of the crew sleeps

below deck. On a nice night, some of them sleep under the stars. I've done it myself a time or two."

Sabine didn't answer right away, too busy looking at everything at once. It was a small glimpse into Malek's life, and she wasn't sure what she'd been expecting. The room was neat and clean but also more ordinary than the fascinating man who slept here.

Pausing at the desk, she ran her fingers over the map of the world and wondered what sort of magic Malek possessed. He could be one of the Merfolk or maybe a shapeshifter of some kind, perhaps one with an affinity for the sea. It would explain the power she detected within him and his decision to captain a ship.

Malek leaned against the wall, seeming content to watch her explore his cabin. She trailed her fingers over the shelves, studying the titles of the books. Many of them appeared to be historical in nature, detailing life at sea or in some other port towns.

"You enjoy reading? I noticed you looking at the books in the councilman's library."

She nodded. "Yes, but they're hard to come by here. The councilman has one of the largest collections in the city. I recognize some of these titles from his library."

A light tap on the door interrupted them. Malek opened it and accepted a covered tray from whomever stood on the opposite side. He closed the door with his foot and carried the tray over to the table. Sabine rolled up the map to give him some room.

"You can put that map in the chest over there, if you'd like," Malek said, uncovering the tray to reveal a small pot of tea, two cups, and a plate of biscuits.

Curious, Sabine opened the chest to find several other rolled parchments, most likely also maps. She placed it inside and noticed a small painted mask in the corner of the chest.

"Oh," she murmured, carefully lifting the mask to examine it. Small shells had been affixed to it, each one giving another splash of color and depth to an already remarkable creation. Tilting it to catch the light, she admired the intricate workmanship of the artist who had crafted and painted it.

"Ah, I see you found one of the gifts I plan to give to my sister," Malek said with a chuckle and poured some tea into the cups. "She fancies herself as an artist. Between you and me, she's probably more likely to collect works of art instead of creating them. She loses interest too quickly, but she's always had an eye for it."

"It's beautiful," Sabine admitted, looking for an artist's mark or signature. "I've never seen anything like it before. Where did you get it?"

"I picked it up in Karga about a month ago. The seller claimed he acquired it from a local tribal shaman. It's supposed to imbue the wearer with good fortune and luck."

She carefully replaced the mask, making sure it wouldn't get damaged in transit. Standing, she accepted the cup Malek held out to her. She inhaled the familiar aroma of several flowering plants designed to promote relaxation, and her mouth curved into a smile. "This is one of Esme's special blends, isn't it?"

Malek chuckled and took a sip of his tea. "I wondered if you would recognize it. I told Levin about her shop, and he decided to check it out. Your witch friend is very talented and quite charming. I think Levin spent quite a bit of coin there."

Sabine laughed, thinking about how Esmelle would preen when she heard the compliment. "I'll remind you about that if she ever decides to try out some of her experimental mixtures. Those can be a little... interesting."

"Your warning is noted," Malek said with a grin and took

a drink. "But it's difficult to imagine after tasting this mixture."

"Mmm," she agreed, her gaze roaming over the rest of the cabin and falling on the chest again. "Will you tell me more about your sister?"

"Kaia?" Malek asked, his expression turning curious. "What would you like to know?"

Looking down at her cup, she realized she just wanted to know more about him. Sometimes learning more about a person's loved ones and how they spoke about them was an insight into who they were as a person. Perhaps it would provide her with some clarity into her own situation.

"Did you always get along with your sister?"

He studied her for a long time and placed his cup on the table. "Not always. There's a significant difference in our ages. I was tasked with acting as her guardian and protector quite a bit. She resented it when she was younger, and I didn't care much for constantly having to bail her out of trouble."

"But that changed?"

Malek nodded. "It wasn't overnight. I started spending more time away from home, and the distance helped our relationship grow. We both matured. We've always cared about each other, but I'm much closer to her now than I used to be."

Sabine studied the books on the shelf again. The eclectic mix of titles indicated Malek had an interest in various cultures and races. There were very few stories, but more about the history of their world. Running her fingertips over the spine of a book about the Fae, she said, "I told you I have a brother."

Malek fell silent for a long time. "I'd heard siblings among the Fae are uncommon."

"They are," she agreed, walking over to the desk to put

her cup down. The tea had helped steady her a bit, but she still needed to figure out what to do about the situation with Rhys. "My people aren't as prolific as humans. Multiple children are rare enough, but twins are almost unheard of."

Malek's eyebrows rose in surprise. "You have a *twin* brother?"

Sabine nodded and wrapped her arms around herself as though it could protect against her emotions. Only Dax, Bane, and Esmelle knew about her brother, and each of them had sworn a blood oath to keep it secret. She'd never been tempted to trust anyone else, but Malek spoke to something inside her and she wanted a deeper connection with him.

"When we were very young, we spent every waking moment together. The other few children were either much older or younger. Rhys and I were more than siblings. We were friends. Playmates. Confidants. We were inseparable."

"But that changed?" Malek guessed, sitting halfway on the edge of the desk.

"It did," she said quietly, running her fingers over the rim of her cup on the desk. "When our abilities began to emerge, the Elders began marking us in accordance with our budding powers. Each mark is created by infusing our blood with our magic below the skin. No matter what happens, we can draw upon the marks and the power locked within them."

Malek nodded. "I saw the markings when you lowered your glamour. It looked like it had taken a long time."

"Hours upon hours," she said quietly, remembering the pain. It was a rite of passage, but the agony of each mark was a type of sacrifice that could fuel one's magic to even greater heights. "A Fae's markings are a sign of growing power and the complexity of the magic contained within their blood. My brother's markings weren't as extensive as mine. I gained power at a much faster rate. Almost as soon as one Elder finished a mark, another began. My father was convinced I'd stolen some of my brother's magic while we shared a womb."

Malek shook his head, his confusion apparent. He placed his hand over hers in a comforting gesture. "I don't understand. Magic can't be stolen, only gifted. Why would your father blame you?"

She studied his hand over hers. It was such a small thing, but it meant far more to her than it probably should. Turning over her hand, she interlaced her fingers with his. "How much do you know about the Fae and how we form family bonds?"

He hesitated. "Not much. My grandmother was Fae, but she came to live with us later in life. She wasn't a blood relative, but my grandfather cared for her deeply. She was the greatest love of his life, even though he'd met her toward the end of his."

Sabine blinked up at him in surprise. "That's how you know the language of the Fae and the oath of no harm?"

Malek nodded. "Even though I wasn't related to her, she took a shine to me. Much of my childhood was spent at her home, and she'd frequently tell me stories while she gardened. That's where I first met pixies."

Sabine smiled, envisioning an Elder telling fairytales to a dark-haired little boy. He was probably just as charming as a child as he was as an adult. She suspected she would have found it impossible to resist him. Children were always a fascination to the Fae, probably because they were so rare. Her people still occasionally spirited away an unwanted or partially magical child, bringing them to Faerie and raising them there. It didn't occur as often now that their territory was so small, but it still happened.

"My parents weren't so fortunate. They had an arrangement between them. It wasn't a love match, but rather a way to consolidate power."

He frowned. "Is that common?"

Sabine shrugged. "It's not uncommon. Ever since the Dragon War, my people have struggled to grow our numbers. Unlike humans, we simply don't produce enough children. A couple may be fortunate to have one child in a century, but some go most of their lives without conceiving. Our Elders began arranging pairings based on what they believed would maximize the chances for a child."

"I'd heard something to that effect. But if children are precious to the Fae, why would your father have blamed you for being more powerful than your brother? You still share the same blood."

Sabine shook her head. "I shared more in common with my mother and her type of magic. I can draw upon the magic from my father's line, but my mother's magic has always been stronger for me. She claimed me as her heir, leaving my brother to follow my father. That would have been acceptable, but Rhys, my brother, could only tap into our father's line. The shadows have never claimed him as one of theirs."

"You're Unseelie," Malek murmured, studying her thoughtfully.

She sighed. So many outside the Fae had preconceived notions about the Unseelie and Seelie. They were essentially from the same fountain of power but had different facets and purposes. The Unseelie worked better in the darkness, while the sunlight was the dominion of the Seelie.

"Not exactly. My mother was Unseelie, but my father was Seelie. I can draw upon the powers of the light *and* the dark. My father viewed it as a taint upon his magic, that his pure Seelie blood should be skewed by the dark." She frowned, studying their entwined hands and the contrast of her pale skin with his more golden tones. "I don't know why the Elders decided to pair my parents together. It may have resulted in two children, but my father always resented their edict."

Malek straightened, his hand tightening around hers. "That's why you had to leave your home."

Sabine gave a half-hearted shrug. It wasn't the whole truth, but she wasn't willing to share everything—not yet, maybe not ever. "When I left, it was with the understanding my father wanted me dead. Since we're twins, my brother should inherit my magic once I'm gone from this world."

"But you said your brother has never shown an affinity for it," Malek pointed out with a frown.

"No, not for my Unseelie magic. But he *could* take my Seelie magic and entwine it with his. At least, that's what some Seelie Elders suggested to my father. It was enough for him to believe it." She paused, staring at the closed port window that overlooked the ocean. All of this seemed like a lifetime ago, but she knew her father would never rest until she was dead. Even if Rhys never acquired her mother's magic, Sabine's existence was a shadow upon her father's Seelie name.

With a sigh, she said, "After my mother died, I didn't have a choice except to leave. I wasn't strong enough to fight my father and survive. A Beastman who swore a life oath to my mother's line helped me escape from the Silver Forest. He was the one who brought me here."

"To a city of stone and metal, surrounded by humans, where the Fae would never consider looking," Malek murmured.

Sabine looked up at him. The compassion and under-standing in his gaze were nearly her undoing. She swallowed, trying to bury her tumultuous emotions.

Malek reached over and cupped her face in his hands. "You did what you needed to do to survive, Sabine. I can't imagine how difficult living here must be for you. In my wildest dreams, I never imagined finding someone like you."

Her heart soared at his words, mirroring her own feelings for him. Placing her hands against his chest, she said, "I'm glad you decided to come to Akros, Malek. I never imagined meeting someone like you either."

Without another word, he lowered his head, claiming her with his mouth. His kiss took her breath away as barely restrained passion and need erupted between them. She whimpered, and he pulled her closer, consuming her with his heat. She wanted him, needed the understanding and compassion he offered like she needed her next breath. This is what she'd been missing, this feeling of connection.

His power called to hers, and she desperately wanted to unleash her own. Running her hands under his shirt to touch his heated skin, she infused her touch with a trace of her magic. Through the mark she'd given him, the power between them flared to life.

His kiss became even more demanding, and he lifted her into his arms. Wanting more and everything he promised, she wrapped her legs around him as he carried her to the bed. They fell onto it, and something jabbed into her side.

She broke their kiss with a laugh. "Weapons."

Malek chuckled and tossed his sword aside, and then his clever fingers disarmed her in less time than she expected. His hand brushed against the edge of her shirt and slid underneath, caressing her bare skin. She wanted his hands everywhere, but there were too many clothes between them. Reaching down, she tugged his shirt up in a silent demand. He pulled it off, tossing it aside, and she ran her hands over his bare chest. His skin was warm, hotter than she expected, and she felt the power nestled within him flare to the surface. A medallion around his neck began to glow. Before she could touch it, he grabbed her wrists, breathing heavily as he stared down at her.

She blinked up at him in surprise, and he took a ragged breath, his expression tormented. He was gentle, holding her in place, but it was obvious he struggled with an internal battle of some kind. With another curse, he pulled away and climbed off the bed. Sabine frowned and pushed herself up as he ran a hand over his head and paced the length of the cabin. The medallion around his neck began to dim, and she arched her brow, waiting expectantly.

He continued pacing for another few minutes, and Sabine settled back, taking the opportunity to admire his muscular physique. He wasn't wearing glamour. She'd thought maybe he possessed a form of it, but whatever Malek was hiding didn't translate to that type of illusion magic. He was a delicious specimen all on his own, and Sabine swept her gaze over him again. If the top half was any indication of what she might expect from the rest, she looked forward to exploring every inch of him.

Malek halted, his heated gaze perusing her as she watched him from his bed. He shook his head. "This wasn't how I planned this, but I can't seem to think clearly when you're around."

She laughed and sat up. Reaching down, she started unlacing her shirt. "Thinking is overrated, Malek. What I want to do with you doesn't require much… thought. Only sensation."

"I can't," he whispered, a trace of a growl in his voice as she slowly untied the bindings of her shirt. His medallion began to glow again, and he squeezed his eyes shut as though in pain.

Sabine paused, tilting her head to study him. Lowering her hands to the bed, she asked, "All right. Why don't you tell me what's going on?"

"I want you," he whispered, opening his eyes and taking a step in her direction. "Your taste, the smell of your skin, every inch of you. I see your face every time I close my eyes. I want you in every way imaginable. You're all I've been thinking about lately."

Although his words made her stomach flutter, Sabine waited for him to finish. He was barely keeping hold of his inclinations, and while the thought of causing him to lose control was thrilling, she wasn't willing to push too far until she knew what was affecting him.

"I'm not human," he admitted, gesturing to the medallion that had been hidden under his shirt. "I hired a witch to create a ward that would allow me to hide my magic."

She glanced at the disc around his neck and nodded. "I figured that out a while ago."

He paused, his frown deepening. "You did?"

She gave him a small smile. "I realized you were wearing a ward when I had to keep refreshing your mark. I don't know what you are, but we all have our secrets. I'm not asking for yours."

The conflicting emotions in Malek's gaze tugged at her heart. She wouldn't push him, but she wanted him to know how she felt. Keeping her voice soft, she said, "I want you, Malek. I wouldn't be here with you if I didn't think you wanted me too. But your secrets aren't part of that, unless you want to share them."

Malek shook his head and wrapped his fist around the medallion. "You're irresistible, Sabine. I've wanted to have you here like this, in my bed, since the moment we met. I've thought of a hundred different ways to tell you the truth, but I haven't been able to bring myself to say the words."

"Why not?" Her first thought had been he might possess Fae magic, but the few traces of his power that had filtered through the mark were unlike anything she'd experienced before. It was a strong and complementary magic of a sort, but the overall flavor of it was different. It was closer to Bane and Dax's power than hers.

He sighed and crossed the room toward her. Sitting on the edge of the bed, he said, "I don't think you'll forgive me once you learn the truth."

Sabine frowned, surprised by the depth of concern she saw in his eyes. Malek didn't strike her as someone who would worry for naught. Reaching up, she placed her hand against his cheek. "You're worried this will change how I feel about you?"

"Yes," he admitted as though the words pained him. "I hope it doesn't, but it will."

The concern in his gaze touched her, but it also reaffirmed her earlier belief Malek had a good heart. It was enough to make her willing to abandon caution, despite living a lifetime of it over the past several years. If things were about to change between them, she wasn't in a hurry to speed it along.

"Will your secret keep for a while longer?"

Malek hesitated. He tucked her hair behind her ear, trailing his fingers over her skin. "Do you have any idea how tempting you are?"

When she smiled, he leaned in closer and kissed her again. Her eyes fluttered closed, and he cupped her face, easing her back onto the bed. A pounding on the door interrupted them.

Malek pulled back with a loud curse and threatened to tear the limbs off whomever was on the other side of the door. He stood, and Sabine sat up again with a sigh.

Someone shouted, and the door crashed open. Sabine dove for her weapons. Twisting her body, she gripped the hilt of her knife and prepared to throw, halting at the sight of

Bane standing in the doorway. Levin stood behind him with a weapon drawn and aimed in Bane's direction.

She blinked up at Bane. Ignoring Levin as though his threat was inconsequential, Bane glanced over at her and then turned to Malek with a thunderous expression.

"You didn't tell her," Bane said with a growl, his eyes flashing to silver.

"I was about to tell her before you broke down the damn door," Malek retorted, glaring at Bane. The medallion around his neck began to glow softly, and Sabine frowned.

Pushing up from the bed, she stepped between the two men. "Why are you here, Bane?"

His jaw clenched, and she waited, taking the opportunity to fasten the laces on her shirt. After a moment, Bane took a shuddering breath and his eyes reverted to their usual amber color. She could tell his anger simmered just below the surface. It wouldn't take much to send him back to that jagged edge.

"Your ship captain is a dragon. When I realized you'd gone with him, I knew he hadn't told you the truth."

Sabine froze. She blinked, turning to stare at Malek with a combination of shock, horror, and underneath... fear. It couldn't be possible. The dragons never descended this far south, preferring to remain closer to their Sky Cities. She studied Malek, her gaze gravitating toward the medallion and remembering his offer to travel with him. Had he wanted to bring her to his ship so he could take her back to the Sky Cities?

"Take off the medallion," she whispered, desperate for Bane to be wrong about this.

Malek didn't say anything, but his expression was pained. He reached up to unfasten the necklace and dropped it onto the bed. The moment it was removed, power, foreign and alien, filled the cabin. She took a half-step backward. By the gods. It was true. He really was a dragon in human form. She'd heard the stories about how they had two forms, but she'd never met a dragon before. There could only be one reason he was here.

"Sabine," Malek began and started to walk toward her. "I never—"

Before he could finish that thought, she raised her hand and blasted him backward against the wall of the cabin. She couldn't risk him getting close again. Not now. The books on the wall tumbled down, the wooden shelves broken beyond repair. Malek, however, was unharmed, likely protected by his own magic. Her hand trembled as she lowered it, and she curled it into a fist to stop it from shaking. In a match against a dragon, she wasn't sure she'd survive. She'd never considered this to be in the realm of possibilities. In all the stories she'd heard, it had taken several Fae working together to bring down one dragon.

Behind her, the sound of Bane drawing his weapon caught her attention, but Malek held up his hand. "That's not necessary, Bane. No one will harm Sabine. Levin, put away your weapon too."

Malek continued to hold her gaze, but he made no effort to stand. "I never intended to deceive you, Sabine. My oath to you still holds true. I won't harm you."

Bane snorted behind her, but she ignored him. Having the demon at her back helped give her the strength to remain standing. Otherwise, she'd be running as far and fast as possible. "Why are you here in Akros?"

"May I stand? It's a little uncomfortable here."

Sabine hesitated and then inclined her head, watching as he got to his feet. Malek kept his movements slow and deliberate. Her hands flexed outward and then curved into fists again, more to stop the tremors and magic that wanted to be used. It wasn't wise to admit her increasing fear when surrounded by predators.

A dragon. The man she'd started to fall for was a dragon. He was one of the creatures who had slaughtered thousands of her people, almost to the point of extinction.

Sabine swallowed, her mouth impossibly dry as she thought back to every conversation they'd shared. "Your Fae grandmother. The one who told you the stories. She was a captive, wasn't she?"

Malek winced and nodded. "Initially, yes. When my grandfather met her, he fell in love with her. I believe she loved him too. At the end, she wasn't a captive. She *chose* to remain with him."

Sabine made a small noise of despair, kicking herself for her foolishness. She'd trusted Malek, but dragons would always be enemies of the Fae. It wasn't simply a matter of liking the persona Malek had shown her. If it were that simple, it wouldn't matter what he was. Dragons hoarded power and magic, just like they collected shiny trinkets, gems, and gold. The Fae had suffered for centuries when dragons imprisoned them as part of their hoard.

It was no wonder his "grandmother" hadn't returned to her people. Even if she wasn't a captive in the conventional sense, Sabine had never heard of a dragon relinquishing their hold on someone once they fell into their clutches. Then again, Malek *had* saved her—more than once. She wouldn't have been able to escape the councilman's home and gotten back to Dax without his help. He could have taken her back to his ship or done whatever he wanted while she'd been unconscious, but he hadn't. He'd protected her instead.

A flash of a memory tickled in the back of her mind. She remembered waking up to a pleasant warmth and seeing Malek's face when she opened her eyes. Lifting her hand, she brushed her fingertips against her lips, recalling a kiss and the taste of his foreign magic. "You kissed me after you brought me back to the tavern. What did you do to me?"

His brow furrowed and then he sighed. "You were dying, Sabine. Your glamour was draining you. I infused you with dragonfire to give you enough power to wake up. Bane did the rest."

She stared at him in shock, hearing the ring of truth in his words. *Dragonfire?* Desperate for him to be lying, she looked over at Bane, and he gave her a curt nod, indicating Malek spoke the truth. This had the potential to be disastrous. She'd been little more than a teenager when she'd fled her homeland, and she didn't have enough training or experience to know how her magic might be affected. She'd need to speak with Balkin at the earliest opportunity to see if he knew what lingering effects dragonfire might have on her.

Unfortunately, there was another matter that now needed to be handled. The heaviness of a debt between them weighed upon her shoulders, demanding repayment. Another debt. This one a life debt… to a *dragon*.

"There is no debt between us for such a thing," Malek said quietly, correctly guessing one of the sources of her unease. "You were injured as a result of my request to acquire the chalice. I won't ask you for more."

Sabine paused, feeling as though the universe was weighing his release. After a moment, the heaviness lessened and the tight band around her chest eased enough to allow her to take a full breath. Relieved, Sabine nodded in acceptance of his words, but the thought of what could have happened left her disconcerted.

Malek started to take a step toward her. She shook her head in warning and lifted her hand again, wary about allowing him too close just yet. He frowned but remained where he stood.

"Why did you really come to Akros, Malek?"

"For you," he admitted with a sigh. "But not for the reasons you may think."

"He needs a Fae," Bane said beside her.

Malek narrowed his eyes at Bane, but when he answered, he focused only on her. "I heard rumors the leader of the local thieves' guild had a penchant for finding rare magical artifacts, particularly those of Fae origins. I thought Dax might have a contact who was Fae or he might have an affinity for Fae magic. I never expected to find *you*."

Sabine frowned and lowered her hand. "The chalice? Why are you looking for Fae artifacts?"

"Not just any artifacts," Malek said, rubbing his hands over his face. "I'm looking for the artifacts that were once used to seal the Dragon Portal."

Sabine stared at him in shock and horror. The portal was a gateway between dimensions. No one knew who had first created it—most likely the gods. It allowed the denizens of this world and others to pass back and forth. As the war for supremacy progressed between the dragons and gods, their world began dying. To battle against the dragons, the gods drew upon the magic of this world to fuel their attack, which ended up crippling and killing the magical races who were dependent upon the magic to survive. Even now, the Fae were still struggling to regain their previous level of power.

Understanding their world would be doomed if the war continued, one of the gods met in secret with representatives from some magical races and gifted them with the knowledge on how to end it. Several artifacts were created and then used to seal the portal, thus ending the war. Unfortunately, it also trapped everyone where they happened to be—including some humans, dragons, and other creatures not native to this world. No one knew if the battle continued in other dimensions or if any of the magical races from this world were still trapped on others.

The closing of the portal may have ended the war and prevented this world from dying, but it had come at a great cost. Some races had disappeared completely. The Fae and those closely related to them still hadn't fully recovered. With the magic of the gods suddenly disappearing from the world, they might never return to their former glory.

Sabine didn't know all the details about the artifacts or how they worked. Most of what she knew had been passed down in stories, with the Keepers of Knowledge protecting the precious tomes that detailed the Fae's history. Supposedly, the artifacts had been hidden after they'd been used to seal the portal. She didn't know where or even what they looked like.

From what she could recall of the stories she'd heard, the artifacts Malek mentioned could be used to remove the enchantment on the portal. That was why they'd been split up and hidden. If the seals on the portal were removed, it would allow the war between the dragons and gods to resume. Only this time, the dragons would have the upper hand since the gods wouldn't be expecting the attack. If that happened and the last of the magic faded from this world, everyone tied to it would die, especially her people. The Fae were the caretakers of this world, and they wouldn't survive its loss.

Her nails dug into the palms of her hand, and she shook her head. "I won't help you kill the gods."

"I'm not asking for that," he said quickly, lifting his hands in a peaceable gesture. "The portal seals are failing, Sabine. Everyone in the Sky Cities feels it. The magic from the other realms is beginning to filter through. I came here to find the items that were used to close it so we can ensure another war never happens again."

Bane snorted. "You can't be suggesting the dragons want the portal to stay sealed."

"Not all, no," Malek admitted. "Many of my brethren are eager at the opportunity to once again take to the skies and leave this dimension. I don't believe we can risk another war. For good or ill, we're part of this world. We need to protect it. Allowing the portal to open again will cause widespread destruction."

Sabine frowned. "You would turn against your people?"

Malek shook his head. "Not exactly. I'm not alone in my thinking. In addition to my family, several other dragon clans believe the same thing. We're a minority, which is why I left the Sky Cities in secret and have been masquerading as a smuggler while I conduct my search."

Bane crossed his arms over his chest. "Have you discovered any of the artifacts yet?"

"Not for certain, but I believe the chalice may have been one of the artifacts entrusted to the Fae for safekeeping. I won't know until Dax turns it over to me."

Sabine frowned. The chalice was old enough to be from that time, but she couldn't say whether it had been used to seal the portal. All she knew was that it was an object of power.

Malek focused on her again. "Sabine, I can't imagine what you must be thinking right now. I apologize for not telling you sooner. I never expected to find a Fae here, only someone with trace amounts of power or someone with Fae ancestry. I wasn't sure that would be enough, but I needed to start somewhere. Then I met you, and I held off telling you the truth because I wanted to get to you know you better."

His words had the resonance of truth, but she wasn't sure she could trust him. He was still a dragon, and all the stories she knew were of terrible creatures who'd unleashed death and destruction upon their world. She didn't want him harmed, but he knew her identity and *that* knowledge was dangerous.

"If Dax agrees to give you the chalice, will you leave Akros?"

Malek hesitated. Her heart thundered in her chest, waiting for his response. He held her gaze and took a cautious step toward her, keeping his hands at his side where she could see them. She *wanted* to trust him, but she was still wary of his intentions. He was taking great pains to make himself appear nonthreatening, which helped a bit.

"If necessary, yes. But I'd like your help to locate the remaining objects. The information I've gathered over the last year indicates only a Fae who possesses the magic of the gods can wield the objects. Someone from each of the original magical races will be needed to work the actual spell to reseal the portal, but you're the only one who can locate them. I've compiled years of research that detail my findings and found a few old scraps of notes that allude to it, but I'm afraid I haven't been able to sort out everything yet. I can show you what I've learned, if you're willing to consider it."

Sabine didn't answer right away. She was tempted to refuse, but part of her was curious. She might want to believe Malek, but he was right; everything had changed between them. Trusting a dragon, especially one as likeable as Malek, would require careful consideration.

"I'm willing to review your notes and take another look at the chalice. Beyond that, I won't commit to anything more right now."

Malek nodded and his shoulders relaxed as though a weight had lifted from him. Apparently, her agreement had given him a great deal of hope. "If you plan to return to the tavern, I can bring them over shortly. Or I can deliver them to Esme's shop."

"The tavern will be fine."

Bane put his hand on her back. "We should get back. Balkin brought more news he needs to discuss with you."

She nodded but didn't make any move to leave. Instead, she searched Malek's expression. Nothing in his face or body language indicated he was being anything less than truthful. He hadn't harmed her, even when she'd used her magic against him. Instead, he'd protected her—not once, but several times. The only flaw was the fact he'd hidden his identity from her. It was impossible to fault him for that.

If she'd been in Malek's shoes, she probably would have done the same thing. Only a few people in the city knew her real identity, so it wasn't fair of her to be angry at Malek for hiding himself. Dragons weren't trusted anywhere in the southern cities. And he tried to tell her the truth before allowing things between them to become even more entangled.

Unwilling to leave things so unsettled between them, Sabine slowly approached Malek. He didn't move, but he seemed surprised as she continued to move closer. She probably wouldn't have been so brave if Bane hadn't been standing at her back. Reaching down, she took Malek's hand in hers. Without the medallion around his neck, his power flared against hers. She jerked her head up to meet his gaze.

"You have nothing to fear from me, Sabine," he said gently but made no other move toward her. "It's been difficult wearing the medallion when you're around. Your power calls to mine and has from the moment you first touched me. That's what you're feeling now."

She didn't respond, too busy focusing on the nuances of his magic. It was stronger than she expected, even more potent than some Fae magic. Like he said, his power called to hers too, and she had a moment to wonder what it would be like between them without the medallion in the way. Tracing her fingertips over the mark on his wrist, she infused her magic into it, feeling it seal properly this time. Liquid fire heated her skin in the same location of his mark, but it was a small price to pay.

Malek placed his hand over hers and squeezed it gently. "Does this mean I still get to have that dinner with you?"

"As long as I'm not the main course," she said, only halfway kidding.

Malek chuckled and lifted her hand, placing a soft kiss against it. "I promise."

She offered him a small smile before withdrawing her hand and turning away. If Malek was typical of dragons, maybe her people had made a mistake. Perhaps they weren't as evil as the Fae believed. For now, she'd withhold final judgment. But she'd still remain cautious.

Without saying another word, she walked past Levin and off the ship with Bane following behind her.

Chapter Fifteen

Sabine walked back into the tavern's meeting room with Bane. Dax and Balkin were sitting at a table someone must have found and brought downstairs. The splinters and pieces from the old table had been removed, leaving no hint Dax had thrown a fit earlier. The chalice was on the table in front of them, and they were both studying it but neither of them touched it.

Balkin looked up when she entered. "Good. You've returned. Your protector informed me you've been communing with dragons."

"It would have been nice if someone had shared that with me earlier," Sabine grumbled and slid into a seat. "But yes. He's sworn a blood oath not to harm me, but he's a subject best discussed another day."

"A dragon as an ally may give you an advantage in dealing with the Fae," Balkin suggested, his golden eyes gleaming.

Sabine frowned. "Only if the dragon decides to eat them. They'll be more inclined to double their efforts in killing me if they think I'm friendly with the enemy."

Bane chuckled and placed a glass of wine on the table in front of her. "You were kinder to him than I expected, although I did enjoy watching you toss him into the side of his ship."

Dax's mouth curved into a satisfied smile. Before he could say anything, Sabine pinned him with a glare. "Don't start."

Balkin's whiskers twitched, and he gestured to the chalice in front of them. "Tell me your impressions when you first touched it, my darling kitten."

She sighed and picked up the wine Bane had poured for her. Taking a sip, she studied the chalice sitting in the center of the table. It was pretty enough and valuable on its own merit, but now she had to wonder if it was truly one of the artifacts Malek was hunting.

"It all happened very quickly. Dax picked it up first, and it was obvious he'd been caught in a trap. There were layers of magic wrapped around it, and I could see the power trying to bind him. I'd only seen a lich ward once before when Elder Thoma'vertina demonstrated it. The binding on the chalice was similar."

Balkin nodded and gestured for her to continue.

She tilted her head, considering the artifact and trying to piece together her memories. "I believe the lich ward was the last magic applied, and Dax was its intended target. I was able to transfer the lich ward to myself by using the pact you formed between us. From there, I was able to neutralize it with my blood like Elder Thoma'vertina had shown me. But when I did, it… the chalice somehow recognized me." She shook her head, not sure how to explain. "It's different, Balkin. It's neither Seelie nor Unseelie, but both somehow. I think it recognized my magic as being similar. I was hoping you might know more about it."

"Malek believes it's one of the artifacts used to seal the Dragon Portal," Bane said, dropping into one of the empty chairs.

"Interesting," Balkin murmured, his tone a little too mild. "What do you believe, my darling kitten? Was this object crafted before the portal was sealed?"

Sabine took a sip of the wine. It was from another bottle of Faerie wine, but this one had a gold cap, indicating it had more substantial power in it. Bane had likely poured it so she could compare the magic within it to the power in the chalice. There was no comparison. The wine was Seelie magic and nothing more.

"I think it's possible. Before the portal was closed, the Fae were one people—neither Seelie nor Unseelie. I don't know how different Fae magic was back then, but it was much closer to the true magic of the gods. I sensed something similar from the chalice when I picked it up."

Balkin nodded and leaned back. "One of the artifacts was rumored to be a chalice."

Sabine's eyes widened, and she studied it again in a new light. "My mother told me stories about the artifacts of power, but she never told me what they were. If this is the same one from legend, why would it have been hidden in a human city? I assumed it would have been kept with our Keepers of Knowledge."

Balkin steepled his clawed hands together as his eyes took on a faraway slant. It was entirely possible he was trying to recall something from long ago. Balkin had lived longer than everyone in the room combined. Occasionally, it took him a while to sort through his memories.

He tapped his claws, clicking them together lightly.

Sabine had witnessed him rip apart intruders with those claws when they'd trespassed into the Silver Forest. Yet she'd never been afraid of him. Balkin was the one person she trusted most in this world.

After a long time, Balkin said, "The Fae may have been given the gift of knowledge to create and wield the chalice, but it was later entrusted to my people for safekeeping. We hid it in a place where we believed none of the magical races would look, should the fighting amongst them lead to temptation in releasing the gods from their prison."

Dax arched his brow. "Were you there, old man?"

"No, but my father was the one who had been tasked with hiding it," Balkin said, his eyes shimmering with the golden light commonly seen when Beastpeople experienced a strong emotion.

Sabine lowered her wineglass and placed it on the table. "That's why you brought me here. You knew the chalice had been safe here for centuries, so you believed I would be safe here too."

"You are as much a treasure as the chalice," Balkin said gently.

Sabine blinked away tears. "I've missed you, Balkin."

"As I have missed you, my darling kitten."

Dax drummed his fingers on the table. "I'll rescind the deal made with the dragon. I have no intention of allowing this item to fall into their hands. They may intend to organize a sneak attack and attempt to eliminate the gods for good this time."

"Malek claims the portal is already failing," Bane said with a shrug. "He's hunting the artifacts to ensure they can keep the portal sealed and to prevent another war."

Balkin's gaze sharpened on her. "I have heard whispers about the portal magic fading. What are your impressions of this dragon?"

Sabine hesitated and folded her hands in her lap. "I don't know. He's come to my aid more than once without attempting to make any undue demands. I want to believe him, but I don't know enough about dragons. Can they lie?"

"Not like humans," Balkin said, rubbing his chin in thought. "They can lie by omission or misdirection, much like the Fae. Perhaps he is a different sort than the dragons from legend. I will speak with this dragon of yours before I make a decision."

No one questioned Balkin about his right to determine the fate of the chalice. If it had been entrusted to Balkin's father and he'd been the one to hide it, Balkin was the rightful bearer of it.

Sabine nodded. "Malek should be arriving shortly. He claims to have some information about the other artifacts. He's going to bring it here so I can review it."

"He wants her help to locate the other items," Bane said with a scowl. "Among other things."

"No," Dax said firmly, crossing his arms over his chest. "She will do no such thing."

She arched her brow. Before she could remind Dax about the dangers of trying to subject her to his will, Balkin sprung from his chair and threw Dax against the wall. His claws were at the demon's throat before anyone could react.

"You dare speak to her that way," Balkin hissed, his words barely recognizable as his claws started to dig into Dax's neck. "She is a Faerie Royal, the last of her mother's line and direct descendant to the Unseelie throne. You will get on your knees and beg for her forgiveness, or I will rip out your throat."

Sabine slowly stood. "No, Balkin. Not here. We're in Dax's den, and he needs to retain his power here. You will not demand this from him."

"I will not permit him to treat you as less than you are," Balkin growled.

"Dax is not my enemy," she said gently, motioning for Bane to remain where he was and not get involved. Balkin was trying to protect her, and she was the only one he'd listen to. Sabine didn't know the entire history between Balkin and Dax, except the Beastman had saved the demon's life and brought him and Bane to the surface years before she'd fled her home. It was Balkin who'd helped establish the two brothers in the city, and both of them were somehow permanently tied to the Beastman. Or at least Dax was. She didn't know what hold, if any, Balkin had over Bane.

Walking over to the Beastman, Sabine placed her hand on his arm. "Dax and I have reached an understanding. I have conceded not to interfere in his den when he's present, and he has agreed to respect my boundaries. We have been able to coexist only because we both agreed to these terms. He does not make decisions for me, but I do respect his opinion —as I do yours. You chose well when you named him my protector."

The reminder Balkin had been the one to form the pact between them was enough to encourage him to retract his claws. He released Dax but didn't move away. Dax crumpled to the ground, blinking rapidly as he tried to fight off the effects from Balkin's poisoned claws.

Sabine pulled out her knife and pricked her finger, allowing her blood to well to the surface. She bent down, offering her blood to Dax. He wrapped his hand around her wrist eagerly, pulling her hand closer and accepting her gift. Balkin's claws weren't poisonous to her or to any of the Fae, and her blood was also an antidote.

"You would reward him for his insolence?" Balkin muttered in disgust. "He would not have died from so little poison, but perhaps he might learn a lesson."

"No, it wouldn't kill him," she agreed and stood, watching as Dax shook off the lingering effects. "Dax is stronger than that. But I will not have my protector weakened when I need him at full strength. You taught me that, Balkin. I remember your lessons."

"Very well." Balkin frowned and glared at Dax who was still on the ground. "You will remember your life is a gift only because my mistress wills it."

"Understood," Dax said, pushing up from the floor.

Sabine hooked her arm through Balkin's and led him back to the table and away from Dax. Even on the best of days, Dax had a way of getting under people's skin.

"I'm pleased to see you again, but I wish it were under better circumstances. The message you sent to Dax was vague. Will you tell me about the seer's vision that brought you here?"

He patted her hand idly. "Usagi is very old. She spends much of her time in dreams, rarely awakening. When she does, her confusion makes it difficult to separate her visions from reality. She came to me under the cover of darkness several days ago and told me of whispers from the spirit world. I came to you immediately."

A sense of foreboding fell over Sabine. Usagi was more than just old; she'd lived through the worst of the Dragon War and had seen the portal collapse. As one of the most ancient Elders, Usagi held a special place of honor amongst the Beastpeople. Even the Fae treated her with no small amount of respect. Usagi's visions had foretold the death of Sabine's mother, and any warnings from her needed to be taken seriously.

Sabine frowned. "What did she tell you?"

"She dreamed of a battle on stone streets. The moon fell into darkness. An ancient iron blade forged in dragonfire. Death. Plots within plots. A crossroads and a choice." Balkin paused, staring at the chalice still untouched on the table. "When she awakened from her vision, Usagi was more clear-headed than I have seen in a century. She urged me to find you with great haste, warning me you were in danger."

Sabine blanched. "She named me specifically?"

Balkin gave her a curt nod. "She spoke your name, Sabin'theoria. Twice the moon will be shrouded in darkness. The third time heralds the return of the Wild Hunt."

Bane stood and walked over to her, his frown deepening. "You've cloaked the moon twice now, haven't you, little one?"

Sabine managed to nod, thoroughly shaken. "Yes. The night I was ambushed, I hid the moon and was forced to pull power through the ground to escape. The second was the night we stole the chalice. I lost my glamour that night when I broke the lich ward. I wasn't shielded either time." She muttered a curse at her carelessness. She'd known it was a risk both times, but her options had been limited. "My father must have sensed my magic. Either that, or he still has people searching for me."

"Your father will *never* stop hunting you," Balkin said, his tone sharp and biting. "As long as you are alive, you will remain a threat to your father and brother. Do not grow so accustomed to pretending to be human you forget yourself and the danger surrounding you."

Sabine looked away and didn't respond. It was impossible to forget she wasn't one of them, but it wasn't as difficult to slide into the role of pretending to be human anymore. She'd blurred the lines for so long that wearing the glamour had become second nature. The most challenging aspect had been tempering her magic and relying upon it less.

She may have stunted her magical growth, but she'd enriched herself in other ways and strengthened some of her lesser talents. She'd always been mediocre with weapons, but Dax and Bane had insisted upon daily training for years.

Now she was as competent with a blade as she was with her magic, but still lacking in both compared to many of her enemies.

"How can we stop the Wild Hunt?" Dax approached the table and kept a respectful distance from Balkin. He appeared fully recovered from the poison, but he likely wasn't willing to risk angering the Beastman a second time.

Sabine shook her head, remembering the terrible stories she'd heard as a child. The Wild Hunt was the Fae's most terrible and fearsome enforcer. The sacrifice to summon it was costly, and only the target's death would stop it. "You can't. It can only be Called with blood and magic, and once unleashed, it will not stop until the contract has been fulfilled."

Balkin was quiet for a long time. "It *can* be stopped if the summoner falls."

Sabine squeezed her eyes shut. It all came back to her brother's death. Even if she agreed to mark both demons and allowed them to go after Rhys, she wasn't sure they would make it past the Silver Forest. It wasn't just the trees that protected the heart of Faerie. Major magic would be required to encourage the forest to accept a demonic presence, and the Fae would be alerted the moment she lowered her protections.

Part of her still desperately wanted to believe Rhys hadn't been the one to demand her death. As long as there was a chance, she wasn't willing to agree to end his life. She wasn't sure she could do it even if he truly wanted her dead. He was still her brother.

A knock on the door interrupted them, and Dax frowned. "That must be Esme."

He walked over to the door and flung it open. Esmelle breezed into the room, patting Dax's cheek affectionately as she moved past him in a swirl of colorful skirts. In her other arm, she carried a small flowering pot filled with lavender. Dax's eye twitched in irritation, but he slammed the door shut and muttered something under his breath about stinky plants.

Blossom darted out from the plant, spotted Sabine, and dove into her hair. The tiny pixie pressed up against her neck, getting as close as possible and whispered loudly, "He's a dragon, Sabine! Your ship captain is a dragon! Esme says so!"

Sabine's mouth twitched in a smile, and she arched her brow at Esmelle. "Indeed. It might have been helpful to know that a little *earlier*."

The witch shrugged. "Malek made us promise not to tell you, but I didn't make any such promise about keeping it from the pixies. Blossom volunteered to share the news, so I brought her here."

"Tricky witch," Bane said with something that looked like approval in his eyes. "You knew the pixies would tell her the truth and you could get around the agreement. We planned something similar but shared our information with Balkin."

"Looks like I'm not the only tricky one," Esmelle said with a grin and winked at him. Turning back to Sabine, she added, "The other pixies were terrified Dax or Bane might eat them if they came here, but Blossom said she'd be safe. You wouldn't allow anyone to eat her."

"Esme's right. I won't allow you to be eaten," Sabine said, more for Dax and Bane's benefit than for Blossom.

Pixies possessed powerful nature magic and were considered delicacies by most demons. Since they didn't have the same offensive abilities as the Fae, demons had been known to eat entire pixie clans as a snack before lunch. She didn't *think* they would eat Blossom, but it was better to keep them separate. Just in case.

Dax snorted and finished pouring himself a drink. "A pity. It's been a while since I tasted pixie."

Blossom squeaked and covered herself with Sabine's hair. Sabine sighed and reached up to send a trace of reassuring magic over Blossom, knowing Dax was just poking fun at her.

Balkin studied the pixie. "How did the pixies manage to find you in the city? Their kind don't usually leave the forests."

"Her magic called to us," Blossom said from her perch on Sabine's shoulder. "She summoned another pixie clan too. They arrived a couple of days ago, but they haven't met Sabine yet." In a quieter voice meant for Sabine's ears alone, Blossom added, "I don't think they're worthy of your magic. They tried harvesting flowers before the moon was in alignment. If they do, it'll upset the balance of the garden and kill the flowers. My sisters want to chase them off."

Sabine froze as the hidden meaning in Blossom's words registered. It was one more reference to the moon and death, presumably hers. Whatever news the pixie clan had to share didn't bode well for her. "I see. That's... unfortunate. It sounds as though I'll need to have a talk with these pixies soon."

"Keeping them with you is risky, my darling kitten. Pixies are not always trustworthy. Many are spies."

Blossom bristled at Balkin's words. "I would *never* betray Sabine. She protects us."

Esmelle took a seat in an empty chair and arranged her skirt around her. "I have to agree with Blossom, Balkin. They've been living in my garden for years. They're all enamored with Sabine. They won't betray her."

Sabine sighed and sat in the chair again. A faint trace of pixie magic floated over her as Blossom smoothed out her hair and started braiding it. At least the task would keep the pixie calm and busy for a while until Sabine got her back to the garden.

Focusing again on Balkin, she said, "Dax and Bane help quite a bit, but it's still not easy being surrounded by stone, metal, and dead wood. Blossom and her family help mitigate the negative effects of living in the city. I trust them."

Blossom trilled happily at Sabine's words and continued braiding. Balkin frowned, but he didn't dispute her words.

Esmelle cocked her head, studying the artifact on the table. "So that's the chalice, huh? It's prettier than I expected, especially with all that magic swirling around it. What are you going to do with it?"

Balkin's eyebrows rose. "You can see the magic, little witch?"

Esmelle grinned and leaned forward in her chair. "Oh, Balkin. I've missed having you around, you stuffy old Beastman. Yes, I can see most magic. It's a fairly new ability, and I'm still learning my way around it. Sabine's been helping me. The colors surrounding the chalice are almost identical to Sabine's power. Well, when she's not hiding behind layers and layers of glamour."

"You have grown more skilled." Balkin walked over and patted Esmelle on the head as though she were a small child.

Sabine bit back a smile at Esmelle's nonplussed expression. Balkin thought highly of Esmelle and her abilities, but he tended to treat everyone like children. Granted, part of that was probably because they were little more than toddlers compared to him. But Esmelle was a witch in her prime. Even though she'd live an extended life beyond most mundane humans, she wouldn't be as long-lived as other magical races.

Other than Malek, only the people in this room had seen her without glamour. Esme had been instrumental in helping Sabine adjust her illusion to appear more human. The witch was the first human Sabine had ever met, which was part of the reason Balkin had enlisted her aid. Those first lessons in sloughing off her Fae mannerisms and becoming proficient in the common tongue had been mostly handled by Esme. In exchange, Sabine had agreed to teach the witch additional magic.

Balkin continued walking around the table to Sabine. "To answer your question, I have not yet decided what I shall do with the chalice." He paused, placing his hand on Sabine's shoulder and squeezed gently. "Despite our efforts, I am afraid none of my treasures may be safe here in the city. I will not risk losing either of them."

Bane and Dax tensed at his words. Sabine lowered her gaze and took a steadying breath, suspecting Balkin was right. The thought of leaving the people she'd grown to care so much about caused her heart to stutter in her chest. But staying would endanger all of them. If—no, when—the Wild Hunt made their appearance, casualties were considered acceptable as long as the Hunt fulfilled its purpose. Humans, especially the defenseless children in Akros, wouldn't stand a chance.

Esmelle frowned. "We can fight it, can't we? If we all stand together, we should be able to protect Sabine. She escaped from it once before."

"That was different," Sabine admitted and picked up her glass of wine. "The Hunt was once formed from Unseelie magic. Over time, it developed its own awareness and changed. The magic has become wild, not something controlled by the Fae."

Sabine took a sip of her wine, absorbing the magic within it and infusing it with hers. The unpleasant thoughts in her head made the wine taste like ash. Setting it aside, she folded her hands in her lap again and continued, "After my mother died, the Wild Hunt came for me with the intention of returning me to Faerie so I might take the Unseelie throne. That was one of its original purposes, to determine the right of succession. Balkin managed to turn it away with an oath to the Huntsman that I would return one day and take my rightful place. If I return to Faerie now, I won't survive it. My father will see me dead, and I don't believe I'm strong enough yet to stand against him."

"Oh," Esmelle muttered, and her shoulders slumped. "Well, drat. What are our options? Should we make plans to take Sabine away from the city?"

Sabine studied her hands, wishing there were a clear solution. "I don't know if leaving and hiding elsewhere is a viable option. I've never heard of anyone being able to outrun the Wild Hunt, and I won't risk allowing anyone here to stand beside me when it comes. I'm not sure what can be done."

Bane scowled. "Absolutely not. Sabine, do not even think about sacrifi—"

At Balkin's threatening growl, Sabine held Bane's gaze and shook her head in warning. The demon glanced over at Balkin, his eyes flashing to silver briefly. Bane wasn't happy at her request for silence, but she didn't want another confrontation with Balkin. Even if the Beastman could be a little overbearing at times, he had more experience in these matters than any of them. While she might rely upon and trust Dax and Bane, Balkin didn't have the same sort of relationship with them. She *needed* Balkin's help. He'd managed to keep her alive this long. Hopefully, he might have some insight into how she could escape from this mess.

Someone knocked on the door, and Dax pushed away from the table. He strolled over to the door, opened it a crack, and snapped, "I told you no interruptions. The next person who knocks on this door will have their head removed from their shoulders."

The slightest trace of hesitation colored Javyn's words as he said, "A-apologies, Dax. I know you don't wish to be disturbed, but the ship captain has returned. He claims Sabine is expecting him."

"Fine. Send him in," Dax said with disgust and turned away, prowling over to the far side of the room where he kept a selection of liquor. "I should have killed the ship captain when he first arrived."

Javyn stepped aside, allowing Malek to enter the room, and then closed the door behind him. If Malek had heard Dax's remark, he chose not to comment. Instead, Malek paused, taking in the room's occupants before his gaze fell on Sabine. His expression softened, and a trace of lingering regret filled his eyes. In that moment, Sabine knew she'd been right about trusting him, despite the secrets they'd kept from each other.

Balkin moved to stand beside her, drawing Malek's attention. Malek gave the Beastman a small nod in greeting, acknowledging his presence but nothing more. If they'd been in a formal Faerie court setting, such a move would have been expected. The fact Malek had known the proper greeting to one of the Beastpeople was surprising and disconcerting. But nothing much should surprise her anymore when it came to Malek. The self-proclaimed ship captain had proven to be skilled at adapting no matter the circumstances.

Before Sabine could address him or introduce Balkin, Blossom abandoned her braiding and darted out from her hair. The tiny pixie fluttered around Malek, inspecting him from various angles. "Are you really a dragon? I heard they smell like burned leaves, but you don't. And where's your tail? Dragons are supposed to have a tail. Big teeth too. And fire magic. Right?"

A laugh bubbled out of Esmelle. Malek glanced over at

Sabine and arched his eyebrow. The deviation from protocol eased the worst of the tension in the room.

Sabine's mouth twitched in a smile. "He's really a dragon, Blossom. The warding medallion around his neck is still active. Maybe you can convince him to take it off later." She gestured to Balkin, who was still in a defensive position beside her and too well-trained to relax over a pixie's wayward comments. "Malek, I'd like you to meet Balkin, my blood-bonded guardian. I believe you already know everyone else."

Malek studied Balkin for a long time and dipped his head even lower, a sign of deep respect. "Well met, Balkin. It's an honor to meet one of the Beastpeople."

A heavy pause filled the room. Balkin prowled around the table toward Malek. "So *you're* the dragon wanting to get his hands on the artifacts used to seal the portal? And you want to use my mistress to do so?"

Sabine remained still, curious how Malek would handle Balkin's questions.

"I am, but only if she is willing," Malek agreed and glanced at Sabine again. He gestured to the small wooden box under his arm. "I brought some of my notes detailing my search. It's my hope Sabine will consent to aid me in my hunt for the missing artifacts. If not, I will continue my search elsewhere. I mean her no harm, regardless of her decision."

Balkin's pelt shifted, smoothing over in the way it did when he eased out of fight mode. It could change instantly, but Malek's comments had in some small way reassured Balkin. The Beastman didn't trust easily, but he was at least willing to hear Malek out. Sabine nodded at Balkin, and he gestured for Malek to place the box on the table.

The box itself was rather unremarkable, but it appeared to have been carved from one solid piece of wood. Runed symbols of protection had been etched into silver locks, the only ornamentation on the container. Malek unfastened the locking mechanism and slid it open. Curious, Sabine walked over to the box and watched as Malek withdrew a large stack of parchment. Her eyes widened in surprise. He'd obviously dedicated a significant amount of time to this endeavor.

Blossom darted back over to Sabine's shoulder and under her hair. Sabine ignored her giggles and the light tugging as the pixie started braiding her hair again. Malek spread out his notes on the table.

"I've brought most of my research, including information acquired by some of my family members over the years. When we first realized the portal was failing, we believed the Fae or the gods themselves had found a way to deactivate it. We've spent years trying to identify and search for the artifacts used in the original workings to seal it."

Sabine picked up one of the loose parchment pieces. It was a sketch of a chalice that bore a striking resemblance to the one currently sitting on the table. "How did you come to learn about this one?"

Malek studied the drawing she held. "When I was a child, my grandmother told me the story about the portal. She saw the chalice once, before it was passed along to the cupbearer to hide. The sketch was made by her hand, years before we realized the portal was becoming active once again. I found the sketch in her belongings after she left this world."

Sabine nodded, staring at the drawing again. The flowing signature at the bottom caught her attention. She didn't recognize the clan name, but the name Elis'andreia was definitely Fae in origin.

Balkin rifled through the papers, skimming over each one briefly before he moved on to the next. He looked at the sketch in Sabine's hand and growled low in his throat. "I recognize that name. It was believed Elis'andreia was killed in a skirmish with the dragons after the portal was closed. You claim she was living in the Sky Cities?"

Malek nodded. "She was captured but later freed. The story I heard was she'd been injured by an iron blade and left for dead. My grandfather found her after the battle had been won. He was so enamored with her beauty, he brought her back to the Sky Cities and offered a boon to any healer who managed to save her life."

Sabine looked up at Malek in surprise. Any wounds made from an iron weapon usually acted like a lethal poison to a Fae, moving throughout their bloodstream and cutting off their ties to their magic. Iron wasn't native to this world, but the dragons had found a way to bring the rocks from the heavens and through the portal. When combined with dragonfire, these meteorites could be crafted into iron weapons.

"Did she recover fully?"

He smiled down at her and nodded. "Yes. It took a great number of healers and many years before she regained her strength. While she was recovering, my grandfather visited her often. At first, she didn't want anything to do with him. He started bringing her gifts, hoping her feelings toward him would eventually change."

"A dragon parting with their hoard?" Dax scoffed in disbelief and walked to the sidebar to pour himself another drink.

Esmelle wrinkled her nose at Dax. "You're one to talk. How many gifts have you given to Sabine after you've made her angry?"

Ignoring Dax's scowl, Sabine asked, "Was that enough for her feelings to change?"

Malek glanced down at her hand on his arm, and his gaze softened. She hadn't realized she'd reached out to him. "No. She still didn't want anything to do with him. He purchased gifts from merchants who had traveled to the farthest reaches of the world. He offered Elisa jewels, gold, silks, paintings, anything and everything you could imagine. She refused all of them."

Esmelle rested her head in her hands. "So what finally changed her mind?"

"A flower."

Sabine blinked up at him in surprise. "She missed her home, and he offered her a piece of it."

"Yes," he agreed, reaching up to adjust one of the lavender flowers Blossom had tucked into her braids. "He loved her too much to force her to remain in the Sky Cities. So he went to her one last time with nothing more than a flower from the Silver Forest and an offer of freedom. He told her he would arrange for safe passage back to Faerie, if she wanted to return. And if not, he said his ship would take her anywhere in the world if she wanted to travel."

"But she didn't want to go. She'd fallen in love with him too," Sabine guessed, wondering how she would have handled it if she'd been in the same position. Leaving Faerie had changed Sabine so much she wasn't sure how she would adapt when the time came for her to return. She'd seen and done too much to fall back easily into that way of life, even if part of her desperately missed it.

Malek nodded. "Elisa used her magic on the flower, making it grow and designing an entire garden in tribute to it. That garden thrived for the rest of her life and was a constant source of enjoyment for our family. My grandfather frequently kept an eye out for more plants from the Silver Forest, and Elisa added them to her garden."

"That's how the pixies found her, isn't it?" Sabine asked, recalling pieces of the story Malek had already shared.

"I believe so. One day, they just appeared in her garden, and my grandmother was thrilled. She used to say she had her very own piece of Faerie right in the Sky Cities."

Bane arched his brow. "A charming yet somewhat senti-mental tale. I've heard other much more believable stories about dragons and their Fae captives, not to mention the ugly reality of everything that entailed. It's unlikely he would have allowed her to leave."

Sabine paused and pulled her hand away from Malek in acknowledgment of Bane's warning. "You don't believe he could have charmed her?"

"Anything is possible," Bane admitted, picking up her wine and bringing it over to where Sabine stood. "But this story is one that was probably told to an impressionable child—a child who would have wanted to believe in the romance of the tale, rather than the harsh truth about his family or how a Fae captive could have been brutalized in the hands of the dragons."

Unsettled at the thought, Sabine accepted the wine from him and took a sip, the memory of Fae magic sharp on her tongue. She replayed the story Malek had just shared in her mind. Perhaps Bane was right; truth was often written by the victors, and it probably wasn't as romantic as Malek's story suggested. But maybe there was an element of truth somewhere.

Malek looked down at Sabine. "I wasn't there, so I can only share with you what I've heard. That was the version of the story my grandmother told me. One day, I asked her if she missed her home and wanted to go back. She told me she didn't. My grandfather had even offered to send word to her family, letting them know she was alive and well, but she refused. She didn't think they would understand her decision to stay. It was better, she said, for them to think she had perished during the battle."

"Elis'andreia was correct," Balkin said, putting the parch-ment he'd been reviewing back in the box. "I did not know her personally, but I heard stories. Elis'andreia was skilled in nature magic and was able to communicate directly with the Silver Trees. It was by her blood and magic that one of the strongest rings of protective trees was grown and became sentient in the Silver Forest. They were her children. When the trees attacked the invading dragons, the dragons burned that area of the forest to the ground."

Sabine shook her head, her heart breaking for the loss of the forest. "I've never understood why they attacked the trees. They're only part of Faerie's defense, not designed for an offensive attack."

Balkin patted her shoulder in understanding. "It was a different time, my darling kitten. The magic of this world was being used by the gods to battle the dragons in the heavens, and very little was leftover for the creatures here trying to defend the world. The Fae were dying at an alarming rate and this world along with them. They needed the Silver Forest and the Beastpeople to help protect them from extinction."

"I think I'm missing something," Esmelle said with a frown. "Why would the dragons have focused on the Fae and the Silver Forest? It's such a small piece of territory. I thought their war was with the gods."

Sabine gave her a sad smile, recalling the lessons from her youth. "It was, but the Fae have always been the caretakers of this world. We were gifted with the magic of the gods, and as we nurtured this world, our power grew, as did that of the gods. Once, at the height of our power, the Silver Forests covered much of this continent and far beyond it. But as Balkin mentioned, the trees weren't always sentient. That was done out of necessity after the dragons began targeting our people to try to diminish the power of the gods. My people were forced to withdraw to a very small and more defensible position. There, they have remained—nurturing the heart of Faerie."

"A lot of the pixie clans died too," Blossom said as she darted over to grab another bunch of lavender flowers. She buried her nose in the petals and added, "When the forests and flowers died, we didn't have anywhere to go. Nothing would grow in the sand or without the Fae to give life to the soil. It was the Starving Times. We remember."

At the sight of Blossom's distress, Sabine held out her hand. Blossom landed on her palm, and Sabine sent a light wave of reassuring magic over the tiny pixie. It wasn't just the Fae who had suffered during the war. The effects had spread far and wide, blanketing large portions of the world and rendering some areas mostly barren. Even after the portal had been closed, the Fae were reluctant to venture far from Faerie. It was too dangerous, and their numbers were too few. The world had suffered as a result.

"I haven't heard it referred to as the Starving Times for many years. The pixie's correct though. That was why the demons and dwarves made an alliance with the Unseelie Fae," Bane said, reaching over to refill Sabine's wine glass. "We embraced their darker magics and allowed them refuge in our underground cities. The Unseelie were generous in sharing their magic with us, while the pretentious Seelie got a sunburn." He gave her a mocking courtly bow usually only seen in Faerie. "Unless they're called Sabine and deign to bring us into the light along with her."

Sabine's mouth twitched in a hint of a smile, and she shook her head in exasperation. "Behave."

Malek's brow furrowed. "I haven't heard most of this. I admit, information can be somewhat skewed depending on the source. My grandmother rarely spoke about the time she spent living with the Fae. She said it was too painful to remember."

Dax sneered. "Convenient you only remember the sentimental and romantic parts of the story, especially given your desire for Sabine to assist you." He put his mug on the table with a *clank* and gestured to Sabine. "Regardless of what you claim, your presence here and knowing Sabine's identity puts her in danger. And that, I will *not* tolerate."

Malek arched his brow. "No more a danger than consorting with demons."

Dax slapped his hand to his weapon. Sabine tensed and started to intervene, but Balkin moved in front of Dax.

"Enough," Balkin said, a trace of a growl in his voice. "I will speak with this dragon in private. Dax, you will escort the witch, the pixie, and your brother elsewhere until my business is concluded."

Dax's eyes flared to silver as he studied Malek. A wicked smile curved the corners of his mouth as though pleased at what Balkin's request might mean for the ship captain. Sabine frowned, but Malek didn't seem concerned. She didn't know why Balkin wanted to speak with him alone, nor did she know Malek well enough to be confident he wouldn't offend the Beastman. Even if she was still unsure about Malek, she didn't want him harmed.

Esmelle hesitated, glancing back and forth between them. Finally, she shrugged. "Right. I'm thinking this probably isn't the best place to be right now. Blossom, you want to come with me?"

Sabine nodded at the pixie. Blossom smiled shyly and dove back under the cover of the lavender plant. Esmelle picked up the pot and said, "We'll wait for you in the kitchen. I think Martha might have some honey cakes for Blossom."

Blossom trilled happily as Esmelle headed out of the room. Dax started to follow but paused, arching his brow at Bane who hadn't moved. Bane returned his wordless stare with a meaningful look. Dax chuckled and gave him a curt nod before heading for the door. Sabine frowned. It had been several years since they'd engaged in their wordless communication, and it usually indicated impending trouble.

"I don't follow your orders, Beastman," Bane said, crossing his arms over his chest. "My agreement is only with Sabine. If she stays, I will remain with her."

Sabine hesitated, glancing back and forth between Balkin and Bane. This had the potential to be very bad. Bane was usually much more levelheaded and controlled about things, but he was acting more like Dax. It wasn't entirely within his character.

Balkin narrowed his eyes on the demon. "You believe I'm not capable of protecting the daughter of my heart?"

"I believe your absence has affected her more than you want to admit. You left her here in this city and did not think she would form equally strong bonds with those who stayed by her side?"

"Bane," Sabine said quietly and placed her hand on his heated arm. Bane might be trying to protect her, but not at the expense of hurting Balkin. "Don't do this. I will not have you at odds with each other."

Bane placed his hand over hers, holding her to him. He leaned down and brushed his nose against hers. "I told you there would be consequences of your Calling, little one. You have trusted me with your safety not once, but more than thrice. I will not step aside and allow anyone to send me away from you, unless *you* request it or accompany me."

"Your demon is within his rights," Balkin said before she could argue with Bane or tell him to leave. Surprised, Sabine turned to face the Beastman who had protected her most of her life.

He walked over to her and pressed a kiss against her forehead. "It is difficult for me to relinquish control over your safety to another, but you have done what is necessary to survive here. I was unsure you would ever willingly gift a mark to either Dax or Bane, which was why I bound Dax to you. But your mark on Bane's skin indicates he's earned the right to be at your side."

Sabine fell silent, a sliver of suspicion entering her mind. Bane wasn't usually so overbearing, and Balkin could be sneaky when it suited him. Something else was going on under the surface.

Taking Balkin's clawed hands in hers, Sabine said, "You will always be my guardian, Balkin. Yours was the first face I remember, your claws protecting and caring for me. I trust you with my life, and that will never change. But I'm getting the impression you and Bane are purposely picking a fight with each other. Are you trying to manipulate me so I'll leave too?"

Balkin's gaze softened, his lips curving in a smile that showed a hint of his fangs. "For generations, I have served your family out of respect and duty, placing their protection and welfare above my own. From the moment you were first placed in my arms, I also began to serve out of love. I would ask, my darling kitten and child of my heart, that you allow me a moment of privacy with this dragon."

She turned toward Malek, who watched them with no small measure of curiosity. He didn't seem troubled or concerned over Balkin's request to speak with him privately, and she didn't have the impression Balkin meant him any harm.

After a long interval, she nodded and kissed Balkin's cheek. In the language of her birth, she said, "You will always be the father of my heart as well, Balkin Lioneyes."

His eyes filled with unspoken emotion, and he gave her a curt nod as she turned away. Taking Bane's arm, she headed out of the room. Bane closed the door behind them and led her down the hallway in the direction of the kitchen.

"I will not apologize for what I said to him," Bane said in a low voice.

"I didn't expect you would, but either one of you could have asked me to go," Sabine said with a sigh, her thoughts considering different possibilities about why Balkin wanted to speak with Malek.

Balkin couldn't order her to leave, since her rank surpassed his. The Beastpeople and even most of the Fae were sticklers for protocol and social niceties. Her experiences in Akros had stripped her of much of that. The learning curve upon arrival in the city had been steep. She'd been more than a little arrogant and self-assured. Dax and Bane had both delighted in teaching her the errors of her ways.

"You don't need to worry. He won't kill the dragon."

Sabine paused, turning to look up at Bane. "Then I was right about that being a ruse to get rid of me. Do you know why he wanted to speak with Malek alone?"

Bane inclined his head and continued walking. She glared at his retreating figure, knowing he was purposely being difficult so she would follow him.

Bane glanced at her over his shoulder with a teasing grin on his face. "You coming?"

"At least Balkin *tries* to give me the illusion he's listening to me," she grumbled but continued down the hall.

He slowed his footsteps until she caught up. "You've always known who and what I am, little one. If you strongly objected to our desire to give Balkin privacy with the dragon, you never would have agreed to leave that room."

She shrugged. "You think I'm foolish for wanting to trust Malek, don't you?"

Bane hesitated. "Not foolish, but it's not wise either. I know you miss your own kind, Sabine. The issues between Dax and myself have only made things more difficult for you.

Malek possesses powerful magic, and he knows some of the truth about you. I imagine that's very appealing."

Sabine didn't answer right away. Bane had always had a talent for cutting to the heart of the matter, a trait that had proven to make him an effective assassin. And one that was annoying in every other situation.

"You believe I'm looking to him as a possible replacement for what I've lost?"

"Haven't you?" he asked mildly, putting his hand on her back and leading her down the hall. "If you were still living amongst your people and surrounded by their magic, would you even consider opening your heart and memories to a dragon? Or a demon, for that matter?"

When she frowned, Bane continued, "You've marked both of us, little one. While mine is permanent, you've made repeated efforts to reapply Malek's marker. I've never known you to leave an unclaimed mark in place for so long, especially one that's most likely trivial in nature. You *want* that connection with him. That small trace of his magic filtering through your mark reminds you of home."

Sabine stopped walking and squeezed her eyes shut as his words crashed over her. "How long have you known?"

"I suspected when I drank of your shared wine," he said quietly. "It was confirmed when Dax told me how often you'd been reapplying Malek's debt marker. What agreement does it represent?"

Sabine blew out a breath, somewhat surprised Dax hadn't killed Malek when he'd learned what she'd done. "Nothing more than an intent to share dinner. I tried to tell myself I wanted to protect him from Dax. That was only part of the truth." Sabine lowered her gaze to stare at the cold, stone floor. "You're right. About all of it. Malek reminded me of everything I've lost. The first words he spoke to me were in

Fae and in an oath of no harm. It was as though he recognized me, even with the glamour."

Bane tipped her chin back so he could look into her eyes. "I know neither Dax nor I can give you what you truly need. We speak to the Unseelie magic in your heart, and that's only one aspect to you. I won't pretend to understand the rest of your desires, but I don't know if a dragon can either."

Sabine wrapped her hand around Bane's wrist. "You told Balkin everything, didn't you? That's why he wanted to speak to Malek alone?"

"If we cannot find an outlet for your Seelie magic, I fear we may lose you," Bane admitted, resting his forehead against hers. "Your powers hadn't fully developed when you left Faerie. Both aspects of your magic are still growing and evolving, and we don't have an Elder who can help harness your abilities by etching your skin. The pixies and Esmelle's garden are no longer enough to sustain you."

She frowned, unsure if the tattooed marks on her skin would be enough at this point. She could only pour so much of her magic into Esme's garden before people started to notice. Magic needed an outlet, and she'd been pretending to be human and repressing hers for far too long. "Balkin believes Malek might be able to temper my Seelie magic?"

Bane sighed. "I'm still of the mind the only tolerable dragon is a dead one. Dax agrees with that sentiment, but Balkin was intrigued by the possibility, especially when he learned how Malek was able to revive you with dragonfire. I suspect that's partly how Elis'andreia was able to remain living in the Sky Cities for so long."

Sabine's eyes widened, and she glanced back down the hallway. "Malek's grandmother would have been Seelie. The ability to grow or bring the Silver Trees to awareness is Seelie magic."

"Indeed," Bane said quietly, putting his hand on her back

again to lead her away. "Even if Malek can help offset the effects and hide you from the Fae, you must never forget his true identity. Bind him to you, if you must. But tread carefully, little one. I will see him dead and broken before I allow him to steal you away to the Sky Cities and out of our reach forever. On that, we're all in agreement."

Chapter Sixteen

The sound of voices and Esmelle's laughter could be heard as Sabine and Bane approached the kitchen. It immediately put a smile on her face, and she entered the room to find Esmelle sitting at the table with Dax and Javyn. Blossom was perched on the table in front of one of the largest honey cakes Sabine had ever seen. The look of complete rapture on the pixie's face was comical.

"You're going to get her sick," Sabine warned, trying to suppress a laugh.

"I won't get sick," Blossom said with her cheeks bulging. Although, it sounded more like, "Ah wah geh 'ick."

Esmelle laughed again. "Sabine's right. You really should consider taking either smaller bites or slowing down. Martha said that cake was meant to feed your whole family."

Blossom swallowed and wiped her mouth with the back of her hand. "Nope. They don't get cake. They were too scared of the demons to tell Sabine the truth. It's my cake now."

Sabine shook her head and walked over to the counter. Picking up a small saucer, she filled it with water and brought it over to the table for the pixie. "Pace yourself, Blossom. You can eat your fill and still have enough to take some to your family and the new pixie clan."

"Tried to pick flowers. Wrong moon. They don't get cake either," Blossom said and broke off another chunk of the honey cake. She dunked it into the water and shoved it into her mouth. Her cheeks bulged at the oversized bite again, and she started chewing.

Sabine sighed. It looked like she was going to have to deal with a sick pixie.

Dax grinned. "If the pixie's too sick to fly, I'm keeping her. I have an ale that will go quite nicely with the tart taste of pixies."

Blossom's eyes widened. She squeaked, causing cake crumbs to fly out of her mouth and over the table. She dove into Sabine's hair and up against her neck, trembling in fear.

"You're *not* eating Blossom," Sabine said as Blossom hugged her neck. "And you, Blossom, had better not be getting crumbs in my hair."

"Ahm nah," Blossom said, which Sabine guessed meant, "I'm not."

She rolled her eyes, not believing that for a minute.

Esmelle laughed again and leaned forward, tearing off a piece of the honey cake for herself. "Dax and I were taking bets over whether you and Bane would come out here together. Looks like I lost."

Dax leaned back in his chair, his expression smug. "Want to know what I won, Sabine?"

"Nope. I've had enough experience with your bets that I don't want to know the answer." She pointed at Esmelle.

"You should know better too. Dax doesn't bet on anything unless he knows he's going to win."

Javyn chuckled. "She knows you well."

Dax grinned and took another sip of his ale. Bane walked around the table and toward the window, staring out into the waning sunlight. Sabine frowned and approached him, curious about what had caught his attention. He tensed, grabbed her arm, and hauled her backward.

"City guards," he said quietly, jerking his head toward the window. "A lot of them. A few mercenaries too, based on their clothing. They're surrounding the tavern."

Without a word, Dax leapt across the table and peered out the window. "They're not any of mine. It's that damned councilman. I don't like the timing of this. They're hitting us right before the tavern is about to open for regular business."

Javyn's hand flew to the sword strapped to his waist. "Orders?"

Without turning, Dax said, "Bane, escort Sabine and Esmelle to the tunnels. I want them out of here. Javyn, clear the upper floors of the tavern. Tell Martha and Henry we've got company. They know what to do."

Javyn turned, his boots silent as he ran from the room.

Sabine frowned at Dax. He usually slept during the day in his room below the tavern. If they were doing this now, the councilman must have another mole inside Dax's organization. "Martha and Henry won't be able to stall them for long, Dax. If they're here during daylight hours and before your men arrive, they must know you're here without your usual support. I can seal the stairwell behind us, preventing them from searching it."

"Do it." Dax waved her toward the door. "Get her out of here, Bane. Quickly. It looks like they're almost in position."

Bane grabbed her arm, but she jerked away from him and snapped, "I am *not* sealing the stairwell without you behind it, Dax. The councilman is working with a magic user strong enough to create a lich ward."

Dax muttered a curse under his breath and stepped away from the window. "Fine. Let's go. We need to grab Balkin too."

Sabine nodded and ran back down the hallway toward the war room. Balkin and Malek looked up the moment she pushed open the door. Balkin's hand immediately flew to his weapon. He glanced over at Dax and ordered, "Report."

"At least six squads of city guards are moving into position around the tavern. We're leaving. Sabine will seal the tunnel to the stairway as soon as we're out. Javyn's evacuating the upper floors and taking everyone out through the secondary tunnels."

While Dax explained the plan, Sabine darted over to the table. Malek started gathering his papers and putting them back in the box. She grabbed the bag and snatched up the chalice, intending to dump it inside. Magic coiled around her arms and her skin began to glow. She hissed as her glamour began to falter, flashing her thorned tattoos. They didn't have time for this.

"Mistress?" Balkin questioned, taking a step toward her.

She ignored him, busy concentrating on the chalice and the layers of magic encircling it. Belatedly, she realized she should have used the bag to pick it up. The lich ward was gone, but the distant sound of drums pounded in her ears. Turning the chalice in her hands, the glow of the flames from the candlelight caught the facets of the gems embedded on the surface, almost hypnotizing her as the power moved across her skin.

A sudden realization hit her, staggering her in shock. The chalice *wanted* to be used. It was sentient, aware of the approaching danger. It had claimed her as worthy of possessing it. If she needed help defending her friends, the chalice offered its assistance. But like most Fae magic, this wasn't a gift. It demanded a sacrifice, a binding of sorts, for it to be hers. She swallowed, unable to tear her eyes away from it.

"Sabine?" Malek asked, approaching her quietly. "Can you release it?"

Daughter. Accept this gift. You will be blessed.

"It knows me," she whispered, shocked to her core at the familiar voice. Dimly, she was aware she'd spoken in Fae, the same language it had used when speaking to her. The chalice warmed in her hand, but it didn't burn her. Its magical tendrils continued moving upward along her skin, exploring and tasting her magic. She closed her eyes, falling into the magic and exploring it in the same way it was doing to her.

Peace, unlike anything she'd known outside of Faerie, filled her as the remaining vestiges of her glamour fall away. A sacrifice was due. A demand for recognition of her magic and blood. Reaching down, she withdrew her knife and sliced open her palm. Blood, heady with the scent of her magic, welled to the surface and dripped from the wound. Her hand pressed over the top of the chalice, allowing the dark red liquid to spill into it.

Power infused her words as she spoke the oath whispered to her by the chalice. "I claim you, by blood and magic. In tribute to the gods and the last sacrifice of the goddess Lachlina, I swear by all I am and the last of the magic of this world to uphold my family's oath in defense from those who would see this world destroyed."

The chalice began to glow brighter and sharper until it became nearly blinding. It lifted from her hand, hovering in the air overhead, heating her blood within it. The sound of drums pounded in her temples, beating a staccato rhythm in time with her heartbeat.

As I will it, the pact is sealed.

Light and magic exploded from the chalice, dropping Sabine to her knees. Her knife clattered to the ground, and she took a staggered breath as the power of the chalice settled over her like a thick blanket. It raced up her arms and down the rest of her body, the marks on her arms glowing and pulsing in time with her heartbeat and the drums. She lowered her head, her partially unbound silvered hair falling over her face.

Pain. Liquid fire. It seared over her skin, forming a new mark. An image of the chalice seared into the flesh on the inside of her wrist, glowing in the same way of her existing marks. She gritted her teeth from the pain, accepting this binding and the power it represented. Memories, sharp and bitter, flooded her mind as the hours of the Elders' markings became alive again. It was as though the magic of the chalice was using those years of pain to solidify this binding.

When it finished, only the faint pulse of the new mark on her skin remained. Sabine took a shaky breath and lifted her gaze to stare at the chalice now resting at the edge of the table. It was only a symbol, a vessel designed to contain the source of power capable of sealing the portal closed. The magic of the chalice was now part of her, as evidenced by the new mark on her skin. Even if she was no longer touching it, she could draw upon its strength. For all intents and purposes, *she* was now the chalice.

Picking up her fallen weapon, she slid it back in its sheath and pushed herself up from the ground. Her wound was healed. The blood that had coated the inside of the chalice was also gone, consumed by the magic of the ancient artifact. She picked up the chalice, staring at it in wonder. The mark on her wrist pulsed once, and the chalice warmed in her hand before it cooled again. It had gifted her with some unknown form of magic, but it now lay dormant in her hands. The chalice was still sentient, but it would be patient to wait until she was willing to use it.

She slid it into the velvet bag and then turned, staring at the room in shock. Whatever magic had been unleashed had rolled the entire room, and everyone was struggling to shake off the effects. Even Malek had collapsed to the ground and was shaking his head as though in a daze. Blossom flew out from underneath the table, her eyes wide.

"The goddess told me you're going to restore the balance!"

Sabine frowned at the pixie and tied the bag containing the chalice to her belt. Before she could respond, a loud crash sounded somewhere close. "Quickly, we need to get out of here. They're almost here."

Leaning down, she gripped Balkin's clawed hand and pulled him to his feet. He blinked his golden eyes at her and immediately turned to Esmelle, helping her get to her feet.

Sabine dropped down beside Malek. "Can you stand?"

He nodded and pushed up from the ground, glancing down at the bag containing the chalice. "Are you all right? What did it do to you?"

"Nothing that wasn't required," she said, turning to help Bane while Balkin assisted Dax.

"Your glamour," Bane managed, shaking off the worst of the effects.

She glanced down at her skin glowing with power and the thorned tattoos winding up her arms. Focusing inwardly, she fumbled, trying to reapply her glamour, but it slid away before she could pin it in place.

"The goddess doesn't think you need to hide anymore," Blossom said, fluttering in front of her.

Sabine scowled with impatience and snapped, "With respect to the goddess, she doesn't know the Wild Hunt is searching for me and wants me dead, nor does she know we have enemies approaching. I *cannot* risk being recognized here."

At her words, her glamour settled across her skin and fixed itself in place.

Blossom shrugged. "She says you can kill them. They're human. They don't belong in our world."

"I will *not* kill the humans," Sabine said, picking up the potted plant of lavender Esme had dropped. "I've been tasked with protecting this world, and they've become part of it."

"I don't think she likes that, but she will trust your judgment," Blossom said and waited until Sabine pushed open the door.

Sabine ignored the pixie and everyone else, placing the potted plant on the floor in the hallway. She'd initially planned to seal the entry to the stairs, but she wasn't sure what else Dax had hidden on this level. Turning toward Esmelle who had followed her, she asked, "Are you strong enough to combine magic with me?"

Esmelle nodded and held out her hand. Sabine took it and accepted the nature magic Esmelle sent toward her. Infusing it with her power, Sabine grew the lavender plant until the size had overshadowed the entire hallway. She could have done it on her own, but the chalice had left her somewhat shaken. Releasing Esme's hand, she withdrew her knife, cut her fingertip, and squeezed a drop of her blood onto the plant.

"*Crescero*," she whispered, and the plant shimmered. It solidified, becoming more substantial, and took on the appearance of a stone wall. She cut into another finger and etched a locking rune into the wall. It flared with a greenish light and dimmed as the magic settled into place.

"To me," she ordered Blossom, and the pixie dove into her hair again. Balkin nodded at her and took up the rear as she followed Dax down the hallway. They descended the stairs, and she turned as the door closed behind them. Sabine repeated the action she'd taken upstairs, cutting into her finger and tracing another rune into the door. It flared with a red glow, sealing it with a death curse, and Sabine turned away. No one except those who knew the appropriate rune could pass this doorway. Only a handful of people, including Javyn, could open it.

"You stole the moon again," Blossom whispered in her ear. "Should we tell Balkin?"

Sabine stumbled, her hand hitting the wall as she caught herself before she fell. "What? The sun hasn't set yet. There's no moon."

Blossom giggled as though she'd said something incredibly funny. "The moon is always there. You just can't see it. But you stole the moon when you accepted the chalice."

Balkin frowned at her. "What's wrong?"

"The moon," she whispered, suddenly terrified about what this meant. "Blossom said it disappeared when I claimed the chalice. I didn't realize—"

Balkin muttered a curse, his hand flying to his weapon. "The Wild Hunt comes."

Malek's gaze flew to her and then settled on Blossom. "Are you sure?"

Blossom nodded. "Sabine called it down with blood and magic. Her magic likes the moon. It obeys her."

"Balkin," Sabine whispered, fear stealing her strength.

He grabbed her arm and pulled her down the tunnel. "Focus, my kitten. The battle is not lost yet. As long as you are alive, we keep fighting. *Now move.*"

Power infused his last words, and she nodded. Pushing aside her fear, she ran down the tunnel toward the sewers and closer to their escape. She'd originally planned to take them to the crypts, but that was no longer an option. If she'd managed to alert the Wild Hunt to her location, she wasn't about to bring danger upon the children she'd spent the last several years protecting.

Nowhere in the city would be completely safe, but they needed to go *somewhere*. Esmelle's shop was out. The crypt wasn't an option.

"Take us to my building on the south end of town," Bane said behind her.

She nodded. They could hole up in Bane's lair temporarily, but he was being targeted too. The stolen ledger she'd found in Terrance's home had been proof of that. Still, it was their best option until they figured out an alternative. Bane's men were used to dealing in death.

At the entrance to the sewers, Sabine stopped and faced the stone wall. Her knife was still in her hand, and she used it to cut another finger. Using her blood, she traced another rune in the wall and pushed her magic outward. The rune began to glow red and the wall shifted, disappearing from sight. She motioned for everyone to follow her.

"Walk in my footsteps," she ordered, sending some of her magic into the floor and causing it to glow beneath her steps to light their path. The magic was temporary, no more than a small amount of illumination to guide her companions.

She felt more than heard the door seal shut behind Balkin after everyone had passed through. The magic that guided her wasn't something she'd ever been able to fully explain. It wasn't her power, but rather the magic of the gods who had been the founders of this city. She was moving all of them through space and time, somewhere outside the normal realm that couldn't be accessed by any mundane means. Unfortunately, they couldn't linger. If they stopped, they risked being trapped here forever.

Only Bane had ever been able to move within this space, but only through the mark she'd gifted him. It was part of the magic of the gods before they'd been exiled. Discovering the secrets of the city had been an accident, but she'd quickly realized the potential benefits and decided to use it for her own purposes.

Sabine paused outside another wall, some innate part of her *knowing* this was the correct location. It had taken more than a year to teach Bane how to listen to the whispers of the darkness so he could navigate these passages. Toby had picked it up within weeks. She'd assigned him the task of gatekeeper, a job he was intensely proud to hold. Toby kept watch in the temple area and behind the burial stones, guiding the newer children into the safety of the crypts. She suspected he'd been able to learn it so easily because she'd given much of her own magic when she'd saved his life more than a year ago.

Sabine cut into another finger, recognizing she would need to rest soon. The power required to move this many people through space and time was quickly wearing upon her. If the Wild Hunt was approaching, she needed to conserve her strength, but she needed to get everyone to safety first.

Tracing another rune into the wall, the wall shimmered and fell away. Sabine entered a room with stone walls, recognizing they were once again back within the confines of Akros's reality. She leaned against the wall, trying to catch her breath as everyone filed through. The wall closed behind Balkin, but it was Malek who turned to her first and asked, "You're performing major magic again. Are you all right?"

"Just tired, but I'll recover soon enough." She pushed away from the wall.

Bane had taken the lead, recognizing the basement as part of the building he owned. He ran up the stairs with everyone following behind him. Balkin held out his hand toward her, and she accepted the strength he offered, infusing some of his power with hers. The magic of the Beastpeople was complementary, especially when they were sworn to serve a particular family. Sabine gave him a nod to indicate it was enough. He released her hand, waiting for her to head up the stairs.

Bane shouted orders to Evo and some of his men, who were busy equipping weapons and planning how they'd eliminate the city guards surrounding the tavern. Sabine walked into the large dining hall and slumped down in a chair, taking the opportunity to catch her breath.

Blossom scooted close to her ear and said, "The goddess says the city is on fire."

"What?" she managed, pushing herself back out of the chair. Sabine rushed toward the window and gasped. The sky had prematurely darkened to the deepest clutches of night, with neither the moon nor the sun anywhere in sight. Magic prickled along her skin, warning the darkness consuming the city wasn't natural in design. A golden glow rose from some distant part of the city, in the direction of the tavern.

"No," she whispered, pressing her palm against the window.

Malek approached her. "What is it?"

"The city's on fire. I don't… I'm not sure…" Sabine swallowed, uncertain and confused. The magic she'd sensed couldn't be from that glow. Could it? Turning to the pixie, she asked, "Blossom? Did the goddess tell you who is burning the city?"

Malek's gaze sharpened on Blossom. "Pixies can speak to the gods?"

Blossom ignored him and fluttered out of her hair to stare out the window. "She says it's the humans. But the Wild Hunt comes too. She can help you kill the humans, but she doesn't have enough stored magic yet to destroy the Hunt."

Sabine frowned. This goddess was a little too eager to kill off the humans. Lachlina was the goddess who had betrayed the other gods to provide information on how to close the portal. If her essence had been trapped within the chalice for centuries and then buried in the catacombs, she probably didn't realize how much the world had changed. That would be something to consider later.

Esmelle's face paled as she watched the golden glow. "They set the tavern on fire to flush everyone out, but the buildings there are too close together. Those idiots are going to destroy the city."

"Probably," Dax agreed, staring out the window with barely restrained fury. "If the tavern goes, the entire neighborhood will go with it. I've got enough magical objects in my vault to level that entire part of the city."

"My shop," Esmelle whispered, horror on her face.

Sabine swallowed. "Blossom, you need to get to your family and tell them to escape. They're too close to the flames."

Blossom landed on her shoulder and leaned against her. "It's okay. They know. The goddess said she'll tell Barley. He'll get the pixies out of the city. They'll be okay. I'm supposed to stay with you. The Hunt is searching for you."

She barely managed to nod, turning to look at Malek whose expression had hardened as he stared at the flames on the horizon. "The fire is in the direction of the docks. If the wind shifts, it'll catch the entire wharf."

"You should warn your crew and move your ship," Sabine said, searching the skies for any signs of the Wild Hunt.

Malek shook his head. "I'm not leaving you. If you come with me, I can get you and your friends safely out of the city."

"What?"

He captured her hand and squeezed it. "Come with me, Sabine. I can protect you and help mask your presence from the Wild Hunt. At the very least, I can give you space to decide your next move. You can't stay here if they're hunting you."

Pulling away from him, she shook her head. Dax moved between them and glared at Malek. "Back off, dragon. She's not yours."

"Nor is she yours," Malek said, his eyes narrowing on Dax.

Dax's eyes turned silver, and Malek's hand reached up to grasp the medallion around his neck. With a hard pull, Malek yanked it off and dragon power flooded the room. Sabine gasped, backing away from both of them. The power output of both men clashed as a sharp mixture of sulfur and burning embers filled the air. The Beastman moved protectively in front of her, claws extended and crouching in a battle stance.

"Seriously?" Esmelle snapped, glaring at all of them. "You're going to pull this nonsense now? We're under siege here. Pull your heads out of your asses and focus, people. We don't need to be fighting amongst ourselves."

A hysterical laugh bubbled out of Sabine, and she clamped a hand over her mouth. The Wild Hunt was approaching, the city was on fire, and a demon and a dragon were facing each other down and trying to claim her for themselves. And a witch—a *human*—was the only one with a shred of common sense among them.

"Esme's right," Sabine managed, throwing a grateful look toward her friend. "We don't have time for this. Bane's people might be able to take out the city guards, but they can't stop the Wild Hunt and the city is still on fire. Whatever we're going to do, we need to figure it out soon."

"Dax'than Versed, son of Kal'thorz," Balkin said, his voice infused with power, "I call your life debt due."

Dax's silver eyes turned to Balkin. The demon dropped to his knees in front of Balkin and lowered his head. "It will be done."

Fear, cold and insidious, slithered across Sabine's skin. If Balkin was calling Dax's debt due, that meant Dax was preparing to sacrifice himself. "Balkin, no. You can't do this. I never agreed to this."

Balkin's jaw clenched, and he didn't respond. Dax rose to his feet, his eyes still silver, and he stalked toward her. Without a word, he yanked her close and pressed his lips against hers. She tried to struggle, but the demon held her tightly, siphoning off her Unseelie magic through the debt marker Balkin had accepted when she was born. The connection between the Beastman and Sabine flared to life as magic rushed outward through it and into Dax. Balkin was the bridge connecting them, and he was stealing part of her essence.

Malek rushed toward them, but Balkin hauled him backward and whispered something she couldn't hear.

Tears streamed down her cheeks, blinding her. Sabine's hands clawed at the demon, trying to scratch or touch any part of Dax's skin to blast him with her magic. He took everything she threw at him, stealing it for himself and bundling her raw power with his. With Balkin's connection active, she couldn't harm him. Panic, potent and staggering, filled her as she continued to fight him, desperate not to give in.

She reached downward, fumbling for her weapon, but someone yanked it out of her grasp before she could use it. Her mind screamed, knowing what they were trying to do. This shouldn't be possible. Magic was supposed to be a gift. But this had always been part of Balkin's plan, a last resort if his attempts at hiding her should ever fail.

After what felt like an eternity, Dax pulled away, swaying from the rush of her power that now filled him. Dizziness swept over her and darkness crept into the corners of her vision. She felt... empty. The chalice at her waist warmed and pulsed in time with the new mark it had placed on her wrist. The worst of the effects passed, stabilizing her. She'd been weakened. Significantly.

Sabine trembled, her teeth chattering as she stared up at Dax. She'd never begged him for anything, but she was willing to do so now. "Please, Dax. Don't do this. I don't want to lose you."

He pressed his forehead against hers and murmured, "This has always been the plan. Did you think it was a coincidence I swore to serve you through Balkin? I would have died years ago if it hadn't been for this pact. You allowed me a chance to live."

She reached up to cup his face. "This isn't your sacrifice to make. Give me back my magic, Dax. I know you don't want to die. It doesn't have to be like this."

"Dax, you must go now," Balkin said, his voice colder than she'd heard in a long time. "The magic won't fool them for long."

Dax gave him a curt nod and pressed a brief kiss against her lips. He winked at her and said, "If I live through this, I'm locking you in my room for a week."

"Dax!" she yelled, reaching for him as he pulled away.

Bane appeared suddenly. He wrapped his arm around her and hauled her against him. Nuzzling her neck, he said, "Calm yourself, Sabine. This must be done."

She shook her head, blinking back tears as Esmelle approached Dax. The sharp and aromatic scent of crushed herbs filled the room, the telltale sign of nature magic at work. Esmelle waved her hands, and Dax's image flickered and shifted, changing the demon's appearance to one almost identical to Sabine's. This was the reason Esmelle had helped craft her human illusion. It wasn't just so Sabine could hide amongst the humans. It was also so the witch could determine how to replicate it.

"Esme, please," she begged. "Don't do this."

Esmelle squeezed her eyes shut. "I'm sorry, Sabine. We all knew this would happen one day, and we prepared for this eventuality. We couldn't risk telling you. We knew you would never agree."

Sparing her one last glance, Dax drew his weapons and ran from the room, a mirrored image of her human form. A choked sob broke out of her, and she slumped against Bane. His arms tightened around her in reassurance and to restrain her.

Balkin turned to Malek. "You made a blood oath to protect Sabine from harm. The final part is yours."

Malek hesitated. He held her gaze, searching her expression. "Sabine, I'm—"

"No," she whispered, knowing what was coming and the real reason Balkin had wanted to speak with Malek alone. "You don't owe Balkin anything. There is no debt between you two. There is no gift he can offer that's greater than what I can provide."

Balkin's expression became thunderous. She ignored him, focused on the dragon who had intrigued her from the first moment they'd met.

"The chalice is fused to me and my will, Malek. If you try to take my Seelie magic through my mark, I will *never* help you find the remaining artifacts. I swear, by blood and magic, I will spend the rest of my life doing everything within my power to end you and the rest of the dragons. Or I can be your ally. The choice is yours."

Dimly, she recalled the seer's warning. *"A battle on stone streets. The moon fell into darkness. An ancient iron blade forged in dragonfire. Death. Plots within plots. A crossroads and a choice."*

This must be the crossroads and choice Usagi had talked about. But it wasn't hers to make. It was Malek's decision whether to embrace her as friend or foe. The air in the room took on a strange weight as though even the universe held its breath while it awaited Malek's decision.

Malek froze, searching her expression for a long time. After what felt an eternity, he shook his head. "I refuse. I won't betray you nor will I force this upon you, Sabine. You have nothing to fear from me. I will be your ally, if you're willing."

Relief flooded through her. She nodded in acceptance of his vow. Of all the likely places to find a potential ally, a dragon was the only one able or willing to support her wishes and stand against the Beastman.

Balkin's jaw clenched as he approached her. Reaching out his hand, he cupped her face. "Almost a millennium ago, I swore an oath to protect your family—even from themselves. I will not be forsworn."

Sabine held Balkin's gaze and hissed, "*Separare.*"

Balkin flinched and jerked his hand away from her as though burned. "Our bond is not so easily broken, my darling kitten. I will take your magic and protect you by force, if necessary."

Her heart clenched, knowing he would do what he promised. Balkin still harbored guilt for not being there to protect her mother, but no one could have predicted the depths of her father's treachery. It didn't matter what she said or did. Balkin was determined to save her, even at the expense of everyone she held dear. She wouldn't allow it.

Sabine closed her eyes, feeling the weight of the chalice at her side. Siphoning the power of the goddess into herself, she expelled it in a shocking blast, scattering everyone away from her. They collapsed, and she darted out of the room in the same direction Dax had gone. She had only seconds until they recovered and started hunting her.

She ran into what appeared to be a large gathering room. It was empty, with abandoned weapon containers and sharpening stones scattered everywhere. She could hear noises from downstairs, indicating everyone was already recovering from the magical blast. Sabine pushed open door after door, trying to find the exit. Only having been inside a few times when she'd visited Bane, Sabine didn't know the layout of the building.

After what seemed like an eternity, she located the exit and stumbled out onto the street. The sky was cloaked in inky darkness, the moon nowhere to be found. The streets were also empty, as though potential violence hung heavily in the air and acted as a deterrent for anyone considering walking the city streets.

Blossom landed on her shoulder. "I don't think that was a good idea, Sabine. Balkin's really mad."

Sabine didn't respond, too busy staring at the golden glow on the western side of the city. It was much larger than it had been, indicating the fire was spreading. Scanning the sky again, she caught sight of what appeared to be an approaching storm far off in the distance. It was little more than a flicker of silver amongst the clouds to the east and in the direction of Faerie. She inhaled sharply, recognizing it as wild magic. It was true. The Wild Hunt was stalking her once again, only this time, it would only be satisfied when she and the magic sustaining her was destroyed.

Pushing aside her fears, she ran toward the direction of the fire. Dax would have gone to help Bane's people protect his territory, trying to draw the Wild Hunt toward him in his magical illusion. She knew he intended to try to use the wild magic to take out some of the city guards and mercenaries threatening his people. Dax had always been practical when it came to killing his enemies.

Abandoning all pretense of being human, Sabine leapt over a stone wall, using the momentum as a springboard to push herself up to the roof. Her foot landed awkwardly, but she ignored the sharp pain and continued running across the rooftops.

Blossom had fluttered off her shoulder at some point, but Sabine could sense the pixie's magic behind her. Jumping across the space between two buildings, Sabine slipped, forcing her body into a roll to prevent injury. Reaching outward, her fingers caught the edge of the roof before she fell over the side. Her breath caught in her throat, and she swung her leg back up and onto the roof.

The dark clouds of the Wild Hunt were approaching faster than she'd dreamed possible. Lightning flashed, and she could make out the faint outline of individual figures. Tentacles and hooves were visible for a split second before the darkness swallowed them again.

The seer's warning about the moon's disappearance came to mind. Sabine may have alerted the magic of Faerie when she tapped into the power of the chalice, but it was the Wild Hunt who was tapping into the power of the moon now.

The Wild Hunt was fueled by the magic of the darkness and moonlight—Unseelie power—the same kind Dax had stolen from her. But neither her brother nor her father could summon the Wild Hunt using Unseelie magic. It was a power they couldn't access, gifted to her through her mother's bloodline. They would be using Seelie magic, the same power that still filled her and that Dax had never been able to touch. That was the link the Wild Hunt was following, and she was still in full possession of her Seelie magic.

They were all fools, most of all Balkin. He'd forced Dax to steal her magic for no reason, and his miscalculation might actually get her killed.

Sabine inhaled sharply, using the momentum to push herself upright and run. This time, she ran back toward Bane's lair and everyone she'd left behind. Dax would be safe enough, provided he didn't do something stupid to get himself killed fighting the city guards. She wasn't too concerned. Fueled by her Unseelie magic, Dax would fight like a… well, like a demon. Sabine almost snorted, but she barely had enough air left in her lungs to breathe.

Jumping across another chasm, Sabine dropped to the next building and pushed up off the clay tiles. Part of her was surprised she was still upright. Normally, when Dax took her magic—

Sabine staggered to a full stop, almost collapsing as she tried to catch her breath. She should be much weaker with only half of her magic fueling her. The first time she'd touched the chalice, it had nearly stripped her magic to the point of almost killing her. This time, after losing most of her Unseelie power, she was still able to race across the rooftops.

Sabine rubbed the sharp pain in her side from running too hard, but it was a physical ailment, not a magical one. Lightning flashed in the distance, and thunder followed a few seconds later. Only this thunder had the same cadence as the hooves from Faerie mounts, the sound that heralded the Hunt's imminent arrival.

She shook her head, lowering her chin and running again. The chalice had done something to her. Either that, or it was Malek's dragonfire. Those were the only two explanations, but she didn't have time to evaluate. She had to get to—

A roar and a huge set of wings shot up from the ground in front of the rooftop she was on. Sabine stumbled in shock. She fell backward, sliding toward the edge of the roof. A scream ripped out of her, and she scrambled, trying to find purchase to stop her rapid descent. Hitting the edge of the roof, she started to fall, barely catching herself before tumbling to the ground. The momentum was enough to slam her against the adjacent wall, forcing a strangled cry from her throat.

A clawed hand wrapped around her wrist and hauled her

onto the roof. She blinked up at Balkin, and the Beastman dropped down beside her. He wrapped her in his embrace, and she held on, burying her face against his pelt. Despite their differences, Balkin had always been there for her. Once again, he'd come to her rescue.

Huge wings flapped overhead and a streak of fire lit up the sky, offering either a warning or challenge. Sabine stared and shook her head in disbelief.

"Balkin," she whispered, part of her hoping she was dreaming.

He leaned back, scanning her up and down. "Are you unhurt, mistress?"

She opened her mouth and then closed it. A hysterical laugh bubbled out of her. "He really *is* a dragon. I almost slept with a dragon!"

Blossom landed on her shoulder. "I *knew* you were going to take him as a lover!"

Sabine jerked her head and frowned at the pixie. When Blossom grinned at her, she shook her head and looked up at the sky again. The Wild Hunt would be here any moment, and her Seelie magic was a beacon in the storm calling them toward her. Despite the approaching danger, it was next to impossible to tear her gaze away from the enormous creature from legend.

It was huge, its wingspan more expansive than the width of the tavern and Esmelle's shop combined. The dragon's skin appeared leathery, its darker colors blending against the night sky. It moved with an undeniable grace, flapping its wings as it soared above the city. Despite the fear the dragon evoked, Sabine had to admit the creature was beautiful. The dragon screamed, fire pouring forth from its throat and lighting up the sky.

Sabine shook her head. Malek must be trying to distract the Wild Hunt to try to protect her. She bit her lip, doubtful even a dragon as large and powerful as Malek could stand against wild Fae magic. She just hoped the sight of a dragon might help tip the battle near the tavern in Dax's favor. She doubted the city guards or mercenaries would stick around for long with the threat of a dragon hovering in the skies.

"You never should have asked Malek to steal my magic," Sabine said to Balkin. "The Wild Hunt won't confuse Malek's dragonfire with my power. I don't believe one dragon could ever stand against the Hunt, not even one as fearsome as Malek."

"No, but he *will* serve as a distraction. I'm assuming Bane told you some of my plans, despite my orders. You surprise me, Sabin'theoria. You somehow managed to bind two demons and a witch far better than I expected." Balkin continued staring overhead at Malek in dragon form as he soared over the city. "Now it appears my darling kitten has charmed a dragon—one who is trying to draw on your Seelie power through your mark and fuel it with his dragonfire."

She frowned and narrowed her eyes on the dragon. He could try to use her magic, but only trace amounts were able to slip through. "It won't be enough, and your suggestion may end up getting Malek killed."

Balkin patted her shoulder. "You will rule the Seelie and Unseelie as your mother planned, should you manage to harden your heart and grow sharper claws. Your mother would be pleased to know her machinations are finally bearing fruit."

"I'm *not* my mother," Sabine snapped. "I will not use and discard those I trust and consider friends. You never should have demanded such from them. Dax stole my Unseelie magic, but the Wild Hunt was summoned with Seelie magic. That's what it's using to track me."

"I know," he agreed with a sly grin. "Now your allies

know the lengths you'll go to protect them, even at risk to yourself."

"You manipulative bastard," she whispered, staring at him in shock. "People are going to die because you're still playing politics."

Balkin's golden lion eyes began to glow with something akin to satisfaction. "Hold tight to that anger and allow it to strengthen your resolve, my darling kitten. If your mother had managed to bind her allies tighter through something other than just fear, perhaps she would have survived your father's treachery. I won't see the same happen to you, Sabin'theoria. You *will* live. And I'll see you combine both thrones to rule all of Faerie as you were meant to do."

Sabine stilled. A thousand retorts fluttered through her mind. Lightning flashed overhead and a hot raindrop splashed on her face. Sabine wiped it off, the dark-red color of fresh blood a sharp contrast against her pale, glowing skin. Sabine inhaled sharply, catching the scent of night-blooming flowers. It wasn't rain. It was her blood, or rather her family's blood. Her skin began to glow, and the tattoos entwining her arms pulsed with power to the rhythm of her heartbeat. Overhead, the lightning began flashing in the same pattern, faster and faster as her magic and blood called to the creatures of the dark.

It was true.

Her brother had summoned the Wild Hunt, using their shared blood and magic to unleash it. The last shred of hope about her brother's innocence shattered. He wanted her dead.

Balkin stared at the droplet, his mouth turning grim. "We are out of time. You must find an outlet for your Seelie magic. Go. Now."

Sabine turned and ran. The enormous dragon overhead roared, the sound piercing the night. Another streak of dragonfire lit up the sky, illuminating the creatures of nightmares that lurked in the darkness. It figured it was her Seelie magic, the magic of the light, that was now calling to the creatures of the dark. In Sabine's experience, the most terrible monsters weren't always the ones confined to the dark. Her only living family was proof of that.

Jumping across the rooftop, Sabine missed the edge and rolled again. This time, she caught herself before Balkin did, although she heard him a handful of steps behind her. Somewhere nearby and below her, she could feel Bane rapidly approaching. Dropping onto a balcony, she grabbed the edge of a trellis and slid to the ground.

The thundering in the air was almost deafening. It sounded as though some of the Faerie mounts had landed and were now racing through the city streets. Sabine ran toward the oldest section of the city. She was leading the Wild Hunt closer than she wanted to where the children were hiding in the crypt, but she didn't have a choice. There was only one possibility that might save everyone, and the rapidly approaching hooves warned she wouldn't have enough time to make it out of the city.

She ran down empty streets in the direction of the temple. The magic of the Wild Hunt was such that ordinary people, those not drawn into the violence of the night, obeyed the whispers of the darkness encouraging them to stay inside and hide. They were the same whispers a child hears in their nightmares—they were all part of the Wild Hunt.

Sabine turned a corner, spotting the temple ahead. Malek dove toward the temple and then upward, as though trying to steer the Hunt away from the children. Sabine blinked away the emotion gathering in her eyes. She'd sorely misjudged a dragon, believing the stories she'd grown up hearing. Malek was once again proving to her with actions and words who he truly was. She should have known better. She wasn't what people believed of the Fae either.

Leaping over the fence that led into the temple, she darted across the grass and toward the burial stones. Toby stood there, staring overhead with an expression of shock and petrifying terror. The Wild Hunt could easily steal someone's will if they weren't strong enough to stand against it. She would *not* allow him to die. Racing up to him, she wrapped her arm around him and yanked him against her body. Her shoulder slammed against the wall. Withdrawing her knife, she sliced the palm of her hand and hastily etched a rune.

The wall dissolved, and she shoved Toby inside, resealing the wall behind him with a death rune. The children knew how to deactivate it, but they'd know not to risk it until it was safe. Spinning around, the sight of some of Faerie's most fearsome creatures raced toward her. Horses, with coats the color of midnight and manes of fire, stampeded in her direction. The riders, with their billowing dark wings, whipped through the air as the specters of the night hunted her. Tentacles, silver and sinewy, peeked out from beneath their robes, tasting the air in search of her magic.

The horses and riders were equally beautiful and terrible, nearly cruel in their ability to beguile anyone who witnessed their awesome power. Few people ever survived laying their eyes on them, and this wasn't the first time she'd faced them down.

"Now, Sabin'theoria! Or all is lost!" Balkin shouted over the sound of their thundering hooves.

Sabine slapped her hand against the ground, the blood from the cut on her palm rushing to meet the rich soil. The magic of the gods lapped against her in this place of power, and she fortified her strength with it. Shoving her Seelie magic into the ground, she screamed as it poured out of her.

The ground trembled as seeds and plants sprouted to life and shot up to impossible heights. Flowers exploded in a kaleidoscope of colors, their heady perfume filling the air. The trees shot upward, turning their limbs toward her, reaching and stretching as though they were trying to touch the sun.

It still wasn't enough. Sabine cut her other hand and placed her palm against the ground. The Wild Hunt had slowed, but they still approached. Sabine closed her eyes, pouring everything she was into the earth. The soil accepted all of it, eager for what she offered. It had been far too long since the magic of the gods had touched this place, but it still recognized her. It was *hungry*.

When the last vestiges of her strength and magic left her, she slumped, falling onto the ground. Balkin swept her into his arms, racing away from the temple and the enormous forest she'd brought to life in the middle of the city. A thunderous blast filled the air as her forest caught on fire.

Sabine screamed.

Pain unlike anything she'd ever felt ripped through her as the Wild Hunt began destroying her creation and magic. The riders cut down the trees and plants, the fiery manes of the horses burning away any trace of the magic that had been used to fuel the forest's birth.

A hooded rider skidded to a halt in front of her and Balkin. His mount pranced in place, tossing its head angrily as the rider gripped the reins with skeletal hands. He turned his glowing red eyes upon her, the rider's physical appearance bearing more of a resemblance to the demons than to the Fae.

"He seeks the death of your magic."

The mental voice was like velvet, wrapping around her mind and exploring her essence. Sabine managed to take a jagged breath, the pain from the destruction of her forest making it difficult to focus. Balkin opened his mouth to speak, but she pressed her hand against his chest to stop him. This was more than a simple rider. The Huntsman was the spokesman for the Wild Hunt and the leader in charge of pursuing its quarry. She couldn't risk Balkin speaking for her this time.

She inclined her head in acknowledgment of his words, wishing she had the power to stand on her own. Balkin was still carrying her, his arms tightening uncomfortably around her. The Huntsman stared at her for a long time, not moving. Waiting.

The chalice at her side warmed, and the mark on her wrist flared. She inhaled sharply as the goddess's power flowed through her. It cradled the tiny embers of her Seelie and Unseelie magic that were nearly extinguished, wrapping them in a protective coating. Instinctively, Sabine knew the chalice was trying to hide her presence from the Wild Hunt so it might fulfill its pact without killing her. But the magic wouldn't last. She needed to run.

Little goddess. We see *you. The magic you offer shall be sacrificed, fulfilling our bargain with the young prince. We eagerly await the return of our one true queen.*

With those words, the Huntsman bowed his head and withdrew from her mind. Large black wings erupted from the rider's back and his mount reared. Pushing up from the ground, the rider and mount raced toward the temple.

"Go. The chalice is trying to hide my remaining magic, but it won't last," she whispered to Balkin, and he took off, running down the street with her in his arms.

Balkin stopped in an alley and laid her on the ground. "Hurry. We have to get her out of here before her Seelie magic returns. She managed to buy us a few minutes, but our subterfuge won't last."

Sabine was dimly aware of Esmelle and Bane dropping to

the ground beside her. Bane lifted each of her hands, his power wrapping around her and healing her wounds. Sabine whimpered, still feeling the life of the garden dying but unable to do anything to stop it. The pain in her hands was insignificant compared to the agony of her magic being destroyed. The Huntsman had agreed to exploit a loophole in the pact her brother had used to summon the Hunt. If she wasn't away before the forest was destroyed, all would be lost.

The scent of Esmelle's witchy magic tickled Sabine's nose as an illusion spell settled over her. It itched, but she was too tired and hurt to care overly much or protest. It wasn't glamour but some other form of hybrid magic that allowed witches to emulate Fae magic.

Esmelle patted her arm. "Huh. You look pretty good, Esme."

Sabine blinked at Esmelle and managed a half-hearted smile. "Yeah? I always wanted to try out red hair. Is it curly too?"

"Gorgeous," Esmelle said with a grin. "We need to dress you better in the future. You need more color."

Balkin leaned over her. "Good. It will have to be enough. Bane, take her to Malek's ship. The dragon will meet you there as soon as he changes form."

Bane lifted her into his arms, and Sabine looked around. "Wait. Where's Blossom?"

"I'm here," Blossom said, landing on her chest. Tears streamed down the pixie's cheeks. "They're killing your beautiful forest, Sabine. Your brother is killing your magic."

"I know," she whispered, unable to send any magic toward Blossom to reassure her. Pixies were highly sensitive to nature magic, and the destruction of hers would affect all of them.

"I must return to Faerie to protect your interests there,

my darling kitten." Balkin pressed a kiss against her forehead. "I will find you as soon as it is safe to do so. In the meantime, Bane and Esmelle will join you on the dragon's ship."

"What about Dax?" she asked, not wanting to leave her other protector.

"He must remain here for now," Balkin said, a trace of an apology in his voice. "Your Unseelie magic will help him remain aboveground for a time, but I'm sure he will find you again at some point. Or you may seek him out once it's safe."

"Don't let him die, Balkin," she said, unable to even infuse her words with power. It came out as a weak request.

Balkin nodded. "I will ensure he lives this night. Now go. Don't squander our efforts to ensure *your* survival."

Without another word, Bane carried her toward the docks and the ship that was waiting.

Chapter Seventeen

Sabine leaned heavily against the railing, watching the city grow smaller as the ship moved deeper into the ocean waters. Most of the buildings around the docks were still on fire, and she stared at the flames rising over the rooftops as Akros continued to burn. It would take years for the city to recover.

Humans were resilient, far more than many of the other magical races. It would take time, but they'd eventually manage to rebuild. Before she'd ever come to Akros, she wouldn't have believed such a thing was possible. Her experiences here had taught her the magic contained within the human spirit couldn't be destroyed. It would survive and one day, thrive again.

Blossom landed on her shoulder, her weight a comforting presence. "Do you think you'll ever go back to the city?"

"I don't know," Sabine admitted, somewhat surprised by

her mixed feelings. She'd lived in Akros for more than ten years. It had been difficult living amongst the humans at times, but she'd miss parts of it. "I'm not sure when it'll be safe to return or even if it's a good idea. I know Edvar and Talia will look after the children for me. Dax can handle himself and his people too."

"Esme's going to miss her shop, but she wants to learn more about your magic," Blossom said quietly. "Are you angry with her for working with Balkin against your wishes?"

Sabine sighed, more weary than anything. "No. I'm not angry with Dax or Bane either. If you hadn't warned me years ago about the agreement they made with Balkin, I'm not sure I would have been able to forgive them. I expected something like what happened, but I wish there had been another way. I didn't want them to have leave their homes or lives."

Blossom giggled. "Balkin thinks all pixies are spies."

Sabine's mouth curved in a hint of a smile. "You are, but you're *my* spies—and you're the best spymaster I could ask for."

The pixie patted her cheek affectionately. "I'm sorry I couldn't warn you about your brother sooner. The other pixies tried to get here with the news as fast as they could. Barley and my sisters are escorting them back to your father's court. They can watch Balkin too, if you want."

She nodded, recalling Blossom's cryptic warning in the tavern basement. The pixie hadn't been able to speak freely in front of everyone, but Sabine had understood her message. "Keep an eye on Balkin in case anyone becomes suspicious of him, but my father and brother need to be the primary focus. We also need to start determining which families have split loyalties and may consider supporting me against my father and brother. Can you get a message to your family while we're on the ship?"

"It's harder to access the in-between, but I can do it."

"I'll see about getting a few plants for you at the first place we dock," Sabine promised, making a mental list of everything else they'd need. Money was going to be something of a problem, but they'd figure something out. Malek still wanted her help to locate the artifacts, so they could probably come to an agreement between them.

Sabine shivered. It was a warm night, but the absence of her magic would continue to keep her chilled for a while longer. The chalice shielded the tiny embers of her magic, but it wouldn't last. It couldn't do anything about the chill inside her either.

"The demon comes," Blossom whispered and buried herself in Sabine's hair.

A heavy blanket was placed over her shoulders, and she glanced up at Bane before focusing again on the city. Bane sighed. "I won't apologize for my hand in what happened, but I am sorry it hurt you."

"I didn't expect you would," she admitted, wrapping the blanket tighter around her. It helped alleviate the worst of the chill. "But if you ever follow Balkin's orders again instead of mine, I will see our pact at an end." She lifted her gaze to regard him, needing him to understand she wouldn't tolerate another betrayal. She placed her hand over the mark on his wrist. "You're *mine*, Bane. I don't want to lose you, but I need to be able to trust you."

Bane exhaled slowly and nodded in acceptance, placing his hand over hers. She turned back to stare out across the water and in the direction of the burning city. It was growing increasingly smaller, and she no longer felt the prickle of wild magic on her skin. The Wild Hunt would likely abandon their pursuit for now, but it was only a matter of time before her family realized she was still alive.

They stood in silence for a long time, the only sound was of the crew working and the crashing of the waves as the ship moved steadily through the water. The moon had reappeared, casting a silvery glow over the ocean.

Bane sighed and leaned heavily against the railing. "The dragon believes you're angry with him. You should consider speaking to him when you feel up to it."

Sabine turned to look across the ship. Malek's crew worked diligently doing... whatever it was to make the ship move. Malek stood at the giant wheel, staring across the horizon. His black hair was tied back, but a few strands had escaped, the inky darkness contrasting with his golden skin. He was a beautiful man, but an extraordinary dragon. She'd never forget the way his wings had seemed to swallow the sky whole or how he'd tried to divert the Wild Hunt away from the children hiding near the ancient temple.

As though sensing her quiet observation, Malek's gaze landed on her and remained there. She hadn't spoken to him since she was brought on board the ship. Things had happened rather quickly while they set sail, but they'd have time soon enough.

She gave him a small smile and dipped her head in appreciation for everything he'd done. He might be one of the fearsome creatures from legend that had almost destroyed her people, but Malek was different. He *cared*.

Malek's eyes warmed at the gesture, and he smiled. He angled his head in acknowledgment, and a pleasurable warmth spread through her.

A dragon. She almost laughed, recalling her near hysteria as he'd flown across the sky. Balkin had claimed she'd charmed a dragon, but she wasn't quite so sure. In her mind, Malek had been the one who had charmed *her*.

"Dax will come for you as soon as he can escape Balkin's orders," Bane said, still staring in the direction of Akros. "Will you bind him to you as well?"

"I don't know," she admitted, unsure about anything right now. "I'd hoped to do it before I had to leave Akros, but we haven't found a balance between us yet. I'm not strong enough to hold him if he keeps challenging me, and I have no wish to see him broken. I need strong allies, not more adversaries."

Bane nodded as though he'd guessed her answer. "Perhaps the distance is for the best then. It may be the only thing that breaks the strength of his will. My brother has always been foolishly stubborn."

Sabine placed her hand over Bane's again. "I'm sorry I took you away from Akros."

With a chuckle, he lifted her hand and kissed it. "I'm not. I hated that city. It will be good to see more of the world."

"Do you know where we're heading?"

"The dwarven city," Bane said, glancing over at Malek at the ship's wheel. "Balkin told the dragon one of the artifacts was hidden there centuries ago. He gave us the name of someone to speak to once we arrive. It's unknown whether it's still there, but at least it's a lead to follow."

Despite the precariousness of their new situation, Sabine smiled. She'd always dreamed of traveling to the dwarven city, and now she'd be able to see it for herself. Although, Balkin never did anything without good reason.

"Balkin wants me to forge an alliance with the dwarves, doesn't he?"

Bane nodded. "You need more allies. If we're going to make you Queen of Faerie in truth, you'll need every resource we can manage. Having the Unseelie stand behind you won't be enough."

The chalice attached to her belt warmed in response to

Bane's words. Sabine frowned. "I made an oath when I accepted the power of the chalice, Bane. My first priority is to ensure this world is protected. Faerie politics and my duplicitous family will need to wait until the immediate threat is handled. If our world is destroyed by another war, it won't matter who holds the throne."

"They may not be willing to wait," Bane warned, his hands tightening on the railing. "If you wish to help the dragon acquire the artifacts to lock down the portal, it will be done. But you may need to eliminate the threats against you first, or risk facing the Wild Hunt again. It's unlikely we'll be able to escape them a second time. Only the gods themselves know what's coming, and they're not talking."

Blossom tugged gently on Sabine's hair, and she smiled at the reminder. The gods hadn't stopped talking to anyone. The portal closing had simply made it more difficult for most people to listen. Fortunately, pixies had always been very good at listening—even when they shouldn't.

Sabine squeezed Bane's hand. "I think I'll go speak with the ship captain. If we're traveling all the way to the dwarven city, we'll need to see about acquiring some supplies."

Without waiting for a response, she turned away from the demon and walked toward a dragon. And behind her, the city continued to burn.

ABOUT THE AUTHOR

Jamie A. Waters is an award-winning writer of science fiction and fantasy romance. Her first novel, Beneath the Fallen City, was a winner of the Readers' Favorite Award in Science Fiction/Fantasy Romance and the CIPA EVVY Award in Science Fiction.

Jamie currently resides in Florida with a murder of crows in her backyard and two neurotic dogs who enjoy stealing socks. When she's not pursuing her passion of writing, she's usually trying to learn new and interesting random things (like how to pick locks or use the self-cleaning feature of the oven without setting off the fire alarm). In her downtime, she enjoys reading, playing computer games, painting, or acting as a referee between the dragons and fairies currently at war inside the closet. Learn more about her at jamieawaters.com.

Printed in Great Britain
by Amazon